THE CROSSED KEYS

THE BELFAST CRIME SERIES

PHILLIP JORDAN

FIVE FOUR PUBLISHING

Get Exclusive Material

GET EXCLUSIVE NEWS AND UPDATES FROM THE AUTHOR

Thank-you for choosing to read this book.

Sign-up for more details about my life growing up on the same streets as Veronica Taylor and Tom Shepard and get an exclusive e-book containing an in-depth interview and a selection of True Crime stories about the flawed but fabulous city that inspired me to write, *all for free.*

Details can be found at the end of **THE CROSSED KEYS.**

For those who continue to fight for their right
to justice

Prologue

There was a non-uniform uniformity about the two boys hiding in the dark.

Each was dressed in the same regulation grey sweatshirt and pants and their feet were shod in identical black plimsolls. The shoes were made of black canvas with rubber soles and no laces.

Definitely no laces. Laces would have made them much too dangerous.

"Stop making so much noise," hissed the taller of the two youths. His attempt to quell his friend's excessive noise was louder than the actual offence. He wore his sweatshirt untucked, hanging over the waistband of his joggers in an act of rebellion. He had his sleeves rolled up, revealing pale skinny wrists and a razor blade and biro ink tattoo, the ragged motif a childish affectation attempting to display a maturity that hadn't yet developed physically.

"I can't help it, Stumpy. It's these bloody wrappers." The smaller boy nibbled at the paper wrapper stuck to his candy. "Could you not have nicked something easier to open?"

Stumpy sighed and started to scoop up the haul of stolen Fruit Salad and Black Jack chews strewn on the rough wooden floor between them.

"It's not the wrappers. It's your gob slapping like a wet fart —"

"No, it isn't. Here, give me some more of—"

"Shut up, Monk—"

"Don't be so bloody selfish, you wee dick."

The boy's nicknames, like the subtle rebellion against dress code was just another meek resistance against authority, one born from the alteration of a surname, the other a cruel reminder of a physical defect. Monk reached for the treats that were disappearing into Stumpy's pockets, but his attempts were blocked as the bigger boy scooted forward, balling a fist in the material of his sweatshirt worn as regulations demanded, tucked into his joggers which were tied tight with a looping bow.

Stumpy put his free hand over Monk's mouth and the boy's eyes widened in alarm before he gave a short nod of understanding.

An initially unheard sound now drifted to his ears.

"Shush," Stumpy warned, his breath hot and smelling of aniseed.

The march of hobnailed boots was marked in time by the clip of a brass-tipped cane.

Both boys held their breath.

They had each felt the impact of those heavy boots, both to their ribs and the bony ridges on the small of their backs, but it was the burning lash of the brass cane tip that had left welts and scars that would never heal. Lifelong reminders of punishment for misdemeanours that had been both real and imagined.

Stumpy pressed his hand tighter over his friend's mouth, feeling the boy's body tense as the footsteps closed and then passed to continue along the corridor, the material of a curtain the only thing that protected them from discovery and further correction.

The beatings were routine, the violence sudden and shocking but preferable to the other abuse that left no marks but would burn forever in their psyches.

The small alcove into which they were cramped was an architectural anomaly in the old school building; a dead spot formed between an old classroom storage space and the corridor that led to a stairwell linking the gymnasium, which had been repurposed to serve as their dormitory, and the rest of the former school site.

Their hidey-hole offered a spot of sanctuary, one where the boys could be free to enjoy carefree camaraderie away from the intense scrutiny of those charged with their care and rehabilitation, and it allowed a view of the comings and goings beyond their confinement through a metal grille inset in the brickwork.

Stumpy waited another minute and a half before he eased position.

"It's okay. I think they're away," he said, releasing his grip. He could feel the heat in Monk's face which shone pale in the gloom.

"It's okay," he said again, a reassuring hand on his friend's, both of them ignoring the warm wash of urine that had soaked through the leg of Stumpy's joggers.

"We need to get back to bed."

"What about Busby?" said Monk, his voice tight.

"He'll have to do without his share of the sweets tonight." Stumpy eased aside the heavy curtain which smelled of mildew and dust.

"Stumpy," Monk's voice was a squeak.

The hiss of tyres on tarmac sounded through the ventilation grate a second before a kaleidoscope of headlamps danced across the wall.

"Come on, that's them coming back. We need to go. Now."

Stumpy took his friend by the wrist and they hurried along the dark corridor towards the door with the big brass knob which led to the stairs.

They were able to travel quietly, their plimsolls robbing the high ceilings and tile floor of the chance to betray their passing. In the courtyard below, the column of cars that stank of sweat and cigarettes was bringing back the boys who had been selected earlier in the day for an evening excursion.

Stumpy and Monk scurried across the main corridor and into the side annexe housing the dormitory.

The sound of car doors slamming outside preceded angry voices.

Stumpy eased the dormitory door open seven inches and squeezed through; opening it any further and the rusty hinge would cry out an alarm.

The two boys crept silently around the edge of the draughty space. In the rafters above, a pigeon fluttered at the disruption.

Stumpy pulled back Monk's woollen blanket and gave him a peck on the top of his head as his friend flopped in.

"Quiet now," he breathed.

Monk's nod was imperceptible.

Stumpy flicked back his own blanket, but before he could drop to the thin mattress the searching beam of a flashlight picked him out in the darkness.

"The eyes of the Lord are in every place, watching the evil and the good." The voice that spoke from behind the torchlight had a thick brogue.

Stumpy straightened to attention, searching for any movement or whimper from Monk.

"Are you off somewhere there, mister?"

"No, sir," said Stumpy.

"It looks like you are, so you better be quick and explain yourself." The beam wavered as footsteps and the click of a cane approached.

"I had an accident, sir." Stumpy turned, displaying the stained crotch and thigh of his joggers.

"Woe to he who is filthy and polluted," said the voice. The footsteps stopped a few feet away, his torch beam chasing up and down the boy's rail-thin body.

"Ugh, you're a dirty wee beast."

"Yes, sir."

"Gather those up."

Stumpy frowned in confusion as the torch illuminated the bed adjacent.

"But—"

Under the glare of the torch, he didn't see the whip of the cane. Its burning bite however devoured his shin and he fell to the floor in agony.

"Strip the bed you wicked little boy and bring the clothes in there too." The voice was cruel and bitter, the cane rapping the wooden box secreted under each bed that contained the occupant's working clothes and underwear.

Stumpy hobbled across to where his friend Busby would sleep and did as instructed, his hands shaking as he pulled the sheets and pillowcases off.

"Hurry up." Impatience was accompanied by a rap of the cane. "And the clothes. Wrap it all in the sheets and come with me."

"But where is—"

Stumpy flinched as his tormentor wheeled on him, his breath smelled of tooth decay and whiskey. Lowering his gaze in submission, Stumpy allowed a rough hand to drag him forward. The torchlight blazed in his face.

"Not another word. Now move."

Thrust forward, Stumpy waddled along in advance of the man with the big bundle of bedclothes and personal items balled in front of his chest and the torch beam leading the way.

The cane prodded him out of the dormitory and right, along the corridor away from the main entrance where voices harsh with recrimination continued to argue outside.

As they moved deeper into the building's interior, they passed the old cloakrooms that now served as storage and the minor hall where they took their meals. The smell of cooking fat and food waste hung in the air as they skirted the kitchen, its stale smells overpowered by the fresher scent of detergents and starch as the torch beam directed Stumpy down a narrow flight of concrete steps, through the laundry and along another narrow corridor until it ended in a wooden door.

"Wait there," said the man.

Stumpy did as instructed. His guide moved forward to unshackle the padlock. The task complete, he motioned the boy forward with a grunt. The corridor beyond was low and arched and Stumpy could feel a tremor underfoot.

Thick pipework ran along the walls and the air was stuffy and warm. It was a short walk and then the corridor opened into a large room dominated by a huge steel boiler and water tank. Pumps and filtration systems festooned the brickwork and adjacent to the boiler's expansion tank the orange mouth of an incinerator yawned below a cylindrical combustion chamber.

Stumpy felt sweat bead his forehead and trickle down his back. The man had picked up a pair of thickly insulated gloves and wielding a curved fire iron he unlatched and heaved open the loading door.

The roar of the incinerator erupted into the space as the man raised the iron and his voice.

"Put them in," he instructed.

Stumpy cautiously stepped forward, the heat licking at his exposed face and hands. Getting as close as possible, his eyes clenched shut and teeth gritted against the intensity of the flames he threw everything in, the fire's voracious appetite immediately consuming the material.

The door clanged shut and Stumpy's ears rang.

He backed away wiping perspiration from his face, brow knotted in confusion. Had Busby been let go? Run off? Lashed out? The thought of what punishments would be meted out if he had chilled him despite the heat of the furnace raging a few feet away.

They all dreaded being one of the chosen few to be selected for the evening excursions but there was no getting out of it. Each boy had to take their turn. The ordeal began with a communal shower before they dressed in fresh uniforms to be chauffeured in convoy to the various private clubs and houses dotted around the city and beyond. Some, like Busby, were more favoured than the others and thereby endured the trips much more frequently.

A rough shove startled Stumpy, knocking him sideways against the thick metal guard rail protecting the fresh water tank.

Two of the men he recognised as chaperones carried a rolled rug between them, its woven backing stained and threadbare with age, ambling alongside them was one of the older boys who had been selected for the evening's excursion. He carried a bundle of material, his expression was vacant, his eyes reddened by tears. Stumpy recognised the load as a dress uniform of blazer, slacks and striped tie.

The roar of the incinerator erupted again as his guide to the boiler room opened the heavy door.

"Christ!" The second man stumbled on the uneven concrete, lost his footing, and the unbalanced load fell to the floor, the rug rolling open to reveal its gory contents.

"Mind your blasphemy!"

Stumpy's hands flew up to cover his mouth and stifle a scream.

The stoicism he had cultivated in the face of the home's escalating brutality failed him and he felt his bladder release again as the two men calmly rolled up the carpet and contents and with the aid of their accomplice and the boy fed it into the furnace.

Stumpy shook. The iron door slammed closed but failed to shut away the image of charred flesh and the cruel double-headed brand seared into the corpse's pale flesh. His eyes remained riveted on the glowing window as the flames devoured his friend.

The shuffle of movement drew him back from the horror.

Three faces illuminated by the incinerator's hellish glow stared at him. Behind them lurked the older boy unsure if he was to be called on to assist or participate. His guide into the bowels of the old school was the first to step forward, a fiendish sneer on his narrow face.

"You dirty wee beast," he said, pointing the fire iron at Stumpy's soiled joggers. The boy's blood ran cold as the three men encircled him.

"Take them off then."

"Can you not follow a simple instruction? Take them off!"

Stumpy bit down on his tongue, blinking back the threat of hot tears.

"Take them off your desk and down to Derek. The files? Are you listening to me? I gave them to you to take down." The supervisor's voice rose an octave, her pitch and level of irritation rising at Stumpy's inability to answer the simple query. She snatched up the top folder and slapped the paperwork against his shoulder.

"I…" Stumpy began, a lump in his throat blocking further excuse for the delay.

"Aye, what? You didn't hear me, or you chose to ignore me?" Sheena Broderick growled. She was four foot five in high heels and there was more meat on a butcher's pencil but her tongue was cleaver sharp and her real power, and the one by which she dominated her subordinates, was the unshakeable rumour she was shagging the regional commercial director.

"Those files are earmarked for destruction and the subcontractors are here. We can't just hang onto them for another bloody six years, where are we going to store them now Cooper Investments are taking over the second floor, huh? Do you not think we're going to be cramped enough without hanging onto years of shit we're no longer obligated to keep."

Panic threatened to consume Stumpy, the files wavering an inch in front of his face. Empty files, in the sense that the information inside them was useless. Old client transactions and audit information that was out of date and earmarked for the incinerator.

Stumpy's skin crawled because he knew the binder in Broderick's hand was stuffed full of spurious account information and padding, the original contents destined for destruction glared accusingly from the recycling box beside his desk. If Broderick looked down. If she just took notice for a second and made a closer examination the game was up. He felt sick.

"I'm sorry, I got caught up with something in the Mercer account," said Stumpy, half out of his chair now, head dipped in submission. He held out a hand. "I'll take them right away."

Broderick passed the files across, holding onto them in a silent tug-of-war for an uncomfortable few seconds. The rest of the office had hushed and Stumpy was aware of his reddening complexion as all eyes watched, engrossed in the confrontation. The supervisor's lips brushed his ear as she leaned closer.

"Get your shit together. Let this be the last time I have to come to you personally to make sure you've done what I asked when I asked," said Broderick in a threatening purr.

He nodded mutely, stumbling as she suddenly released her grip on the paperwork and turned on a stiletto heel, sashaying back towards her glass-walled, square office.

Stumpy's hand trembled and he fumbled for his identification badge to unlock the security door leading to the basement storage space. The lift would have been quicker but he needed headspace. Time to think. To get his emotions under control. The weight of the useless files under his arm felt too light and the thought of those under his desk waiting to be discovered crippled him with anxiety.

Reaching the half landing he stopped, peering up and down the stairs before he took out the burner phone that had been left on the table at his usual breakfast haunt.

His source had been insistent. No contact by any other means. The risk of a leak was too great. Stumpy thumbed the one saved number and waited for the call to connect.

"Yes."

"Thank God," wheezed Stumpy, leaning over the handrail, one ear on the familiar voice, the other ensuring he was alone. "It's me. I got what you wanted."

"Can you get them out tonight?"

"I… I think so."

"It needs to be tonight."

"Okay, but where will I—"

"Don't worry about that now. I'll be in touch later. You've been very brave."

Stumpy swallowed hard, fighting the surge of fear and adrenaline flooding his nervous system and pushing back darker thoughts of the evils which had brought him here.

"This is going to work, isn't it? He's not going to walk away again, not after you use this, none of them will, will they?"

"I'll worry about that. Just you get what we need to expose them."

Stumpy nodded silently as the call ended, pushing down the familiar feelings of dread, futility and hopelessness that followed all previous attempts to force authorities to acknowledge the immorality and violation imposed on so many innocent lives.

Their exposure was all he had ever strived for, ever since they had stolen his childhood and thrown his friend into the furnace.

1

The Volvo rolled to a stop beside red, white and blue painted kerbstones, tyres crunching across a rutted roadway of broken glass beer bottles.

"The king is dead," observed the driver.

"Long live the king," said Detective Inspector Veronica 'Ronnie' Taylor.

Twenty yards ahead, a youth of about fourteen years old stood at the top of a ladder which leaned precariously against a lamppost. His safety and well-being were in the hands of a slightly older boy who stood at the foot, engrossed by the screen of his mobile phone. The boys' BMX bikes had been discarded in the middle of the road.

"He's giving me palpitations looking at him," said Detective Sergeant Robert 'Doc' Macpherson as the younger lad reached higher to snip off the cable ties holding a faded and weather-beaten flag in place.

"Are you sure it's him and not the belly buster you just put away?" said Taylor.

"If a man is to be fit for his work he has to eat, Ronnie." Macpherson planted two huge hands across an ample stomach, his stature along with his jolly red cheeks having earned him the moniker of one of Snow White's famous friends. His face broke into a satisfied smile as he recalled the Butler's breakfast special he had recently demolished.

"The only thing you'll be fit for if you keep eating like that is a heart attack." Taylor unfastened her seatbelt, opened the passenger door and stepped out.

"I've the constitution of a man half my age," said Macpherson joining her at the Volvo's bonnet.

"You've the waist size of someone twice it."

"You could do with eating the odd fry yourself," he said, ignoring the jibe to give her a concerned look which she chose to ignore. Her appetite for food, drink and company had diminished over recent weeks as she fought to shake off a flatness that had become pervasive in the aftermath of their last case.

The maroon paramilitary flag now freed from its mooring fluttered to the ground and the youth began the ordeal of replacing it with an almost identical one. As the two detectives approached he caught sight of them and whistled down to his mate who barely glanced up from his phone.

"Bit dangerous isn't it, lads?" said Macpherson, making a show of craning his neck to look up at the youngster fastening new ties to the stake holding a brand new banner featuring the crest of a fringe Loyalist group.

"Who are they? The health and safety?" shouted the boy up the ladder.

"Pigs, mate," said his friend putting the phone away and giving a grudging jerk of his chin. "Is there a problem, officers?"

"Off the top of my head?" said Taylor. "Obstructing the public highway for one and breach of the peace a close second." She pointed first to the bikes and then the flags.

The boy's face pinched in irritation.

"We know our rights," he said, head wobbling on a scrawny neck adorned with thick gold chains.

"You're the worst-dressed human rights lawyer I've ever come across," said Macpherson with a chuckle.

"You lot can't stop us expressing our culture."

"You'd be right if they weren't inciting sectarian hatred," said Macpherson, once again pointing out the flag bearing the crest of the outlawed group.

"Piss off. In this estate?" said the second boy, clambering down to join his outraged friend.

"Can we see your permit then?" added Taylor.

Two mouths hung open for a second and then they spoke, one voice talking over the other.

"You're a melter. Like you need a permit for putting up flags."

"Away up the Falls and ask them for a permit. You two buck eejits can kiss my…—"

"We've the right to our identity…"

Taylor held up a hand, and the tirade against the oppression of the Loyalist identity, the harassment of the youth of the Fearon Estate and the greater threat to the Union stuttered to a stop.

"Look, lads, we've heard it all before. Just pick up your bikes and pedal away before one of you falls and hurts yourself," she said.

The boy wearing the chains who had been the more vocal of the two opened his mouth to speak but closed it again as a black BMW X6 pulled into the street. The car was lowered so its arches skimmed the wheels. The dull thud of bass from its sound system poured out from open windows.

It stopped a hundred yards short, the occupants obscured behind a tinted windscreen, and then it gave a short blast of the horn. The boys shared a look.

"Aye, whatever then," said the flag erector, signalling to his friend that the argument was over. Between them they dropped the ladder, shouldered it and collected their bikes, weaving awkwardly down the street.

"The wee buggers are getting younger," observed Macpherson.

"And more brazen." Taylor watched the two pause briefly by the car. They looked back up the street, leaving no doubt about who was the topic of discussion. Just as quickly as they had stopped they left, bumping fists with the passenger.

The BMW clunked into gear and the big SUV began a swooping one eighty to go back the way it had come. From the open passenger window, a face regarded them with a sneer, the young man inside raised a hand above the door sill to point to a gable wall, and the fingers then closed to form an imitation pistol.

"Looks like the battle to win hearts and minds rages on," said Macpherson.

Taylor read the lines of scribbled graffiti on the end wall of the decrepit flats and sighed. The slogan which had been spray painted in black paint stood two feet high and the letters had bled slightly. FCB SAYS NO TO IRISH SEA BORDER. The sentiments had been springing up across the city's Loyalist communities in the wake of Brexit and following the impact of the Northern Ireland protocol on trade.

A summer of violence was the response to customs checks on goods entering the province from the rest of the United Kingdom which was, in the eyes of Unionists, precipitating a constitutional change that would shift control of the contested six counties back to Dublin and place the Good Friday Agreement in jeopardy. In the vacuum of no political deal to remedy the situation, the threat of a return to the dark days of the Troubles simmered just below the surface, unhelpfully fuelled by the rhetoric spouted by both sides.

The crumbling tower blocks and the sprawling terraces and alleyways of the cramped post-war Fearon housing estate offered the perfect breeding ground for those who wished to exploit those tensions and weaponise a youth already struggling in the aftermath of a pandemic, with chronic educational and social failings and the lack of investment in blue-collar jobs. The impact of the protocol and the enforcement of repeated lockdowns had given time to idle hands and was resulting in growing protests, bus burnings and a steady increase in antisocial behaviour and interface violence which in reality was just a vent for the frustrations felt by the gang masters over steadily declining profits.

Lockdown had increased demand for the supply of illicit drugs but travel restrictions and extensive import checks had crippled the importation routes, the double whammy arriving on the back of Taylor closing her most recent case involving the murder of a local criminal, an international human trafficking ring and the shooting of her nemesis, the city's most notorious narcotics importer and business mogul Gordon 'Monster' Beattie.

The news that Beattie's alleged criminal infrastructure had been chopped to the root was initially viewed as a good result however, with the godfather lying in a coma recuperating from his wounds and with no greater threat to keep the minnows in check, the void he left behind had spawned tit for tat violence and a vicious turf war to claim what spartan product was left to trade now the more traditional means of underworld financing like extortion, protection rackets and door security had been choked off by enforced business closures.

In a concerning turn of events, an increasing number of adolescents had been caught up in the conflict, the glamour and prestige of running with the gangs ending abruptly in violence. Their mutilated bodies were dumped unceremoniously in back alleys or on building sites, ironically, at times, alongside their own victims of the insidious black market trade.

Taylor watched the SUV turn left at the end of the road and

filter into the light traffic of the A2. Beyond the road, the dull blue-green waters of Belfast Lough churned under a shroud of grey sky. Her eyes tracked to the southwest, her thoughts split between the former soldier who had made the ultimate sacrifice in helping her break the trafficking ring, his body residing somewhere beneath the galloping white caps, and a few miles away to the west to the man who occupied a single side ward of the Royal Victoria Hospital.

She had visited Beattie twice in the aftermath of events at Hoey Cargo. The first, she told herself, was to inspect security and ensure he wasn't about to walk off the ward and onto the next plane bound for the south of Spain. An unlikely possibility given the extent of his injuries but given their long and chequered history, and with the gangster having slipped the noose of prosecution and the grim reaper more than once, she wasn't about to give him the chance to steal a march. The second time, she swore she was going to unplug the bastard. But she didn't. When he woke she would have questions.

Taylor thrust her hands into the pockets of her jacket and glanced at her colleague. Macpherson was oblivious to the events that had transpired in the subterranean tunnels under the cargo warehouse culminating in the death of Assistant Chief Constable Ken Wallace, and the longer she kept the truth from him the more guilty she felt, regardless of it being potentially safer all round that way. The revelations Beattie and Wallace had divulged implicated faceless mandarins, politicians and the police in concealing the truth of the troubled province's path to peace behind a sinister code of silence.

Macpherson poked a little finger into a molar, taking a second to inspect the remnant of his breakfast which he managed to fish out on the fingernail before flicking it away.

"Back to it?" she said, pushing her worry, guilt and desire for answers to the back of her mind.

"We might as well. A few broken windows are just what we need to start the week."

Taylor chuckled in spite of her mood as they got into the car.

"Did anyone ever tell you that you're a lot more positive when you've a full belly?"

"Anything to keep us out from under the chief super's feet, even if it is a wild goose chase." Macpherson fussed with his seatbelt and then crunched the Volvo into gear. "Up here?"

Taylor pointed ahead.

"Next one on the left and then up past the derelict ground. There's a row of garages that back onto the flats."

As Macpherson made the turn she considered his words. Solving a spate of wanton vandalism was perhaps just the thing to occupy her thoughts for the time being. The task was significantly more mundane than the troubles that were keeping her awake at night.

Macpherson guided the Volvo carefully around broken bottles and potholes. The Fearon Estate was a warren of entries, winding narrow paths, and council housing that had been abandoned to the point of dereliction; at one point the Volvo's headlamps illuminated a battlefield where a conflict raged between a thriving expansion of weeds and the decayed bones of several burnt-out maisonettes.

There were a hundred places in the maze where the man they were looking for could have gone to ground but Finn Abbott was a creature of habit, a petty criminal whose journey through the justice system had begun with an early stint in reform school and then juvenile detention, accumulating on the road to adulthood an impressive record of anti-social disorder, theft and minor drug offences. Regardless of whatever scam he was involved in though, on a Tuesday morning, he could always be relied upon to pay a visit to the sole surviving member of his extended family. To say it was a coincidence that his visit just so happened to coincide with payday would be a stretch.

"You know what's sadder than this reprobate conning an old man out of his pension?" said Macpherson as the car bobbled over an uneven patch of tarmac.

Taylor shook her head, her eyes scanning for signs of Abbott flitting from the mouth of the entries or along the boarded-up street. Macpherson jerked his chin towards a couple of old timers linking up to walk towards the row of shops at the end of the road.

"If Abbott didn't fleece him of a cut, the bookies would take every brass penny."

2

"All rise."

Observing the usher's instruction the rumble of feet and rustle of gowns of those sitting in the well of the court greeted the entrance of The Honourable Mr Justice Pollock who climbed awkwardly to his raised position at the head of court four before taking his seat at the bench and clearing his throat with a phlegmy cough.

"Good morning, everyone. Mr Gamble, please proceed."

The court clerk sitting below the judge's bench dipped his head in a formal bow and glanced down at the legal documents in front of him. A stifled sneeze came from the back of the defence benches and a murmur of quiet conversation died in the public gallery.

"Crown versus Casey," announced Gamble to the court before angling slightly to face the dock. "Colm Casey, you are charged with conspiracy to solicit murder contrary to the Criminal Law Act. Primarily you are charged with orchestrating the murders of prison officers Bartholomew Townsend and Richard Timothy Plymouth and with murder contrary to the Common Law in respect of the death of Pastor James Phelan." The clerk paused to confirm the accuracy of his statement, the silence offering a dramatic pause to the solemn proceedings, then facing the defendant again he added, "How do you plead?"

Colm Casey gazed out from behind the glass of the dock

with an expression of disdain for the archaic spectacle unfolding on the other side of the security partition. A step behind Casey, standing at ease at each of his shoulders, two G4S security guards were dwarfed by the broad-shouldered and ruddy-faced West Belfast bruiser.

"It's bollocks, so it is," sneered Casey.

The clerk blushed beetroot at the response and Casey's deep laugh erupted from his belly.

Mr Justice Pollock rapped the bench with his knuckles, his expression frosty.

"Mr Casey, you'll reserve some respect for this court or we'll add contempt to that list."

Casey gave a short shake of his head.

"Fuc…"

"Your worship," the call from the defence benches cut over Casey's oath but did little to dismiss Pollock's dissatisfaction.

"My client wishes to plead not guilty to all charges."

Casey's aptly named defence barrister, Margaret Jury KC offered an apologetic and deferential half nod and half shake of her head to the presiding judge. "He also offers his sincere apologies to the bench for his outburst."

Casey rocked on his heels, an expression of amusement on his face as he came under the disdainful scrutiny of Jury, his best attempt to honour her pledge of contrition displayed in a recalcitrant shrug.

"Is that correct, Mr Casey?" said Pollock, with a sniff of irritation.

"Aye."

"Enter it in, Mr Gamble. The defendant may sit," instructed the judge. "Mr Callander, what say you?"

The barrister for the prosecution rose to his feet and gave his learned colleague on the defence and the judge a dour dip of the head.

"Your worship," said Damien Callander. The King's

Council for the prosecution was ably assisted at his bench by a shy-looking young man with mousey hair peeking out from below his horsehair wig and a pair of spectacles that perpetually slipped down his long narrow nose. Regulars of the court knew that although the two men sat at odds physically and each despised the other in equal measure, they nonetheless comprised a formidable team, one renowned for its fastidious ruthlessness in closing cases for the public prosecution service, but a duo also shrouded in ignominy for allowing one particular rat to slip their snare on more than one occasion.

Callander declined his junior's notes with a shake of his big square head, continuing his performance in a confident baritone that sailed close to condescension, presenting with a gravitas honed over the course of hundreds of trials. "My colleague, Mr Crothers and I will provide witnesses and evidence to you that will demonstrate beyond reasonable doubt that Mr Casey is guilty on all counts…"

Colm Casey pressed back in his seat and peered out of the dock at the pompous figure representing those who had tried and failed to bring him to justice before.

The third son of the fabled Joe Casey, a prominent trade union figurehead through the sixties and seventies, he had struggled in his early years to live up to the family reputation. As his father organised and mobilised protests and demonstrations against the British occupation, his two older brothers Joe Jr and Enda rose through the ranks of the IRA's Belfast brigade, spearheading intelligence gathering operations against RUC officers and weapon smuggling from Europe. The younger Casey's attempts to emulate his brothers' bravado, however, ended in failure. Caught up in petty crime and the rampaging street violence, Colm had been apprehended and spent two years in juvenile detention. The stint inside had hardened the boy and in the years after his incarceration buoyed by rage and impotent frustration, Colm's fists and temper had earned him a fearsome reputation enforcing the paramilitary gang's rule in the west of the city. It was the killing of his father and eldest brother however that set him on a new trajectory, one that eventually would bring him full circle and back to the attention of the authorities.

At the time of his murder by the hand of Loyalist paramilitaries, Joe Casey had built up one of the most successful coal, oil and gas import and distribution businesses on the island of Ireland. Two dozen Bedford trucks and liveried oil tankers darted around the capital city and surrounding areas ferrying their cargo to homes, businesses and healthcare facilities while also satisfying a full spectrum of government contracts. Such was the demand for Casey products the company's two boats could be seen sailing into Belfast Lough three times a week.

Stepping into his father's shoes, Colm Casey began to understand and appreciate the wiliness of his old man, and how Casey Bulk Fuel had achieved such an aggressive expansion. Behind the front of heating supplies, they were heavily involved in illegal fuel production, tobacco smuggling and the shipping of weapons and explosives to assist the armed rebellion that had swept the north of the island of Ireland through the seventies and eighties.

As Colm took the reins however the advent of peace and the signing of the Belfast agreement saw a sudden need to diversify, replacing the loss of revenue from the arms shipments with other illegal products, the most lucrative of which were the illicit trafficking of waste, the facilitation of illegal immigration, and drugs.

As the Casey family business continued to prosper while competitors found their bottom line cut by market forces and the rise in wholesale costs, HM Revenue and Customs assisted by the PSNI Economic Crime Unit began to put Colm Casey under the microscope and it was during the investigation into a multitude of shell companies and suppliers linked to Casey Bulk Fuel the investigation team had been gifted evidence of the crimes which had placed him in the dock, namely murder and the orchestration of it.

Casey returned his attention to the court and to each of the persons present, not wholly surprised to find that the one face he expected to be there to see the spectacle was absent, but then as he considered it, with the drone of Callander's speech rising in the background as he laboured a point, it made sense that the minister would be trying to avoid adding to the speculation of political prejudice and more awkward questions regarding their well-documented and shared history.

Next to the dock, and to the left of the prosecution benches, the press gallery was empty. The public benches adjacent held a handful of stern-faced men and women in business attire, identification lanyards hung around their necks. Casey recognised them as solicitors' associates acting for the prosecution and members of the police service. A thin smile creased the bristles of his unshaven face as he caught the eye of one woman and gave a short nod.

Detective Chief Inspector Gillian Reed didn't return the gesture, instead impassively returning her attention to the winding up of Callander's summation.

"Thank you, Mr Callander," said Pollock. "Mr Casey, please stand."

As Casey lumbered to his feet, the court clerk rose and approached the bench, offering up a sheaf of documents. The judge mumbled his gratitude and shuffled the papers, drawing out an extravagant signature across several of the pages.

"Colm Casey you are remanded in custody with a trial

date set for the fourteenth."

Pollock gave the defendant a look over the rim of his spectacles and then raised a hand to the security guards. "Take him down."

3

If the one hundred and six inmates who had been forced to walk in chains from Carrickfergus Prison could see what had become of the black basalt Victorian penitentiary where once they had been incarcerated for crimes of stealing food and threadbare clothing they would no doubt be aghast in disbelief. Their destination, HMP Belfast, Crumlin Road Gaol, colloquially known as The Crum had changed little in appearance but dramatically in application during the intervening hundred and seventy years since those first patrons experienced the bitter cold and cruelty inside the stern walls and ended their lives trapped behind metalled portals which deterred the most ardent attempts to escape from the suffering haunting the halls.

In contrast, people were now flocking to enter the prison.

On the circular landing of steel beams and concrete staircases, light poured in from arched windows giving the main floor the air of a theatrical amphitheatre. The four wings which had housed the general population were separated from the space by glossy black iron grilles and the rows of cell doors along each were set into pristine whitewashed walls and polished floors, all latched open for inspection by the curious tourist or those seeking the macabre thrill of seeing the hangman's chambers.

Banners hanging from the balustrades offered such diverse delights as 'Troubles Tours', the 'Ultimate Gaol Experience' and bizarrely extolled the old prison as a 'Unique Wedding Venue', but rather than the strained cries of a wedding singer or the din of guard and inmate, it was the call of the press pack that echoed.

"Colm Casey is facing his arraignment this morning. Should you not be there to…."

"Minister, does your personal relationship with Colm Casey put the prosecution in danger of…"

"Is it true that you have blocked attempts by HM Revenue and the Economic Crime Unit to seize the assets of Casey Bulk Fuel…"

Minister for Justice, Oliver Maddox unbuttoned his suit coat and allowed the wave of questions to wash over him. To his left, the visitor attractions managing director blanched under the barrage of flashbulbs and onslaught of demands, while to his right the head of the Northern Ireland Prison Service (NIPS) Michael Nendrum glowered at the mob. Behind him a row of prison officers stood at attention, bookending a mix of a dozen students and reformed prisoners, all of them unsure of what to make of the spectacle and each trying unsuccessfully to fade into the old walls.

"Okay, okay. Settle down. I won't be answering questions on Colm Casey today or any day. The matter sits with the Northern Ireland Courts Service and the defendant will be tried without prejudice regardless of what lurid speculation certain sections of the media feel compelled to report."

Maddox placed his hands shoulder-width apart on the balcony's iron railing and gave a genial smile. At six foot four and an active member of the NIPS old boys rugby team, the justice minister cut an imposing figure. His sandy hair was shorn to the skull, minimising the visual impact of a receded hairline, and a chiselled jawline added to his air of masculine charm. Exhaling through a nose which had seen one too many scrums, Maddox waited patiently for the interruptions to die down.

"Thank you," he said, quieting the remaining murmurs. "While I appreciate the interest surrounding the impending court case we are here today to focus on the positive reforms we've been working on to combat a scourge affecting our colleagues in the service, the people in our care and the wider community at large."

Maddox beckoned one of the former prisoners and an officer forward, welcoming both into the sudden clatter of camera shutters with a reassuring smile and a clap on the shoulder.

"As you know from my previous role, the Prison Service is close to my heart. I served many happy years there and made good friends and acquaintances whom, I'm glad to report, have continued to move forward in their lives and assist us all with their community work and efforts to discourage others from emulating their mistakes."

The former inmate to Maddox's left blushed as the justice minister put an arm around his shoulders.

"These two men represent opposite sides of our system. You may look at them and think they have nothing in common, but these brave men stand before us today with a shared story. A tale that is tragically familiar throughout the service and sadly permeates the fabric of our society at this present time, it is a tragedy which we have the power to prevent and one we must, regardless of cost, intervene to end."

A flurry of flashbulbs illuminated Maddox as he straightened, his face a mask of solemnity.

"Both these men tried to take their own life. One prisoner and one prison officer. In the briefing notes presented to you the statistics of death in detention and in the service make for grim reading. Worse still are the statistics regarding the suicide of young people across this city and this province who see death as their only way out. Out of what, you may ask. Despair? Debt? Well, our research shows there are many factors and while this briefing today is focused on announcing reforms to encourage a new direction in how we as a service address mental health education and treatment for staff and prisoners because I still hear all too often from colleagues in the executive, the public"—Maddox drifted an open palm left to right across the assembly—"from headlines in your own newspapers and editorials that prison should be a place of punishment. I want to make it absolutely clear that those who find themselves convicted by the courts and serving sentences are there as punishment, not for it. The measures I intend to push through later this week will be a starting point for reform, education and safety for all within the walls."

A smattering of applause led by Michael Nendrum rippled from behind the justice minister.

"There is however one other matter before I take questions."

Maddox's handsome face soured as he spoke, lips pursed and eyebrows drawing down to form an exasperated frown.

"We are living through a unique set of crises. The pandemic has decimated lives and livelihoods at a time when the cost of living is becoming unmanageable across a large section of our demographic groups. Add to that the constitutional threat raised by the Northern Ireland Protocol which has increased tensions between communities and it is not difficult to see how the powder keg of frustration could reignite a wider return to violence."

Maddox gave a slow shake of his head as his words drifted back to him from across the central reception area.

"We know from recent events at the city docks that we have a problem with organised criminal gangs who may or may not operate under the same flag or follow old doctrines but let me be clear, their reach and their rule is not confined to the housing estates or the high-rises but seeps into society wherever they can exploit the individual or the organisation to gain advantage."

Maddox paused, the focus of his gaze lingering on each camera barrel pointed at him

"Territorial advantage, financial advantage. Political advantage."

Flashes illuminated the balcony amid a barrage of camera shutters.

"Root and branch reform to policing, the prison service and the courts are challenging but cannot be shirked if we are to ensure the foundations of the last twenty years continue to be built upon and not undermined by the ambitions and the stranglehold of those organisations seeking to grow their illicit operations through corruption or the spread of their illegal wealth. Equally, for too long partisan politics have held us back, encouraging division and threatening the hard-won devolved institutions that we all have fought for. This brinkmanship cannot be allowed to continue."

Maddox took a breath, acutely aware of the weight of the decision he had come to through many sleepless nights and the implications his next words may have.

"As justice minister, the defining mission for my department is to ensure a safer community for all and the respect of law and order. With that in the forefront of my mind, I'm here today to call time on all those engaged in the pursuit of organised crime, their facilitators and their enablers."

The low murmur of voices below began to grow again in intensity and just as the wall of flashbulbs exploded to dazzle him, Maddox saw the silhouette of a lone figure peel away from the back of the crowd and quietly exit.

4

"In the name of God, is there a fire or what?"

The exasperated voice came from a now wide-open window of the second-floor apartment. Old man Abbott's neighbour was bleary-eyed, what hair he had left was standing on end, and his chin and cheeks looked like they hadn't seen the edge of a razor in at least a month.

"We're looking for Duncan," said Macpherson, taking a few short steps back from the ground-floor door with its peeling paintwork to look up.

"Aye well, you've the right door at any rate." The neighbour made to close the window.

"Is he in?" said Taylor, holding up her police identification.

"You've been rattling that bloody door for fifteen minutes, love, what do you think?" The man exhaled loudly and gave a short shake of his head, the motion causing his complexion to suddenly blanch and Taylor took a step to the side just in case last night's carry-out made a reappearance. "Any wonder this estate is away to hell if Belfast's finest can't work that one out."

Macpherson balled his fists and tipped back on his heels.

"We'll have less of your lip, fella, if you know what's good for you," he said. "Has he had any visitors? We're looking for his nephew if you've seen him knocking about lately?"

"Youse are looking for that wee scrote?"

"Can you help us if we are?" said Macpherson, losing

patience.

The neighbour gave his untidy beard a scratch and then poked a finger up his nose as he considered the question.

"I might be able to now, aye," he said after a long pause.

"Well spit it out before my whiskers reach my knees, man."

Taylor held in a chuckle as she watched her DS stomp a pace forward and fix the man peering down with a glare that would curdle milk.

"That Finn lad is a waste of oxygen you know—"

"Have you seen him is what I asked you," growled Macpherson, cutting off further comment.

The neighbour jerked his chin in the direction of the main road.

"He was here this morning. Took off down the street with the old fella in his wheelchair about half an hour ago."

"You've been very helpful," grunted Macpherson turning and trudging back to the pavement.

"Pension or pints?" said Macpherson as Taylor eased open the Volvo's passenger side door.

"He'll need the one before the other," she said.

They could see the commotion at the small row of shops which served the estate as they exited Abbott's street. A rapid flash of blue light strobed across the caged windows of the convenience store and Post Office and a small crowd had gathered at the edge of the communal square of muddy ground and scorched grass impersonating the estate's only green space. The bystanders were swapping their attention between an unseen misfortune and the ambulance crew busying themselves with their bags of kit.

"What have we got here then?" said Macpherson, parking up across from where the paramedics had bumped their vehicle up on the pavement.

Taylor stepped out of the car and into the murmur of

voices. In the distance, another siren wailed.

"Can we help?" she said, moving towards the huddle of figures grouped nearest the door to the convenience. Macpherson followed.

"The ambulance people are here now but—" The woman who spoke was in her fifties, her hand shaking as she dragged on a cigarette.

"What happened?" said Taylor peeping into the shop's interior to see the two ambulance crew fussing around the slumped figure of an old man in a wheelchair. Macpherson shot her a glance and slipped inside

"He only came in for his pension the poor craiter. I've been serving him for years," said the woman continuing to tremble.

"Do you think he's... you know? Dead?" A girl in her teens wearing the same bright yellow tabard as the woman edged closer to the doorway, peering through the grimy glass in morbid fascination at the spectacle unfolding inside.

"I'm losing bloody custom here you know. Can they not wheel him out or something?"

Taylor turned her attention to the man sitting on the shop's windowsill with his back to the scene inside. He was older than the woman, with a complexion ravaged by drink, and eyes that suggested he was still fuelled by a skinful. His fleece jacket was grubby and had the motif of the shop's branding on the breast. He wore it zipped up to a stubbly turkey neck and rubbed his palms on his thighs; his right foot tapped rapidly on the pavement.

Taylor took a second to consider if it was in agitation at the disruption to business or in anticipation of his next drink and settled on the latter. "With an attitude like that you'll have no bother winning a customer service award this year," She flipped her identification open. "What happened?"

The man peered at her warrant card.

"You tell me, detective."

Taylor frowned in annoyance and glanced back towards the shop door just as Macpherson stepped outside. As he made his way towards her she looked around at the diverse mix of bystanders. There were several young women with pushchairs wearing heavy outdoor coats over pyjamas, untamed hair piled on top of their heads. They had the prams circled like wagons with a clutch of toddlers corralled in the centre.

On the pavement, leaning against the shuttered and graffiti-covered frontage of a Chinese takeaway, a group of youths who should have been at school already sipped energy drinks and munched on sausage rolls, their occasional raucous banter drawing ire from a band of old-timers standing nearby, the youthful catcalling interrupting the study of the Racing Posts they clutched in their bony hands as they waited for the bookies to open.

Every eye she met turned away quickly.

"Give over, Mervyn, she's only doing her job." The woman flicked her cigarette butt to the kerb and gave Macpherson a nod as he approached.

"Stroke," he said matter-of-factly as he reached Taylor.

She saw the shopkeeper flinch and could feel the ears of the crowd twitch as they sought another titbit they could share over the course of their day.

"Is he alive?" she said.

Macpherson nodded. "Just about. Paramedics reckon it's been some time since it hit him though."

Taylor turned her attention back to the shopkeeper. He looked at her blankly and she began to feel frustration bubble up. Coolness towards the police was par for the course in places like the Fearon Estate but when you added in all that had been happening across the political landscape in the last few months and then doubled down with the ongoing turf war between disparate groups of local hoods, any support that may have been forthcoming had chilled, becoming uncooperative at best and outright hostile at worst.

"Poor Duncan," said the woman, sparking up another cigarette. "I can't believe that wee bastard just upped and left him."

"What do you expect from the likes of that toerag." Mervyn McGurk, proprietor, as the shop signage identified him, sighed and stood up. He looked at Macpherson. "Did they say if they'll be much longer in there?"

"There's no grass growing under you is there," said Macpherson, rolling his eyes.

"It's hard enough to make a living around here without being closed half the bloody day," snapped the shopkeeper.

Taylor raised a placating palm, her frustration tempered by the truth behind McGurk's complaints. Those who lived in the shadow of Fearon House were, without a choice, under the protection of those that ran the estate. Mervyn McGurk did need his shop open and the till singing so he could claw together enough in revenue to pay the protection money demanded by the faceless men who would arrive at his door once a week to collect their subscription. For McGurk and those like him, there was little choice. Authorities be damned, the gangs and criminal groups administered law and order and woe betide those seen to openly be cooperating with the PSNI, no matter how trivial the misdemeanour.

Taylor gritted her teeth; same old story. Whatever you say, say nothing. See no evil, hear no evil, speak no evil. She might have managed to cut one head off the beast but two more had grown out of the gore. With that thought at the forefront of her mind, she checked her watch. If she wanted to find Finn Abbott she better be quick about it because the window was now closing.

The blare and wail of a siren rose in pitch as a rapid

response car rolled to a stop on the road beside them. A doctor in a hi-vis jacket and carrying a bag quickly exited to be met at the door of the shop by one of the paramedics.

"We were told his nephew brought him out this morning?" said Taylor.

McGurk gave a short nod.

"Same as every week. Wheels him in and wheels him out minus half his pension. Duncan had a soft spot for him though, God knows why. Finn's been nothing but trouble his whole worthless life."

"Family is family," said the woman, exhaling the final dregs of her cigarette.

"Maybe to Duncan…" said Taylor, letting the thoughts of what Abbott might have done sink in.

"Do you think he knew he'd had a stroke before he brought him in?"

"Shut up, Maggie." McGurk paced in a circle, clenching and unclenching his hands, answering his employee's question. "Of course he knew. All he wanted was the old fella's money so he could get off his face."

"Do you know where he'd go?" said Taylor, her tone and expression firm.

McGurk hesitated and then caught her look, but before he could answer the young girl stepped forward and pointed back across the muddy green to a point in the lee of Fearon House.

"He'll be where they all go since the old score houses got burnt down."

Taylor and Macpherson followed the direction of her finger to where a chain-link fence protected a row of concrete carcasses and exposed roof timbers making up an abandoned development of new build homes.

5

It always struck Tom Shepard as ironic that the majority of those who stood outside the emergency department inhaling carcinogens were those charged with the care of the patients within.

The groups dressed in scrubs and health service uniforms puffed away with no regard to the clear signage announcing that the Royal Hospital Belfast site was a no-smoking zone nor did they seem to be too concerned for the patients who joined them in partaking of their pleasure, some of whom were clad in little more than surgical gowns, flimsy pyjamas or nightdresses, and hooked up to mobile drip stands.

The wail of an incoming siren redirected Shepard's attention away from the smokers as an ambulance raced into the drop-off bay adjacent to the ED's entrance.

Tom took a sip of takeaway coffee which had long since gone cold, the scene across the road playing out as it had a hundred times before during his extended period of observation. First, the driver jumped out and opened the rear doors. He, or she, would then lower the access ramp before disappearing inside the vehicle. Moments or minutes later depending on the complications faced within, both paramedics and the trolley-bound patient would lead a concerned relative past the oblivious smokers and into the hospital building.

Shepard tossed his empty cup into a waste bin, his eyes

drifting up the steel and glass facade of the recently redeveloped acute services building to settle on the eighth floor where the man responsible for the murder of his wife and child recovered from his injuries.

If it hadn't been for the quick intervention of police officers, the wounds would have ended Gordon 'Monster' Beattie's life and the city would have been done a service but as it stood he still drew breath, and if anything positive could be taken away from that fact, Shepard decided it was the small consolation that the bullets which had failed to kill him may have ended his reign of terror. That uplifting thought, no matter how often he tried to frame it, gave him no comfort. Not when the imagined images of his family's fate and that of Beattie's other countless victims haunted his nightmares, and not when he now knew the man he had come home to kill was a link in a much longer chain of corruption.

The former special forces soldier let his mind drift back to how his plan for simple revenge had segued into something greater. Memories flashed back to the shock of sudden impact as the big Manitou telehandler plunged into the lough and the rush of chilly water filled the cab. His escape from what could have been a watery grave had been calm and professional, his head breaching the surface of Belfast Lough to bob in the choppy water as the blue strobes of the police and ambulance vehicles lit up the shoreline and storage containers of Hoey Cargo in an ongoing operation to mop up what had been an extensive human trafficking, drug and weapons trade. The spotlight of the overhead police helicopter had missed him as it sought out the running lights of retreating speedboats before banking sharply to return its attention to the shore, lending assistance to colleagues on the ground who were recovering the child victims that Shepard's final desperate act had saved.

The next morning the city had woken to the shock news of

an assistant chief constable killed in the line of duty and the suicide of a city councillor whose crime of embezzling public funds had been exposed. The headlines became more lurid as the day wore on and news broke of the scandal that a respected charitable organisation had been implicated as a front for the money laundering and as the vehicle for trafficking and exploitation of young women and girls on an industrial scale.

There had been arrests but it didn't take a razor-sharp mind to appreciate that those named weren't the architects and once again the hands holding the strings were free to continue their manipulations and powerplays to quietly infect and undermine the institutions appointed to uphold democracy and social order.

Shepard continued to watch the comings and goings around the ED entrance as he weighed up his options. Money wasn't an issue. He had taken enough loot from Beattie's cronies to see him through for some time, and to all intents and purposes, he was missing, presumed dead. Even if that hadn't been the case, his military career had furnished him with the contacts, documentation and skillset to slip out of the city to the UK mainland where he could then drop off the radar. Long before Brexit, the focus of the border force and their partner agencies had been on the deluge of those trying to enter the country illegally. With that situation exacerbated and the numbers overwhelming, there weren't too many people left with time to worry about who was sneaking out.

The thought of leaving brought a sense of failure and frustration that gnawed in the pit of his stomach. While no longer a clear and present danger, Beattie was still alive and as much as Shepard wanted to walk into the ward and finish what he had started he now also wanted to know more. The tear-stained face of a young mother and then the other women and children he had liberated from the burning food factory crept into his mind, those faces blurring into yet another. Detective Inspector Veronica Taylor.

He had watched the police press conference the day after events at the docks, perched on the edge of the bed in the small holiday let he had taken as his current base.

Taylor stood behind her chief superintendent and detective chief inspector as they briefed the television news crews on the violent week that had befallen the city. Something about the detective inspector's body language and the pinch of her brow as the late Assistant Chief Constable Ken Wallace was mentioned piqued his interest, his own expression mirroring hers when Chief Superintendent William Law spoke of an unnamed source currently being treated for injuries who, when sufficiently recovered, could shed significant light on events and help shape any potential future investigations. The senior officers signed off with reassurances to the public that the immediate crisis was over and order had once again been restored to the streets of the capital.

As the press rattled off their questions, Shepard mulled over what he had gleaned from reading between the lines. The extent of the operation he had seen at Hoey Cargo suggested Beattie had thrown his hand in with some big hitters in transnational organised crime and, supposing the source Law spoke of was Beattie himself, it suggested one of two things: a legitimate deal had been struck which would once again see Beattie slip off the hook and avoid justice in return for cooperation or, as so often had been the case over the course of Northern Ireland's troubled history, those infected by the cancer of collusion were bolting the door and drawing the curtains to ensure no further light could be shone on their sordid schemes and further damage illicit trade and impact profit margins.

Shepard weighed up the chances the former might be true. Given what he knew of Beattie's talent for self-preservation there was a slim probability. The primary risk in taking that course however was the target it would paint on his back. The latter, given how the police were beginning to downplay events, the swiftness in how the public prosecution service had come to agree plea deals with a group of foreign nationals arrested during the incident, and how several politicians from across the green and orange divide were trying to sweep events surrounding Beattie, the suicide of Councillor Howard, and the charity scandal off the front pages tugged at the cynic in him.

Who had Beattie gotten into bed with? Who had escaped the police raid on Hoey Cargo and who were the faceless backers and enablers willing to risk routing guns, drugs and flesh out of Belfast? Ultimately though, what the hell did it have to do with him?

As he once again pondered that thought, Veronica Taylor came to mind. The detective inspector, her history in pursuit of Beattie, and the failed court case against the business magnate and his organisation had made more than the footnotes in recent days, and Shepard wondered how she felt at once again being the subject of intense press and peer scrutiny. If there was a deal on the cards could she, would she, toe the line?

They were both, in their own way, victims of Beattie, the detective's career consumed in her pursuit of justice at the expense of a personal life and her reputation, he in the loss of his family, each of them bound together in pursuit of a perpetrator yet to face any significant consequences.

While Taylor had the motive, means and opportunity to continue her dogged quest, the overwhelming question in Shepard's mind was the decision of if he could live with just being a bystander.

The blip of a siren and flashing blue strobe interrupted his brooding. A liveried PSNI Skoda speeding through the hospital gates negotiated across lanes to bypass the cars lined up for the public car parks, swerving into a yellow hatched spot beside the ambulance bay. As the two officers inside exited the vehicle, Shepard perked up from his slouch against the car park railings. Exiting from the hospital and stealing a glance at the police car, two figures took the steps down to the footway. The shorter and stockier of the two sparked up a cigarette, his head tucked into the crook of his elbow to protect the flame before coming up a second later to exhale heavily, his hand gesticulating the glowing tip towards his larger companion in a series of sharp stabbing motions.

Shepard recognised both the stocky Albanian gangster, Amir Kazazi and Beattie's heavy-set enforcer, Harry Carruthers who swigged the dregs from a bottle of cola, jabbing the empty vessel in a defiant gesture before dropping his waste into the road. Whatever they were in a heated discussion over was lost to distance and the background drone of traffic, but it was unlikely the two were debating who forgot to bring the grapes or get well soon card.

As the two men parted with brusque nods, Shepard took the only decision he knew would give him peace at night. He had left his city to the grip of terrorists, gangsters and violence once to pursue a career at the tip of the spear fighting other people's wars. All those years had honed an appreciation of what happened when those entrusted with keeping society safe stood idle, allowing themselves to be blinded by division and partisan politics long enough to let the virus of corruption and kleptocracy gain a stranglehold over the powers and governing institutions who were meant to protect the citizens. Beattie lay in a hospital bed instead of a cell, or better yet an unmarked grave but he hadn't risen to his position of influence by accident.

As Carruthers lumbered into the road, shortcutting the railed walkway that led to the underground car park, he spat a curse and threw up an aggressive fist at the honk of an angry motorist who had been forced to slam on her brakes.

Shepard peeled away from his post. If he couldn't reach the puppet master perhaps he could grind some answers from the monkey.

6

Macpherson reached out with his oversized hands and hauled aside the temporary fencing that poorly secured the building site.

"What a bloody waste. Look at the state of the place," he said as Taylor crunched across the threshold of crushed stone, pausing to poke a toe at an abandoned and dented metal sign that had been ripped from the site boundary declaring 'DANGER – STRICTLY NO ADMITTANCE.'

A mock-up image of what had been planned for the derelict site remained mounted on a wooden billboard. It showed a row of modern townhouses alongside a block of contemporary apartments surrounded by luxury landscaping and the gleam of turnkey interiors. She didn't give the strapline a second look as she passed.

'GBH HOMES *presents a luxury development of 2 bedroom homes and modern apartment living just a stone's throw from the city.*'

"That needs to be looked at by the Trade Descriptions lot. They might actually have something to lift him for," muttered Macpherson. GBH, Gordon Beattie Holdings, the DS imagined the gangster's smug grin as he had dreamt up the tongue-in-cheek slogan.

"We'll start up in here and work our way along," said Taylor. She stood in the centre of the site's turning circle and pointed towards the first of the half-built dwellings.

"You take the front and I'll take the back," said Macpherson. Taylor gave a nod of acknowledgement and moved to enter the first premises.

There was no front door, just the raw and rotting architrave surrounding where it should have been. Graffiti marred the exterior red brickwork and the bare concrete interior smelled of damp and urine.

The hall was empty but for some general waste that had blown in and as she explored further she found the entire ground floor vacant. Macpherson met her as she exited the space that had been designated as the lounge to enter that of the small galley kitchen.

"I'll take a juke upstairs," he said.

"Okay. Be careful."

Taylor cast her eyes around the incomplete room. Bare blockwork was scarred with spray-painted Loyalist slogans and more personal attacks on unknown individuals: Pete was a pedo, Davy loved dick and her personal favourite; FUCK THE POLISE!

Incomplete stud walls had been vandalised with either huge holes bashed in them or entire sections of plasterboard ripped down to expose the wooden framework. Above, she could hear Macpherson clump from room to room.

The sight was depressing. The vision of what should have been a family home given over to despair and drug abuse. The estate remained riddled with the scourge of powder and pill, and while some tried to make a stand those involved in the business of addiction enforced their dominance through intimidation and violence. A child's football bearing the logo of a popular film franchise lay amid the broken ruins of what should have been a safe haven.

Macpherson appeared on the other side of the open wall. "There's not a sinner here," he said. For that Taylor was grateful. With the increasing number of overdoses and gang-related deaths plaguing the city, the last thing she needed was to discover yet another corpse.

There was nothing of note in the next four properties they searched either, so they turned their attention to the three-storey apartment building. Of all the derelict sites it was the most complete, if window frames with shattered glass hanging like broken bat wings counted, and it had a front door, albeit the safety glass panels were missing and it was absent any visible locks.

Stepping inside they found the communal hallway was empty but littered with the detritus of recent use. Takeaway cartons of half-eaten food, crushed cans of pilsner and empty bottles of supermarket spirits presented a path to the stairs. Once again the fixtures were vandalised and the walls and ceiling daubed in gang motifs and graffiti. Moving through the ground floor it wasn't long before they began to find evidence the apartments were being used as a doss house for drug abuse.

Foil wraps and homemade crack pipes carpeted the entrance porch of the first apartment. The broken glass of lightbulbs and second-hand syringes glittered in the light that poured through the flat's bathroom window. Taylor carefully stepped around the worst of it, entering the space set aside for the lounge to find three figures slumped on sagging and threadbare sofas.

"You'd be better taking them out for the bonfire," said Macpherson, jutting his chin at the furniture, his expression dark and hands thrust deep in his jacket pockets.

Two of the heads remained slumped in stupor. The third, that of a young woman, peered up. Her eyes were glassy and a stream of drool had dried on her chin.

"We're looking for Finn Abbott," said Taylor.

The woman's mouth opened and closed but nothing more than a guttural grunt escaped.

"His uncle has had a wee turn," offered Macpherson in a tone attempting compassion. "He's had to go to the hospital. Is Finn here?"

Her eyes rolled into the back of her skull and her head slumped back against the dirty couch, her response coming in shallow snores.

"Thanks for your help." Macpherson snorted in irritation, his nose crinkling at the fug of urine and body odour souring the room. Taylor took a few steps closer to the trio and peered down. The floor between them was littered with the debris of their addiction but thankfully, judging from the slow rise of their chests and the soft snuffles all three were still breathing.

"Come on, it looks like we're heading in the right direction at least," said Taylor, leading the way back out into the communal hallway.

The sound of shuffling feet and dry coughs echoed from the landing above. Taylor led the way to the stairs. The rubbish and paraphernalia associated with the misery of dependency seemed to get worse as they made their way along the first floor and they were met by similar scenes to that below inside every doorway. Bodies of the living dead crashed out on filthy sleeping bags or heavily stained mattresses, but worse yet were the backed-up facilities. The smashed windows exposed the tiny bathrooms to the outside elements but the damage did little to ventilate the heady stink of excrement and vomit.

Their search took them the whole way to the last apartment on the first floor before they found who they were searching for.

"Finn Abbott?" said Taylor.

The figure was crouched over an upturned milk crate and he had his back to the hallway. The waistband of his jeans hung low exposing bony hips and an emaciated spine. He spun around in surprise, Taylor confirming on seeing the sallow face it was indeed the man they were looking for.

Abbott stumbled away from where he had been cooking up a hit of heroin, backing against the wall like a cornered animal, then easing his way along towards the windows. His movements were erratic and his mumbling, at first incoherent, became more agitated as he called out for help.

"Get away from me... don't you be coming any closer!" His grip on the blackened tablespoon tightened and he waved it like a dagger.

"Help. Anybody. Help me... they're going to kill me." As Abbott called out, his eyes darted frantically around the room for an exit.

Taylor raised open palms to her sides in a gesture she hoped he would recognise as non-threatening. Macpherson stayed back, maintaining his blockade on the apartment's only escape route.

"We're not here to hurt you... it's okay, Finn, no—" Taylor quickly shot up a restraining palm as, when reaching for her identification, Abbott's eyes bulged and he took a half-step forward raising the spoon aggressively.

"We're the police," she said calmly. "We need to talk to you about some vandalism to a new building development across town. We'd like you to verify where you where at the time so we can rule you out of our inquiries,"

"I know why you're here and I'm not talking to you!" Abbott shrank back again, one hand guiding him along the wall to the open archway leading to the apartment's small kitchen.

Finn Abbott was thirty-eight but looked younger and older at the same time. His habit had ravaged a tall and gangly frame to the point of malnutrition giving him an air of adolescent underdevelopment which was in contrast to his pallor and the paranoid stare of a much older addict. He was clean shaven and wore an oversized dark green sweatshirt and cheap training shoes.

"It will help everybody if you calm down and tell us your side of the story. Look, have a seat." Taylor gave the milk crate a soft kick, the container sliding across the bare concrete floor towards Abbott.

"How do I know you're the police?"

Taylor slowly extended her warrant card. Abbott shook his head, clawing a hand across his face and through his hair.

"Doesn't matter, I mean, so what if you are? They have the police in their back pocket… Jesus… Fucking Stumpy. I knew this would happen." His voice rose in pitch as he paced left and right, Taylor deducing he was already heavily under the influence with a mental state teetering on the edge of delusion. Abbott continued to mutter to himself.

"Finn," said Taylor, waiting until her repeated call drew his attention. "I need to talk to you about your uncle."

Abbott had tears in his eyes, one arm was wrapped around his tummy and the other pointed the spoon.

"Did they do that to him to get to me?"

"No, Finn." Taylor shook her head, trying to maintain a calm facade and keep the quizzical expression from her face. "You took him to the shops, remember? He's had a stroke but he's been taken to the hospital. We can take you there and talk about this other stuff in the car?"

"No. No, he didn't have a stroke. D'you think I'm stupid? I'm not getting in any car," His eyes widened as if suddenly understanding. "You're one of them." He jabbed the spoon towards the floor, each thrust punctuating his words.

"Right, son. That's enough of that. You're coming with us either to the hospital or to the nick. Last chance to make it your own choice."

"If I get in your car no one will see me again. I'll end up like wee Barry Toms." Spittle flecked from Abbott's mouth and he doubled over as if in agony.

Taylor cast Macpherson a quizzical look as he huffed out a loud scoff.

"Barry Toms was a story the people round here used to get their kids to come in at night," he said, easing away from the door to close down the room.

Abbott backed away, his movements feral and his teeth gritted in anger.

"You'll be telling us next the bogeyman is after you," continued Macpherson, moving slowly forward. "Come on, lad, you don't have to make this harder than it needs to be. Let us get you some help."

"Finn, it's obvious you've taken something. We'll take you to the hospital to get checked out and maybe we'll get to see your uncle while we're there. When you're ready you can tell us what riled you up so much you had to trash that building site?" Taylor offered a palm towards the open door, her tone encouraging and her expression reassuring, Macpherson took another slow step forward.

"Get back!" Abbott threw the spoon at him and scrambled to pick up the milk crate, waving it menacingly from side to side. "I know what I saw and I know those bastards want us out of the way because we're trying to tell people who they are."

"Finn, I need you to calm down." Taylor took a step back to offer him some space, gesturing for Macpherson to follow suit.

Abbott glared at Macpherson, the anger in his voice cracking to grief.

"You're letting it happen again," he sobbed. "And all these youngsters. Why won't you stop them?"

"Stop who, Finn?" said Taylor, backing a further half step away in an attempt to defuse Abbott's increasingly erratic behaviour.

"All of them," screamed Abbott, before his wracked sobs

were punctuated by more babbling. "Fucking Stumpy. I told him they'd use you lot to get us. Same old fucking story, isn't it? Who's going to believe the troublemakers and the drug addicts?"

"Finn, I give you my word. If you come with us I can—"

"You're a liar! We've tried to tell the police. We've tried to tell everybody."

Taylor spun away as Abbott launched the crate at her. The plastic container deflected off her shoulder to clatter across the floor. As she swung back anticipating a further attack Abbott instead ran across the room and hurled himself out of a broken window.

She was at the sill a second after Macpherson, the two sharing a stunned look before peering out, expecting the worst. As they looked down at the crumpled figure spread out on the ground, rail-thin limbs began to untangle themselves. Taylor pushed away and darted from the apartment, the echo of her footfalls fading as she hurtled towards the stairs.

Macpherson closed his eyes and gave a resigned sigh.

"Why do they always have to run?" he muttered, watching as Abbott pushed himself up from the ground and started to limp away.

7

'The Union Snack' held the flanking position in a row of small commercial units on the northern fringe of the Fearon Estate.

The chip shop was separated from a Chinese takeout by an off-licence and a home bakery. The next unit to that was currently empty, its shutters covered in abstract swirls and the acute angles of unreadable graffiti tags, some of which had been vandalised by thick-tipped marker pen and a single white splatter of paint bomb, the dried drip trails curling from a long-ago impact towards the gum scarred pavement.

Harry Carruthers swung his legs from the Range Rover, his feet thumping to the pavement in an awkward half step, half leap. He wasn't tall but he was broad of shoulder and had the build of a man who divided his time between the barbell and the beer barrel. Short arms pumped each side of an impressive belly as he strode towards the chippy, eyes darting to surveil the road as he covered the short distance from the car. The shop's front window was dominated by a cartoon cod in an orange collarette and bowler hat, union flag in one hand and a three-pronged fork in the other. Shouldering the door open, he was greeted by an electronic chime and the warm waft of fried food.

"Harry. What about you?" The man behind the fryers gave a nod of greeting.

"Send me in the usual will you, Jimmy," said Carruthers, raising the hatch to step behind the counter.

If there had been any other customers present they may have noted Jimmy was evidently ready for the request, already moving to slop a cod fillet out of the fryer and deposit it onto a drip tray under the amber glow of a warming rack.

Carruthers' trainers squeaked as he walked across the greasy floor towards the rear of the property, and roughly pushing aside a beaded curtain he stepped into a narrow prep space, the curtain's brightly coloured plastic orbs clacking in his wake. Chest freezers and tall refrigerated larder cupboards lined the walls. Stainless steel countertops were littered with cartons of sauces and multi-coloured chopping boards. Ahead, a short corridor extended towards the door to the yard, which was jammed open, funnelling a draught of warm air out from the frying area. The door to the cramped toilet that doubled as a cleaning store was mercifully closed although the underlying stink of dirty mop heads and stagnant water lingered.

Carruthers shook out a bunch of keys and opened the office, crossing to the desk where he flopped down in a wheeled faux leather chair.

"Jimmy, any chance? My stomach thinks my throat's been cut," he bellowed, jerking open the bottom desk drawer, pulling out a bottle of Vodka and snatching up the glass standing beside the antiquated monitor and keyboard. After a testing sniff, he thwacked it down and glugged in a generous measure of the spirit, immediately taking a long pull before topping the glass back up.

The bleep of electronic chimes sounded from a duplicate speaker in the corridor outside the office as a customer entered. Carruthers gave the CCTV monitor mounted in the corner of the room a cursory glance, its split screen showing the shop front and the yard at the rear.

"Jimmy, bring mine in here before you see to anyone else,

will you?"

He could hear the irritation in his voice and it wasn't just down to hunger. Things were not going well and his meeting with his Albanian counterpart at the hospital which he had hoped might offer a solution to address their mutual predicament, had proven fruitless.

First, it had been the murder of Rab Millar and now with Beattie incapacitated and Freaky Johnstone dead, the sharks were circling, sensing blood in the water and whipped into a frenzy at the prospect of an easy kill. The last two weeks had been a war of attrition as he had sought to hold onto as many street corners and customers as possible while at the same time ensuring that those loyal to the Beattie organisation received reassurance that their investment remained sound or left in no doubt of what might happen if they chose to cash out or throw their support behind one of the multiple new personalities testing the strength of the organisation's embattled defences.

He took another swig, the welcome burn pushing back the anxieties that had been creeping from sleepless nights into his waking hours. The one thing he had always taken for granted was the security of hierarchy, comfortable in his abilities and accepting that his role was to follow orders rather than undertake the burden of organisation and command. The transition from follower to leader didn't come naturally nor did he wear the mantle well, his inexperience coming to a head in recent days in the punishment of a vocal mid-level dissenter. Unable to foresee the secondary and tertiary effect of his violence, Carruthers had quickly found taking a hammer to his victim's knees and elbows had not only martyred the man but garnered wider sympathy and a backlash from those who sought new leadership. All in all, it was a classic backfire, and Gordon Beattie had not been happy.

The former paramilitary godfather had only recently been declared fit enough to receive visitors and Carruthers had been shocked when he saw his boss. He looked like death. His injuries and the time in isolation had taken their toll; Beattie's healthy complexion was now gaunt, and weeks of relying on the assistance of machinery and medical intervention had left him physically weakened. None of it had blunted his mind nor the edge of his tongue though. Carruthers and Kazazi had left Beattie's bedside in full knowledge of what he needed to be done to ensure the survival of the organisation, and neither of them had been happy about it.

The clack of the bead curtain rattling in the corridor interrupted his reflections.

"About bloody ti—"

"Is it not a bit early in the day for the hard stuff?"

Carruthers, in his haste to get up, caught his belly on the desk and his feet in the chair's wheelbase. Pens scattered from a desk tidy across the Formica work surface, momentum sliding him several feet backwards on the castors. His mouth hung agape as he came to rest.

"You look like you've seen a ghost, Harry," said Shepard, stepping closer and sampling a chip from the box he held in his hand. He gave a satisfied nod and then offered the box across the desk. Carruthers gave a shake of the head that was barely perceptible, his knuckles white as he clutched the armrests.

"I guess you've lost your appetite?" Shepard placed the food on the desk, noting Carruthers' eyes flash to the CCTV monitor. He took a seat on the edge of the desk, drawing a compact M9A1 pistol from inside his jacket and resting the grip on his thigh, the stubby barrel aimed at Carruthers' gut.

"I'm afraid it's just us, Harry," said Shepard. "And I want to know who your boss has cut a deal with to keep him in a hospital bed and out of a jail cell."

8

"...the development which was due for ribbon-cutting in the next month has been so extensively damaged that it will now be impossible to open without significant remedial works... Pastor Nigel Hinds told us of his disappointment but offered reassurance to his worshippers that they would still be able to undertake their spiritual guidance at a sister site nearby... We reached out to Corry Developments for comment regarding the recent spate of attacks on their portfolio but no one was available for comment..."

Steven Scott listened to the rest of the report with a tight-lipped smile on his face. As the news anchor cut away from the reporter and the carnage of broken windows and ruptured water pipes to go to the weather he dropped the remote control to the sofa and picked up his tie.

Serves the bastard right, he thought, nodding at his reflection in the mirror while fastening the knot. The practised movements did little to quiet a mind preoccupied with Geordie Corry, his entrepreneurial enterprise and his other long-time cronies. It may have only been a small setback to the firm but it was another bloody nick in a thousand tiny cuts, the campaign designed to deter investors, frustrate shareholders and infuriate the board. Scott forced a chuckle; more fool them if they didn't think the past would catch up to them.

Tie fastened, he took a step back to check his appearance. Dark hair with no hint of grey, clean shaven and although just shy of six foot he was of average build with forgettable features. Unremarkable. Anyone visiting the ground floor apartment would quickly deduce it was a bachelor pad, the light touch of home furnishings and fresh flowers not quite offering a sense of the female touch, instead marking the gentleman resident as someone of more sophisticated tastes. The abstract artwork, classical CD collection and bookcase of biographies and professional finance tomes added to the sense of the individual.

Scott checked the time and decided it was time to get a move on if he wanted to get to the office before his bitch of a supervisor could haul him over the coals again. Making a start on his daily tasks and managing some headway through his workload calmed his nerves before he continued to fulfil his surreptitious obligations to an old acquaintance in what had become a mutually beneficial arrangement.

With both parties having a clear focus on what was needed to achieve their shared goal, Scott's involvement had begun with the relatively innocuous retrieval of information destined for destruction. Soon though, it had expanded to the procurement of sensitive commercial information and the smuggling out of hard copies and the occasional data drive brimming with secrets.

For the layman, what he had uncovered during the previous week spent auditing ledgers and invoices wouldn't have made very interesting reading but to Scott, the numerical columns and dissemination of the financial transactions were illuminating. To his partner, they offered the means of absolution.

Pausing at the kitchen counter, Scott pressed two Seroxat pills from a silver blister pack and washed them down with the dregs of his breakfast tea. As he reached for his jacket the doorbell buzzed and barely a second later it was followed by the triple rap of the letterbox.

"I'm coming," he called.

The buzzer again harshly called for attention.

"Christ's sake."

Walking down the short hall he could see the outline of a figure wearing a hi-vis vest on the other side of the privacy glass. It was too early for the postman and he wasn't waiting on a delivery so what was this? A courier to pick up the stolen documents and his reports. It would have been nice to have been warned. He opened the door.

"Yes."

The figure in the hi-vis turned out to be a woman and she took a step back, raising the barrel of a high-end Nikon camera in a smooth arc.

Scott made to close the door but was obstructed by a heavy-set man in an anorak; the jacket was the colour of dried blood and the branded logo gleamed bright on the breast like a fresh wound. His suit trousers were shiny from age and at odds with the work boots he wore, one of which barred the door from shutting.

"Steven Scott?"

"Get off my—"

The rapid staccato of a camera shutter and the strobe of a flash drew his eye and attention, giving the invader a chance to press a meaty fist against the doorframe. The hand was close enough for Scott to count the forest of fine black hairs and smell cheese and onion crisps.

"Steven." The man had a slight lisp and it took a moment for Scott to adjust his hearing to compensate. "Reg McGarrity. Belfast Echo. Have you any comment to make on the Colm Casey trial?"

"No." His face flushed and the cold wash of fear flooded his abdomen.

"Will you make any comment on the rumour that you have been stealing inside information on Casey and asked to assist with witness tampering?"

"What rumour? You can't do this—"

"Does your prior history with Oliver Maddox cloud your ability to ensure Mr Casey gets a fair trial?"

The camera continued to snap and strobe. Scott felt light-headed.

"Get the fuck away from me," he screamed, pushing the tabloid reporter back and slamming the door closed.

The questions, now muffled, continued.

"Did Oliver Maddox threaten to reveal things about you if you didn't help him…"

Scott slumped to the skirting and put his hands over his ears to block out the accusations, the drumbeat of blood pumping through his skull exacerbating painful memories.

"Steven, how old were you when…"

The reporter's face was squashed against the glass. The letterbox flapped open and the camera flash illuminated the narrow hallway.

Scott doubled over, unable to hold back the nausea and the sudden rush of vomit.

9

"Do you think barging in here waving a gun in my face scares me?" said Carruthers, the tone of his voice lacking the conviction of his words.

"Rab Miller said something similar before I killed him so spare me the bravado, Harry."

Shepard thought back briefly to the evening he had killed Beattie's right-hand man. The drug dealer and pimp had been belligerent to the last and the first to die in his rampage of revenge against the group responsible for the murder of his family. He picked up another chip and took a bite. "You sure you don't want one?"

"Fuck off."

Shepard shrugged and popped the other half in his mouth. The potato was crisp and smothered in salt and vinegar.

"How's the Monster doing?"

"He'll live."

"How long do you think that'll last?"

"If that's a threat I'll pass it on. I'm sure he'll be quaking in his hospital gown." Carruthers gave a small laugh. "You'll not get near him."

"Who says it'll be me?" said Shepard with a shrug. "It looked to me like some nasty bastards missed out on a big payday. I wouldn't like to be lying vulnerable in a hospital bed while they're out there wondering who's to blame for the balls-up."

"You don't know what's going on," sneered Carruthers.

"Then why don't you enlighten me?" Shepard gave a nod towards the CCTV monitor. "Not exactly rush hour is it?"

Carruthers followed the glance, wondering what had happened to Jimmy before settling on the probability the yellow bastard took to his heels at the first sight of a gun.

"Fuc—"

"I get it, Harry. You're not a tout."

The muscles along Carruthers' jaw rippled as he clenched his teeth, chin jutting defiantly.

"Let me lay out what's going to happen here." Shepard pushed the chips aside and stood. "I came back to make sure Monster and the rest of his mates paid for what they did to my family. So far, so good. But then he had you snatch an innocent woman and her daughter off the street to get at me and I realised he's not for changing." Shepard's mouth pursed in distaste. "I can't let that go, not when I saw with my own eyes what was planned for them and not while he's still breathing."

"What are you? A one-man army?" said Carruthers, his words dripping with sarcasm.

"You'd be surprised at the damage I can do when I put my mind to it."

"Monster didn't know…"

Shepard raised his eyebrows as Caruthers refrained from further protest. His face was red and he was sweating profusely.

"Didn't know what was going on? Do me a favour, Harry."

"Believe what you want. I'm saying nothing else."

Shepard snatched a biro from the table top and took a quick step forward, slamming the pen into the middle of Carruthers' right thigh.

He let out a yowl of pain.

Shepard kept pressure on the wound, his other hand

pressing Carruthers into the seat as he tried to wriggle free. The pen was buried an inch into the meat of his quadricep and a bloom of blood had begun to seep through his jeans.

"I'm not messing about, Harry. Who was Beattie working with and why has he not been arrested?"

"He's sick—"

"Sick in the head," snarled Shepard. The two men faced off, inches apart. Carruthers' breath was sour from stress and his features warped in a grimace of pain as Shepard put more pressure on the pen.

"Talk to me, Harry. Hoey Cargo was a setback but it wouldn't have been enough to have Beattie's backers pull the parachute."

Caruthers' reply was inaudible through gritted teeth.

"Where were the weapons going? It wasn't for your lot. Was it for dissidents? Christ, there was enough hardware there to start a war."

"Get off me!"

"What has he asked you and the Albanian to do? Neither of you looked too happy earlier."

"So you're spying on us now?"

"Absolutely, and I'll be on your back every damn day from now until I put Beattie in a box and burn his business to the ground."

The electronic bleep-bleep of the entrance chime sounded. The two men's attention snapped to the CCTV monitor in unison.

"Hello. Shop?"

The screen displayed the images of two customers, the distinctive bulk of body armour and their caps marking them out as police.

"Hello?"

Carruthers reacted a millisecond before Shepard, pressing upward with every ounce of strength he could muster.

Mashing his feet into the floor, he levered himself up from the chair as though driven by pistons, the crown of his head smashing into Shepard's jaw and knocking him aside.

Stumbling awkwardly, Carruthers fell against the desk, the impact enough to upend the monitor and send it crashing to the floor. With a grunt, he ripped the pen from his leg and limped for the door.

Shepard shook off the impact but tasted the coppery tang of blood in his mouth. The bright spots blurring his vision cleared as Carruthers exited the office using the frame and the wall for support, turning left towards the rear yard.

The ringing in his ears abated enough to hear sudden concerned calls from the counter.

"Police. Is everything okay back there?"

Shepard shoved the abandoned chair out of the way and started his pursuit before the query turned into a confrontation. Rushing out into the yard, he saw the gate to the alleyway beyond swing closed. The space ahead was littered with stacks of plastic produce trays, old cooking oil barrels and an overflowing waste bin smelling of rot.

"Stop! Police!" The order was firm and came in the same instant an engine spluttered to life beyond the gate.

Glancing back inside, Shepard saw the two officers cast in shadow as they rapidly approached and he felt suddenly trapped between complying with the instruction and allowing Carruthers to escape.

A TETRA radio blared with static, the words emanating and the reply distorted by the acoustics of the corridor.

Shepard launched himself at the heavy back door, both hands slamming it closed before scrambling to secure the sturdy galvanised locking bolt. As it snapped into position heavy thuds crashed in futility against the now secure exit, the angry voices inside urgent but muffled.

Wrestling the gate open he rushed out into the alley. His

motorcycle remained semi-hidden behind a row of three large industrial waste bins belonging to the other units. To his right, the grind of missed gearing gave him just enough time to see a flare of brake lights before a rusting delivery van took the corner and disappeared from view.

10

"Which way did he go?"

Taylor sucked in a breath. Her heart thumped against her chest and a sheen of sweat glistened on her brow. Having arrived at the rear of the building she was met with more piles of dereliction but no Finn Abbott.

Macpherson peered out of the shattered window above her, pointing across the broken ground towards a rusted site container and a row of felt-roofed outhouses on the far side of some more damaged fencing. "The wee shite squeezed through there. Go on, I'll get the car."

Taylor gave a nod and took off, each step a battle as her feet were sucked into the coarse granular aggregate of the unfinished groundworks. The rasp and crunch of her strides masked the huff of her laboured breathing.

She pulled the damaged fence aside and squeezed through, getting momentarily caught up on the sharp tines of snipped chain links before the material of her jacket gave in and ripped free. Inspecting the tear and feeling frustration well up she stepped into the road seeking a sign of her quarry.

There was none.

The deep baritone bark of a dog sounded farther along where the outhouses bordered a rutted track that led to the rear of the estate community centre and then doubled back onto the communal green. As she started to jog in that direction, the crash of a dustbin and more aggressive barking boomed out.

"Finn. Finn, stop!"

Taylor entered the narrow moss-covered lane to see Abbott crabbing backwards along the ground, protected from the snaps and snarls of a German Shepherd by flimsy fence panels, the wood quivering as the dog thudded against it. There was terror in Abbott's eyes as he scrambled to his feet and limped away, clinging to the wall opposite the baying dog.

"Finn," implored Taylor, her jog now reduced to a walk.

As Abbott neared the end of the lane a car screeched to a stop. The driver's door flung open.

"Right you are, son. Give it up." Macpherson defended the end of the path like an undersized and overweight goalkeeper.

Abbott searched frantically for a way to escape but the walls were too high and the slavering of the big dog behind the fence too dangerous.

"Finn, it's okay. Come on, listen to me." Taylor slowed her pace and adopted a posture she hoped looked unthreatening and sincere. Abbott continued to pace and thump a tattoo on the walls with the heel of his fists.

"Finn, let's get you to the hospital. Look you're bleeding."

"No! No hospitals. I'm not going back there. No more pills."

Macpherson looked past the rambling figure to Taylor, the two locking eyes with unspoken words of concern for the safety of each other and that of the man in between. A cornered animal was unpredictable and could be deadly.

"It's okay, son. Come on. We'll not let any harm come to you. Just get in—"

Abbott wheeled on Macpherson, saliva spraying from his mouth as he screamed in anger and frustration.

"That's what they tell you!" His fists balled at his sides and blood dripped from his scraped hands and fell in droplets at his feet. "It's for your own good. You'll be safe and then…" Abbott doubled over in a fit of wracking sobs.

"Finn?" Taylor's tone was soft as she took a few steps closer. The dog had shut up but continued to snort and sniff through the narrow gaps in the fence.

"I should have stayed away from them. I should never have listened."

"If someone has hurt or threatened you, Finn, I promise we can help you, but only if you talk to us." Taylor caught herself mid stride, Abbott suddenly rearing up in rage again, his words directed at her but the venom of his thrusting finger aimed at Macpherson.

"He said Barry was a fairy tale! Youse are just like the others. No one wants to hear the truth of what they did to us. You say you want to help and then you'll hear what I have to say and call it the ravings of an addict. I'm not doing another second in any psych ward again. I'll kill myself first."

"Finn, I promise—"

"If you won't believe me go and ask Stumpy!"

"We don't know who Stumpy is Finn," said Taylor. She could see Abbott's mental state was deteriorating by the second. Whatever trauma he was alluding to and the stress and anxieties it was bringing to the surface had him on the edge of a full-blown panic attack.

"Steven Scott," shouted Abbott as if they should know the name. "He'll tell you why we smashed that place up and what I'm saying about wee Barry and those kids is the truth," He screamed the last word, setting the dog off again.

Several windows opened and voices shouted out in irritation at the ongoing commotion. Abbott slumped against the wall, his face beetroot and his chest heaving. Then, quietly, he said, "Nobody takes a dope fiend like me seriously. He's unreliable, he can't be trusted. That's what they say, you know." A snort of callous laughter sent snot spraying from his nose. "So ask Stumpy about Glenrafferty. You'll believe him." Abbott affected a mocking tone at Taylor's seeming ignorance of the name. "Go and ask your bloody star witness."

"Steven Scott?" said Taylor, looking past Abbott towards Macpherson who looked like he had just seen a ghost.

"Doc?"

Macpherson blinked rapidly but any words were drowned out by the sudden blare of a siren in the distance.

"You bastards!"

"Finn, wait." Taylor took a step forward but he wheeled away.

"You set me up. Kept me talking while you got backup."

"No, we didn't. Those sirens aren't for you."

"Liar!"

The sudden speed at which Abbott spun and pulled into a sprint caught Taylor off guard. Macpherson, emerging from the quagmire of memory which had swamped him made a valiant grab but the younger man stiff-armed the detective sergeant away and swerved around the front of the blocking Volvo onto the road. He shot a single glance over his shoulder, sprinting towards the expanse of the communal green.

The impact was sickening.

It was the same wet crunching whump that had traumatised Taylor on fishing trips with her grandfather so many years before. A sound of pliable flesh and small bones being bashed against the concrete pier. A shudder coursed through her as the feel of a slimy tail and the smell of salt and fish guts came flooding back.

Frozen to the spot, she watched in horrified fascination as Abbott's broken body jackknifed over the bonnet of the speeding van, the impact hurling him fifteen feet into the air and over the roof before he slammed into the road in a tangle of broken limbs.

She didn't need to get any closer to know he was dead.

11

Shepard slammed on the brakes so hard the rear wheel of the powerful Honda motorcycle lifted off the road and he had to wrestle the bike back under control, the rubber slamming to the tarmac in the same instant as the body a few hundred yards ahead.

There wasn't so much as a flicker of brake lights as the van sped on, spewing out a cloud of black smoke and a throaty backfire as it turned along the edge of the common and raced towards the entrance to the estate and the main roads beyond.

Whoever the victim of Carruthers' hit and run was they weren't getting back up. Their head was as misshapen as a bashed-in boiled egg and blood oozed from the ears, nose and mouth.

Shepard swore under his breath, knocking the bike out of gear as a bystander ran into the road, closely followed by another figure emerging from an adjacent entry.

"You've got to be kidding me," he groaned.

Veronica Taylor was on the phone, her attention focused in the direction of the fleeing van, no doubt rattling off a description, direction and the number plate if she had managed to get a decent view of it.

In the few moments it took for her to relay the information, close the call and turn back, her stalwart DS had risen from inspecting the body and was giving her a sombre shake of the head. Taylor slammed her palm on the roof of the Volvo parked kerbside. In the distance, from the direction of The Union Snack, sirens wailed.

Shepard walked the bike through ninety degrees and then gunned the throttle, leaving the scene and the two detectives in his wake. Glancing in the wing mirror he caught Taylor peering at his retreat and then crouching to do her own examination of the body.

Within seconds he was putting distance between himself and the incident, losing himself in the warren of backstreets as he circumnavigated the estate, eventually coming out on the western fringe and gunning the bike beyond the speed limit in the hope he could catch up to, or snatch a glimpse of Carruthers' getaway van. Ideally, the fleeing vehicle would be caught up in the column of traffic filtering into the city centre but weaving between cars and crossing into the oncoming lane when a gap in traffic appeared offered no immediate success, and so, by the time he reached the Cityside Retail Park and York Street interchange, Shepard had accepted his efforts were in vain and Carruthers was gone.

Sweeping the bike through a tight turn he cut across two lanes, heading country bound towards Holywood and the loughside holiday let that was his temporary refuge. His route took him over the M3 bridge and as he reached the apex of the overpass he glanced left over the ruins of old memories and the wounds of the recent past. A ribbon of road was just about all that was left of Sailortown, that and a few redbrick terraces and the old spire of St Josephs, the once thriving community now almost completely buried under towering architectural tributes to modernity. Those vestiges that did remain were fighting a losing battle against the drumbeat of progress and a rampant surge of redevelopment.

Beyond the gleaming high-rise apartments, business parks and building sites, Belfast Lough bled into the Irish Sea.

Along the western bank, the docklands were encircled by the shining ribbon of the M2 motorway heading north, the multi-lane carriageway hemming in the warehouses which rose up on land reclaimed from the water and while he couldn't see Hoey Cargo, he could make out the marker buoy where he had caught his breath before swimming ashore a mile farther inland.

The traffic thinned out along the Sydenham bypass and as the iconic yellow cranes of Samson and Goliath rose into view he thought again of Veronica Taylor, wondering if she had ever given thought to what had happened to him in the chaotic aftermath of the police raid.

The media had reported the ongoing sea searches in the days after but the police had remained tight lipped on what they hoped to find, alluding to nothing beyond a connection to the ongoing investigation. When the divers scaled back a few days later, and with nothing to report, press speculation fell behind newer headlines.

He had considered reaching out to Taylor more than once, mostly to gauge her reaction to Beattie remaining free but also to let her know that he had survived and wasn't about to abandon his quest for retribution against the man they both despised. He felt the need to press her for information on what remained of Beattie's organisation, his accomplices, those who had been released on petty charges, and the others who had escaped altogether.

Each time he had reconsidered. Taylor had discovered who he was and what he had done to Billy MacBride, Rab Millar, Freaky Jackson and the rest, and, she was a cop, bound by oath and duty. He was a killer. A killer of killers right enough but that wouldn't change anything in the eyes of a judge and jury.

Easing back on the acceleration Shepard turned the motorcycle into a narrow shrub-lined lane that led to the holiday cottage and wondered about the detective's connection to Carruthers' most recent victim. Who had he been and what did she want with him? Was it in connection to the raid or completely unrelated?

As he pulled to a stop and kicked down the motorcycle's stand, his overriding thought was to throw caution to the wind and make contact. Quid pro quo. He would tell her who she should be looking for in exchange for information on the Monster and his minions. Information that would assist in his continuing war against Beattie and the organised crime gangs.

A war the police service, in their desire to dampen the embers of recent events, seemed to have chosen to concede.

12

"You might want to ease up before you rub a hole through that. It's practically an antique."

"I'm sorry?" said Taylor, startled from her thoughts.

Father Michael Keane gestured towards the trellis table and the spot she had been obsessively wiping down.

"Eadie McReedy from number eighty-four donated this on her deathbed." The old priest laid a liver-spotted hand on the pitted surface. "Do you know it's seen five jubilees, goodness knows how many royal weddings, a presidential visit and"— he reached out to take the damp cloth from Taylor and chuckled—"I've a feeling it will outlast me."

Taylor blushed under the warmth of the grandfatherly concern in Keane's eyes. "Are you alright, Veronica?"

"I'm… yes. Sorry," she said. "I had one of those days yesterday."

"Well, a problem shared is a problem halved, so they say. Come on away of that now. You've served enough tea today to have earned one yourself."

"But, what about…" Taylor made for the basin of mismatched cups and saucers she had been collecting.

"Bernie will see to them. Don't worry, there'll be plenty more when you get back." Keane laid a hand on her forearm and gave it a gentle pat, before guiding her away from the tables set out to receive St Joseph's honoured guests.

On the morning of every second Tuesday St Joseph's

opened its doors to welcome those in the wider community who either through loneliness, circumstance or on the recommendation of other charitable organisations availed themselves of the companionship, compassion, spiritual guidance and the warm, dry space and hot cup of tea that was offered.

Since the operation at Hoey Cargo and when her day off coincided, Taylor had made a point of volunteering to help.

Keane led her through the small gathering which looked larger than it was in the confines of the small hall, pausing on occasion to mutter a word of prayer or pass comment or compliment as was needed to those who had come in from the cold. Taylor recognised some of the faces as regulars, but there was always someone new and while most were warm and appreciative there were several who quickly shifted eye contact or shrank back in the crowd as she approached.

"Survival instinct," said Keane, squeezing her bicep. "They sense a lion amongst the lambs."

"I'm off duty."

"Ack, sure it's me you're talking to. You're never off duty." Keane chuckled, beckoning over a young man in a grubby yellow puffer jacket. "Liam? Come here till I see you. Where have you been?"

Liam froze, his eyes narrowed in suspicion long enough for the biscuit he held to crumble into his tea before his manners kicked in and he forced a smile.

"Father. Hello," said Liam, taking Keane's outstretched hand. "I've been moving around a bit. Found somewhere to stay for a while but well, they got a bit preachy, you know…"

Keane gave a throaty laugh and then an understanding dip of the head. "Well, you'll not have anything forced down your throat here. You're very welcome back. This is Veronica," he said, and then in a whisper. "She's a police officer."

Liam kept his hand by his side. "I... yes, I know. I saw you on the news."

"She's helping out for a while so do an old fella a favour and pass it around she's not here to lift anybody. Okay?"

Liam swallowed, eyes darting from Keane and back to Taylor. "Yeah?"

"I'm only here to pour the tea," confirmed Taylor.

"Aye, right enough then. Good to meet you," said Liam with a nod. Keane reciprocated and let him slink back into the safety of the crowd.

"I don't think he believed you," said Taylor, pulling out a seat at an empty table and helping the old priest to sit.

"Liam's alright but God love him he's one of too many desperate cases that come and go." Keane started to pour milk into two tea cups, Taylor palming the urn to check it was still hot.

"He's living on the street?" she asked, taking each cup and drawing off the stewed contents, adding two sugars to sweeten the brew.

Keane nodded. "Yes. A story you'll know well enough. Broken home, truancy, limited life choices. Drugs."

Taylor's lips twisted in a sympathetic grimace as Keane laid out the evolution of the route into petty crime, a cycle of violence and a potential premature death.

"There are those who try to make a direct intervention but you have to come to a decision on your own, I think. I just hope Liam reaches that point before his choices take him down a path he can't return from."

Taylor sipped her tea, the sickening crunch of Abbott's body hitting the tarmac replaying in her ears. She caught Liam sneaking a peek at her before he was lost again in the throng.

"So, tell this old man your woes," said Keane.

"Do you ever feel you're wasting your time?" said Taylor.

Keane's eyes narrowed over the brim of his cup, and after taking a moment to swallow he placed it on the table. Over the past weeks, she had grown fond of the old priest, his wit and wisdom sometimes the sole source of comfort in the turmoil that churned in her subconscious. His charity in arranging a safe place for the women and girls rescued from Hoey Cargo had been gracious and unexpected, extending to her when in the following days he had reached out to follow up on her well-being which offered a timely distraction from press conferences, debriefs and brooding. The spectre of the man who had drawn them together had yet to be raised beyond brief queries from Keane which she met with semi-official responses. As yet, she hadn't raised her own questions about the priest's past.

"Well, my faith allows me to see beyond the immediate, Veronica," he said. "And considering your recent achievements, I should think you could be more forgiving of yourself. There's a lot of people moving away from terrible trauma thanks to you."

"But for every one of them, there's ten of…" Taylor inclined her head in Liam's general direction.

"You can only save the world one soul at a time."

"Maybe it's easier to tell yourself that when you're making a positive difference," Taylor gave a tired smile, the bright hubbub of the hall washing over her. She stared into her cup. "I lost another one yesterday."

"I'm sorry," said Keane, placing a hand over her own. "What happened?"

"It was a hit and run, but the victim," she sighed. "He wasn't unlike Liam."

"I see."

"Just another young man who'd lost his way but the awful thing is I think we failed him. The system, I mean."

"Society bears a collective responsibility. Family, the

church, local government. You're a smart woman, you know he didn't end up where he was by accident and you know there was nothing you could do to prevent him from taking the road he chose."

"I know, it's just—"

"You are a good police officer, Veronica. You make a difference, maybe not to this young man in life but you can certainly find out who ran him down and offer an example to someone else who finds themselves wondering what is the right choice."

"Maybe—"

"Maybe nothing, and besides," said Keane. "You're better off out there doing that than in here making tea." Keane pushed his cup aside. "This is terrible."

Taylor shook her head as the old priest wheezed a laugh. "Come on, I've a few more people I'd like you to meet and it'll take your mind off your woes."

He stood and offered an arm so she could guide him back through the crowded hall. "Have faith in yourself to do the right thing when it's called for, Veronica. I have."

13

The whiteboard which hung by the entrance to Professor Thompson's office had neither the gallows of the hangman nor the hash etchings of noughts and crosses that usually marked the surface, the game boards replaced by neat initials: PM. FA and the number 1015.

"Come in." Thompson's voice called out a response to Taylor's firm rap.

The pathologist's office was every inch the lair of the busy professional, and he gestured towards two chairs for the visitors while clearing a rough space on his desk, dropping and then opening a folder containing the pinned pages of a forensic report and selection of high-quality digital prints. The clock on the wall behind him said it was two o'clock

Taylor's day off felt long distant as the morning and early afternoon blurred together, the former taken up establishing any leads on the vehicle involved in the hit and run and then engaged in debate to ascertain if Abbott's passing could be classed as a death in police custody, which for the moment remained a firm no. A round-up of the remaining caseload took up the time immediately after a quick lunch until it was time to make the short journey across town.

"Prof," said Macpherson flopping down with a nod of greeting. Taylor took the seat nearest the wall, quietly studying the space and finding it unchanged since her last visit.

A list of contact numbers and anatomy charts were pinned to the walls, and a bookcase sagged under the weight of medical manuals and periodicals. A mug declaring 'I'd find you more interesting if you were dead' sat beside a grinning skull, bookended by a photograph of a younger Thompson and an elderly woman, and framed diplomas.

"Thanks for squeezing us in, Professor. We know you're busy so it's very much appreciated."

Thompson waved away Taylor's gratitude.

"No need, Inspector. We're all on the same team at the end of the day and in any event"—He prodded the pages in front of him—"This one has most certainly piqued my interest."

Attendance to The Royal Belfast Hospital Regional Forensic Mortuary was something Taylor considered an occupational hazard, the facility being a place of personal and professional pain scattered with the memories of lives cut short. Those same recollections were often tainted by the cutting room's faint odour of raw meat mingling with disinfectant and the teeth jarring sounds as Thompson put the tools of his trade to work in determining cause of death. Taylor, although ever desperate for the guidance and the crucial evidence his examinations provided, had never quite been able to see the detached clinical brutality as anything but a secondary desecration to an already violated victim.

Thompson slid out a page. A generic illustration of a human body was marked with a number of checkmarks and neatly printed comments arrowed to the location of each. Beside this, the pathologist placed two photographs, one from the scene and one taken on the autopsy table. Taylor noted the absence of the classic Y-shaped incision suggesting the image was one of the first taken.

"Your victim died as a result of blunt force trauma to the

head." Thompson pointed his pen at the diagram and then the photograph of Finn Abbott's misshaped skull. "It's my hypothesis that the initial impact with the vehicle fractured the skull causing sudden and catastrophic brain injuries. The tissue of the frontal lobe shows evidence of tearing and bleeding with bruising as deep as the cerebellum." The pathologist shook his head sadly, then continued. "Further damage was consistent with the type of injuries we would expect from man versus vehicle. Broken left wrist, clavicle displacement and a fractured pelvis, as well as the obligatory cuts and contusions which come from an unrestrained impact with the road surface." Thompson's lips pulled into a tight line as he indicated each.

"Sounds cut and dried, Prof," said Macpherson, with an arch look of suspicion that the pathologist had not quite played all his cards.

"Open and shut, sergeant. This man's death was as a direct result of injuries sustained by vehicular impact."

"But?" said Taylor, catching the same whiff that something was being held back.

"But these aren't the injuries that interest me."

"Okay…" Taylor patiently waited for Thompson to expand.

"Did you know this man? I suppose I mean to say are you aware of his history?"

Taylor cocked her head to the side and Macpherson nodded slowly.

"Finn Abbott. Juvenile delinquent graduating to adult pain in the arsehole. He had cautions for anti-social behaviour, petty theft and fraud and more recently a couple of custodial sentences for minor drug offences. It's fair to say he wasn't exactly an angel but he was no Tony Soprano either."

"Abbott was someone we were aware of, Professor," said Taylor. "Why do you ask?"

Thompson slid his initial drawing away, replacing it with another. The notes and indicating marks doubled those of the previous.

"On examination, we found thirty-four areas of previous injury."

"Self-harm?"

"I'm afraid not. These range from scars I'd associate with repeated physical beatings, cigarette burns and"—Thompson pointed to a V-shaped section marked up on the posterior illustration—"at some point, he had an iron held against his back and both buttocks."

"Jesus!" Macpherson breathed.

"I'd be confident saying Mr Abbott had at one point in his life been a victim of long-term physical abuse."

Taylor felt a chill run through her. Abbott's frantic protests and paranoid ramblings carried a different tone with the benefit of hindsight.

"Can you have a guess at—"

"When these occurred?" said Thompson, nodding as Taylor indicated that was what she had been about to say. "Don't quote me just yet but anywhere from the age of eight to thirteen."

"I don't understand?" said Taylor, a frown deepening.

Thompson pulled a selection of images from his document folder.

"Aside from the old wounds I noticed during the physical examination, some of his measurements were off so I had the cadaver X-rayed prior to dissection. It's not that uncommon," he added as Taylor looked surprised. "These are images of the left arm, right leg and spine. You can see in both limbs historical fractures that have not healed correctly. It suggests to me that your victim didn't receive adequate medical attention at the time of the injury and the breaks were left to heal on their own."

"How can you tell?" said Taylor. The black-and-white images of the limbs were clear enough but her experience at deciphering the detail fell somewhat short of Thompson's.

"This"—Thompson held up the image of Abbott's left arm —"is a torsion fracture, sometimes called a spiral fracture. See the detail?"

Taylor nodded that she did. Glancing at Macpherson she noticed the colour had drained from his cheeks.

"It would commonly occur when force is applied along the axis of the bone."

"His arm was twisted violently," said Macpherson with an eerie edge of disquiet to his tone.

"Yes," agreed Thompson.

"But how do you date it?" asked Taylor with a brief glimpse of concern at her colleague who had sat back in his chair with an odd look of unease plastered across his face. Macpherson gave a short dip of his chin acknowledging he would be fine.

Thompson indicated the X-ray image of the right leg.

"This is a classical metaphysical lesion." Thompson traced the location of the injury with the tip of a pen. "It's an injury common in nearly fifty per cent of child abuse cases. You can see the corner fracture of the proximal tibia has impacted the growth plate of the right leg so I'd assume your victim had a limp or certainly some physical impairment as a result."

"And those?" said Taylor.

"The sixth to the tenth thoracic vertebrae. Signs of more historic fracturing, possibly from a fall or, if we take it in the context of these other injuries, a prolonged or vicious beating."

Taylor blew out a breath as she considered the trauma he had been through. Macpherson was right, Abbott had been no angel but to have had to endure all that at such an early age? Was it any wonder he took to self-medicating considering the physical toll and psychological damage it must have wrought on a young body and mind?

"I'm afraid that's it, inspector. Your man didn't have a very pleasant start in a life that has been tragically cut short."

"Thanks, Professor." Taylor reached out a hand.

"I'll have the report drawn up and have Irene send it across." Thompson took her hand, giving it a short professional pump. Macpherson followed. The DS was distracted as they left the pathologist's office and made their way back to the car park.

"Are you alright?" said Taylor, the note of concern in her voice triggering a dismissive wave and shake of the head from Macpherson.

"Aye. Listening to all that?" He jerked a thumb over his shoulder and rubbed a palm over his tummy. "It ruined any joy I had after my brunch bap. Give me a minute will you?"

Taylor nodded as he headed for the men's room. "I'll meet you at the car," she said.

Watching him disappear inside she knew Abbott's death and the pathologist's findings had triggered something for her colleague and as she wondered what it could be, the troubling secrets she was keeping from him began to churn in the pit of her stomach.

Exiting the lobby into the underground parking bay she thought back to Michael Keane's advice and knew the time was coming that she would have to trust Macpherson with what she knew and have faith he would understand why she had stayed silent. Even if just to unload the burden that was keeping her awake at night.

14

In the end, Taylor didn't go directly to the car. She walked up the vehicle ramps until she reached ground level and then took a minute to let the afternoon's stiff breeze blow the clinging scent of the mortuary from her clothes and hair.

Her phone buzzed with a text message from Macpherson. She replied in the affirmative to his offer of coffee and decided if he didn't bring up the subject of what was bothering him, she would come clean about what had happened in the undercroft of Hoey Cargo.

It didn't feel all that long ago that she had descended into this car park to identify the body of Rab Millar. A descent that mirrored the dread she was feeling that her career, her identity, and her life's work could be stripped away in the aftermath of the failed prosecution against Gordon Beattie. Millar's murder had set in motion a chain of events that restored her reputation, broke up a trafficking ring and took a vast quantity of arms and narcotics off the street. So why did the emptiness remain? Looking across the hospital grounds and up at the soaring ward block she knew why. She sighed, turned her back on the sight and headed back towards the car.

"Penny for them?"

Taylor started at the sudden intrusion into her thoughts. A previously unseen figure peeled away from the structural H-beam they had been resting against to intercept her.

"You look surprisingly well for a dead man." Taylor didn't break stride until she came to a stop two feet away.

"I'll take that as a compliment." Tom Shepard offered a warm smile. "It's good to see you, inspector."

"Likewise, Tom," she said returning the smile. "You know my chief super will be doing a jig when I bring him in a multiple murderer."

Shepard laughed.

"You couldn't bring me in the last time and you had me in handcuffs."

"That's because you played dirty but I know what to expect this time."

"You're seriously going to stand there and tell me you're going to take me down after all the help I gave you."

"All the *help*…" said Taylor, incredulous. "You sparked off a bloody war on the streets and you're lucky you didn't get both of us killed."

"Aye well, look on the bright side."

"Why are you here, Tom?" said Taylor.

"What makes you think it's anything other than to wish our friend a speedy recovery." Shepard cocked his head in the direction of the main hospital.

"Because you forgot the grapes."

Car tyres screeched on painted tarmac as a vehicle drove down the ramp, the driver peering at them briefly before refocusing her attention on seeking out a parking space.

"How is he?" said Shepard, his expression darkening.

"He'll live."

"I see, so how come you've got him in there and not on a prison medical wing."

Taylor knew as soon as the subject of Beattie was raised Shepard would question the criminal's continued liberty.

"It's complicated."

Shepard scoffed, giving an irritated shake of his head.

"You're not writing a Facebook post, Veronica. Christ, you've caught the bastard red-handed." He held up two fingers. "Twice."

"It's not just you the bastard has wronged, Tom, and you've a cheek to be giving out to me about anyone needing locking up after what you've done so get down off your high horse."

Shepard was briefly taken aback by the ferocity of her riposte.

"It's complicated. What happened down there..." Taylor trailed off as a car immobiliser blipped and a pedestrian made their way towards their parked car.

"Well, what did happen down there? Do you not owe me that much?" said Shepard. Taylor gave an exasperated shrug.

"I can't talk about it. I especially can't talk about it with you."

"For God's sake, Veronica."

"You killed those men in cold blood, Tom."

"Are you telling me they didn't deserve it? They wouldn't have thought twice about killing you or me or any of those women and kids if push came to shove."

"I'm saying they deserved to be made an example of. To be brought before the courts—"

"Like Beattie?"

After everything that had happened, after ACC Wallace had assisted in the escape of his co-conspirators, after the secrets Beattie had revealed in the undercroft, the lies, the half-truths and the conspiracy pressed down on her and she felt the fragility of her argument, the tent poles of her convictions beginning to sag under the weight of the accusation. Shepard continued as she struggled to protest further.

"You can't put them in front of the bench because either your precious constabulary has more rotten apples than

Nutts Corner market or the people that decide if there's a case to be answered have too many vested interests in the shady dealings behind the scenes."

"That's not fair—"

"Isn't it?"

"No." Taylor took a step forward. "It isn't and I'll see Beattie gets what he's due but…"

"But what, Veronica?"

Taylor turned away. Shepard sighed and reached out, placing a hand on her forearm. "Veronica?" She shrugged him off.

"What if I was able to help you?"

"Help me?" said Taylor. "With what?"

"The hit and run."

Taylor's eyes narrowed in suspicion.

"I know who was driving the van. I'll tell you who and you can clear up a death by dangerous but you need to give me something on who Beattie was working with."

"Nice try."

"I'm not bluffing, I was there, on United Terrace." He paused to let that sink in. "I saw the guy run into the road and get hit by the van. Your DS checked him over and you called it in."

Taylor studied his features. Nothing about his manner suggested a bluff, that and the accuracy of his statement bolstered the claim so she considered his words. To take his trade would only muddy her own sense of morality and potentially lead to further mayhem or murder. The memory of a retreating motorcycle flashed into her mind closely followed by Professor Thompson's medical report on Finn Abbott.

"Who?"

"Do we have a deal?" said Shepard.

"Who?" Taylor asked again with the slightest of nods.

"Harry Carruthers. He worked for Rab Millar, and then as a gopher for Beattie. Right now he's up to something with Beattie's Albanian contacts."

"How do you know all this?"

Shepard tapped the side of his nose.

"Quid pro quo, inspector."

Taylor could see the scheme play out in her mind's eye. "So, correct me if I'm wrong then. You tracked down this Carruthers to turn up the heat and find out what you can about Beattie," said Taylor, her frown deepening.

Shepard turned down his lower lip, not committing to any further explanation of his actions. The inspector shook her head, irritability simmering towards anger.

"And then at some point in your conversation, Carruthers fled, pursued by you and he managed to kill my suspect."

Shepard shook his head. "No comment?"

"This isn't a joke, Tom."

"You're frigging right it's not." Shepard's tone was clipped. "I was in that warehouse, Veronica. I saw the quantity and the quality of the weapons and the scale of human misery with my own eyes. It doesn't take a genius to work out how lucrative that is."

"I know."

"So what are you doing about it?" said Shepard

"There's nothing I can do about it!" Taylor snapped. Her eyes dropped from his gaze and she shook out her hair. The empty ache in her stomach intensified as her thoughts turned to Finn Abbott, the misery he had endured and the dead end at which she now found herself in both instances.

"I thought you were different."

"Tom—"

"Don't start trying to make excuses."

"I can't do anything, okay? I can't." The burden of her fears and the frustrations of the last weeks weighed down heavily.

The suppression of what she now knew and the pressure of her silence had left her feeling as though she was drowning. Panic began to rise in her chest as repressed memories of being trapped in a whirling maelstrom of raging river and the sensation of impending death washed over her.

When her head snapped back up her words burst out with urgency.

"I can't do anything because I don't know who else might still be involved." Finally speaking the truth to someone else felt like a blessed relief. "The ACC wasn't the hero the PR department want you to believe. He was up to his eye teeth in it. Beattie's man on the inside. It was Ken Wallace who lured Martin Copeland to his death, a change of leadership in the name of securing peace was how they tried to spin it to me." She shook her head in dismay. "That was the night your wife and son died."

Shepard's expression darkened.

"I'm sorry they were caught up in what happened."

Shepard didn't reply. His features slipped into a mask of resolve, the commitment that his retribution was not complete hardening.

Taylor's voice sounded detached as she continued. "Neither of the two could have risen to that level if the corruption didn't go deeper, so yes, you're probably right about the rotten apples. Christ, Tom. The scale of what we found at Hoey Cargo was…" Taylor threw up her hands in a gesture of exasperation.

"Industrial," said Shepard.

"Trafficking, weapons, drugs? You don't bring three deals like that under one roof unless you're positive that you're getting away with it."

"So what do we do?"

"We?" said Taylor.

"I swore I'd put Beattie in a box for the part he played in

what happened to my family, him and anyone else that was even remotely involved, so, if the cancer has spread deeper then it's time to carve it out."

"Can I remind you that you're a suspect in at least three murders?"

"No, I'm missing. Presumed dead. Which by the sounds of it, makes me more useful to you."

"I can't let you be involved in this—"

"I'm already involved."

Taylor's phone began to ring. She glanced down. It was Macpherson.

"If there's any chance of flushing these people out and securing convictions you cannot be a part of it, Tom."

The incoming call rang off. Shepard nodded slowly. Plea bargains and pre-trial hearings were the last thing on his mind.

"Then I'll bring you Carruthers for the hit and run. After that, it's over to you to flip those charges and find out what he knows."

"You said it yourself, he's a gopher."

"That he is, but he's been in with the Monster nearly every day for the last fortnight and I'll bet you a pound to a penny it wasn't to hear about his bed baths."

The phone started to ring again. Taylor hit call cancel.

"So we just hope that whatever he's being tasked to do gives us another link in the chain?" she said.

"Beattie's deal tanked and he's on the ropes. You make sure Carruthers gives you something you can take to Beattie to use as leverage."

The phone started a third incessant ring.

"You'd better get that," said Shepard. "I'll be in touch when I track down Carruthers."

"Tom?"

Shepard had already turned to leave. When he looked back

Taylor hadn't moved, her thumb hovered above the call connect icon. She gave a short nod.

"Be careful."

15

The broad flagstones that lined the mall outside Belfast Royal Courts of Justice were damp from a brief shower that had swept in off Belfast Lough, the sudden deluge passing just as quickly as it had arrived left a clear blue sky in its wake. The neoclassical facade of the building glowed in the sunlight, the Portland stone and Corinthian columns shimmering almost white in the sun's glare.

Oliver Maddox took the sudden turn as a good omen, first, the rain to wash away the sin and then the herald of golden light to offer redemption.

In any event, it offered a much more photogenic backdrop than the dreary grey of thunderclouds or winter waves the walls projected when the weather was more malign.

A light breeze rustled the needles of tall firs ensconced in ornamental concrete pots on either side of the great black gates, nature's whisper competing with the low murmur of the assembled press pack standing in a loose arc around the Justice Minister.

Maddox raised his hands and a flurry of flashbulbs rippled from the photographers' cameras.

"Ladies and gentlemen, thanks for waiting." He offered a humble smile, his voice carrying across the mall to the ears of the assembly without the aid of a megaphone.

To the left of the media scrum, several members of the public sat on seating cubes observing the scene with varied degrees of interest, and a court service security guard waited patiently on the steps of the entrance to escort the minister back inside once he had made his statement.

"I've read a number of articles and I'm aware that a number of your outlets and commentators have been questioning my commitment to a recent statement regarding a more robust stance on organised crime in the city and on those engaged in, and benefitting from it." Maddox let his eyes drift across the faces, some expressions amused and some just bored, attending out of necessity in the hope of a soundbite or the snap that would help pay the monthly bills. "Specifically comments around my personal history with Colm Casey. I have never denied Casey and I grew up a street apart or shared a classroom, nor that we were on the same youth sports teams. I share that history with many other boys, but, none of them sit accused of being at the head of a company channelling illicit cargo into this city, nor are they behind the barbaric murder of three innocent men—"

"Are you able to address the rumour your party leader isn't too happy with your crusade and called for you to desist until an independent investigation can gather more evidence on any third-party business and political links to the Casey family?"

Maddox raised his hands for quiet as the speculation rang out from an unseen source. You bet the old bastard isn't happy, he thought, picturing the wrinkled old schoolmaster being forced to admit his stance as a staunch defender of the Union had been helped along by inducements and kickbacks from Casey and others of his ilk.

"I'm not going to add weight to rumour, but I can tell you that I have not sought a case against Casey as revenge for some slight or to further my own political ambitions. I have no grudge to bear nor quarrel to resolve. It is the function of my office to ensure those who seek to feather their beds with the proceeds of crime are brought before a jury of their peers.

It is the weight of evidence and the prosecution's carefully constructed case that will win the day here, not the powers of office or the influence of personality."

Maddox's eye was drawn to the corner of the mall as a small crowd rounded the corner of the Laganside Court Complex. Beyond them, traffic had slowed to a crawl along Oxford Street as the lights at Lanyon Place changed to red. Blurred faces behind the grimy windows of a double-decker Citybus peered down at the placard-waving mob.

"I'm here today impartially, to witness from the public gallery the first step in dismantling a criminal enterprise that has peddled untold misery and been detrimental to health and security across all sections of our community. This particular case is about Colm Casey, but as of today, I've instructed officers of the PSNI Economic Crime Unit to begin a thorough investigation into those companies aligned with Casey Bulk Fuel—" Maddox's words were interrupted by catcalls and jeers and the attention of the press pack and the public spectators began to shift focus to the approaching group. The first placard to catch the Justice Minister's eye cried out 'SHAME' in large blood-red letters. The next sent his heart plummeting to his stomach, 'MADDOX THE MOLESTER'.

The assembled press pack began to fall into disarray as the scent of scandal suddenly filled the mall. Their calls mixed with the chants of the group, whose accusation was roared in unison and echoed off the walls of the courthouse.

"*PAEDO! PAEDO! PAEDO!*"

Maddox jumped as a hand gripped his upper arm. Blinking under the sudden onslaught of camera flashes and shouts of accusation and frantic questions, he let the security guard drag him to the safety of the court steps and hustle him up and through the screening barrier into the sanctity of the courts and out of reach of the baying mob.

16

"You look like you've lost a pound and found a penny, sir. May I?"

Detective Chief Inspector Gillian Reed took the offered seat opposite her superior's desk and crossed her legs, hoping the man wasn't about to suffer an aneurysm. Chief Superintendent William Law replaced the telephone handset and slumped back in his chair.

"That was the PPS," he said. "The judge has adjourned Casey's trial until there has been a case review to alleviate any doubt that the test of prosecution hasn't been compromised."

The DCI gave a thoughtful nod. There goes Casey then, she thought. The story had already hit the news websites and social media channels and by the time the evening news rolled around, the events outside the courts and their repercussions would be felt high and low.

"Oh, and Casey has been bailed," Law added, his words delivered with the intonation she expected he would also have related news of an acquittal, that of bitter disappointment.

Gillian Reed's appearance exuded nothing but calm professionalism considering the mushroom cloud of erupting scandal, the potential extent of its fallout and the accusations that would be brewing as efforts to shirk the blame of failure ramped up, and that was all before the lambasting to come over due diligence, oversight, and wasted budgets.

Immaculate in a pinstripe designer trouser suit and matching heels, she may have looked more like an accountant than a tough detective but a bean counter, she was not.

"How in God's name did the Echo manage to get wind of this before us?" Law pinched the bridge of his nose, his question rhetorical. "Who put this Scott forward as a witness?"

"Scott was a whistleblower," said Reed. "He worked for a firm of accountants used by Casey and offered up information he had discovered on money laundering and other illegal trades he thought may implicate himself and the business in fraud or criminal intent if it wasn't declared."

"Do we have any idea if these accusations levelled against him and Oliver Maddox can be corroborated? I mean seriously, or is it a bloody ham-fisted stitch-up?"

Reed adjusted her horn-rimmed glasses with a manicured fingertip.

"At the moment we only have what Reg McGarrity has put up on the Echo's website. I'd expect he's holding most of the juicy details back for when his scoop hits the newsagents in the evening editions. I'll have Scott pulled in and put somewhere safe before anyone else gets to him."

"That would be all we would need, another bloody sleazy hack offering him a few quid to cast more aspersions."

"I was thinking about the fact he'd put the finger on Colm Casey, sir. That's the sort of thing that earns you a one-way trip to the bottom of the lough," said Reed.

Law pulled a sour expression and leaned forward, uncharacteristically putting his elbows on the desk. "That sounds like the sort of wit I'd expect from Detective Sergeant Macpherson, Gillian."

"Doesn't make it any less accurate, sir. People are shot dead for less."

"Indeed."

Reed let the silence hang in the air for a second, Law preoccupied with his thoughts.

"Will someone be speaking to the minister?" she said finally.

"I suppose I'll have to." Law didn't sound like it was a conversation he wanted to have, and she empathised. No one would want to have that conversation and equally, where did you start? Sorry, the Casey prosecution has fallen on its backside but by the way is it true that when you were in a previous position of trust you sexually abused the prosecution's key witness, yes, that same individual it's now claimed was coerced into fabricating evidence against the defendant so you could pursue a personal vendetta. No thanks, she thought, then cleared her throat.

"To add to our troubles, I've had Geordie Corry's solicitor on, asking why there isn't more being done to protect his developments and apprehend the vandals."

Law rolled his eyes, half-heartedly scattering some paperwork. "It never rains but it pours. Yes, I read the report."

"Our prime suspect died at the scene. DI Taylor is following up on the hit and run but we've just been informed that due to the circumstances, the Police Ombudsman is assigning an SIO to review."

Law sighed and rose from his desk, stretching out the kinks in his back. "We may as well rent them a bloody office the amount of time they've spent here recently."

He took a few steps to the window and looked out across the city. "See they receive our full cooperation, please."

"Yes, sir."

Reed smoothed out the material of her trousers and stood. "If that's all I'll get back to the team for an update and see what I can do to appease Mr Corry."

Law nodded and Reed retreated to the door. As she turned the handle the chief superintendent spoke.

"Gillian?

"Sir?"

"Make sure DS Macpherson is on his best behaviour, I don't want to get so much as a whiff he is antagonising our guest or being anything but obliging in his assistance."

Reed acknowledged his request and as she closed the door, it was her turn to sigh.

17

Detective Constable Carrie Cook placed the last slice of homemade Victoria sponge cake onto a plate and was pleasantly surprised to find the sink empty for a change. The sign Sellotaped to the mug cupboard politely asking 'respect the facilities' was pristine, its tea-spotted and water-marked predecessor having been banished to the bin in someone's uncharacteristic fit of cleaning. Carrie rinsed the knife under hot water, gave it a dry with a paper towel and dropped it with a clatter back into the cutlery drawer just as the kettle clicked off.

"Hi, Carrie. You've been busy again," said Taylor, observing the stack of Tupperware and wedges of cake that set the mouth watering. She placed a thin folder on top of the fridge and made to offer a helping hand. "You know you'll ruin their dinner?"

"Ack, it's not much and besides"–She leaned in conspiratorially—"It'll keep the sarge from moaning about all that paperwork."

Taylor gave a small chuckle at the truth in the DC's words. If there was one way to distract Macpherson's descent into gloom and despair when administrative duties became a priority it was to appeal to his stomach, and Carrie Cook was a feeder.

Cook brushed icing sugar from her fingertips, scuffing the excess off on the hips of check trousers that today had replaced one of her regular high street skirt suits. Sensible shoes remained though, as did the cheap charm bracelet she treasured as though it was a Faberge.

Taylor helped her lay out cups for the team, Cook dropping in a teabag or scoop of instant coffee granules as the order demanded. The DC had anchored her position within the team when seconded during an investigation into a domestic slavery ring. Her inherent aptitude for investigation, a sharp eye for detail, IT abilities and empathy were all attributes Taylor admired and was keen to put to use. Her skills as a pastry chef and master baker ensured she had a friend for life in Macpherson.

"Everything alright?" said Cook, looping a strand of mousey hair behind an ear as she stirred milk into a coffee picking up on something of an atmosphere.

"Actually, I wanted you to do something for me on the QT," admitted Taylor, taking the offered cup and placing it on a tea tray.

"No bother. Fire away."

Taylor retrieved the folder she had placed on the fridge and passed it across. Cook opened and skimmed the front page as Taylor transferred the rest of the cups.

"Harry Carruthers?"

"I need you to do some digging. Aliases and associates, last known address, possible haunts."

"Is this to do with... oh..." The question died on Cook's lips as she caught a familiar name amid the brief.

"It could be to do with a lot of things, Carrie," said Taylor. "That's why I need discretion for the time being."

Cook nodded, continuing to flick through the presented information. Taylor picked up the tray of cups and flicked an elbow towards the slices of cake.

"Right, you grab that and bring it out before we get back to find out there's been a mutiny."

❖❖❖

"Why does he always get the biggest piece?"

"For God's sake dry your bloody eyes, man," mumbled Macpherson through a grin and a mouthful of cake, then, wagging a finger at the complainant as he washed down the treat with some tea. "You youngsters need to be quicker off the mark. Oh aye, and who snaffled the extra sausage the last time we went to Butlers for breakfast, eh? Answer us that one, Detective Constable Walker."

Chris Walker blushed as the other people around the conference table turned to him and Macpherson harrumphed at his lack of an immediate response.

The younger man took a gulp of coffee and launched into a familiar nervous tick, fussing at the edges of his receding hairline, brushing the fringe forward as valuable seconds ticked by in the struggle for a witty riposte.

"He was only trying to do your shirt buttons a favour, Doc. Jesus, there are cables in the shipyard under less tension," said Detective Constable Erin Reilly with a wink at Walker who returned the glimmer of a grateful smile.

Macpherson spluttered into his tea, then glanced down at the arc of his belly and the gaping mouths that yawned between the buttons, each revealing a glimpse of a white undershirt. Quickly rearranging his tie he put down his tea in preparation for a broadside against the angel-faced Reilly, but Walker, in response to the sergeant's attempt at distraction fired first.

"Seriously, sarge, moving your tie about is like putting a sticking plaster over a bullet wound."

Reilly, moving to sit beside her partner, clapped him on the shoulder and chuckled. "Nice one, Chris. Oh, and the vertical stripes aren't flattering you by the way," she added.

"What are you talking about? They make me look taller," protested Macpherson as he inspected his shirt, sitting up straighter and pulling in his gut. "I like this shirt."

"You should try a block of pastel or maybe a nice floral print."

Macpherson, aghast at the prospect, turned to face Carrie Cook as she weighed in on the unexpected debate.

"Floral—"

"Yes. It would take years off you," Cook's expression was deadpan.

"It would take stones off him you mean," said Walker and the three detective constables collapsed in fits of giggles.

"You can't fatten a thoroughbred. You should all know that."

The assembled team looked up as Taylor approached and sat down.

"You tell them, Ronnie. They're undermining the chain of command here," Macpherson scolded, giving his tie another tug. "Bloody insubordinate is what that is. You need to tell them, respect the stripes."

"Right, give my head peace or I'll send you over to Slick Simpson for a few pointers on what's what in this season's trends," said Taylor as she dished out briefing notes. Macpherson peered around the blue fabric screen that separated their section of the CID suite from the others. He couldn't see the coiffured and preened DC from Inspector MacDonald's unit but there was a whiff of Dolce and Gabbana cologne in the air.

"From Slick? Sure he's all winkle pickers and those big braces. The same boy must have got Musgrave Street mixed up with Wall Street." The DS accepted his briefing and grimaced. "This is turning into a bloody ball ache, isn't it?"

"I wouldn't know, but thanks for pointing out the obvious," said Taylor with an arch look, then to the assembled team more generally. "You'll have heard the news already. Finn Abbott died as a result of injuries sustained in the hit and run. Because of that, we will be receiving a visit from the Ombudsman's office. Our accounts of what happened have been submitted"—She motioned a finger between herself and Macpherson—"But before we leave tonight can we make sure the associated documentation is right up to date, initial call transcripts, eye witness reports of Abbott fleeing the scene and anything that might tie him to the vandalism and harassment of Corry Developments more generally. Carrie, just on that, can you see if anything has come back from Seapark about the forensics and, Chris, contact the social housing provider for Abbott's address and try to arrange access, please?"

Both nodded and added a note in the margins of their respective briefs as Taylor continued.

"Uniform have been issued with a description and the partial number plate of the van. As yet, no sign and no reported thefts of a matching vehicle around the time." Taylor gave Cook a meaningful look. "I've asked that any information coming in on the van or driver is handled by Carrie." She didn't elaborate and no one passed comment.

"Now, this is where things become a little complicated." Taylor placed a copy of the late edition of the *Belfast Echo* on the tabletop. A blurred photo of the justice minister being hurried from the mall outside the Royal Courts of Justice by a security guard took up the bulk of the tabloid's front page. The headline screamed *ABUSE SCANDAL* alongside an equally gratuitous cutline hinting at what could be found in the special report on pages two, three and four. Almost as an afterthought, a tiny column highlighted a story of concerned parents and victims' families rallying to pressure the PSNI into opening a review into the ongoing deaths of alleged adolescent gang members and victims of the city's current opiate epidemic.

Adjacent to the story were two smaller pictures. One of a

young Oliver Maddox marked out amidst a group of boys, the second a recent surveillance shot of a man crossing Chichester Street carrying a laptop bag.

"The *Echo* has outed Maddox as a serial predator of young boys. Proving the veracity of that isn't going to fall to us yet, *but*, the reporter has identified this man as Steven Scott." She tapped the second image. "Mr Scott was the whistleblower who provided the gateway for the prosecution of Colm Casey. He was due to testify that he had uncovered messages and payment schedules implicating Casey and others in the murders of two prison officers and an evangelical pastor."

"I skim-read the *Echo* website earlier," said Walker, nodding. "Maddox was an officer in the eastern youth justice centre. Scott and the boys in that photo served time there and that's when—" He cut off, the news copy offering explanation enough of what was being alleged.

"How do either of them factor into what we're looking at?" asked Reilly, leaning forward on her elbows and scanning the story.

"Finn Abbott told us before he died that Scott, or Stumpy as he called him, could give us a motive behind the vandalism of Geordie Corry's developments."

"Really?" Reilly looked sceptical.

"Abbott's behaviour was erratic and he was clearly under the influence but he also implied that Scott may be able to shed light on a cold case." Taylor offered the floor to Macpherson and his expression once again darkened. He reached out and prodded a finger into the picture of Maddox and the boys.

"This boy here is Finn Abbott and this other scrawny runt is called Barry Toms."

"He's not mentioned in this," said Reilly glancing up as she flipped a page.

"Toms is a bit of an urban legend," explained Macpherson.

The team, apart from Taylor who he had filled in over coffee at the Royal, now sat in rapt attention as he continued. "Toms was a wee hallion. Never out of trouble." Macpherson shook his head. "Housebreaking, shoplifting, handbag snatching, you name it he had form for it."

"He looks like butter wouldn't melt in his mouth," observed Cook. "What age is he here, ten, eleven?"

"Aye, about that," agreed Macpherson. "His da was dead. His ma had six other youngsters to worry about and didn't have the means or the patience to control him. He was in and out of the care system until one day he disappeared."

"Ran away?"

"That's what the staff at the boys' home said. Backed it up with a file an inch thick detailing all the times Toms had previously absconded and his record of behaviour, or rather misbehaviour and disobedience. He was frequently in solitary for biting and spitting on staff, for self-harming, and for catching and torturing wildlife. I heard it didn't make for good reading. "

"You investigated?"

"I was only involved in some of the initial searches. To be honest, it was mostly for show. At the time we were in the grip of the Troubles and both the staff at the home and the boys at the top of CID had decided Toms had done a bunk south or across to the mainland. Whichever, he wasn't seen again and most weren't shedding any tears for the fact."

"So how is he an urban myth?" said Walker, confusion creeping across his brow. Macpherson took a gulp of his tea and licked his lips, his complexion paling a little.

"About eighteen months later the dismembered torso of a young boy was found in a coal sack on the edge of the Drumkeen Estate. There were signs of torture to the body. The head and limbs were never recovered, the victim was never identified, and no one was ever caught." The DS paused, recalling the incident and the revulsion that rippled out across all sections of the community in the weeks and months that followed. The barbaric and brutal murder of the child was a new low for a city that had become used to daily carnage and an endless cycle of sectarian murder.

"Kids weren't allowed out on their own after that. Certainly not after dark. The rumours of animal cruelty had leaked and some told their kids it was Barry Toms back. It gave the bogeyman a name and put the fear of God up them." Macpherson gave a shrug. "Others used it as the carrot and stick, "Be good or you'll end up like that bad wee boy who hurt the animals."

"Horrendous," groaned Walker, the jovial banter of earlier vanishing.

Macpherson pushed the plate of cake across the table. "Do you still want the rest of this?" The look on Walker's face said that he didn't.

"Abbott was in a paranoid state," said Taylor. "Incoherent and rambling about what had been done to him, to Barry Toms, and to unspecified others. We knew before those headlines that historical abuse was rife in some quarters, and we now have that image which goes some way to corroborating that Abbott did know Toms."

"And the justice minister," murmured Walker, the uncomfortable tension around the table clicking up a notch as all eyes rested on the damning image.

"Let's not go jumping to any conclusions just yet, Chris. The DCI has given the go-ahead for Doc and me to pick up Mr Scott in the morning. Considering he's been named as the man responsible for putting Casey in the dock, he should be glad to be brought somewhere safe. We'll see if he is equally forthcoming about his relationship with Abbott and Toms and a potential motive for the harassment of Geordie Corry."

"And us?" said Reilly, flipping the paper closed and easing

back from the table.

"You and Chris follow up with Corry, on the pretext it's by way of an update. See if he offers any ideas why his developments are being targeted but really, we want to be looking for something that links him to Abbott or the others. Past employment, social networks, anything. At the minute I don't care how tenuous it is."

The two DCs confirmed their instruction with stiff nods.

"I wonder where that was taken?" said Cook, turning the newspaper to face her; the image of Maddox and the boys was grainy.

Macpherson reached out. "I know because I've been there." His chubby finger traced the cast iron railings behind the group. On either side two stone columns were topped with the original gas carriage lights and the gates had a decorative swirl of leaf and shamrock. He pulled his hand back as though it had been scalded.

"It's the Glenrafferty Home for Troubled Boys."

18

"Welcome to the O2 answer service…"

Steven Scott swore, hurled the handset onto the pillow, and upended the contents of a sports holdall onto the floor, replacing the gym towel and deodorant inside with the items strewn across his bed, not taking any care to fold the clothes, instead just balling them, underwear and socks into any spare space.

Scott tensed as a beam of car headlights flashed across the ceiling, most of the glare blocked out by the closed curtains. He took a quick peek outside, but the car had travelled on.

Get a grip of yourself, Steven.

As he repeated the mantra, a drumbeat of stress and anxiety beat a tattoo in his temples. He felt sick but at least the door had stopped hammering and the landline, now disconnected from the wall socket, couldn't taunt him with its shrill electronic accusation of being ignored. For the moment he had the uninterrupted but time-limited luxury to hastily shove enough possessions in a bag to flee the city for a few days.

Who are you kidding, he thought, picking up the phone and stabbing redial. He put the call on speaker and dropped to his knees, hauling open a bedside drawer and scattering its contents on the carpet, searching frantically through the mess of bills, loose change, and pill packets for his passport.

"Hello?"

Scott snatched up the phone. "Where the hell have you been? Have you not seen the news?"

He was only half listening to the response, muttering in triumph as he seized the passport from its hiding place. He clambered to his feet and tossed the document into the holdall and headed for the en suite to grab some toiletries.

"Look, it doesn't matter. I need some help… No, it isn't bloody money. My face is all over the frigging news. That weasel McGarrity has fucked me right over."

Scott emptied the contents of the bathroom cabinet into the sink and grabbed the essentials. Toothbrush, toothpaste, and a razor. He leaned across and grabbed a bottle of shower gel from the edge of the bath.

"I need to get away," Scott cut in as the recipient of his call relayed their own problems. "Your place up the coast? What are you doing there?"

Scott listened to the reply as he shovelled the remaining items into the holdall and zipped it up, then scanned around for his wallet and car keys.

"Well? Is it alright if I keep you company for a bit?"

He hefted the holdall and carried it to the lounge, setting it beside the bookcase. As an afterthought, he grabbed a book, just in case it was more than a few days.

"Don't be getting cagey now, your lot fucking owe me remember…"

Scott pinched the bridge of his nose, feeling the pressure increase behind his eyes.

"Look, it's bad enough the Provo's know I'm the rat that squealed on Casey but other shit has hit the fan too—" Scott felt a sting of phantom pain and flinched, pressing a hand over his lower abdomen where beneath his clothes and the tattoos were the scars that mapped out the horrors of his youth.

"Now it's out and now they know—" He bit back a sob

and cleared his throat.

"I'm a dead man walking."

19

The next day began earlier than expected for Taylor. The hair at the nape of her neck was still wet from her interrupted shower and had soaked the collar of her blouse.

She opened the door of the Volvo and eased carefully into the passenger seat.

"Black, no sugar? You're sure?" she said, passing the takeaway tea across.

"Can a fella not make a healthy switch without being bloody questioned on it?" said Macpherson.

Taylor indicated a confectionery wrapper balled in the centre console beside his phone. Macpherson grunted.

"'Go to work on an egg' says the advert." He crunched the car into gear and pulled away from the kerb.

"I don't think they meant a chocolate fondant one, Doc."

The DS chose not to bite and Taylor hid a smirk behind the rim of her cup as he weaved the car across the lanes of the M2 northbound. Off to the right lay the sprawl of the Duncrue Industrial Estate and the docks, at the same time sweeping by on the left beyond the railway tracks carrying commuters into the city lay the Victorian terraces of York Road and the dominating structure of Thompson and Sons.

The animal feed factory loomed over the red brick streets, on a good day wafting the warmth of fried cereals and on a bad, something akin to rotting fish mixed with Marmite. Thompson's original structures, destroyed when Belfast was blitzed during the Second World War, had been rebuilt. The familiar blue and grey corrugated cladding and concrete that had stood since the sixties was at odds with its neighbouring survivor of the Luftwaffe bombs.

Jennymount Mill retained the architectural beauty of an older time. Built from red Belfast brick, the mill soared above the terraced streets that had once been home to its workforce, a physical reminder of when Belfast had held the moniker, Linenopolis and was a jewel in the crown of the British Empire, renowned and respected as the largest producer of the fabric throughout the world.

The two buildings, hunkered side by side along the edge of the M2 motorway had stood long enough to have overseen two world wars, a time of trouble and a fragile peace, and now bore witness as the juggernaut of modernity fought its own battle to co-exist with their precious past.

The traffic was light as Macpherson took the offslip for Belfast Zoo, the Shore Road cutting back against the flow of the motorway. The first landmark they passed was the old RUC barracks. All that remained were the concrete blast walls and high fencing still topped with barbed wire. The site was derelict, overgrown and up for sale. Cutting right across traffic Macpherson headed north, the barren hulk of Cavehill filled the windscreen, newer social housing and turn-of-the-century semis passing on each side until the road bisected the fourth and the sixteenth holes of Fortwilliam Golf Club, and then eventually they emerged to cross the Antrim Road and along a street of old-money villas.

Palm trees and blooming bougainvillea dominated the gardens which were set between detached period properties, manicured hedges and intricate cast iron fences, the beauty of the scene scarred somewhat by the glare of blue lights and fluttering police tape that stretched between lampposts at the end of the road.

"DI Taylor. DS Macpherson."

Taylor had her window rolled down and presented her warrant card to the constable who had stepped forward from the cordon.

"Do you want to just park it here? It's a bit chaotic up at the house," he said.

"Anywhere?" said Macpherson. The constable peered in, nodded, and the DS ratcheted on the handbrake and killed the ignition. The engine clanked and rattled to a noisy death.

After they had presented their credentials and signed in with the scene coordinator the two detectives ducked under the tape and walked the last thirty yards up to the house that was the hub of the activity.

An ambulance sat kerbside, the paramedics packing up. Taylor noticed as the two medics loaded their kit that none of it seemed to have been needed. Her observation was confirmed a few seconds later when she saw the tinted windows of an undertaker's van parked at the end of the drive, the last vehicle in a line of others snaking up to the house.

"Nice spot," said Macpherson, taking in the manicured grounds and property's sweeping vista across Belfast Lough to the Holywood hills and the County Down coastline to Bangor on the opposite shore.

An inner cordon extended from the porch out and around a yew tree and the wing mirror of a patrol car. Outside the tape stood another pair of uniformed constables and to the right, two Tyvek-suited crime scene investigators were stacking step plates back into their van. A third was swigging from a bottle of flavoured water as she inspected images on her phone. She turned and shook her head in disbelief as the detectives approached.

"Do they still have you saddled with this reprobate?"

"Better the devil you know, Diane," said Taylor, accepting

the woman's hand.

"You can't teach an old dog new tricks you know."

Macpherson affected an irritated tone as the woman then turned to greet him. "I'm wounded," he said, adding with a smile. "And for your information, I don't need any new tricks, the old ones are still the best."

The SOCO laughed. "It's good to see you, Doc."

Diane Pearson was the Forensic Science Service senior crime scene investigator. The foundations for the trio's trusted and professional respect for each other had been laid over many shared cases, the two detectives often deferring to the SOCO's lead and her near psychic ability to decipher and analyse the evidential patterns left behind at a crime scene.

"What do we have?" said Macpherson, cutting to the chase.

Pearson took another swig of water, using the time to work out how best to phrase her answer, tousling hair that had been tucked under the hood of her oversuit, some of the ash blonde strands at her temples darkened by sweat. When she spoke it wasn't to Macpherson.

"Mal?" A junior crime scene tech peeked around the back doors of the van. "Get this pair some overshoes." Then to the detectives, she said, "You'd better see this one for yourselves."

There was a scent inside not dissimilar to how the animal feed factory smelled on a bad day which sat at odds with how neat and tidy the home was. There was a place for everything and everything was in its place, in a minimalist kind of way. The fabrics and furnishings were neutral which gave more impact to the bold wall hangings and abstract sculptures. The carpets and rugs bore parallel vacuum marks, tramlines that ran along their length as carefully as if they were the pitch at Windsor Park stadium.

The wide hall opened into an open-plan kitchen diner while on the left lay a drawing room in the same pale shades that a colour chart may call Creamy Linen or Elephant's Breath. To the right, a formal lounge hosted two occupants, neither was the homeowner.

A uniformed PC sat beside another woman and the two detectives immediately recognised their colleague.

"PC Arnold," greeted Taylor.

"Guv." Leigh-Anne Arnold had a youthful complexion and big blue eyes set in a baby face and looked much too young to be a police officer. Beside her sat an older, red-eyed lady who stifled her sobs behind a tissue. Half a dozen others were crumpled beside a tea cup on a chrome and glass-topped coffee table. "Sarge," added Arnold, acknowledging Macpherson before continuing. "This is Eleanor Hammond. Miss Hammond discovered the body." This set the woman off again, the choking sob beginning somewhere in the back of her throat to release in a strangled snort behind her tissue.

"Miss Hammond, I'll be back in just a moment," said Taylor, any further explanation as to back from where moot.

Leigh-Anne Arnold gave the woman's hand a reassuring pat. Taylor and Macpherson followed Diane Pearson back into the hallway and up the staircase to a wide landing.

"Watch your step," said Pearson indicating a puddle of vomit, then said in explanation. "Miss Hammond's. You wouldn't think to look at her she'd hold that much, would you?"

Taylor stepped past the sick, and although breathing through her mouth caught its acrid tang. Macpherson, more shrewd, placed the cuff of his jacket over his mouth and nose.

"The body is in the master suite," said Pearson, indicating a door and leading the way.

"Anything suspicious?" said Taylor, apprehensive that the usually fastidious Pearson had opted for overshoes instead of the full Tyvek overall. The door to the master bedroom stood open. Pearson's expression was deadpan.

"Yes and no," was her cryptic answer, offering the way into the room in the manner a maître d' might present a table.

Taylor led, Macpherson followed and Pearson stood in the doorway. The room was well lit, sunlight flooding in through a large bay window, the sway of the trees outside occasionally dappling the beams. The room was masculine, the furnishings including the king-size bed's headboard were black walnut, the drapes and bedding dark grey damask. By the window, next to a drinks trolley topped with a stoppered decanter and heavy glasses sat an Eames lounge chair. The scent of an expensive musk mingled with fouler smells.

Taylor didn't take any of that in at first. Her attention was fixed on Oliver Maddox.

The justice minister hung by the neck from the door to his en suite, hairless and naked and as a newborn save for a black nitrile glove that covered his right hand. Around his throat not a knotted tie nor a cutting of electrical cable but a section of braided black rope.

"Christ on a bike," muttered Macpherson.

"You asked if there was anything suspicious?" said Pearson from the doorway, but Taylor was only half listening, her ears ringing with Professor Thompson's report on Finn Abbott.

"Ronnie?" Macpherson placed a restraining hand on her forearm as she took a step closer.

"Yes, be careful," added Pearson as she gestured to the small, numbered markers on the floor in front of Maddox. "We'll take the syringe and have the contents analysed." The SOCO pulled a face. "And, as far as I can tell that is semen on the floor. Mal has a sample but try not to step in it."

Taylor didn't reply but took an extra step away from the nearest yellow A-frame marker, focused on the body. Oliver

Maddox was tattooed with old scars and healed injuries from his shoulders to his knees, nothing that could be attributed to his love for rugby. Instead, they were the puckered pink edges of old cuts and deep gouges suffered a lifetime ago. A line of dimpled craters snaked around his abdomen, the evil circular scars evidence of deep and deliberate cigarette burns. Of abuse. Of torment.

Each of the injuries paled though against the one to which all eyes were drawn in horrified fascination.

Seared into the flesh above Maddox's pubic bone was an icon, a raised scar much darker than the surrounding undamaged skin. The super-heated branding iron which had left its indelible mark had been forged in a distinct shape.

Two crossed keys.

20

People experienced pressure in different ways and to varied degrees. To some, it built up slowly ending with the realisation a once-tailored collar could no longer encompass a neck bloated by gluttony. To others, it was immediate, the sudden sharp jab of a pebble crept into the sole of a handmade Italian brogue.

John Barrett held no truck with pressure, it was for tyres and meteorological discussion, but his current experience comprised a suffocating oppression not unlike the minutes before a thunderstorm or the irritation of being stranded kerbside by a random nail slipped through the ribs of a brand new Pirelli.

Exiting his official car, Barrett strode silently past the welcoming commissionaire and ghosted through the lobby of Castle Buildings, choosing to eschew the bank of lifts and instead take the bland concrete fire escape stairs, leveraging the odds this might grant him the privacy of his own thoughts as he returned to his lair. The meeting, a mile down the road from which he was returning, had been predictable, not just in delegates but by discourse.

Those who knew Oliver Maddox the least heaped platitude on top of anguish for a life lost too soon. Those of the deceased justice minister's own party were more careful in their lamentations lest the headlines of the last few days prove true and there was guilt by association, and as for those who knew him best? Barrett had observed nothing from them but dispassionate relief.

Exiting the stairwell he strode along a corridor that was appropriately utilitarian for a government building and towards the sanctuary of his office, the eyrie from which the senior civil servant orchestrated the real power behind the facade of democracy. He was the unknown face who ensured those in ascension had their secrets buried and those who fell would plummet in ignorance of the fact it was he who had cut the strings. Politicians came and went, their careers book-ended in success or scandal and Barrett's tactic to ensure which was which was as old as time: divide and conquer.

The scandal and sudden death of the justice minister was providing enough of a lever to assist with the former but also offered a means to redirect attention away from the real reason Barrett was more saturnine than usual. To those for whom he kept the keys, it was near exposure rather than the loss of revenue which had brought disquiet and reprimand from on high. His masters, a consortium of shadowy individuals whose reach stretched like an invisible web across borders and jurisdictions, held influence that cut to the heart of political ideology and played the strings of government through an insidious corruption of democratically elected executives, law enforcement organisations and the judiciary. A secretive cabal of men and women operating in the shadows, bolstering their coffers through the assiduous manipulation of geopolitical conflict and by agitating historic tensions. Tensions that those claiming to represent the constituents of the north of the island of Ireland gripped like a child's comforter.

Approaching his office, Barrett's attitude shifted. Like any predator, he sensed something in the scene that wasn't right. Neither a sound nor a scent but an anomaly, nonetheless. Noting the door was slightly ajar, he entered without pause.

"John." A man was sitting in the black, buttoned Chesterfield two-seater, the sofa arranged in a corner for less formal meetings or when Barrett required time away from screens to contemplate what pieces he had in play. It took the man a few attempts to rise, doing up his suit jacket as he did so. "I hope you don't mind me waiting," he said, offering a hand.

Barrett ignored it and took the seat behind his desk, wordlessly offering his visitor a less comfortable chair. "It would seem I wasn't given much choice in the matter, Matthew."

Matthew Tearney flopped down, legs akimbo and ignored the barb. "Well?"

Barrett affected a blank expression. "It's a big hole in the ground with water at the bottom, or in some instances a body."

"Don't be crass, John. It doesn't suit you. You know damn well what I mean. How did it go up at the big house?"

The big house. Stoirmhonadh. The place for crossing the mountains. Stormont, the seat of devolved government.

"As it ever does. One set watching their backs while the other lot aim to stick the knife in and those who don't matter expounding their outrage at it all."

Matthew Tearney gave a chuckle that was more of a wheeze.

"So Matthew, tell me. What drags the undersecretary of regional development away from his desk to lurk in the office of this lowly civil servant? It's not just to query how the great and the good mourn their recently deceased, is it?"

Tearney smiled, his grin exacerbating the creases of six chins and his eyes almost disappearing into the folds of his jowly cheeks. Pushing twenty stone, his gluttony had long outpaced his collar size and for want of a tie to fuss with he placed his hands over an ample belly.

"Straight to the point as always," said Tearney. Barrett shrugged. He was a sagacious man and frugal when it came to wasting time talking around a subject.

"It is to do with Oliver actually, or rather the opportunity his unfortunate death now presents."

Barrett steepled his fingers and leaned forward. "His body is still warm, Matthew. There are some who might regard your haste to capitalise callous."

"But not you."

Barrett didn't answer. Both he and Matthew Tearney were cut from the same cloth but unlike Barrett, he held a position above the parapet, what some might still call a 'grey suit'. Tearney was entrusted to ensure that a department with such a wide and varied remit met its aims and responsibilities efficiently and effectively. Tearney had the diplomacy and ruthlessness that many in the current crop of elected officials lacked and he used those traits to great effect, in the background and out of the limelight to direct strategy and maintain critical oversight of policy, performance and finance. He also understood the value of his unique position which was why Barrett and the consortium continued to keep his less desirable proclivities buried in exchange for his compliance.

"The drumbeats suggest that allegations of scandal aside, Oliver Maddox in over-playing his position on Colm Casey has caused the case to somewhat flounder," said Tearney.

"Sinking fast," agreed Barrett. "What brings that debacle into your orbit?"

"Not just that debacle, John. We lost a mutual friend recently, and with another currently rehabilitating, dare I say, some sense the winds of change?"

The newsprint detailing ACC Wallace's sacrifice and Gordon Beattie's predicament flashed through Barrett's mind, and although this latest scandal complicated an agreed-upon solution he meant what he said when he addressed Tierney. "There is no danger of long-term disruption and matters are in hand. I sincerely hope that was not a misjudged threat?"

Tearney held up a fat hand. "No, not at all. Merely that without management and given the current scrutiny those streams are experiencing there may be another way to ensure revenue continues to flow and where new partnerships might be formed in the absence of others."

"Speak plainly, Matthew."

"I've been approached with a proposal. It will involve some finesse, mainly in convincing one party to come to the table but given the headlines of the last few days I believe it to be in all our interests that this sees traction sooner rather than later."

Barrett gave no indication he was interested one way or the other. "Go on."

"The department sub-committee has been approached by a conglomerate wishing to pump significant investment into a cross-community project. I don't have to tell you that sort of proposal sells itself."

Barrett understood what was implied. Grants, loans and social funds would be thrown at anything remotely connected to projects aiming to improve community integration. Tierney continued. "Conveniently, part of the proposal includes the provision of new low-value social housing which the department has been instructed to add to its portfolio over the next five years. The prime market drivers in this are location and of course, cost to the departmental purse and the end client." Tearney removed a handkerchief from his pocket and mopped his brow, continuing. "I have an interested developer who has identified a significant area that could be put to use. It's essentially a derelict brownfield site which bypasses the hold-up that may come from the green lobby. His problem is that the land and property are held by a private investor, and until very recently even if they did want to sell, certain legal restrictions meant they could not."

"Colm Casey," said Barrett after a moment's pause.

"One and the same. The difficulty being it seems he is holding this piece of real estate out of spite. My man cannot get him to the table never mind entertaining talk of a sale."

"And your man is who exactly?"

Tearney gave his nose a quick toot into the handkerchief and weighed up what, if anything, would be lost in the telling.

"Geordie Corry."

Barrett held his own counsel, his expression deadpan.

"A leading Republican won't sell to a Loyalist developer. Hardly newsworthy, Matthew."

Tearney tutted, such intransigence in the face of making obscene profit abhorrent to him. "No indeed, however as I said, in light of recent events there may be impetus for getting this deal done and the construction crews on the ground and underway."

"Why the rush?" said Barrett. "Have you a restricted window to manipulate your budget?" Tearney was shaking his head, chins and cheeks wobbling like half-set jelly.

What he was proposing was a defrauding of the public purse. His inside knowledge had identified a need, and he would propose, appoint and sign off on those who would fulfil the contracts required to implement the department's strategy. Those contracts would be put out to tender but the bids would heavily favour those whom Tearney had hand-picked in advance. Initially, the winning bid would undercut the competition but then additional and inflated supplementary costs would be billed and the excess divided between those who stood to benefit. The consortium would take their percentage while also laundering the proceeds of other transactions through the build schedule. In most cases, there were barriers to be surmounted, timescales to meet, bribes to pay, and suppliers to shake down and that could be a problem when the committee administering the funds expected it to be a cut-and-dried process. When Tearney spoke next it was with a quiet solemnity.

"The estate, the property, and the outbuildings therein are what demand the drive for expediency," he said, adding, "Specifically there are a number of subterranean structures which hold a measure of, well, let's call it sentimental interest for the end client who would like them returned. We are looking to procure both buildings and the extensive estate on which they sit to accommodate the proposed new build while renovating and repurposing some of these older sections so they can be handed back." Tierney paused, hooking a finger to tug against the limiting restriction of his shirt collar. "The client would like a meeting to see if you would be agreeable to discuss terms."

I'm sure they would, thought Barrett, remaining silent, astute enough to be thinking through the potential angles that had for one, brought a direct request for his assistance, and two, deciding if that request was a ruse that may be used to take advantage of him in the future. It wasn't without consequence that with Wallace dead and Beattie off the park for the foreseeable, Oliver Maddox had been put forward by associates as the man to steady the ship, but as it had transpired the justice minister had turned out to be a somewhat reluctant caretaker.

"As an unfortunate aside, the site we are talking about holds a degree of notoriety," said Tierney.

Barrett gave an upward flick of the chin, prompting his visitor for the first time in the conversation to break his gaze and glance at the floor.

"It's the Glenrafferty Home for Troubled Boys."

21

"Do you think I've put on the weight?"

Taylor looked at her detective sergeant who was regarding his reflection in the driver's window of the Volvo. She loved the grizzled old grump who had stepped in as a surrogate father since her own had been killed by an under-car booby trap when she was a girl, so she chose diplomacy.

"I think you could probably consider making a few healthier choices."

"Oh, so you do then?" said Macpherson, sounding affronted.

"I didn't say that." Taylor raised a hand defensively. "And before you eat the face off me for saying so, you asked." As she rounded the rear of the car she stood beside him and looked at their reflections. Seeing her own she tried to ignore the stress-induced weight loss that had given her features a sharper look and carved half a stone from her naturally athletic build.

"That's not the most flattering of surfaces to be making judgements in and anyway, I'm just saying maybe it's time to lay off the belly busters and go for something else every now and again."

"What, like a tofu finger roll?" Macpherson stuck out his tongue and mimed a retch. "Boke."

"Like maybe a wholegrain bacon sandwich instead of a full soda," said Taylor.

"That wouldn't fill a hole in your tooth—"

"And maybe introduce a bit of fruit?"

"Sure I had an apple turnover yesterday and a strawberry tart the day before that."

Taylor sighed. "An actual apple won't kill you, you know?"

"Aye, you say that but look what it did for poor old Adam. Sent him off on the path of self-destruction and got him turfed out of Eden."

Macpherson shook his head at the thought of a dietary overhaul and turned away, changing the subject. "I'm healthier than your man Maddox is," he muttered, then pointing a finger at the cookie-cutter apartment complex across from their parking space. "Which one is it?"

Taylor couldn't argue with his observation, so instead indicated the block on the farthest right of the five identical housing units.

They had travelled across the city, leaving the grim task of cutting Oliver Maddox down and transferring him to the undertaker's vehicle for others. As Pearson and her team had finished up their duties, photographing the corpse in situ and searching for any sign that Maddox had died by anything other than his own hand the two detectives had teased details from Eleanor Hammond. The woman, it turned out, was Maddox's housekeeper and the general conversation revealed nothing out of the ordinary on her arrival that particular morning. The gates were closed, his car was in the drive and the house was locked up. Normal, save her employer was not yet up as he usually would be, and then on checking, Hammond was confronted by the sight of the justice minister naked, suspended by his neck and very dead.

They hadn't gleaned much more from Hammond, Taylor deciding a follow-up in a day or two once she had time to come to terms with her traumatic experience would be more beneficial. It seemed that Maddox had taken the means of relieving the stress and the humiliation of the breaking news into his own hands, one gloved hand at any rate, but unfortunately for him and, as far as Pearson would hypothesise until the full report was compiled, it looked as though Maddox's indulgence of auto-erotic asphyxiation had gone badly wrong.

The justice minister's body was to be taken to the Royal Victoria Hospital prior to its release to family so Taylor, en route to their current destination had made a call requesting Professor Thompson take a look at the corpse and offer his opinion on any comparisons between the historic wounds he had found on Finn Abbott and those she had seen on Maddox.

While the untimely death had saved the justice minister from facing questions over the allegations made against him, and perhaps offered his political peers a temporary reprieve from further scandal, it also unfortunately, left Taylor absent someone who would have been in a position to corroborate any claim which may be forthcoming once she had spoken to the other person named in the Echo's headlines, Steven Scott, the only surviving link between Finn Abbott, his paranoid rant about the children's home and Oliver Maddox.

Macpherson leaned on the intercom buzzer and then rattled the letterbox flap. When the door opened, it was restrained by a locking chain and the quarter face that peered out was not the expected homeowner.

"We're looking for Mr Scott," said Taylor brandishing her warrant card.

"Police?"

"Detective Inspector Taylor. DS Macpherson. Can we come in?"

A second later the door was unbarred and they stood in the hallway.

"Sorry, the press are still nosing past every few hours," explained the man who beckoned them on into the apartment. "The phone is pulled out of the wall too, so if you were ringing ahead…" He shrugged.

"We weren't and there's no need to apologise," said Taylor entering an open-plan kitchen lounge.

"Where are my manners, I'm Neil. Neil Graham."

"Friend, family?" asked Taylor.

Graham gave a snorting chuckle. "Friend, I suppose. Some would call what Steven and I have a situationship."

"A what's that, now?" said Macpherson, his attention which had been roaming the well-ordered room coming back to Graham who gave another chuckle. Graham was short and hiding a bit of a paunch below an untucked paisley-patterned silk shirt. He had a youthful expression that seemed to have been aided by Botox and a floppy fringe of brown hair which he swept to the left every half minute or so. Between his wrinkle-free complexion and dress sense, it was hard to tell if he fell into the same age bracket as Steven Scott or was maybe a little older. There was a carefree bonhomie about the man.

"Friends without benefits," said Graham.

The term didn't help Macpherson much so Taylor interjected.

"Do you know where Mr Scott might be or when he may be back?"

"I do not, inspector."

"Had your own key did you?" said Macpherson.

Graham tapped his nose. "Third plant pot on the right. "

"Recipe for a burglary," growled the DS. "I'll send crime prevention round with a leaflet and a lecture."

Graham exchanged a look with Taylor, then he offered drinks.

"Thanks but no," she said. "Have you spoken with Mr Scott about—"

"What that bloody rag is saying? No, he didn't mention the court case or any relationship with the minister, consensual or otherwise." His tone shifted as he stressed the word, as though some piece of a puzzle may have fallen into place. In that moment Taylor caught a glimpse of the dynamic between Graham and Scott, one of friendship and burgeoning trust but one yet to take the leap from platonic to intimate. Graham continued. "I've been ringing but Steven wasn't answering, so I called round. I didn't want him to think he was dealing with all this on his own."

"When was the last time you spoke to him?" said Taylor. Macpherson had stepped away and was examining Scott's bookcase. Graham had poured himself a glass of tap water and taken a stool at the breakfast bar.

"A few days ago, just on the phone. In person? We had dinner and a few drinks last weekend and he mentioned he would be busy for a few weeks which I now presume was because of this trial."

"How did he seem?"

"Fine, his usual self." Graham stared into the middle distance. "Maybe a little distracted. He had a bit more wine than usual and he was preoccupied with his phone. Text. Email. I didn't press. He didn't elaborate."

"Did he ever mention anyone called Finn Abbott?"

Graham shook his head. "Not as I recall."

"How did you meet?" said Taylor. She had remained standing while Macpherson, now finished with his browse of the book titles, was regarding a framed smear of monochrome in messy brushstrokes. Several accents of red and trails of black dripped down the canvas. His head cocked from side to side and Graham, pleased by the attention the art was receiving, called across the room.

"It's called 'Deep Inside My Heart' by Emin. It's only a signed reproduction but it's one of Steven's favourites."

"I've no eye for art, Mr Graham, but I can see why your man calls himself Slim Shady," Macpherson tutted. "Stevie Wonder could do a better job, was this painted in the dark or what?" He waggled a disapproving finger. "There's better stuck to my fridge from our Kayleigh." Realising his comment had been met with silence, Macpherson offered an explanation. "She's my niece."

"How did you meet?" repeated Taylor, giving Macpherson a despairing shake of her head.

"I'm in hospitality. The Ristorante Sartarelli," said Graham.

"Away of that with you." Macpherson abandoned his critique of Scott's artwork and crossed to the island. "Sartarelli's?"

Graham nodded. Macpherson puffed out his cheeks and licked his lips. "Oh, the duck ragu and porcini mushroom ravioli is just..." He gathered his thumb and index finger and gave them a loud kiss. "Squisito!"

"Thank you very much. I'm delighted you think so. You should try the pollo Valdostana sometime—"

"Really?" A grin split Macpherson's face like an axe strike. "That's very generous of you. What about this Saturday—"

Taylor cleared her throat. With his initial appreciation stranded at the edges of his eyes and her DS continuing to nod excitedly at the prospect of a free meal the sound quickly brought Graham's attention back to her question.

"Steven came in most days for lunch. He worked across the road in the Quays Buildings, for one of the accountancy firms. We just got talking, turned out we had similar interests. Literature, politics." He gestured at the walls. "Art."

Taylor scowled as Macpherson snorted on mention of the latter.

"I take it you've been here previously?"

Graham answered with a nod.

"Did you notice anything out of the ordinary when you

arrived today? Did Mr Scott leave a note? Was anything out of place."

Graham shook his head, shoulders giving a shrug. "No note. Everything in here is as it usually is. It does look like he has gathered some things and packed in a hurry though." He pushed a thumb over his shoulder. "I can show you?"

Taylor accepted gratefully and the two detectives followed Graham through a short hallway to the primary bedroom. The space was dominated by a queen-sized bed. An alcove along the right-hand wall had been enclosed by floor-to-ceiling sliding doors. One was open revealing a neat and tidy closet space with clothes arranged by colour. Scott's jackets, shirts and slacks hung together on the rails, his shoes and trainers paired up on a rack set into the bottom. Shelves on the opposite wall held some paperbacks and several photos, a few landscapes Taylor recognised as the north coast and a couple of Steven Scott posing in various tourist spots. The general order of the apartment was marred by an upturned drawer and discarded gym clothes strewn on the floor.

"I found it like this. There's a few things lying in the bathroom sink too."

Macpherson stooped and poked through the items on the floor and Taylor went into the en suite. Just as Graham had described, the bathroom cabinet was open, contents discarded in the sink but no sign of a toothbrush.

"Ronnie?"

Taylor returned to the bedroom where Macpherson was nosing through the usual detritus of a bedside drawer. Bills, screwed-up receipts and scribbled notes. A couple of pill packets and a tube of antiseptic ointment. Amidst it all he had singled out a few photographs. The corners of the Polaroids were bent and starting to yellow with age but the images were clear. Impromptu snapshots of a group of boys. Haircuts and fashion from a different era, a few dated by the sponsor on the Glasgow Rangers football shirts they wore. Each face was screwed up in high spirits, cans of super strength lager raised in the air. Behind them stood an unlit bonfire, the stack of wood and tyres leaning precariously under a long shadow cast by Fearon House.

Scott, although younger, was recognisable in the centre of the group, his arm around a boy next to him whose features were immediately familiar.

"Do you mind if we borrow this?" said Taylor.

Neil Graham, the photograph not being his and suddenly realising they were trespassing in his friend's most intimate space, just nodded.

22

The scenic drive along the County Down coast passed through dozens of small seaside towns and villages. In the summer these were places of joy. The blue-green of the Irish Sea glittered under big skies and lapped against long sandy beaches, places for paddling, sandcastles, ninety-nine ice cream cones and a chippy tea.

Ballyhallion was an anomaly. Even on the brightest day, there was a bleakness about it. The most easterly point in Northern Ireland, it was almost within touching distance of Dumfries and Galloway, and it clung desperately to the edge of the coast and its secrets.

It was a one-street place on the way to somewhere else, offering little to entice the passing motorists other than its small harbour, old houses that bore the scars of exposure to the elements and the decay of dereliction. The only significant business of note was a large caravan park that had been an RAF airfield during the Second World War although more recently its infamy lay in the disappearance of a young woman. Her body and her killers had never been found.

The village was also contested ground between opposing factions of Loyalist paramilitary gangs, its proximity to Scotland, tiny harbour, and remoteness marking it as a prime location for smuggling between the UK and the northeast of Ireland.

Loose pebbles sparked off the chassis as a car drove slowly

along the track leading to the caravan site. Potholes and overgrown vegetation caused the driver to weave along the rough road, finally thumping over a scuffed speed hump to follow the one-way system around the site. Nearly all the static holiday homes were shuttered and empty but in the distance, a light marked out his destination.

As the driver pulled up on the adjacent grass verge, the caravan door opened, the wind catching it like a sail and crashing it against the flimsy aluminium siding. A bitter curse and inspection for damage preceded greetings.

"Alright, Stumpy. You found us then?"

Stumpy, no matter how many years passed there were those who still only called him by the nickname. Steven Scott struggled to extricate his holdall and slam the car door shut against another strong gust.

"Yeah, it was no bother. I remembered well enough so I did."

"Come on in then, I've a brew on," said Harry Carruthers, taking a firm grip on the door and ushering Scott inside, pausing for a second to look back along the track to ensure no other vehicles had followed or were loitering.

Inside hadn't changed much since the last time Scott had been there. Half a lifetime had passed but the decor, dated even then, remained. His memory though hazy, recalled with fondness the carefree summer evenings, bonfires, and parties fuelled by vodka and Es, the substances and new friendships helping to blot out a darker past. Now the smell of mildew was mildly overpowered by the scent of a recently demolished fish supper and a pine disinfectant that leached from the trailer's small toilet.

"I read the paper. Bastards they are," said Carruthers, wincing as he bent to pluck a pint of milk from the fridge.

Scott pulled a sour face. The *Echo* and several other local newspapers were spread over the kitchenette table. "What's wrong with your leg? Thanks," he said, reaching out to take the tea.

"Some shite stuck me with a biro." Carruthers waved away the questioning look. "It's a long story, and anyway you have a bit of explaining to do yourself. Is this true?" He prodded a finger at the newsprint, the ghost of a scowl on his face. "You a tout now?"

"Didn't fucking bother you when it was youse that needed a snitch." Scott put the tea down, some of the liquid sloshing over the lip to stain a picture of Oliver Maddox. His elocution which had smoothed out over years slipping to familiar back-street diction.

"Aye, well that got you out of a hole as well so don't be swinging your dick in here like it was all one sided."

Scott dipped his head, Carruthers was right. The big man was a few years older than Scott, and it had been he who approached him on behalf of Gordon Beattie, offering the chance to break free from the cycle of violence and the talons of another predator who had sensed the victim in him. An escape that had likely saved his life from the twisted bastard who had groomed the already damaged youth with booze and compliments until all Scott remembered was waking up in hazy stupors beside men he didn't know and with bruises he couldn't remember receiving.

"Stumpy, this is serious. I've no love for the Fenian bastard but Casey isn't one to be pissing off."

"Look, I know it wasn't exactly above board but all the stuff I passed to Olly was being sent for destruction." Scott waited a beat but getting no response continued. "I swear to God, years of it had been deliberately hidden in the archives by someone inside the firm so that after a while it could be legitimately destroyed."

Carruthers gave a disapproving scowl, irritated that his friend had been implicated so publicly in his involvement while as usual the firm's fat cats and politicians were cowering from the shitstorm under an umbrella of non-disclosure agreements and the data protection act.

"Olly needed me to confirm the transactions and find a corroborating document trail so that he could have Casey brought down," said Scott. "I don't exactly know how but there was money laundering, fraud, paying off regulatory inspectors, loads of it. Casey finding out that I blew the whistle wasn't supposed to happen, but he is as guilty as sin and Olly promised it wouldn't end there either, he could…" Scott felt the tension of the last hours come to a head and hid his trembling hands in his lap. "He *will* implicate all those other evil, twisted, fuc—"

"I wouldn't hold your breath on that happening any time soon." Carruthers jutted his chin at the tea-stained picture of the justice minister.

"What do you think will happen to him?" said Scott, his voice faltering as a blur of memories washed over him. He lifted both hands and wrapped them around his mug, hoping the heat might melt the horrors away.

"What will happen to him?" echoed Carruthers. "He's dead. He's done himself in."

Scott spluttered, his eyes widening as his breath caught, the tea going down the wrong way. When he sneezed it jetted out of his nose.

"That's what the news said." Carruthers stood and snagged some paper towels from the roll beside the sink, then handed them across. "Well, they didn't say that exactly but reading between the lines on Twitter I'll bet you ten to one he did after they outed him as a bloody kiddie fiddler."

Scott wiped his eyes and nose and Carruthers slurped down the last of his tea.

"Stumpy, did he… you know… do what they're saying? To you? "

Steven 'Stumpy' Scott rubbed his palms over his face. Everything he had endured, the risks he had taken, and the revenge he sought bled from his soul to feed the rivulets of despairing tears streaking down his face.

Carruthers grunted awkwardly as he shifted his weight. "If he did, you know you don't need to be on the run. It wasn't you that was in the wrong."

When Scott looked back up at his old friend he wasn't sure where to begin.

23

At a guess, the damage ran to thousands. Maybe tens of thousands if the labour required to rip out the wreckage was taken into consideration on top of the replacement and repair of the fabric and fittings.

So were the thoughts of Erin Reilly as she surveyed the scene of wanton vandalism. Her next observation, travelling hot on the heels of the first was that the old bugger could probably afford it.

Geordie Corry had yet to grace them with the courtesy of his presence even though he had rolled up in a pristine silver Daimler twenty minutes earlier to meet with his insurance assessor and the two men were still shooting the breeze.

"How did they get in?" she said.

Corry's foreman who had introduced himself as Dessie, hissed out a stream of cigarette smoke, his eyes slits while indicating a discarded paving slab. "We've CCTV in the site hut of him climbing the fence and then tossing that against the glass until it gave way. I showed it to the other peelers who were here in case they could get prints." He dropped his spent cigarette and crushed it out underfoot, blowing a final lungful from the side of his mouth. "Did you get him yet?"

Reilly smiled politely. Everyone these days seemed to be an amateur sleuth and keen to offer their expertise on crime scene management, and the paver might have held something if it hadn't been removed from its final resting place to be deposited back amongst a slag heap of a dozen others like it. She chose to answer the question with one of her own. "Did you recognise him? Maybe a former employee or subbie?"

Dessie was shaking his head. "No, didn't know him from Adam."

"How long have you worked for Corry's?"

"It's a right while now, ten years?" The foreman peered at the eaves of the development that would soon house a new community outreach centre as though the exact date might be found up there.

"And does this sort of thing happen a lot?" Reilly gave a nod towards the building.

The front door had both panels of frosted safety glass smashed in, shards carpeting the paved walkway and front lobby like a frosting of ice. Once inside, Abbott, identified by CCTV smashing his way in, had used the tools available to smash through the dry lining, hammer lumps out of the desks and workstations, and trash light fittings and electrical sockets. A battery-powered grinder had severed cabling and water pipes and an abstract of multicoloured paint daubed the walls and pooled in puddles on the newly laid fabric floor tiles.

"Some trouble, kids wanting a chase mainly, but you don't expect this." A cock of the head preceded a wink. "Especially after you've made a donation, if you know what I mean?"

Reilly knew exactly what he meant. It didn't matter on which side of the political fence you sat or what colour the kerbstones were painted, once the local goons spotted a site going up someone would be round, the pitch to donate money to community projects no more than a veiled offer of protection, and it was almost always paid. Those who didn't soon wished they had.

Chris Walker approached, his circuit of the site complete.

When he stopped he jerked his head towards the CCTV eyeball erected on the site container.

"Any chance that picked up the road? Maybe caught our boy getting dropped off or picked up by someone else?"

Dessie's face pinched and he tapped out another cigarette. "Afraid not. Data protection or something. We aren't allowed to record images outside the fence line."

"You've your work cut out to get open now," said Walker, stepping forward to peer into the interior.

Dessie huffed out a breath. "You're not wrong."

"If you're done with my foreman, he has a bit to be getting on with."

The three turned to face a scowling Geordie Corry. He was in his sixties, still had a haircut from the seventies, and sported a bushy Tom Selleck moustache. "Have you caught the wee fucker?" His suit looked Saville Row but his accent was Shankill Road.

"There's been some progress, sir. I'm DC Reilly. This is my colleague, DC Walker."

"I want him done. None of that suspended sentence or community service shite either. Done, and every penny of damage paid back."

"That would be up to the courts, sir," said Reilly.

Corry tutted. "They're a useless bunch of bastards as well. All too happy to throw about noise abatement injunctions and nuisance notices but hand them the likes of this on a silver platter and their bloody balls fall off."

Corry paused to shout instructions to a gang recovering debris from the damaged building and then instructed his foreman what to do with what was salvageable. He continued, with one eye on his workers. "Well, what is progress? Have you got him or not?"

"I'm afraid there was an accident and the man identified as your alleged vandal didn't make it," said Reilly.

Corry wheezed a laugh and clapped his thigh. "That's karma for you, isn't it? Serves him right, although I suppose that means I'll be footing the bill again." There was no smile as he glared at the damage. Dessie, having directed which materials to save and which to skip, was taking the insurance assessor inside.

"You didn't recognise him from the CCTV footage?" said Reilly. Corry turned down his mouth and shook his head.

"His name was Finn Abbott."

"The name means nothing to me."

"Could he have worked for you in the past, directly or otherwise?"

"Do you know how many people work for me?" Corry shook his head. "No, of course you don't. I don't know the name, and his face doesn't ring a bell."

"We understand this isn't the first time your developments have been targeted in one way or another, Mr Corry," said Chris Walker, angling his notebook towards the shattered doors. "Would you have any idea if someone is holding a grudge? We're thinking along the lines of a disgruntled employee, competitor, locals objecting to your build?"

"Pick any number, constable."

"What about the name Steven Scott?" said Reilly. "Stumpy?"

"Who's he? One of the Teletubbies?" scoffed Corry.

"Another name that came up during our enquiries."

Corry shrugged. If there was recognition, Reilly didn't see it reflected in his expression. "I don't know. Look, I've never heard of either of them, but if you want to contact the office, HR can check if they've ever been on our books."

"We appreciate it," said Walker."

"I honestly don't know who did this but some of your theories might have validity." He nodded to Walker. "We've had more objections to planning proposals than normal lately, plus a fair few public demonstrations. They're always the same faces. The tree-hugging, hedgehog-humping brigade and what not. They make a racket and use whatever red tape they can but I've a solid relationship with the council and the DfI."

Reilly nodded, quite sure mention of the council and the Department for Infrastructure was meant to impress Corry's importance and standing on them.

"It's a leap from protest to this," said Reilly.

"Sure that lot all have militant wings, don't they? Environmentalists, animal rights. Even that woman from the family planning centre got red paint tipped over her in the street right before they put the windows in."

Reilly recalled the incident, demonstrations, petitions, and gory placards of aborted foetuses turning to assault and vandalism in the blink of an eye. She said, "I don't suppose you'd be willing to narrow the field a bit?"

Corry squinted past her. Dessie and the assessor were on the way over.

"Any names we could follow up on, perhaps see if they knew of Abbott? Maybe he had been to one of these protests and decided to take matters into his own hands," said Walker.

"Aye, or been put up to it," grunted Corry. "There's a couple of groups under the one banner. They call themselves, SCAR. Stop Construction and Redevelopment. Paul Finnegan is the chief rabble-rouser. Try him."

Corry's body language signalled they were at the end of their conversation.

"We'll be in touch," said Reilly.

On impulse Walker stuck out his hand, Corry shook it, offered a curt nod, and moved off to receive the damage assessment.

"What?" said Reilly. Walker had a wry grin on his face.

"He's part of the funny handshake club."

Reilly watched the three men carry on their discussion as they moved towards the site cabins.

So, Corry was a Freemason, or similar. She filed the detail away and blipped the locks of their car.

24

Shepard wasn't surprised when he found that Harry Carruthers didn't take his security seriously. There was nothing even a magpie would have considered worth stealing. The flat was a tip and the stench was enough to put off any but the most determined burglar. Whatever was in the kitchen bin had either died in there or been abandoned for some time.

He had accessed the communal block using the tradesperson button on the intercom and took the stairwell to the top floor flat, gaining access with the use of a lock-pick, a torsion wrench and an S-rake that made light work of the rudimentary lock.

Given that Beattie's enforcer was not remotely adept at anti-surveillance, Shepard had long since known where Carruthers laid his head but until now he hadn't held any inclination to breach the man's private quarters.

He hadn't been missing much.

The flat was devoid of any charm or character and lay somewhere between student digs and a doss house. The lounge had one three-seater settee set on a filthy laminate floor and dust coated every surface including the screen of a huge seventy-five-inch flat-screen television, the swirl of a palm on the LCD being the only sign of any attempt to clean. A pyramid of lager cans stood at the side of the sofa where a well-worn groove indicated Carruthers preferred seat. Next to the cans, the occupier had been busy building a tower of takeaway pizza boxes.

A space that had been set aside in the sales brochures for a small dining table set housed instead a barbell bench and a selection of dumbbells. A vat-sized tub of chocolate protein powder and a shaker sat on the floor.

As Shepard walked between rooms, he carefully observed everything but saw nothing of immediate significance. A check in the toilet cistern, inside the oven and then under and on top of the kitchen units provided no evidence that Carruthers, contrary to what he had expected, had been stupid enough to stash weapons or narcotics in his home. Not that he was looking for those. He needed a lead on where Beattie's man had fled to and hoped there would be something, anything, that might give him a starting point in his search.

Shepard had made peace with what he had offered to Taylor, and even though the urge to beat a confession from Carruthers remained strong, he was confident that handing him in to face charges of death by dangerous and fleeing the scene would see him take a deal. There was nothing about the man that had shown he had the backbone or the steadfast commitment to rise in Gordon Beattie's organisation. He was a committed minion and he would know that under the right circumstances, he would be used as a convenient scapegoat.

The bed hadn't been slept in. Shepard only knew this because he had kept the flat under observation. The sheets were balled, duvet kicked to the end of the double divan. A set of beside drawers stood on each side, one with an anglepoise lamp the other with a pint glass of water and a couple of protein bar wrappers. Shepard checked the drawers. Some socks and underwear, a few gym shorts in one, the usual credit card and utility bills and bedside junk in another. Crossing to the wardrobe he checked inside. Carruthers' trademark black tee-shirts were balled on the bottom shelf, a bowed rail held dark jeans, some polo shirts, a few brighter designer numbers that would come out when he was off the clock and a charcoal pinstripe suit. Probably for court. The slip-on shoes too. He closed the door on Carruthers limited fashion options and huffed out a sigh, returning through the flat to the lounge. Given the state of the place it would be unfair to call it sterile, but it was in a sense.

The smell in the kitchen was still overpowering and Shepard thought to crack the window in the hope the passage of air may dissipate the stink and let out some of the congregating flies. He opened the fridge instead and immediately wished he hadn't, gagging at the sudden wash of fetid air and buzz of more bluebottles. A clotted jug of milk and the decay of what might have been a couple of steaks left to defrost were the only contents; the meat was thick with mould and maggots. He closed the door quickly, putting a hand over his mouth, thumb and forefinger pinching his nose, thoughts that he had crawled through sewers less contaminated in his mind as he exhaled and focused on breathing through his mouth.

And then he saw it, hidden in plain sight amongst the takeaway menus, council bin collection schedule and a card for a taxi firm. The junk mail was stuck to the fridge door by a magnetic bulldog clip. Shepard pulled the sheaf from the door, dumping it on the drainer.

From the pile, he removed a postcard showing a pleasant seaside scene, deckchairs on the beach and a row of static caravans. He flipped the card over and read the spidery writing but there was nothing incriminating and it amounted to little more than a wish you were here card.

He noted the postmark, then studied the scene again and thought back to the last time he had been that far along the coast, his eyes closed, visualising the winding road that bisected fields of lush crops and the Irish Sea.

Blink and you'd be past it, and perhaps that was what Carruthers was counting on in lying low where everyone was on the way to anywhere else.

Shepard tucked the postcard into his jacket and pulled the front door closed behind him as he left.

25

If John Barrett had any concerns about his meeting they were allayed by the knowledge that it was to take place behind the walls of the prestigious Thirty-One Club. The Old Boys' Club was a private members institution fashioned in the image of those gentrified hangouts of the aristocracy in St James's and Pall Mall and had been a staple of Belfast City since before the Boer War, although its current iteration could only be traced back about twenty years.

The violence of the Troubles, the murder of Lord Mountbatten, and the Brighton bombing had finally put paid to the old guard submitting themselves and their flunkies to the risk of a car bomb or indiscriminate shooting while holed up with a gin and high tea, but once the ceasefires began and relative peace resumed, the building quietly returned to its former use while still maintaining the air of mystery and exclusivity for which it was renowned.

On his arrival, Barrett's remaining unease that the timing and potential inference or conjecture that may arise in being seen at his appointment in the private members' bar or dining room were quashed as he was directed to one of the club's exclusive function rooms. The Long Hall was a misnomer for it was neither long nor a hall. It had been named in honour of two of the club's late members and aside from the panelled walls and oil-painted voyeurs who mutely witnessed all, it was the sworn oath of club members and the staff to maintain the confidentiality of what exact after-dinner proclivities were indulged in inside the closeted rooms.

Barrett was shown to The Long Hall by one of the club's exclusively male front-of-house staff. His guide left him at the door with a curt nod and on entering, Barrett found two people inside. Settled in a buttoned leather wing chair, a wizened old gentleman quietly dismissed the other, a waitress in the process of laying out drinks. She made no eye contact with Barrett as she retreated to the opposite corner of the room, each step scrutinised by her seated patron, an unabashed lascivious leer on his face as he ogled the movement of nylon-covered calves and svelte hips under her satin pencil skirt until she took up a position out of immediate earshot but close enough should she be summoned.

"John." the seated gentleman indicated the table with a liver-spotted hand. There was a melodic clarity to his tone which held the subtle lilt of an Irish brogue. "I took the liberty of ordering for both of us."

Barrett sat, giving a nod that conveyed gratitude and greeting in one gesture. The man opposite was pushing seventy. His suit had been well cut perhaps twenty years ago but the decades had robbed the wearer of width and it now hung a little sadly, likewise, the collar of his shirt gaped and the skin of a bristle-free turkey neck fell loosely from a sagging jawline. His hair was grey, thinning and slicked into a side parting.

"To your health," said Barrett picking up the iced water and offering a toast. "To what do I owe the honour, Your Honour?"

The gentleman didn't reciprocate, nor indicate he found any mirth in Barratt's greeting, his only mannerisms the slow blink of rheumy eyes and a caress on the grip of a walking cane propped against his chair. The judge drew out the silence long enough to indicate his belief he held power over the coming conversation.

"I wished to discuss the unfortunate demise of the minister for justice."

Barrett replaced his glass on a slate coaster and nodded. "You are the second person to approach me in that regard, however, I'm not sure I can offer you any updates other than what is available through the media or what some of your members with more compelling connections might be able to divulge," he said, ignoring that these were facts the old man already knew.

"An honest witness does not deceive, but the false pours out lies." The man's voice carried the weight of a Sunday sermon.

"Proverbs?" said Barrett.

His host ignored him, a shrewd expression on his face as he continued. "We are concerned that scrutiny may find there was more than the minister's own hand involved in this... tragedy?"

"Are you now?"

The man rapped the brass tip of his cane against the parquet floor, the sharp crack drawing a fearful look from the waitress.

"The wicked make of themselves a stench that brings shame upon us all." The tone seethed with righteous fire and brimstone.

"I accepted the minister on your recommendation," said Barrett. "I bear no shame for what has befallen him."

"If any one of us had the foresight that Oliver Maddox was weak, or that he planned to announce his crackdown on organised criminality then we would have dealt with his betrayal with discretion." The last word came out in a harsh hiss. "We cannot be burdened by the consequences of these revelations. The stink you raised to discredit him and protect the interests of your cronies is threatening to soil the reputation of something much greater."

"Your Honour," said Barrett patiently. "If this impromptu meeting is over concerns around Maddox's exposure or the manner of his death, I'd suggest you consider the nature of both to see that any scrutiny will be swiftly quashed."

The judge took a sip of his water, lowering the glass with a hand trembling with age rather than anxiety. When he regarded Barrett again his eyes were drawn into reptilian slits. "And if you are wrong?"

"I am not wrong. Neither the police nor the Executive have any stomach for Maddox's misdeeds to play out for any longer than necessary and they will move to ensure that. He will be a footnote by the weekend."

"From your lips to God's ears," said the judge.

Barrett took another sip of his water. The man seated opposite proclaimed virtue and temperance, however, the civil servant knew that was an act. He was all too aware of the indulgences the man enjoyed behind the hallowed walls of the club with girls like the slip of a waitress. Reading between the lines though, this was about more than that, this was about deeper depraved desires and cruelties that threatened a greater status quo.

"Your Honour, our fate and our fortunes are interlinked, so be assured that the interests and privacy of your fellows is of primary concern to me," said Barrett.

"Indeed, however, I must make it expressly clear what is at stake should this particular genie leave the bottle."

"I understand the potential of this leading to the rebirth of rumour and of innuendo, however, any investigations into historic allegations have been dismissed with all investigative avenues fully and firmly closed down." Barrett leaned in a little closer, staring directly into the judge's watery eyes. "Can I remind you that your latest spoils, which were more of a threat to your group than Mr Maddox's sudden attack of conscience, have also been disappeared," said Barrett, underscoring his point by adding. "In no small part due to pressure brought by the consortium might I add?"

The judge's face pinched, uncomfortable at being beholden to his guest and his masters. "John, your own intimate knowledge and the rewards you have reaped in choosing to exploit that information rather than divulge it to the authorities make you an accessory and co-conspirator, that's setting aside how your deeds may be viewed as blackmail."

Barrett's smile was mirthless. "Is it still blackmail when it suits your personal agenda, Your Honour? I know the part I played, and I know why it had to be done—"

"And you did very well out of it; convenient some say." Colour flushed the judge's vein-flecked cheeks and a bite of venom tainted his tone.

"The primary concern was and always will be ensuring the administration of power can be regulated by means other than the threat of civil disorder or through the crosshairs of an Armalite. If one facet of that control requires you to understand and accept that civil society could at any time open the morning paper to discover the sordid predilections indulged by its administrators, then so be it," said Barrett.

"Still—"

"Still," snapped Barrett. "If it wasn't for twisted base desires and the innate cruelty of man there would be no sins to hold over anybody, would there? Now, I think I've addressed your concerns both historic and most recent so if you'll excuse me, I'll be getting back to it." He rose from his chair and buttoned his suit jacket, his host regarding him with a cool glare and tapping the tip of his cane against the floor.

"I understand Matthew Tierney came to see you?" said the judge.

Barrett chose not to reply but silently acknowledged that his suspicion of who might be behind Tierney's request once Glenrafferty had been mentioned had been correct.

The old judge stared unseeing at the two glasses and when he spoke again his attention was welded in the past. "You would do well to use whatever options you have at your disposal to expedite his request."

He cleared his throat and his attention returned to the room, focused completely now on Barrett. "There is more than a financial incentive in seeing this project overcome the current impasse. To see the site returned to its rightful heirs would go some way to alleviating concerns that your only interests lie in feathering the caps of your masters and their syndicated friends."

"Concerns? You make it sound as though you and your brethren are in a position to negotiate." Barrett snorted a chuckle. "I would respectfully suggest that you clearly communicate to them that unless someone wishes to be the next Oliver Maddox they continue to offer unstinting support when and where it is required."

The judge's mouth twisted in a grimace of bitter loathing. Barrett fixed him with a stern glare.

"Whatever I choose to do, it will be for the benefit of the consortium, and should I fulfil your request and see that ruin redeveloped for whatever twisted purpose you have in mind, be under no illusion, neither your crimes nor the crimes of those you count as your abhorrent friends will disappear under a new pour of concrete or behind a fresh lick of paint." Turning on his heel, the civil servant's parting shot left no room for misinterpretation. "I know you think enough time has passed that people have forgotten or guards have dropped, but that wretched school is not the only place where the bodies of your victims are buried and let's not forget some of them are not yet cold."

No barbed retort or biting comment followed Barrett across the parquet, but as he turned the antiquated brass handle and heaved the door open he heard the rap of cane and the bark of a summons from the old judge.

The clip of heels crossed towards his recently vacated chair. He didn't need to look back to see the girl assume the position. As the door closed, he heard the first lash of a cane across the girl's smooth flesh, the vicious strikes amounting to an angry priming of the pump as the filthy old bastard worked himself up to a point where he could slake his lust.

26

The bar should have been called *The Alleyway and Gables* because that was the limited view through the grimy windows of the lounge.

It had however, been christened *The Laganview* which was somewhat ironic given that it was about half a mile away from the river that cut through the city and any view of the grey-green water was obscured by rows of terrace streets and shops that surrounded the establishment dominating a corner site on a main arterial road junction.

The lounge was a long affair with round tables and chairs arranged around a horseshoe bar, the walls a peculiar hue of magnolia emulsion that came when two different shades were hastily mixed to get the job done.

The smell of food was in the air and genial banter could be heard above the tinny sound of music as the swinging door dividing the rear of the lounge and the kitchen swung back and forth. Ensconced in a corner booth, nursing the dregs of a pint and studying the form for the evening racing sat the man Taylor and Macpherson had come to question.

His nose tested the air like a prey animal sensing danger, but as his eyes snapped up from the paper to scan the bar his face split in a jovial grin.

"Sure, will you look at what the cat's dragged in," he said, raising his glass towards Macpherson. "If you're here for a yarn I'll need to lubricate the old vocal cords so I will." Again the glass waggled back and forth. "Another of the usual, please and thank you."

Taylor slid into the booth as Macpherson diverted to the bar.

"Afternoon, Eddie. How are you?"

Eddie Faulks was a long-limbed, skinny man. His head was too big for his body and he had a shock of straw-like blond hair and a wine stain birthmark running under his nostrils and covering the scar left from a childhood cleft lip. The overall effect had cruelly dubbed him with the nickname Worzel after the walking, talking scarecrow from literature and television.

"All the better for seeing you, Inspector." Worzel's grin, although showing off a row of rotting tombstones, was genial and sincere. "I can't be saying the same for your partner but what he lacks in manners he makes up for with his generosity. I'll give him that."

Macpherson returned with a pint of Tennent's for Worzel and two soft drinks for himself and Taylor.

"Not even a wee cheeky half 'un, sergeant. It's nearly quitting time too, this must be serious."

"I'm not made of money, Worzel," grumbled Macpherson, brandishing a soggy receipt. "What's happened to the prices in here? I've a mind to be lifting the landlord for daylight bloody robbery."

Worzel picked up the pint of lager and toasted the two. "Your good health." He smacked his lips and reached out to study Macpherson's bill, chuckling as he put the glass down. "He's charged you peelers rates," he said, the laugh turning to a deep cackle as he watched the realisation dawn on Macpherson that he had been had.

"The cheeky bas—"

"Eddie, if you have the time, we hoped you'd help us out with something," said Taylor. Macpherson reined in his irritation and embarrassment with a throaty cough and pocketed the receipt.

Worzel, a second draught draining half his pint, checked the watch on his thin wrist. The timepiece was probably right twice a day; its glass was cracked and the leather strap worn shiny. "It was my old man's," he said, noticing the looks and adding, "Fire ahead, it doesn't matter what they say about me I'm all for performing my civic duty when it comes to the pursuit of law and order."

Taylor sincerely doubted that was wholly accurate. Faulks was an old-school D Company reprobate with a jacket as long as his leg of previous form, and custodial sentences that stretched back to childhood. Which, retrieving the photograph from her pocket, she hoped might go some way to explaining how they came to have shared acquaintances. As she placed the image on the table Worzel spluttered into his drink.

"Are youse doing the double with Time Team or what?" he said, wiping drips from his chin and shirt front.

"That is you, isn't it?" said Taylor. Worzel nodded.

"Uphill paper round was it?" said Macpherson with a smirk. Their informant hadn't aged well, but then that was eighty roll-ups a day and a former heroin habit for you.

"That wasn't taken yesterday right enough." There was a wistful look of nostalgia on his face, his drink abandoned and the next race meeting forgotten for the moment. "Where did you get it?"

Taylor tapped the face next to his in the photo.

"Steven Scott."

"Stumpy gave it to you?" Worzel's face screwed up in confusion.

"We found it amongst his possessions."

"Aw, Jesus. He's not dead is he?" There was a note of grief in the tone.

"How much of that paper do you actually read?" said Macpherson.

"Back pages and the racing section," admitted Worzel with a grin, then he shrugged. "Sometimes the problem pages when I need to cheer myself up."

Macpherson reached across the table and flipped the red top over, the headlines on the front page concerned the sudden death of the justice minister and a few by-lines hinted at the expected implosion of Colm Casey's trial. Flipping the pages to the continued coverage, he turned the story and accompanying pictures for Worzel to see. He shook his head sadly.

"That wee lad has always been a magnet for trouble."

"Did you know him well?" said Taylor.

"Aye, well enough. Back then mind, I haven't seen Stumpy for years." Worzel grunted. "He's a stupid bugger for getting himself into the likes of that." He closed the newspaper.

"How did he get the name Stumpy?"

Worzel winced, his eyes falling to the table. Taking a few seconds to ponder he picked up his lager and drained it, holding the empty up to the barman.

"Andy, I'll have another one on the house on account of you ripping off my good friend here." He nodded to Macpherson. "Can I get you something, sergeant?"

Macpherson smiled. "Not while I'm on duty, but send him over a double to chase it, Andy. And thanks, that's very generous of you to acknowledge your mistake."

Worzel cackled at the look on the barman's face, but the steel behind his eyes moved the man towards his optics.

"Stumpy," breathed Worzel. "I used to think it was because he was just a wee fella but then I found out about what went on at the home."

Taylor felt a catch in her throat and noticed Macpherson shift his position. The article hadn't mentioned any specifics.

"The boys were allowed out to play football against the community teams every once in a while. Other times we had to go there." Worzel shuddered at the memory. "Fucking horrible place. It gave me the heebie-jeebies going through the gates."

"This is Glenrafferty?" said Taylor. Worzel confirmed with a slight dip of his head.

"That's where I first met him. It was a few months before I clocked the nickname though. Years before that picture."

The barman arrived to interrupt, setting down lager and chaser with a face like a slapped backside. He ignored Macpherson's repeated thanks and retreated behind the bar.

"He was missing a couple of toes on his right foot." Worzel folded down his pinkie and third finger to demonstrate. "The animals that worked in there beat the kids for stepping out of line, or for the craic when the mood took them if you believe the stories." Worzel's expression soured. "Stumpy skived off for a few ciders after an away game and missed the bus. When they got him back to the home they beat his feet to a pulp and didn't treat the wounds. He lost the toes and the fucker that did it christened him Stumpy. I guess the name just stuck."

Taylor could have noted that Stumpy wouldn't have been old enough to drink or asked why he hadn't reported the brutality and why others hadn't intervened on the boy's behalf but like everyone who had seen the various scandals unfold in the media she was aware of the sordid silence surrounding the history of cruelty and abuse in the care system at that time. If anyone had spoken up, their voice would have been silenced, the accusations ridiculed or made out to be no more than idle fantasy or childish devilment.

"Do you remember this photo being taken?" said Taylor.

"No. It's a right while after he got out of the home though and after…" Worzel's face pinched in distaste. "Well, like I said he was a magnet for trouble."

"What are you not telling us?" said Taylor, feeling Worzel shrink back as he pushed the photo away.

"Good wee bunch of mates we all were then, wasn't always like that though." His eyes moved between the two detectives. "D'you remember the Mad Monk?"

"Billy McBride."

It was Taylor who answered. Billy McBride, the Mad Monk, had been before her time. Brigadier and chief of active operations in the UVF wing's notorious nutting squad. Outspoken, violent and self-serving, he hadn't baulked at the cold-blooded gunning down of Republicans or Loyalists alike leaving the establishment and his own organisation in uproar as his exploits grew in audacity.

With a schism emerging between Loyalist factions and their political representatives who were keen to embrace the Good Friday Agreement, the Monk was deemed surplus to requirements but before he could be liquidated, the leading Loyalist responsible for the action was himself murdered in a hail of gunfire. Although firmly in the frame for the execution the Mad Monk had a rock solid alibi, and the then worsening situation between the clans was only curtailed when the newly minted Brigadier Gordon Beattie put a blowtorch to McBride's balls and told him if he wasn't on the overnight ferry, a few singed pubes and the police would be the least of his worries.

The Mad Monk was now presumed dead, the only evidence he had ever lived a severed finger removed from a recent crime scene and Taylor was the only person at the table who knew the real story that linked McBride's expulsion and Beattie's sudden meteoric rise afterwards.

"He wasn't just put on the boat because he was a wanker," said Worzel.

"But also because he was a rapist?" Macpherson's voice

had a note of steel behind the accusation.

Worzel's jaw flexed and his lips drooped in contempt. "He was a rotten bastard alright."

The two detectives had heard the rumours before. Tales of how McBride enticed young men to his side with the thrill of gangs, guns and drugs only to subvert their loyalty to satisfy his own warped sexual gratification.

"The Council wanted him gone after what happened to Marty Coleman, but they were looking for an excuse long before that. Nobody wanted to have a kiddie fiddler in the club." Worzel swerved his lager and took a deep draw of his whiskey chaser. "Stumpy was one of the Monk's. God knows how, but once he got out of that hellhole of a home he wound up in his wee harem of youngsters. Stumpy was a fucking magnet like I've been telling you. Anyway, long story short, after McBride was sent on his way Stumpy kinda just fell in with us. Not a bad kid, but damaged, as you'd expect after all he'd been through."

"Did he ever talk about it?" said Taylor.

"Not really." Worzel pulled a face. "We wouldn't have wanted to hear about it anyway. Less said the better, you know."

Taylor nodded but inwardly sighed. Northern Ireland's problems in a nutshell, the unbreakable code of silence. See nothing, hear nothing, say nothing.

"What about him?" Taylor pulled up a photo of Finn Abbott on her phone.

"Aye, I know him right enough. Housebreaker, shoplifter, smackhead. I heard he took his dead uncle to collect his pension the other day." Worzel gave a short laugh. "Desperate, eh?"

"The aul lad's fine. He had a stroke and is in hospital," said Macpherson.

"Still. The lengths you go to for a score."

Taylor continued to display the image, allowing Worzel to contemplate whatever it was that he was recollecting from his own days battling the brown. "Any idea if they knew each other?" she said.

"Probably, your lad there was never out of the barracks or the borstal. They're bound to have passed each other."

"And you're certain Stumpy never talked about his time in Glenrafferty or the people who had abused him."

Worzel tipped the last of his whiskey into the pint and took a swig, smacking his lips and nodding.

"Not to me, and not as far as I could tell you to anyone else either."

"And you've never seen this man at any of these matches or on your trips to the home?" She pointed to the front page snaps of Oliver Maddox.

"It was a lifetime ago." Worzel shrugged. "Sorry."

Taylor closed the image and locked her phone, feeling the creep of a dead end frustrate her.

"There's always been something doesn't sit right with me about the whole thing though," said Worzel, easing forward on his stool to lean closer to the two detectives. "The Monk got away with bloody murder and no one pulled his chain over any of it until Copeland bought the bullet. Even then, D Company let him walk rather than planting him in a peat bog." He let a silence hang over the drinks for several seconds.

"The Monk was Teflon. Your lot never got anything to stick, no murders, none of his sick antics and none of the rackets he was running. And our lot? Fuck, they give him free rein to run riot." He took another sip of lager before he offered his final thoughts. "You have to wonder what cards he was holding in his back pocket to get away with all that, don't you?"

27

Steven Scott crushed a beer can and tossed it to the growing pile. Seated to his right, Harry Carruthers sipped cheap convenience store vodka from the bottle, the spirit doing a better job at numbing the nip of pain in his thigh than the five per cent lager had been.

In the distance lightning streaked across the smear of grey where the sea met the clouds, followed long seconds later by a dull rumble of thunder. The scene unfolding in front of the two men was aggressive and oddly alien as the waves swelled to blur against the horizon, the darkening shades bleaching the colour from the seascape and a strengthening wind blowing in off the tide to hurtle between the caravans, creating sounds an overworked imagination might easily place as the shriek of angry sea birds or the ghosts of the dead, the unnatural howl carrying the weight of pain and grief of those lost to the depths.

As the storm drifted ever closer to the Irish coast it brought with it the ominous threat of torrential rain and localised flooding yet the gloom gathering around the men was more forbidding than what Mother Nature was preparing to unleash.

"You could have said no." Carruthers eyed his friend for a second, waiting on a response to his comment before jetting an arc of vodka onto the sandy grass from the side of his mouth.

"It was something I had to do," said Scott finally.

"I know it's been a while but I'd have thought what happens to touts would have stuck with you."

"It was about more than informing on a bloody plastic paramilitary, Harry."

"The Casey mob aren't exactly small fry—"

"Olly asked for my help, and I did it because he was offering something in return."

"Olly, Olly, Olly. Oi. Oi. Oi." Carruthers chanted mirthlessly into the strengthening breeze. "How the fuck do you and the justice minister end up so pally?"

Scott took a deep draught of a new beer. "It's a long story."

"Well, apparently we have a while until either Casey or the papers track you down so why don't you spit it out."

Scott stared out to sea and poured a measure of beer into the sand at his feet.

"I knew Olly Maddox from before… before I came to the estate. From Glenrafferty"

"He was at the home?" said Carruthers, the surprise reaching his eyebrows.

"He was on the staff but he wasn't like the rest. He was kind to me."

"Oh right."

"It wasn't like that, you dick. He did his best to protect us but he was new. Junior." Scott shrugged. "He had to turn a blind eye to a lot of it."

"Convenient that."

"You've no idea what it was like," scolded Scott. "What they did to us and the sort of people involved. The threats that were made, the intimidation. It wasn't just us bad wee boys who suffered."

"I still don't get it," said Carruthers. "So, he knew you half a lifetime ago and suddenly he gets in touch because he has an axe to grind with Casey?"

"Look, I don't know the whole story behind it, or how he found me. Olly wanted Casey put away and he was under pressure to make it happen."

"So what was the sweetener to help out?"

Scott took a swig of beer and his gaze fell shamefully between his knees.

"He was offering me a way to get back at some of the dirty bastards who abused us as children."

Carruthers' eyes widened, the revelation containing the tale of two horrors which his head struggled to categorise into a hierarchy of danger. "He told you who they were?" The pleasant warmth of the vodka suddenly fell away as he realised the potential risks that harbouring his friend may now hold. Scott nodded slowly.

"I knew some because, you know, of who they… came to be." The nod turned into a violent shake. "A lot of it is just a blur."

"And what did you think you were going to do with this information?" snapped Carruthers. "Go public? Or was it going to be set a few fires, slash a few tyres, or maybe you were prepared to go the whole hog?"

Scott shot him a dangerous look. "He was going to help us expose them. These people stole my childhood, my friends' lives. Not one of them has ever been made to pay for what they did."

"Did you ever stop to wonder why that was?" Carruthers levelled a look of equal ire.

"Because we were worthless and no one cares," snarled Scott.

"No, it wasn't. It's because of who they were and who they represented. For fuck's sake, Stumpy, what have you done."

Scott lowered his head and a sudden tear tracked down his cheek.

"I got a friend killed."

"What?"

"Finn Abbott. Olly let slip one of the sleazy bastards who came to the home was now a big-shot developer so we made a plan and Finn went and smashed up one of his building sites. The next day he was killed in a hit and run."

The vodka soured in Carruthers' stomach and the crunch of flesh and bone resounded in his imagination. "Abbott?"

"Don't try telling me it was a coincidence," said Scott, wiping a hand across his face, the gesture serving to graze sand down the side of his cheek. "The same day the story breaks about Olly and they out me in the paper, Finn is run down. Less than twenty-four hours later Olly kills himself? No way. Just no way that makes sense."

"Stumpy, calm down a minute and let me think." Carruthers set his drink on the sand and eased himself slowly to his feet, the spin of emotion and the toll of recent insights leaving him more unsteady than the alcohol. "Come inside." He staggered a few steps towards the duckboard path and the caravans beyond.

Scott called after him. "They're scorching the earth, Harry. I didn't think it through, I thought we could do something small to get our own back while Olly did his work. Piss some of them off, hit their bottom line, make people reconsider their investments. Jesus, I didn't think they would want to kill us."

Carruthers turned and beckoned him off the beach, acknowledging to himself that Scott was not just naive but bone dumb and ignorant to just what exactly he had unleashed, and for the moment that was the one thing preventing him from doing anything even more stupid.

"Get inside, we can't be seen out here."

Scott threw the tin onto the pile with the others and rose to his feet in compliance.

Carruthers cast a nervous look along the sandy bay and up

to the road leading into the site, keeping the rest of his assessment to himself. If Scott thought having his card marked by Colm Casey was bad it was nothing compared to what would happen if the others found him.

28

If it hadn't been so rundown it could have evoked a certain gothic charm but, as it stood, the overgrown weeds, old iron gates and rusting railings served more to dissuade casual visitors rather than welcome any thrillseekers in their macabre search for a glimpse of the buildings and the grisly history that lurked behind the antiquated barriers.

A single iron sign affixed to the railings instructed there was to be, 'NO TRESPASSING', the sentiment underscored by a thick chain and padlock securing the gate.

The headlamps of the Volvo bled between the bars and across the potholed and weed-infested drive beyond.

"Abandon hope all ye who enter here," said Macpherson.

"Dante?" said Taylor, impressed. "I thought you weren't a scholar of the classics?"

"I'm not, it just reminds me of one of those Hammer Horror movies." Macpherson shuddered as he peered through the bars. "All that's missing are the peasants and the pitchforks."

The comparison was close enough, thought Taylor, even without the cautionary inscription there could be no doubt that for the children who had crossed the threshold it had been a passage through the gates to Hell, cast into limbo to suffer the lust, violence and treachery of those who had been charged with their care.

Glenrafferty wasn't unique, nor was it the only cancerous

scab that remained to blight the landscape in the aftermath of the historic institutional abuse scandals that had rocked the country. Reams of newsprint and hours of television and testimony had detailed the horrific seventy-year span of vile psychological and physical abuse meted out by the religious orders and secular bodies who ran the homes. Each distressing account of physical and sexual abuse seemed to unearth another. Report after report detailing more unimaginable horror than the last with harrowing descriptions of how men and women, staff and visitors, had been free to indulge and keep secret cruelty on an industrial scale. It remained a scandal and an insult that none of the revelations had gone any distance in assisting with the apprehension of perpetrators or in offering redress to the victims.

While most of the houses of systemic horror had been razed to the ground and redeveloped or reduced to wasteland hidden behind nondescript hoardings, Glenrafferty's sandstone building which comprised the main reformatory school and dormitories was still in relatively good repair and while it wasn't exactly on the tourist trail it was only a minor detour on the way back to Musgrave Street which was why Taylor had chosen to stop.

Macpherson was still quiet and she wasn't entirely sure that it was just the revulsion she herself felt when thinking about what had gone on in these places of supposed sanctuary. "I can't help but think the last day or two puts some meat on the bones of Finn Abbott's rant," she said.

"A conspiracy to bump off former residents?" Macpherson turned his back on the home, his expression as fraught as his tone.

"The murder of Barry Toms, the historic injuries to Abbott, the scars on Maddox." Taylor chewed her bottom lip. "I've never seen anything like that branding."

Macpherson nodded, made to speak and stopped. Taylor continued.

"The link between the three of them all seems to stem from here," said Taylor. "And from what we've just seen, Maddox looks to be as much a victim as the others."

Macpherson took a long time to speak. "I've heard tell of people being marked like Oliver Maddox."

"When?"

"Years ago." Macpherson studied the rough ground underfoot. When he looked up there was a deep sadness behind his eyes. "It was something I worked on with your da."

"My dad?"

Macpherson nodded. Derek Taylor had been his friend since high school and his colleague since the first day they had entered the Royal Ulster Constabulary as probationary officers until the day an under-car booby trap ended his life.

"A whistleblower made allegations of mistreatment in care homes. They alluded to the abuse being widespread, orchestrated and involving some prominent people of the time." The sergeant shook his head as he recalled events. "This was years before anything came out in the public domain."

Taylor sat on the bonnet of the Volvo, the rush of memories surrounding her father's death and then her mother passing from grief knocking the wind from her.

"The source was a groundsman here and he alleged that part of his job was to transport boys to private parties around the country where they would be abused by groups of men and women. Your da passed the complaint on but it went quiet so he pursued it with the inspector. He was told due to the sensitive nature of what was being alleged it had been passed to Special Branch."

Taylor stood up. This wasn't an old war story she had

heard before and considering the topic she understood why Macpherson had chosen to skip past it.

"Part of the statement claimed there was a cabal of businessmen, MPs, judiciary and senior police officials who frequently attended these parties and there was a persistent rumour one particular group marked their favourites." He paused and scuffed the ground with the toe of his shoe. "I suppose I always thought that meant they gave them a sovereign ring or something, maybe tattooed the poor craiters."

"Christ," breathed Taylor. "The pain Maddox must have…"

Taylor paced towards the railings, caught between thoughts of her family and the brutal brand seared on the justice minister's skin. After a few moments, she turned.

"What did Special Branch find?"

Macpherson shrugged. "I can tell you nothing ever came of it. Your old man raised it to the point he was pulled in and told to forget about it, the allegations had been dropped because the witness wasn't credible. When Derek tried to track down the groundsman it turned out he'd had a nervous breakdown. He was sectioned and strung himself up in Purdysburn not long after."

Taylor ran a hand through her hair. The former psychiatric unit outside Belfast may have replaced the old Belfast Asylum but it had always retained the stigma and although it was now rebuilt, renamed and rebranded as a modernised healthcare park, it didn't stop people making the old associations.

"What Worzel said keeps going around in my head," said Macpherson.

"What about it?"

"That McBride was let off the leash. That he had a thing for wee boys and he was untouchable," said Macpherson.

Taylor felt the palpitations start as she considered what Macpherson was saying; the knowledge revealed to her in the undercroft of Hoey Cargo had at first seemed implausible, this train of thought seemed unthinkable. Her stomach soured as she thought of the depravity that had gone on a few hundred feet away.

"Doc—" she started but Macpherson continued.

"There was always a suspicion McBride was a Special Branch informer. But if he was involved in these circles then it might not have been his paramilitary colleagues he was ratting on." He paused, considering the implications. "If Special Branch knew this was happening, then someone high up the chain of command was either more interested in gathering information on people of influence or bloody protecting reputations rather than stopping what was going on."

"Doc—"

Macpherson, now on a roll, spoke over her. "We're talking individuals, prominent individuals, who if they were members of this syndicate and had the dirt gathered on them could be manipulated at the right time or when the right circumstances presented themselves." Macpherson gave the old home a hard stare as an unexpected gust of wind blew through shaking a murder of crows from their roosts in the treetops. "Maddox held a press conference recently and called time on corruption. Now we've seen he was branded. What if he was one of these chosen few? What if taking the brand showed fealty or granted promotion, protection even? What if in return for his allegiance his rise up the greasy pole was assisted by this cabal to make sure they had friends in high places? If they were prominent then who knows where they ended up."

"Doc!"

Macpherson's train of thought came to a crashing halt as

he saw the colour draining from her face.

Taylor swallowed, forcing down the bile threatening to rise up her throat while at the same time hearing Father Michael Keane's words nagging at her. It was time to have faith, in her sergeant's loyalty and in herself, as she finally admitted that bottling up what she knew was poisoning her soul.

She took a deep breath and told Macpherson everything about the extent of ACC Ken Wallace's corruption, his role in Copeland's fall which had resulted in Gordon Beattie's rise to the top, and of their links to a group working in the shadows to set the agenda across the country's institutions of power and governance and the depths to which they had sunk in the name of securing peace.

When she finished they both sank against the bodywork of the Volvo, silently considering their options in the face of revelations which threatened to suck them into a void no one would wish to be explored.

29

"You left that a bit bloody late."

"Some would say better late than never, and you're welcome by the way." John Barrett kept his hands thrust deep in the pockets of his overcoat, Colm Casey had made no attempt to offer his hand in gratitude or friendship, choosing instead to offer the civil servant a scowl.

"How did we not know Maddox was coming after me? He was supposed to be on our side?"

"Colm, why the minister chose this exact moment to reveal a conscience I do not know, however, I can assure you that those who placed him in post are equally relieved that matters have been brought to a conclusion and they pass on their gratitude."

"They can stick their false sentiments up their arse, John. I've held my silence all these years. I didn't expect to be stabbed in the back for making sure the morals of others didn't derail the gravy train."

"And we are grateful for that," said Barrett.

"So you bloody should be."

Barrett bit back a retort and turned his face away from the breeze that swept in off Belfast Lough. The two men stood on a siding overlooking the Musgrave Channel and the Casey Bulk Fuel operation which was in full swing. The compound was surrounded on three sides by high barbed wire fencing with the northern end open to a concrete jetty where a barge lay low in the water, its shipment of pallets being unloaded by derrick onto the dock. Casey employees scuttled like black beetles handballing sacks of coal from deposited stacks onto the back of flatbed coal lorries, or ferrying pallets of the fuel by forklift to a huge storage shed. Opposite, along the eastern flank, another shed housed bottled gas, the corrugated walls nudging up against a stack of double-height shipping containers that were packed with imported kiln-dried logs.

"I'm sorry you feel that there was a lack of support," said Barrett. "Your resourcefulness has proven you to be someone we can rely upon to get their hands dirty, especially when the cause is mutually beneficial."

Casey held up calloused palms. "Dirty hands have been an occupational hazard my whole life, John. Given the position in which I've now been placed, I expect I'll be blackening them a bit more before too long."

Barrett regarded the fierce look on the man's face. He had watched a feral anger grow behind his eyes over the years. A flame that had been stoked by the knowledge his father had chosen prosperity and his lecherous acquaintances over his own flesh and blood, the choice for a time condemning his third son to the trials of the youth justice system.

"The last thing you need, Colm, is further scrutiny. One seedy suicide can be explained away under the circumstances. More deaths will only create suspicion and if another inquisitive media hound links that and your sudden good fortune in avoiding prosecution for the passing of two prison officers and our dear departed pastor, then conspiracy theories will run amok," said Barrett.

Casey's journey from victim to one of the consortium's acolytes was intricately bound to the legacy left by his father, where family secrets and the source of their affluence required discretion to be paramount. Through the years, Barrett had been aware of their rise and moved to be unswervingly supportive of it, his influence and mentorship surreptitiously guiding the Casey clan away from sectarian activism and meaningless criminality into the consortium's fold, creating a bulwark against actions by more militant republicanism on the consortium's interests. The civil servant eventually and without fanfare anointed them as disciples in his greater cause, bestowing the opportunity for the family business to flourish as they were granted access to those in positions of trust and influence.

Barrett gritted his teeth as he faced the impulsive son of the man who had been altogether more malleable, finding himself once again frustrated by the understanding that when dealing with criminality, soft power had to give way at times to a more overt message to the masses. A harsh reminder that the code of silence was a blood oath to be taken seriously.

Casey laughed scoffingly. "You're asking me to turn the other cheek? Not a chance. Grasses need to be made an example of." He paused, adding, "Especially wee weasels with the ability to point fingers."

"I have people looking for Mr Scott and it's my belief that the fear of consequences will lead to him reaching out to make amends," said Barrett.

"That isn't a gamble I'm willing to take, John."

Barrett thought back to his tense meeting at the Thirty-One Club with the representative of the ultra-secret group whose disregard for consequences had created the current blood trail which ironically they now wanted to disappear. "The Crossed Keys wish to communicate that the situation has got out of hand and discretion must be restored. What should have ended with Pastor Phelan is threatening to reignite a fire that many have taken time and trouble to extinguish."

Casey sneered. "So they're big men when they're preying on wee boys but when the bodies start to fall their balls drop off? You don't let the dogs off the leash and then cry foul when they get their teeth bloody. That's just not how it works and you know it."

Barrett nodded, conceding he did. The Crossed Keys had required a mess to be cleaned up and Casey had achieved that, albeit with more attention than expected. "There has been too much focus brought on consortium affairs recently and we need this to go away." He offered a hopeful gesture. "Just for the time being."

"It's my arse on the line—"

"I've been instructed to offer you extended protection, both personally and to your interests. Of course, this demands certain conditions are met."

Casey turned to fully face Barrett, hands on hips and with an expression of curiosity. He nodded for the civil servant to continue.

"You drop thoughts of any unsanctioned action against Steven Scott or anyone else who may step forward with allegations surrounding the demise of indiscreet former associates. In return, the consortium and our friends in the judiciary will move to call a mistrial and issue a formal apology."

"Throw in some compensation and I'll think about it," grunted Casey.

"There is a proposal on the table offering you a significant financial return which I believe we can thrash out."

Casey's eyes narrowed, suspicion mellowing to curiosity. "A deal to be had? Okay, go on then. Let's hear it."

"A need has been identified. A civic and commercial expansion opportunity which will enable the consortium to advance their interests and offset some recent setbacks."

"That's what's in it for you," snorted Casey.

"It offers a large return to those partners who invest early. You, however, are in a unique position." Barrett offered Casey his open palms. "Without your support, this expansion is stalled. With it, the consortium is offering you an additional twenty per cent over market valuation and their extended insurance against and protection from future prosecution."

Casey's face creased in confusion and he swept a hand across the fuel yard. "You want this?"

"No, we want you to sell the site of the former Glenrafferty Boys Home," said Barrett, watching the penny drop as Casey digested the words.

"To Geordie Corry?"

"Twenty per cent over value and extended protection," repeated Barrett.

"Why?"

"Not your concern." Barrett gave a slight shake of the head. "Can we make a deal or shall I report back there's an issue?"

Casey looked out across his busy yard to the lough beyond, hearing the offer of indemnity and the threat for what they were.

The old home and buildings had been in the family since his old man had struck a deal with the council in the wake of the various care home scandals and he had thought it an odd purchase at the time considering the sullied reputation of the place and his own short time behind the reformatory walls as a youth. The property itself needed a fortune of work if it was ever to be renewed for any purpose and that would only happen if it could shake off the stigma attached. The estate itself though had grown in value over the years, also achieving the incidental benefit of hemming in the burgeoning real estate empire owned by Geordie Corry.

Selling to the Loyalist developer would see encroachment onto the fringes of nationalist soil and Corry was known for formenting tensions that had seen swathes of green assimilated into the orange as thriving local businesses were harassed and starved of custom.

Casey pondered the offer silently, thinking that perhaps there could be more than a simple financial benefit to reap this time, that perhaps it was time to redraw a few borders and stick it to Corry at the same time.

Gulls swooped along the shoreline and as he followed their flight his eye was drawn to a passenger ferry making the slow turn to the terminal, the birds arcing lazily to continue along the York Dock towards the Abercorn Basin where the sun glinted off the pointed hulls of anodised aluminium which made up the imposing facade of the Titanic Museum, the cladding shimmering under the gaze of the city's iconic twin cranes, Samson and Goliath.

Beyond those, the Lagan meandered around the outskirts of East Belfast.

"We can make a deal. But I have some terms of my own," said Casey. Barrett gestured his intention to listen. "I get Steven Scott. If there's no witness, there's no case."

Barrett reluctantly nodded his acceptance. "But no body. Never," he said.

Casey smiled coolly and crossed his heart. Barrett, noting a gleam in his eye, prompted him to continue. "What else?"

"You said it yourself. There have been setbacks and you've lost a valuable partner in the process." Casey gave a shrug. He had heard the stories, watched the news and listened to the rumours. "No great loss, Gordon Beattie had it coming if you ask me. Lost the run of himself and got too big for his boots. Still, it can't be good for your business having the minnows fighting over his scraps."

"The consortium's relationship, if any, with Gordon Beattie is no concern of yours," said Barrett.

"Well, you see, that's where you're wrong, John. I'll sell Geordie Corry the old home and the acreage, lock, stock and barrel. But in return, I want a foot across the river and you need somebody competent enough to step into the mess

Beattie has left and take it in hand. So what do you say? Out with the old and in with the new?"

"I can't risk igniting a turf war between East and West Belfast," said Barrett, shaking his head.

"I won't be repainting the kerbstones or swapping the Union Jack for Tricolours, and I've no interest in construction either," said Casey, pointing downriver to the cranes dotted against the skyline. "I want the Monster's real empire. I want the chance to recover what he managed to throw away."

30

Carrie Cook's fingers rattled across her keyboard and a moment later the information she had gathered during her excavation of the archives and through internet searches appeared on the wall-mounted display monitor. "There have been fourteen complaints of vandalism associated with property or construction sites in the Corry portfolio over the last six months and a further four reports of intimidation," she said.

Reilly and Walker sat at opposite ends of the table in conference room 4.12 listening intently and scanning the update. Opposite Cook and side by side sat Taylor and Macpherson. The DS was unusually subdued following the trip to Glenrafferty and his inspector's revelations of active corrupt elements within the service and beyond.

"Aside from that, the company has also seen disruption to schedules following the discovery of victims of the recent gang violence on or nearby their sites. The last being Dylan Masters."

Each of the detectives around the table knew the story of Dylan Masters. Sixteen years old, A-grade student, active in a local church group and accepted for a summer legal internship. No history of trouble. His body was found half submerged in a neglected river that separated a retail complex and a Corry building development. Cause of death had been marked as misadventure but lurid speculation from anonymised social media accounts ran claims he had been shifting packages and pawning stolen goods for local hoods, something his family and friends vehemently denied.

Cook went on to explain how the Corry portfolio had been snapping up land and property on the periphery of the estates and in interface areas where traditional contractors might baulk at the prospect of losing revenue or seeing their development go up in a blaze of civil unrest. She illustrated each summary with a relevant PowerPoint displayed on the main monitor.

The room was set up for team briefings, and on occasion would be used for informal remote interviews or collaboration between policing districts. The IT equipment and centre console spider phone allowed cooperation between the investigative team, forensics, the medical examiner's office or liaison with the office of the Director of Public Prosecutions. Room 4.12 itself was situated on a dogleg of the corridor between the main CID suite and the lift lobby, offering views across Ann Street and east towards the Lagan Weir and the twin cranes of Samson and Goliath, the panorama presently masked by vertical blinds covering the floor to ceiling windows.

Cook continued to elaborate on what she had discovered to date.

"Before the vandalism, any opposition had been relatively peaceful up to a point. Placards and picket lines protesting against a poor record on environmental protections and expansion into the green belt. Uniform attended on two separate occasions when protestors complained they had been intimidated by site staff, also alleging a number of physical assaults," She skim-read the reports, giving a shrug to summarise. "Handbags at dawn. Contractors forcibly removed protestors who'd secured themselves to the gate by taking an angle grinder to the chains. Name calling. Pushing and shoving. No injuries."

"How did you get on over there?" asked Taylor, addressing her junior detectives. Walker picked up the question.

"No CCTV. No eyewitnesses and a ton of damage as reported," he said, adding as an aside. "I'd say whoever it was did them a favour. For something that's supposed to be a church, the building is an eyesore. It looks like the lovechild of a caravan and one of those out-of-town retail units." The young DC pulled a face. "It might give them a chance to remodel though, to be fair."

"Christ, are you auditioning for a spot on *Grand Designs*, son?" scoffed Macpherson. Taylor shushed him but was grateful the gloom looked to be lifting. She continued her questions.

"Did Corry give up anything on Finn Abbott or Steven Scott?" She kept her tone light, keeping the trip to the boys' home, Macpherson's tale of a secret sexploitation ring and the hypothesis that the justice minister may have been a historic victim or collaborator between the two of them.

"We've a call in to his HR department chasing up ex-employees to see if there was ever any connection between the company and the two men," said Walker. "He did call out an individual he thinks may be behind the recent protests. Paul Finnegan. Organises a group called SCAR," said Reilly.

Cook nodded, dragging up a window for her colleagues around the table. "Finnegan has a number of associations with groups advocating for social mobility and protection of the environment. He's also been vocal in highlighting civil rights abuses and miscarriages of justice and been front and centre at the recent rallies calling for a border poll."

"An all-round pain in the hole then," muttered Macpherson. Cook's highlights of Finnegan's status as an eco-warrior and a wannabe champion of the voiceless included the donning of many hats, most of which it seemed bore a feather railing against the likes of Geordie Corry. He was anti-expansion, anti-British and eager to agitate.

"Are there any membership lists that show links to Abbott or Scott?" said Reilly.

Cook shook her head. "No. A few high profile talking heads like Finnegan but the foot soldiers remain largely anonymous."

"Okay," said Taylor. "Keep looking for any associations between this SCAR group and Abbott and Scott. Social media links, press or intelligence images from any rallies or protests, it also might be worthwhile going back to the sites targeted and sharing their mugshots. Erin, Chris, first thing tomorrow doorstep Finnegan. I'd like to know why his group is so incensed at what Geordie Corry is doing and if he admits to knowing either Abbott or Scott."

"Will do," said Reilly. Walker gave a mute nod.

"Carrie, anything further on Maddox from Seapark or Professor Thompson?" said Taylor.

"Nothing yet. As soon as either present initial findings, I'll drop them across in a mail. By the way, uniform gained access to Finn Abbott's flat with the permission of the housing provider but Sergeant Harris reports they didn't discover anything out of the ordinary."

"Thanks, can you escalate Scott's profile to Sergeant Harris too and have him make the crews aware we are looking for him."

Cook sounded her acceptance of the request.

"Lastly, did you talk to the DPP about Casey and the rumoured personal links to Maddox?"

"They're being tight-lipped," said Cook. "I suppose it's to be expected given there are now questions over the credibility of bringing a case to trial in the first place. I did manage to track down one of the customs officers who led the initial investigation against Casey's business activities before he was rolled up in the conspiracy charges. Do you want me to send the details over? "

"Yes, please." Taylor nodded her gratitude. "Okay, you three wrap up what you can tonight and make sure all the logs are updated. Anything from anyone else?"

Reilly and Walker voiced they had not.

"Just one from me," said Cook. "I had a look at the person of interest you mentioned earlier. Quite a character."

"So I hear," said Taylor. Macpherson sat up a little straighter and eyed Taylor, an unspoken question in the look.

"He has a who's who of close associates including a few names you'll recognise. I've an address for an apartment on the fringes of the Fearon Estate and another out of town."

Cook reeled off the two addresses.

"Thanks, Carrie," said Taylor. "Okay, away and get yourselves sorted and we'll catch up tomorrow around midday to see where we're at."

The detective constables' goodbyes were interrupted by a knock on the door. Before Walker could stand to open it, Detective Chief Inspector Gillian Reed entered.

"DI Taylor, have you got a minute?"

"We're just wrapping up, ma'am."

Reed held the door as Cook, Reilly and Walker gathered their things to leave. Macpherson grumbled a complaint against age and aching limbs as he hauled himself from his seat to follow.

"Stay with us please, sergeant," said Reed. She moved to the head of the table and remained standing after the junior ranks had filed out. Taylor shared a look with her sergeant who slowly lowered himself back down.

"Is everything alright?" asked Taylor, trying to keep the trepidation from her tone as, in the back of her mind, the death of Finn Abbott while being informally questioned was about to land heavily.

"Not really," said Reed. "The super has been in meetings with the chief constable, the deputy first minister and the chair of the Policing Board. To say things have been tense is an understatement. They are all concerned that in the wake of his sudden death, the allegations against Oliver Maddox may now take on a life of their own."

"It's a bit late to be panicking. Now the inference of wrongdoing has been made of course the press will use Maddox's suicide to pile innuendo on top of speculation," said Macpherson with a grunt. "They're bloody vultures."

"You're not wrong, Doc," agreed the DCI. "But that being said, the powers that be are all keen to ensure these allegations are shown to have been taken seriously and that the investigation is robust and transparent. An independent team is to be appointed to carry it out. We"—Reed circled a finger in the air—"will all be obliged to comply and assist with any and all requests for information or evidence that comes to light through any other investigations."

"Ma'am?" Taylor's brow surrendered to a confused frown. Reed's voice softened.

"These allegations besmirch the office of the Department for Justice. They could, at worst, jeopardise convictions or raise the potential of reopening any of the cases Oliver Maddox oversaw in his tenure. Given the allegations against Colm Casey were concocted due to a personal vendetta it's —"

"The Caseys have been a rotten barrel for years," said Macpherson, raising a palm in apology for interrupting. "Colm's hardly an innocent bloody bystander who has been caught up in this car crash."

"You're right, of course," agreed Reed. "But, you were both at the scene. You and a limited number were privy to the corpse in situ." The DCI sighed and sat. "I've seen the initial crime scene review and I'm waiting on Prof. Thompson's report."

"Oliver Maddox was a victim," said Taylor, searching her superior's face for what was as yet unsaid.

"And if that is the case, you know as well as I do that victims can often go on to perpetrate the crimes which they suffered." Reed tucked a strand of hair behind her ear, then placed her elbows on the table.

"The deputy First's office has had requests for statements and the Echo is alluding that they have more on the story to take to print. The Executive and the chief constable want this put to bed and out of the headlines quickly. They aren't happy that Steven Scott is in the wind and want him found before he appears on the front pages or the six o'clock news. If not to ensure he receives support over what he may have endured at the hands of Oliver Maddox, then to question the veracity of his allegations against Casey and if he was put up to it."

"DC Cook has just given me a contact within customs who was undertaking initial scrutiny into Casey's affairs before he was identified as relevant in the triple deaths. It might be worth a call to see if they were aware of any tenuous links?"

"Maybe, but make sure any conversation is recorded in the database so the independent review team has access."

"Of course," said Taylor. "And where do we stand having Scott corroborate the statement given to us by Finn Abbott that he knows the reason behind the attacks on Geordie Corry's property empire and what happened to Barry Toms?" said Taylor.

"Veronica, Finn Abbott was a troubled soul and by your own account was heavily under the influence."

"That doesn't mean that his claims should be ignored—"

"No, it doesn't but the priority is to ensure Scott can do no more damage by making further unverified claims and explain his part in the Casey fiasco."

"So much for transparency," said Macpherson.

"Doc—" said Reed but Taylor cut over her.

"He's right though. What about transparency? Steven Scott offers a valuable lead in an active investigation and an unsolved missing persons."

Reed took off her spectacles and rubbed her eyes before settling a look on her subordinates.

"You don't need me to tell you it's been a hard road lately, Beattie slipping the net, the death of the ACC." She glanced between them before continuing. "That's before the protocol protests and now the demonstrations for a border poll. We, as ever, are caught in the middle."

Taylor saw a weariness to her DCI that hadn't been there in recent times; the result of one too many crises piling up at once was taking a toll.

"I'm not going to lie, this is becoming more political by the hour," Reed continued, pausing another interruption from Macpherson with a raised index finger. "Regardless of that, I'm not about to sweep anything under the carpet for the sake of a politician's career or to ensure their legacy remains unsullied, but we have to pick our battles at the minute and this one is a lost cause. The Maddox case is going independent and there is nothing I can do about it, and that includes anything associated with Steven Scott."

Taylor made to speak but Reed got in first, rising to her feet as she spoke, indicating the meeting was over.

"If you want to be productive, find the hit-and-run driver that killed Abbott and wrap up the vandalism against Geordie Corry before we've another crowd down from Stormont asking why the police are failing to prevent the trashing of their good friend and generous donor's business and putting constituents' jobs at risk."

Reed offered a half-hearted nod, which the two detectives returned.

"Yes, ma'am," said Taylor. "We have a few leads to follow up on both."

"Keep me in the loop."

Reed left, closing the door behind her. Taylor's eyes remained focused on the spot where the DCI had sat moments before. Something was happening. She felt the tremor of déjà vu in the pit of her stomach, an uncomfortable flashback to the handling of ACC Wallace's death and the circling of the wagons in the aftermath.

The quiet of the room was broken by the gurgle of Macpherson's stomach. He placed his hands over his belly and let out a groan as he stretched back in his chair.

"I don't know about you but I could do a Maharaja to cheer myself up after that," he said.

Taylor's unfocused gaze drifted across the conference table, trying to make sense of her conflicted feelings now the DCI had effectively closed down any thought she had of pursuing the links between Abbott, Scott and Maddox to Glenrafferty and its shadowy past.

To keep busy they had Cook's customs official to engage with and, she had promised to follow up with Maddox's housekeeper, Eleanor Hammond. Although that interview, she thought, may now be a step beyond the boundaries that Gillian Reed had just drawn and would be better left to the independent investigators. Her interest in what Professor Thompson had to report regarding Maddox's injuries however might not be so easily assuaged.

She slid Carrie's notes towards her and studied the two addresses her DC had provided.

"How do you fancy a spin up the coast for some fish and chips for a change?" she said.

31

Shepard hadn't passed through Ballyhallion in years and little it seemed had changed. If anything it was bleaker and even more rundown than his memory recalled.

The little row of shorefront houses had suffered the ravages of the sea air and even though the corner store had been given a makeover the gloss had scabbed over, welcoming any trade with a haggard face of peeling paintwork and rusted signage. The whole place was a sorry sight of slow decay and decrepitude. Inside the shop, lights were illuminated but in the hour Shepard had sat astride the Honda motorcycle in the lay-by across the road no one had been in or out.

It was dry at least, with an onshore wind that scattered discarded polystyrene coffee cups and crumpled crisp packets into overgrown hedgerows. The lights of council housing in the Ballyhallion estate were beginning to blink up on the hill with only the occasional car whooshing along the shore road, mostly heading country bound and driven by weary commuters heading for the villages farther along the peninsula. Shepard tried to recall the last time he had passed through; although it was well known to him he only really ever registered the place as a waypoint on the way to Portaferry, a small town that lay at the mouth of Strangford Lough. A place of childhood memories with its aquarium, the annual gala float parade and boat trips to Strangford. Happy memories that merged with those of later years, snapshots aboard the car ferry, the sun on Cara's face, the music of her laugh as the wind whipped her auburn hair into a mess and the swooping gulls dive-bombed their picnics.

Shepard shrugged off the darkness that threatened to shroud the happier memories and tried to swallow the guilt over his failure to fully avenge his wife and son. A frustration that burrowed because even though he had drawn first blood on the men responsible for their murder, those ultimately culpable had been protected by a corrupt system, hiding their actions behind the excuse of fighting a dirty war.

Spiralling thoughts on the depths of the systemic deceit and his next moves against the faceless participants involved were interrupted as the full beam of headlights rounded a corner on the city side of the shore road, the vehicle speeding past the turnoff to the shop and housing estate before the bloom of red brake lights illuminated as it approached the entrance to the imaginatively named Ballyhallion Caravan Park.

The parks were regularly dotted along the shoreline once you hit the scenic roads leaving Bangor to follow the coastal route through the small villages of Groomsport, Donaghadee and Millisle. Most of the parks had names suggesting a grander experience than perhaps would be found down the winding lanes: Sandy Cove, Sea View, Sands End, Silver Bay. Those who had chosen the old airfield at Ballyhallion as home to their rows of rented static homes had, it seemed, realised that adding an appealing honorific would only be a vain attempt to add shine to a turd.

Shepard reached into his jacket and pulled out the postcard he had taken from Carruthers' flat. There was no doubt he was in the right place. The image on the card showed the bend in the road and a shale beach. The boathouse and jetty, however, like everything else, had succumbed to the elements and only rotten stumps and the rubble of broken blockwork remained. The gates at the end of the lane to the caravan park had long since gone but the dry stone gateposts were still there.

Shepard watched the vehicle, a dark blue BMW X7 negotiate the narrow entrance and follow the track towards the caravans. Briefly, he made out the silhouettes of four men inside. It didn't take a man of his experience to mark the quartet and the vehicle as being out of place. Yes, perhaps it was local hoods, or dealers making a drop or collecting a re-up from an out-of-the-way stash but the fact Harry Carruthers was hiding out in one of the off-white berths at the end of the lane couldn't be a coincidence.

His boss may have been lying in a hospital bed but Carruthers was still connected and still doing Beattie's bidding. Shepard's reconnaissance on the big man and his Albanian counterpart attested to that, so either this was backup or maybe even his ride out of the country to escape the heat of the hit and run.

Shepard replaced the postcard and gunned the engine of the Honda, pulling into the road and crawling the short distance to the caravan park entrance. He had given Taylor his word he would deliver Carruthers, but if the rules of the game were to be followed it would be up to her to persuade the enforcer that to save his own neck he would need to offer a way to pressure Beattie to give up something on those who had left him for dead. A deal that might offer a means to pursue the corruption they both knew continued to rot the heart of the establishment. If she could make a case and get her own hierarchy and the DPP on board all well and good, but Shepard had decided he wasn't going to let another golden opportunity slip through his fingers if it didn't pan out.

At the end of the lane, the BMW's headlamps swept left

and the car followed the pot-holed road that threaded around the site. Shepard, his own headlamp extinguished, began to follow.

Five against one wasn't the worst odds he had ever faced. Not when he held the element of surprise, and five mouths would be better than one when it came to extracting the names of those who still lurked in the shadows believing themselves untouchable.

32

If anyone on the site had noticed the big BMW slowly crawling along they paid it no heed. Not a curtain twitched and no doors opened to offer assistance or make enquiry as to the reason why the occupants were scrutinising each berth.

"Do you know where it is?" The rear driver's side passenger leaned between the seats to peer out of the windscreen as he addressed the two men up front.

The caravans were carbon copies of each other, their uniqueness only measured in the detritus of old bicycles or sun loungers propped up along the sidings or the occasional rusting gas barbecue sheltered from the worst of the onshore breezes in the lee of the van.

"Third along from the end. Second row back," said the driver.

"Keep an eye out for a white Volkswagon Caddy too. The boss says that's what he was driving." The front passenger offered the instruction to the others as he scanned out of the windows, peering between the gaps in the caravans and along the grassy embankments for where the vehicle might be parked should their initial information on Carruthers' location be wrong.

The driver hit the brakes unexpectedly and dipped the headlights.

"There it is. Right where he said."

Sure enough, parked up in the gap between the third and

fourth caravan on the second row from the beach sat the white Caddy, squeezed in alongside a dark green Skoda Fabia.

Plain curtains were drawn across the main window overlooking the sea, lamplight bleeding around the frayed hems and as the quartet quietly observed, a shadow passed close within.

"Alright, let's be having it then. You two know what needs to be done," said the passenger, twisting in his seat to fix the two younger occupants in the back with a stern glare.

"Aye, Frankie. No sweat," said the man who had leaned between the seats, a hurl laid across his lap. The flat wooden stick was reinforced with metal and resembled a primitive battle axe. His accomplice lifted a sawn-off shotgun from the gym bag between them.

"Young fella comes with us and the fat lad gets a free cremation," he said, a set of crooked teeth grinning in the light of the dashboard.

"No fucking about, do you hear me?" The passenger raised a warning finger. "Chalky will keep the car running. I'll be keeping dick out the back in case they try and do a runner. Malkie, you put your boot through the door." The finger pointed towards the man with the hurl and then to his accomplice holding the shotgun. "Sean, wave that in their faces and get them under control. Chalky, I'll give you the nod when we're good and you get up there. Once you're outside we hood the wee lad and get him in the boot."

There were nods all round.

"Right then." A low tone bleeped as the passenger opened his door, leaning into the footwell to pick up a pistol of his own before he got out. "Let's get this party started."

33

Shepard freewheeled the Honda to a stop behind a row of large industrial bins which blocked the path to the site's derelict play park. Fifty metres ahead, the BMW had killed its headlights and a few moments later the passenger side and rear doors opened and the occupants stepped out. The soft clunk of doors being closed and then the click of the boot lid being released drifted to his ears.

There was enough light from a single overhanging streetlamp to see the men were armed.

Shepard watched the three casually walk away from the car, the man who had got out of the front passenger side issued an unheard instruction before moving off the road and disappearing between the nearest caravans. The other two continued, Shepard reading a sudden tension in their body language as they focused on a berth at the far end of the path.

Dismounting the motorcycle he moved for a better view. Screened by the bins he was able to cross the pitted tarmac unseen and take cover behind the nearest beachfront caravan, the spot offering a clear view of the idling BMW and the men now creeping up on the second van from the end of the row. The taller dark-haired man reached out to place a palm on the bonnet of a white van parked up on the grass, a vehicle with a human-shaped dent in the bonnet which Shepard recognised. He reassessed what was happening, his initial hypothesis that these men were there for backup or to secure transportation evaporating with each second that passed and along with them the chance to ensure Taylor would receive her bargaining chip and any potential opportunity that may lead further up the ladder of corruption.

The two men had crept up to the door of their targeted van. The shorter of the two, more powerfully built than his counterpart and carrying a hurley stick, placed an ear to the door and then gestured to his accomplice who raised a sawn-off shotgun to firing position.

Shepard was already moving when the first crashing impact obliterated the silence.

❖❖❖

"What shite are you watching?" said Caruthers, absentmindedly glancing up as he stirred three sugars into a mug of tea.

"Have you never seen this?" Scott looked up from his recumbent position on the threadbare couch-come-bed. "Your man from what do you call it is in it. Ack, you know him from that other thing. Him there." Scott pointed to the screen.

Carruthers tossed his teaspoon into the sink, its landing coinciding with a huge crash as the caravan door burst in.

"Jesus!" Carruthers swore, tea slopping over his hand. Scott bolted upright in fear, staring down the double barrel of a sawn-off shotgun rushing towards him.

"Get on the fucking floor!" The gunman crossed the small space and jabbed the gun roughly into Scott's chest

"Who the hell are you?" shouted Caruthers. "What the fuck is going on?"

"You heard him, on the floor before I put you there." A second man had entered, hurl hefted and brandished indicating that he would follow through on his threat.

"You two arseholes picked the wrong van," said Caruthers.

The stocky intruder pulled back the hurl to deliver a swing

but Carruthers reacted first, throwing the scalding tea at the man.

"On the fucking floor!" reiterated the gunman, sweeping his weapon towards the small kitchen as his accomplice twisted away, howling in pain.

Attention distracted, Carruthers drew his own pistol from where it lay under a grotty dishcloth and took aim.

"Put it fucking down!" screamed the gunman, finger tightening around the trigger. Carruthers swept his aim towards the cramped living space and the greater threat.

Scott leapt from his seat and threw himself at the gunman, wrestling for control of the weapon in a vain attempt to force the stubby barrels towards the ceiling.

The noise in the confined space as a shot discharged was deafening.

❖❖❖

Joseph 'Chalky' Whyte flinched at the sound of the gunshot and the sudden flash illuminating the windows of the caravan. The staccato barks of several dogs filled the immediate silence of the initial eerie aftermath

Chalky, swearing to himself, jerked in surprise as the driver's door opened.

"Frankie, what the fuc—"

He never got the opportunity to finish his question.

Shepard drilled a series of short left hooks into the bridge of the stunned driver's nose before hauling him partway out of the car by the hair. Several slams of the BMW's door on the man's head rendered him blissfully unconscious and ended the sudden brutal violence.

Shepard, leaving the door ajar, moved towards the commotion coming from the end of the path, drawing his M91A1 pistol from the retention holster secured at the small of his back.

Angry shouts and the sound of crashing and breaking

glass intensified up ahead. As he got closer to the scene, the door to the van nearest him creaked open, the pale and concerned face of an octogenarian peering out.

"Go back inside," said Shepard as more high-pitched barking came from somewhere deeper in the gloom behind the man.

"It's those bloody drugs again, isn't it?" He gave a shake of his head and a gap-toothed grimace. "Youse should be ashamed of yourselves, terrorising the folk around here."

Shepard waved the Beretta. "Go back inside for your own safety. Now."

The pensioner grunted an unintelligible response and closed the door. As the barking continued, several lights in nearby vans lit up and the odd curtain twitched but everyone else had the sense to follow the code; if you see nothing, you can say nothing.

Two more gunshots cracked off, pistol shots muffled by the walls of the caravan. Shepard dropped to cover behind a rickety storage bin as a shout of pain reached him, the howl preceding a further noisy blast of shotgun fire.

Shepard rose up and out of cover quickly, his weapon in a two-handed grip and trained on the caravan's front door and the sounds of melee within.

Even though he was anticipating it, when the gunfire sounded again, the direction from which it came was unexpected.

The zip of rounds supercharged the air around his ears, thudding into the siding of the van behind and sparking off the rough tarmac road. The shots were delivered not from inside the caravan but from his right flank.

He scrambled forwards into cover offered by an aged and warped set of stairs leading to an elevated deck that surrounded one of the more salubrious berths.

Another barrage of bullets blew chunks out of the weather-stained timber above his head and Shepard ducked low to avoid the splintering woodwork, working to pinpoint the shooter's position while he tried to keep the target caravan in the periphery of his vision.

Whatever the crew's initial intention had been, it had gone swiftly sideways. He now suspected they had arrived believing they held all the key elements for a successful assault: surprise, superior numbers and overwhelming fire power but like a house of cards it only took one small tremble to send the whole deck toppling down.

Urgent shouts came from opposite his cover and he caught a brief glimpse of a figure in dark clothing silhouetted against the starker off-white of the caravan siding. There was a muffled response from inside the trailer, followed by the sounds of violent physical confrontation. The curtain obscuring the interior was swept away and the supporting pole crashed from its anchor points to lie at a haphazard angle across the window frame. The crashing inside ended abruptly with the crack of a gunshot.

Shepard rose and took aim. With an elbow supported on the bullet-riddled timber frame, he loosed off several shots. Neither of his first rounds hit, and his next pair were poorly sighted as he changed target, the sudden appearance of another figure in the doorway of the target van splitting his attention.

He checked his fire and returned to cover as gunfire sounded around him.

The first figure out of the door had been hooded, manhandled from behind and unceremoniously dumped down the steps to faceplant heavily onto the ground. From the build and height, Shepard could tell it wasn't Carruthers.

The two men who had forced their way inside had now joined the gunman, swearing peppering their urgent conversation as they realised their getaway vehicle remained idling thirty metres away. The shorter man, no longer carrying the hurl, brandished a pistol, shoving the weapon into the back of the prone prisoner's neck as he manhandled him to his feet. The two then moved in an awkward tangle of stumbling limbs towards the headlights.

A blast of a shotgun accompanied another half dozen rounds from the gunman as they laid a barrage of suppressing fire to cover their retreat. Shepard fired blindly in return. The farther they moved back up the road towards the car, the greater the angle removed his advantage of cover. Two more rounds struck too close to ignore and he emptied the remainder of the Berretta's clip in the direction of the gunmen.

Backlit by headlamps he could only make out vague shapes as the driver was dragged from his seat and roughly shoved into the back of the BMW. In the lull, the thud of a door closing preceded the rev of the engine.

Shepard slammed his remaining magazine home and took a few strides into the road as the SUV lurched forward, kicking up a spray of loose gravel.

Weapon held in a double-handed grip, he aimed at the driver's side of the windscreen but before he could squeeze off a shot, gunfire from the passenger side window sparked up the road. Shepard sprinted for the safety of the verge and cover between the two vehicles parked alongside Carruthers' caravan. Taking a knee and twisting to aim towards the oncoming vehicle, the threatening roar of the big six-cylinder engine and the glare of headlamps were abruptly eclipsed by a blinding blue-white flash.

A shockwave slammed Shepard against the bodywork of the van, a wave of heat rolling over him. The ear-splitting explosion and the ringing in his ears muted the sound of the BMW as it accelerated away.

Flat on his back, coughing and tasting the acrid air,

Shepard could do little more than watch as the ruptured propane tank that had stood at the front of Carruthers' caravan spewed a mushroom cloud of smoke and flame high into the sky above Ballyhallion.

34

"That's the third chippy you've just drove past," said Macpherson, rubbing his grumbling stomach.

The glowing frontage, displaying prominent signs promising fish, chips, snack boxes and more importantly the key worker discount for which they would qualify as members of the Police Service, disappeared from view as they rounded another bend on the coast road.

"We'll stop on the way back, I promise." Taylor glanced at her colleague. A familiar scepticism clouded his face. Checking the rear-view mirror she saw her own expression held a look of dogged determination.

"Why didn't you tell me about Shepard?" Macpherson stared out of the passenger window as Taylor guided the Volvo out of another one-street village and on towards their destination.

"You'd have tried to talk me out of it."

"You're right I would." Macpherson turned from the darkening seascape to look at her. "For Christ's sake, Ronnie, do you not think we're skating on thin ice as it is? I've done my time, but you've a right few years ahead of you yet. Don't be throwing them away."

"Doc..." Taylor shook her head and sighed. "The information Carruthers was involved in the hit and run came from a confidential informant. That's all anyone needs to know."

"Aye, but have you registered it? Sought and signed off the approvals? Of course you haven't because it's this bloody Shepard character and reading between the lines he isn't finished with his murder spree yet."

"Shepard isn't the—"

"Ronnie, I'm not saying I don't sympathise with what happened to that family and you're not going to hear me complain or cry foul that he's giving those bastards a taste of their own medicine but you can't be involved. Do you really fancy a spell in Hydebank? You know as well as me cops don't do easy years inside."

Taylor concentrated on the road ahead, Macpherson's concerns over her ending up in the women's prison at Hydebank Wood, although no doubt sincere, were, in her mind, premature.

"If Carrie's location pans out and we can pick up Harry Carruthers who knows what he'll offer us on Beattie."

"Ronnie, enough with Gordon bloody Beattie. He's in a hospital bed. He's finished."

"As long as the Monster draws breath he'll never be finished, Doc."

The hum of the tyres on tarmac and a breath of coastal wind filled the silence in the car for a while.

"Look," said Taylor. "Since Hoey Cargo, everything is a mess. You saw what happened there, and you said yourself that this Maddox thing doesn't smell right. If he was about to go toe to toe with this syndicate or whatever it is, then Beattie must know something about who they are. He'll have a contact. A handler. We need leverage."

"It's murky, Ronnie. And it's bloody dangerous."

Taylor gave a silent solemn nod. He didn't need to warn her, not after all she had learned in the bowels of Hoey Cargo and on seeing the international element to the trafficking and shipment of guns and people. This wasn't just former paramilitaries manipulating the amnesties offered by the Good Friday Agreement to diversify their business model. It went much further, and the corruption was much more entrenched.

Cresting the brow of a short hill, Taylor picked out a place name amid the thorny hedgerow, 'Welcome to Ballyhallion'.

"I think this is us," she said.

Macpherson pulled a face. "I thought the last place looked like the rats had left it but—"

A dull crump and sudden flash illuminated the sky on the opposite side of the one-street village cutting his sentence short.

A mushroom of flame and smoke billowed into the late evening sky and Macpherson strained forward against his seatbelt, gazing up at the expanding cloud and falling debris

"Looks like we're just in time for the fireworks again, eh?" he said without enthusiasm.

35

After the initial violence of the blast, a tattoo of debris clattered down on the caravan roofs followed lazily by a layer of burning embers drifting slowly to earth.

Shepard eased himself up on his elbows, shaking off the effects of the concussive shock wave and trying to make sense of the area around him.

Carruthers' van and the other car had sheltered him from the worst of the exploding gas tank. The vehicles themselves though were written off, their windows shattered and the bodywork peppered with shrapnel.

Across the road, curtains and vertical blinds dangled from shattered doorframes, but judging from the state of disrepair it seemed unlikely anyone had been resident. The front of Carruthers' caravan was wrecked.

Fires smouldered in the bay window, flames flickering from the fixtures and furnishings that had once overlooked the road and sea beyond but now spilt from the open wound onto the ground. The front facade and roof had been torn open, leaving just a ragged hole exposing insulation and the bare bones of supporting metal work.

Shepard stood, stumbling the first few steps until he regained his equilibrium. The caravan's door had fallen across the opening so he manhandled it onto the grass. Stepping inside, the interior was a chaos of upturned chairs and a carpet of broken glass and stoneware crockery. Smoke was beginning to fill the cabin so, pulling the remnants of the curtains from their moorings, he heaved the thick material over the smouldering wraparound seating where the threat of fire taking hold seemed most likely, stamping it down in an effort to smother the flames.

Satisfied with the attempt, he turned back to the carnage. It took a moment to notice a foot poking out from underneath the upturned dining table. Grunting in effort, he hefted the furniture aside.

"Alright, Harry, that was some party. Your mates left a right mess behind them," said Shepard.

Carruthers' face was blackened, his shirt torn, and bloody hands pressed down on a gunshot wound on the right-hand side of his belly. Grit and dust filled his eyes and he struggled to squint; a cough wracked his body before he could say anything.

"Looks like you've more to worry about now than me stabbing you in the leg." Shepard teased the hands open and inspected the injury. Rolling the protesting Carruthers to one side, he reached behind, his hand coming away from the exit wound bloodstained.

"This is going to hurt you more than it's going to hurt me," said Shepard.

Carruthers mewled an agonising groan as Shepard pulled him to a seating position and then hauled him into a fireman's carry and retreated outside to carefully lay the wounded man on the grass.

"S-St-Stumpy?" moaned Carruthers.

"If that was your mate, whoever paid you a visit has taken him," said Shepard, pulling open Carruthers' shirt to expose the wound. It wasn't pretty, but he'd seen worse. What he couldn't tell was what structures the bullet had hit on the way through.

Lights had started to flick on inside a few of the caravans

and he could hear the murmur of frightened voices. The arc of headlights swept across the road and illuminated the shore as a car made its way down the entrance lane.

Shepard tore a long strip of fabric from the bloodstained shirt, wadded it, and pressed it against the oozing entry hole.

"Keep pressure on that," said Shepard, before he retreated inside the wreckage, stalking through the small kitchen, emptying cupboards and drawers until he found a roll of clingfilm and a stack of cotton napkins.

Back outside he replaced the strips with the clean linen and wrapped Carruthers' torso in clingfilm.

"What was that all about, Harry?"

Carruthers blew a bubble of bloody froth and grunted.

"Is it to do with Beattie? Is somebody making a move? Cleaning house?"

Shepard hauled over an upended lawn chair and raised Carruthers' legs above his hips.

"Stumpy." The name came out through gritted teeth.

"Who the hell is Stumpy?" said Shepard. He could hear more voices and the sound of more doors opening as curiosity began to overwhelm concern. It wouldn't be long before he had company.

"Harry, I don't have long. Neither do you without some help. I need a name. Who was Beattie working with at the cargo warehouse?"

Carruthers grunted and tried to sit up.

"Stay where you are. You'll make it worse moving," said Shepard.

"You need to go after them. Get the youngster back." Carruthers twisted Shepard's sleeve in a fist. Shepard glanced at the havoc that had been wreaked around them, Carruthers continuing to tug weakly on his arm.

"The fuckers that took him... Stumpy..." he panted. "They're the same—"

"The same people behind the trafficking?"

Carruthers spat out bloody phlegm. "Behind all of it."

Shepard could hear the hiss of tyres on the road, then the squeal of brakes as a vehicle pulled up short of the caravan. He glanced back quickly; they were too far out on the coast for it to be emergency services. The nearest response would have to travel three-quarters of an hour to reach Ballyhallion. He checked the Berretta.

"D'you hear me?" growled Carruthers.

"You're not convincing me," said Shepard, turning back to face an intense expression.

"That youngster can give you names. The real names, the people behind the people the Monster was working for. Don't you get it?"

Shepard could hear cautious footsteps approaching and raised his weapon to cover the corner of the adjacent trailer.

"There's a cartel…" Carruthers let loose another ragged cough. "A consortium. They put Beattie where he is, they have bought up judges and senior police officers, councillors and politicians. They're everywhere, in every organisation."

"Tell me something I don't know," said Shepard. Carruthers' hand slipped from his sleeve.

"You blame the Monster for what happened to your missus and youngster, but it was these bastards. They wanted to take control, they needed change to happen and your family got caught in the crossfire. If you want to change something, go after them."

"So give me a goddamn name," said Shepard, pressing a fist into Carruthers' wound.

"Steven Scott," answered Taylor.

Shepard wheeled around, raising the Berretta.

"Put it down, sonny Jim." A second gruff voice instructed from behind.

Shepard lowered his aim, away from the woman who had

spoken.

"You never do things by half, do you, Tom?" said Taylor.

36

"Who is Steven Scott?" said Shepard.

Taylor ignored the question and knelt down to look Carruthers over.

"There's an ambulance on the way, Harry. You need to hang tough for us, alright?"

Carruthers slumped back on the bloodstained grass, his complexion growing paler by the minute.

"Subtlety isn't your strong point is it, big fella?" said Macpherson, jerking a nod towards what was left of the caravan.

Shepard gave a resigned chuckle. "Believe it or not, that wasn't my doing."

"Wrong place at the wrong time, was it?"

Shepard shrugged at the question. Macpherson scoffed. "You're just unlucky like me then, I guess."

Shepard turned to face Taylor. "Who is Steven Scott?"

"He's a witness in a case against Colm Casey."

Shepard pulled a face indicating he didn't know the name then swept a hand in the air. "How's he related to all this?"

"I'm not quite sure. We pulled this as an address linked to him," said Taylor, pointing to the prone figure between them. "Scott was raised as a person of interest by our hit-and-run victim. He ran with the Fearon Charlie Boys back in the day which ties him to your friend here. He knew him as Stumpy."

"Yeah?"

"Yes. But before that, Stumpy was in and out of the care and juvenile detention system. He ended up on the streets before he fell in with a crew headed by Billy McBride."

"UFF hitman, they called him the Mad Monk," said Macpherson, his expression deadpan.

"I think I might have heard the name. Couldn't put a finger on where exactly," said Shepard.

Taylor said nothing. Macpherson gave an amused snort. The only piece of the gunman ever retrieved was a single hairy digit complete with signature sovereign ring from the aftermath of The Corners bar shooting. Both messages Taylor knew had been sent by Shepard, declaring his intent to go to war with the mob that murdered his family.

"Do you think Casey has snatched Scott to make sure he doesn't take the stand?"

"I think there might be more to it," said Taylor.

"Enough for you to share with me?"

Taylor took a step back from Carruthers and surveyed the scene again. A few bystanders had appeared, mostly clad in dressing gowns or the clothes they had been wearing when woken by the explosion. Sensibly, they all stood at a safe distance.

"Ronnie?" Macpherson cleared his throat. A look passed between the two, her DS, it seemed, still not completely on board with the prospect of utilising an asset with the potential to burn them both.

"Have you seen the *Echo*? Or watched the news in the last few days?" said Taylor.

"I'm not really into current affairs, inspector."

Macpherson gave a rumbling chuckle at the response in spite of himself. Taylor continued.

"The press has run a story that Oliver Maddox and Scott have a complicated history and the evidence putting Casey in the dock was fabricated."

"What kind of history?"

"The allegation is that Maddox, as a former officer in youth justice, was grooming the boys in his care and/or, was aware at least of physical and sexual violence being meted out on them."

Shepard's face darkened. "I watched a speech he made at Crumlin Road Gaol about how he was taking on organised crime and corruption. He was getting my vote."

"Yes, I saw the transcripts," said Taylor. "That's why I think there may be more to this than first meets the eye."

"Have you pulled in Maddox and got his take on it?"

Taylor shook her head. "Apart from the fact he's the justice minister—"

"He's tattie bread. Done himself in," Macpherson finished for her.

Shepard paused and considered the disparate strands that seemed to once again be dissolving before their eyes.

"He didn't strike me as the type, but I suppose you never really know, do you?"

"The victim in the hit and run told us Steven Scott could shed light on the perpetrators of historical abuse, maybe even murder," explained Taylor.

"And dying by his own hand implies Maddox's guilt?" said Shepard. Something in Taylor's expression gave him a second's pause. "But you're not sure?"

Taylor's lips twisted. "There's nothing at all to suggest that it wasn't a simple suicide."

"But it gives his political peers and your bosses a way to distance themselves from the stink? Maddox is dead, let any investigation die with him?"

"There's going to be an investigation but it's being handed over. It will be undertaken independently so we aren't getting within a mile of it."

Shepard scoffed. "Which amounts to the same thing,

doesn't it?" He blew out a frustrated sigh. "It's all beginning to sound very familiar, Taylor. Another whitewash."

"What if we can get Steven Scott back?"

Shepard looked at her, unsure if it was a rhetorical question.

"If we take care of this," she said, indicating the devastation and Carruthers who lay between them. "Can you go after Scott?"

"Well, the lads that took him have one hell of a head start, and that's supposing they're heading back to the city," said Shepard.

"Come on, Tom. It's either Casey or someone who doesn't want their name being plastered across the front pages of the tabloids alongside pictures of Maddox."

Macpherson stepped forward to peer down at Carruthers; although deathly pale, Beattie's lieutenant was still breathing. He set his gaze on Shepard. "Ronnie tells me you're a resourceful SOB?"

Shepard offered no response.

"I'm not happy that she's going out on a limb that could end her career, but I'll stand beside the pair of you." He offered a hand which the former soldier shook.

"Shepard, these people have to be exposed," said Macpherson. "And if this cartel or whatever it is has penetrated as deep as we think, that's never going to happen just by working on the inside. We need to get Scott in front of a TV camera, we need every news network and red-top hack in the country to be digging up as many skeletons as we can give them headstones."

"Sling some mud and hope it sticks?" said Shepard.

Macpherson's shrug turned into a nod.

"What about him?" said Shepard.

"We do what we talked about, see if he'll take a plea on the hit and run in exchange for leverage on Beattie," said Taylor.

"That way we might have a chance at getting more than one name and, at the same time, be working two ends towards the middle."

"It's going to be difficult if he's dead."

"The ambulance service was diverting a unit from Newtownards. They'll be on the way."

Shepard weighed up his options. He wasn't getting anything from Carruthers now, and the longer he was left untreated the less likely he would be able to help, even if he could be persuaded to. This new development, the sudden revelations smearing the justice minister, and then his suicide left a sour taste. He hadn't seen the exposé but he had been quietly impressed as Oliver Maddox had promised reform and action on organised crime and corruption. Had that speech been what sounded his death knell? Was there more to it? Did he want to get involved?

The mission had been to exact revenge on those who had robbed him of Cara and Thomas. He thought on Carruthers' words. Perhaps he had fixated on the trigger men, those directly involved, men like Gordon Beattie who was still owed a reckoning. The parameters had expanded after Hoey Cargo to include those who Beattie had partnered with, those with tangential responsibility, the enablers and facilitators who stood back accepting their dividends from the proceeds of crime and the actions of those perpetrating it.

Did that mean he was now fighting a war against institutional corruption? Could he make an impact or was that best left to people like Veronica Taylor? And what were her chances if the deck was stacked against her?

"Shepard?" said Taylor, breaking into his thoughts. A flicker of blue illuminated the hedgerow above the caravan park and full-beam headlights cut an arc in the gloom of the shore road. Time for pondering had run out.

"I'll do it."

An analogous vision of the hooded figure being bundled away from the caravan combined with his feelings on hearing of Oliver Maddox's death; two events eliciting parallels that those who wished to maintain their secrets held no hesitation in blinding any attempt to shine a light on their illicit affairs by whatever means necessary.

"Shepard, you need to keep us involved," said Macpherson. "We can help as long as you don't—"

"Do what I do best?" said Shepard with a wry grin.

Macpherson reached out a hand. "Just don't get dead."

Shepard shook the DS's big mitt and offered a nod and a tight smile towards Taylor.

"Sure I'm already a ghost," he said.

37

"They got him and are on the way back."

"I hope they have the fucking sense not to bring him here," said Colm Casey as he kicked his feet off his desk and stood, snatching up and draining the shot of brandy he had been nursing.

The man who had entered his office gave a short nod of confirmation. "I was thinking you could do it at the pre-packing plant and then offload the body onto one of the cargo boats. Dump him overboard halfway to Scandinavia?"

Casey considered the suggestion and then smacked his lips, raising the empty glass to emphasise a point. "No, Kevin, I've a better idea. One that will bring this whole fuck-up full circle."

He laid out his instructions and poured another tot of the Hennessy XO for himself, taking a second glass from the drinks trolley. The offered drink was gratefully accepted.

"You should know there were a few… complications."

"What kind of complications?" said Casey, eyes narrowing as he returned to his chair and indicated the seat opposite.

Kevin Cullen sat. He was shorter than Casey and much thinner. The runner's physique which gave him a long-limbed and stretched appearance suggested a frailty that was misleading. Cullen was as hard as granite. Sinews stood out on his neck as he swallowed a sip of his drink. "The information they gave us about the caravan was right, but he had some protection with him. Frankie is sure they worked for the Monster. Things got loud."

Casey considered the news, deciding that making a bang wasn't the worst thing to have had happen. Not now, not given the direction he planned to take and the action he had been mulling over. Barrett's contacts had been able to use cell tower data to locate Scott, allowing Casey's men to make the grab, with instructions to bring back their quarry in one piece. The fact that the touting wee shite had found protection from Gordon Beattie though was a curve ball. Could it mean John Barrett was playing one hand against the other, or had Geordie Corry got wind of their conditions of sale and tipped off his Loyalist mate? Casey didn't like either idea but a confrontation, however unexpected, may just have helped move up the timeline of his plan.

"They had to get rid of the car and then dump Chalky Whyte off at the Royal emergency department. Beattie's lad got the jump and smashed his head in," said Cullen.

"Will he live?" said Carruthers. There was no concern in his voice, only consideration of what Chalky might tell the doctors or the police about what happened to him. The man opposite picked up on the unspoken question.

"There wasn't much inside his big napper to begin with. Chalky is as sound as a pound, he won't have a problem keeping his trap shut."

The two men chuckled and sipped their drinks.

Casey hoped his man was right. Kevin Cullen had been in the family firm for a long time and he trusted his judgement. He had been part of his brother's provisional IRA active service cohort back in the days before Enda's death, and when Colm himself was having trouble adjusting after the trauma of borstal by talking with his fists and generally causing havoc, Joe Jr had despatched Cullen to ensure that his baby brother's liberty remained intact. Something the youngest Casey initially resented.

At other times, Cullen carried out the family's more nefarious tasks, most lately assisting Casey with the business Barrett needed to make disappear. The same business that had resulted in him standing in the dock.

"Are you sure about doing this, Colm?"

Casey didn't answer immediately, it was a decision that he had wrestled with. He knew John Barratt well enough to understand asking for a move across the river was a risk, but to ask for what he really wanted was deranged.

The grey man resided in the shadowy world between the power-sharing elite and those groups who on the surface had been disbanded but in reality, still needed to be courted so the myth of a successful transition to peace could be maintained. Barrett's long-standing relationship with his father and eldest brother had seen the family thrive, so when he arrived with an offer of retribution it was a surprise. Casey hadn't thought twice about accepting but that didn't mean he wasn't worried there may be an ulterior motive.

The whispers surrounding the network who had requested Barrett's services and then, by appointment, Casey's own he knew to be more than rumour. He knew that intimately.

The secretive sect owed their position and power to a clandestine syndicate with influence far greater than could be bestowed by the electorate and whose dominance extended far beyond the shores of Northern Ireland. The sect, The Crossed Keys, was a benign embellishment for an anonymous club of twisted individuals who on the surface projected themselves as pillars of virtue and respectability but in reality, were soaked in the sins of their perversions and bound together in a kinship of secrets which consolidated their grip on the institutions of power.

Casey's personal experience began on his journey through

the Catholic education system and then youth justice when he and other boys in his peer group had been exposed to the shameless perverts with faces he'd never forget who denigrated them to little more than chattels to quench their lusts.

Killing the vile old bastard who had raped him had been a recurring fantasy ever since he had been a teenager. Every opponent, every victim that had fallen under his fists, wore the face of the sleazy old pastor who had forced him onto the altar and then beaten him in shame for what he had done. The two prison officers, whatever their transgressions or involvement, had been marked by Barrett to face a similar fate so Casey had killed them too but not personally. As the head of his organisation, he couldn't risk getting blood on his hands but he was responsible for setting Cullen the task. This time though, he wasn't prepared to sit idle.

"Yes I am," said Casey. "Those bastards used us and then thought they could tie up loose ends by making sure I took the fall for it. The only reason Maddox had a case was through transactions that implicated me. Funny how those were unsealed but the sender's information was corrupted and no onward financials could be traced."

"It didn't do him much good," scoffed Casey. "Just another means to an end." He grimaced. Although holding no care for the deceased justice minister, the way he had been cast aside by his masters disgusted him.

"I'm going to use snatching this wee buck to leverage the profits of sale for their bloody hell-house, and make sure no one gets it in their head to try and fuck us over again." Casey's expression was resolute.

"Are you sure Barrett will hold up his end of the deal after this?" said Cullen.

"I don't trust him as far as I could throw him, but yes, I do."

"And Beattie?" said Cullen.

"Never turn your back on a wounded dog, Kevin."

38

"Detective Inspector Taylor. We followed one of your crews in." She held her identification up against the glass of the Emergency Department reception counter. The mole-like administrative assistant peered at it suspiciously, viewing the presentation as a blunt challenge to her authority in a vain attempt to coerce a way past red tape and the queue of seventy-four other patients waiting to be triaged.

"The patient's name is Carruthers. Harry. Gunshot wound to the abdomen," added Taylor.

The admin's fingers clacked across her keyboard, her expression blank.

"Excuse me, love." Macpherson loomed over Taylor's shoulder. "Your vending machine ate my money and didn't give me my muffin."

A slender finger left the keyboard to point at a notice taped to the glass partition that served as her barricade. Macpherson's face drooped to a scowl as he read.

"Not hospital property?" said Macpherson, scanning the few pointed sentences. "So what am I supposed to do about my muffin? My stomach thinks my throat's been cut."

The barricade served its purpose, the wagging finger remaining protected from Macpherson's growing ire behind the quarter inch of reinforced glass.

"Aye, right enough. And I suppose if I ring them now in the middle of the bloody night they'll be right over?"

The finger tapped pointedly on the last line. Macpherson's face bled from scarlet to puce.

"Leave a message—" he spluttered.

"DI Taylor?"

The swing door partitioning the emergency department waiting area from the ambulance arrival corridor opened and one of the paramedics who had treated Carruthers at the scene looked around the ED. Taylor raised a hand in acknowledgement and was beckoned forward.

The admin assistant began to protest about procedure. Macpherson gave a wry chuckle and pointed at another sign mounted on her screen. In bold letters, it read: 'Zero Tolerance on verbal or physical abuse towards our staff'.

"Sorry, duty calls, but if you ever need anything from us, ring one-oh-one and we'll get someone out… eventually." The last he muttered over his shoulder, a spring in his step as his short legs pumped to catch up with Taylor.

"How is he?" she said. The paramedic shook his head, bemusement etched across his brow as Macpherson rolled to a stop, rocking onto the balls of his feet with a grin on his face.

"He's in a bad way. Lost a lot of blood. If you wait here the doctor will be out in a minute."

"Thanks," said Taylor, giving her sergeant a warning look.

"What?" Macpherson looked behind him, half expecting the admin assistant and a security guard.

"Behave yourself."

"Me?" said Macpherson, "I'm starving and that machine conned me out of three quid."

"I can't believe you were going to pay that much for a week-old muffin."

"Well, I'd have gotten a gravy chip if you hadn't—"

"Inspector?"

The doctor pushed her way through a set of anti-microbial

curtains, peeling off pale blue nitrile gloves which she jettisoned in a pedal bin, pausing to squeeze a dollop of sanitizing foam onto her hands from a wall-mounted dispenser.

"Is he conscious?" said Taylor. The doctor nodded, fussing a blonde fringe over her eyes as she checked the watch fastened to her breast pocket.

"Flitting in and out but that'll be the morphine. He's lost a lot of blood, and to add to his problems the bullet has caused severe abdominal trauma. Primarily to the left kidney and spleen but we can't rule out anything else until he's had a CT scan. We're prepping him for one now and then surgery asap. You can wait, of course, but he's not going to be in a fit state for questions anytime soon."

"What are the chances we'll be able to talk to him eventually?" said Taylor.

"Greater than fifty-fifty, that's for sure. The immediate first aid to pack and dress his wounds certainly helped. You did good with that under the circumstances."

"Thanks, doctor."

Macpherson cleared his throat, his lips forming a tight line as he returned the medic's slight nod as she made to depart.

"I'll get back in unless you have any other questions?"

Taylor shook her head, offering a smile of gratitude. "I'll leave my details at the reception; if you could let me know when he comes through the operation?"

"Sure." She reached for the curtain.

"Ah, doctor?" said Macpherson, clearing his throat.

"Yes?"

"Is there somewhere we can maybe get a wee bite to eat?"

❖❖❖

"Are you not eating your crusts?" said Macpherson.

Taylor absentmindedly glanced down at the cardboard wrapper.

"They're stale."

"Waste not, want not." Macpherson swooped a hand across and snatched up the arches of bread like a starved seagull. "What now?" he mumbled through chews.

Carruthers' doctor had directed them to a small rest area for visitors halfway down a corridor on the first floor. The place was dead, the ward entrances securely locked for the night, and there was little noise bar the gurgle of heating from antiquated pipes. The seating area consisted of hardback chairs, bolted together in a U-shape facing a selection of vending machines which offered a limited choice of sandwiches, wraps and hot and cold drinks. Taylor picked up her tepid coffee and sipped.

It had been three hours since Carruthers had been loaded into the Mercedes Ambulance and they had followed the rig to the Royal, dawn just beginning to announce itself as a yellowing bruise against the blackness as they arrived. Taylor had focused on the rear lights as they whipped through the small villages and towns back to the city, it was only when she killed the engine and pulled the handbrake she realised she had drawn blood, having gnawed on her lower lip in thought and frustration. Her dominant feelings were those of the sensory quagmire experienced during a bad dream, of not being able to shout loud enough for help, not being able to run fast enough from danger, trapped by the rules of the sleeping universe set up to prevent the action needed to drive change.

Shepard, she thought, may have understood it better than she; perhaps was even used to it as a military man. Lives and limbs were thrown against the grinder of an ideal, the fulfilment of a political whim, and once the winds of foreign policy changed direction or the eyes of government imagined a new and emerging threat, interest and appetite shifted to a shiny new bauble and the game started again. It was endless, there was no goal, no out, just a continuing bloody fight which, at least in the main, was overt. There was an acknowledgement that the battle was engaged and while the true agenda may be blurred, there was a narrative outcome.

"Ronnie?" Macpherson's voice cut into her morose musing. "You're miles away. Did you hear me?"

Taylor nodded as she pushed away her wrapper and slumped back, rolling her neck.

"What's next?" she sighed, brow furrowing. "We found the hit-and-run driver so the DCI should be pleased with that. What she won't be happy with is finding out he's connected to the big man upstairs and had been sheltering Steven Scott." She aimed a finger at the ceiling where, somewhere above, lay Gordon Beattie. "Hopefully he recovers and we can persuade her to consider offering a deal to testify against Beattie."

"We?" said Macpherson, lips smacking and sounding a grunt as he finished the crusts.

"Yeah, not really your skillset is it? You can offer moral support."

"Do you think she'll go for it?" said Macpherson, ripping open a bag of chocolate and honeycomb sweets and shovelling a handful into his mouth.

"If the information is strong enough and can be corroborated, I don't see why not?"

Taylor quietly wondered how true her statement might be. Would the DCI see fit to have another crack? The question more likely was could she move the needle? Garnering support from her superiors and then convincing those in justice who might still be disposed to move against Beattie after the first failure and now on the back of another high-profile collapse, seemed slim to non-existent.

The narrow hope out of another dead end was Shepard recovering Steven Scott from his captors. If that could be achieved then perhaps the opportunity to nudge the first domino and start a chain reaction to collapse the tower of corruption that loomed over investigative efforts against Beattie and his enablers and shaded those who hid in plain sight manipulating the rule of law and preying on innocents like Finn Abbott and Barry Toms would be the first action in lancing the boil.

There was no magic bullet but shining the lamp of Scott's testimony may well illuminate a target, one that could bring about the beginnings of a catalyst for change.

"So, one for one with a result on our hit and run. What are we doing about Geordie Corry?" said Macpherson, a look of surprise on his face as he peered into the confectionery bag to find the chocolates were gone.

Taylor checked her watch, God, was that really the time? A wave of fatigue crashed over her.

"Erin and Chris will be following up on Finnegan and SCAR in a few hours. You and I should get some kip before we go in and debrief on Ballyhallion." She crumpled her cup and aimed it at the waste bin, the shot landing short.

"We'll review the follow-up reports and any eyewitness statements that might place Abbott or Steven Scott at any of the other sites. Carrie should have the employee and sub-contractor list by then." Taylor sighed. "And I still want to talk to Professor Thompson about similarities between Abbott's and Maddox's injuries."

"You sure you want to follow that up?"

"There's still something in those connections even if nobody wants to look for it," said Taylor, confirming her intent with a nod.

Macpherson unfolded himself from the seat, a dozen bones creaking as he dumped his trash and bent to pick up Taylor's cup. Thumbing another coin into the vending machine, he made the selections for a second packet of sweets.

"God, I'm getting too old to be working these hours," he said, watching the machine's mechanical innards stir to life

"DI Taylor?"

The two police officers turned to see a nurse in blue scrubs hurrying down the corridor.

"Yes, that's me," said Taylor.

"Could you follow me, please?"

"Is it Harry Carruthers?"

The nurse gave nothing away, perhaps because she didn't know or maybe it was a skill earned in her professional capacity. A sweet smile and a proffered hand indicated the way back along the corridor to a bank of lifts. They followed, pausing as she unspooled a smart card from a lanyard around her neck and badged a card reader. Somewhere beyond, the lift clunked to life.

"Do you know—"

"I'm not able to tell you anything, inspector. I'm sorry. Please, after you."

Taylor and Macpherson stepped into the lift, the nurse paused at the door then reached in and selected a floor, badging the card reader again.

"Follow the yellow line along the corridor to the right when you exit. Go through the double doors at the end, and someone will meet you there to explain."

The lift doors swished shut before Taylor could say anything more. The two detectives shared a look as the car lurched and began to descend.

Macpherson's expression had darkened.

"Since when did you have a thing about lifts?" said Taylor.

"I don't. I've just realised I left my bloody sweeties in that machine."

As Taylor stifled a chuckle the lift car rumbled to a stop.

39

Shepard felt a sense of déjà vu creep across the back of his skull as he observed the compound below him.

Not that long ago, on the opposite side of Belfast Lough, the target premises had been a meat packing plant, however, the real business of Signal Foods, a front operated by an Albanian gang, was smuggling.

Tracking a shipment of Beattie's narcotics to the plant, Shepard had inadvertently stumbled on more than he bargained for, discovering and then freeing a group of trafficked workers destined for domestic servitude or prostitution, and then finding himself apprehended, albeit temporarily, by Detective Inspector Veronica Taylor.

The difference between this time and that was there would be no violent incursion, at least not right away.

He snapped a few wide-angle shots of the coal yard on his phone, which would enhance any online map searches he would carry out once back at the cottage.

It had only been a few hours since he rolled the bike out of Ballyhallion Caravan Park, heading back along the coast road to the city. Too much time had passed to run down the escaped BMW but the miles allowed him to mull over what had happened and to digest the information both Carruthers and Taylor had divulged.

Arriving at the outskirts, he stopped at a twenty-four-hour service station. At the hatch he ordered a coffee and a power bar which he ate sitting kerbside in the empty parking lot while skimming internet news sites for stories covering Oliver Maddox's death, the alleged scandal involving Steven Scott and the imploding case against Colm Casey. By the time he crushed his coffee cup and jettisoned it into a nearby waste receptacle he had decided on his destination, spending a final few minutes in location research and to allow his instincts to confirm the tiny details he had gleaned at Ballyhallion.

Decades of vigilance and hyper-awareness in theatre and on operations, where he had to collate on-the-fly data and assimilate it to inform situational awareness allowed Shepard to make split-second decisions; live or die calls as to whether the vehicle speeding towards his checkpoint was a threat or someone seeking the shelter of the green zone. Did the gait of the figure under the burka seem off, was there a little too much masculinity in the stride, or enough cues in the environment to suggest the standing of the hairs on his neck had been raised by a sniper's reticule?

Disconnected data from Ballyhallion came back in short flashes. The driver of the BMW wore a signet ring, gold coloured and bearing the logo of Glasgow Celtic football club. A copy of the *Irish Times* was folded in the door pocket and the vehicle's bodywork was coated in a film of gritty dust that had left a sooty black smear on his hand.

Before the confrontation he had thought the men were there to protect Carruthers or offer a route to sanctuary. Now he was almost sure that Beattie's lieutenant happened to be caught on the sidelines of something else.

Even though his surveillance at the Royal suggested all was not rosy between Carruthers and the Albanians, the evidence wasn't pointing to them now, nor a Loyalist faction wanting to strike a death blow against the Monster's ailing organisation. This was the other side. A team from the west of the city, intentionally or not, had gunned down someone with keen Loyalist connections. Operations like that didn't usually end well and as he looked down on Colm Casey's bulk fuel business, Shepard considered what sort of trouble warranted Scott's abduction and would cause Casey to risk the potential green-on-orange fallout of such an action.

The bulk fuel yard wasn't exactly a hive of activity at that time of the morning. Several figures wrapped up against the early morning chill and wearing hi-vis coveralls moved between the large storage units that housed the various coal products. Beyond those, a black coal barge wallowed in the deeply dredged landing station at the end of a wide concrete jetty. The absence of shoremen alongside or aboard suggested the operation to unload its cargo was not scheduled to begin for some time yet.

In the gatehouse, a minimum wage security guard sat with his feet up watching a small portable television and the administration building forty feet away was shut down for the night. All the offices, save one, lay in darkness and as Shepard's eye lingered on the spot, unable to see beyond the closed blinds, until this too was extinguished.

The car park harboured a few vehicles but there was no sign of the BMW, it could, of course, be parked up in one of the large storage sheds but after the fireworks at Ballyhallion, Shepard's gut told him Casey was smart enough to make sure Scott had been taken somewhere more discreet and he hoped that the impetuous nature for which he had read Casey was famous, may lead him to Taylor's witness.

An automatic floodlight bloomed over the admin block entrance doors as two men stepped out into the pool of light and Shepard immediately recognised Casey from his image searches. The other man was shorter, his suit jacket pulled tight across the shoulders of a compact, lean frame.

After a short exchange and without further preamble the two separated and made their way to their cars, a pearlescent white Maserati Quattroporte for Casey and a Firenze Red Jaguar F-PACE for the other.

Shepard settled onto the saddle of his motorcycle and prepared to follow.

The driver of the F-PACE flashed Casey out of his space and as the Maserati pulled up at the gatehouse, Casey beeped impatiently, rousing the guard. A moment later the white barrier shuddered to life.

The Maserati's exhaust billowed in the chill air as it accelerated away and at the end of the short drive the two cars left in different directions.

Shepard watched both for several seconds then fired up his ignition and set off in pursuit.

40

When the lift opened, the corridor outside was unremarkable, with an unpainted poured concrete floor marked with coloured directional indicators. One-third of the wall surface was covered to protect against the collision of delivery trolleys in scuffed Acrovyn, while overhead electrical cable trays and pipework were exposed to view.

Taylor and Macpherson followed the yellow line as instructed, arriving quickly at a set of double doors. The wall-mounted smart card reader blinked green, suggesting the magnetic locks were disengaged. With a final glance at each other, it was Taylor who led the way, entering the space beyond and taking a sharp intake of breath.

"Hello, Veronica."

Gordon 'Monster' Beattie sat in a wheelchair. A thick woollen blanket in a plaid tartan was draped across his knees and he wore a dark crew neck sweater, the collar of a lighter-coloured polo peeking from underneath. He had lost weight, his skin was sallow and his eyes, although more deep set than she remembered, were still piercing. The timbre of his voice and the intensity of his demeanour remained unchanged.

"I hear you've been checking in on me? I'm touched by the concern." He smiled, and the gesture looked genuine to Taylor who remained fixed. "You alright there, Doc?" said Beattie, angling his head in greeting.

"Nice wheels." Macpherson's observation was delivered

deadpan, the surprise which had caught both Taylor and himself off guard covered by a sarcastic quick wit.

Beattie's laugh echoed in the large goods inward space.

"Aye." He glanced down and caressed the large rims. "Not up to my usual luxurious standards but sure they get me around and I don't have to pay a driver."

Macpherson grunted.

Behind Beattie, the only other person in the space cleared his throat. The sound, which began as an avalanche of skittering rocks deepened to the gravel one might associate with an eighty-a-day habit.

"Detective inspector, I've advised my client against talking to you, but it is on his insistence this meeting is taking place. For clarity, it is off the record and he shall not be expanding on anything you discuss in a formal statement."

Taylor gave a short nod. In contrast to the somewhat diminished figure of Beattie, his solicitor Solomon Reeves was, as always, immaculately tailored and coiffured. He returned her gesture, adding a brief acknowledgement to Macpherson before taking a step back, pursing his lips, and absentmindedly smoothing down his expensive silk tie, and Taylor sensed the usually unflappable legal heavyweight was uncomfortable with the circumstances of the meeting.

"You look well," she said to Beattie. "Considering."

"And you're still fighting the good fight." Beattie made a show of raising a prize fighter's fist. "Upholding law and order in our fine city." He gave another wry chuckle, fixing his eyes on his long-time adversary. " So, I guess the bastards didn't get their way with either of us in the end."

"What's with the cloak and dagger, Monster? What do you want?"

"That's what I like about you, Veronica. Straight to the point. No bullshit. Come on."

Beattie twisted his chair around and self-propelled across

the near-empty goods area towards a small office in the northeast corner. Taylor and Macpherson followed wordlessly, Beattie pausing to allow Reeves to handle the door before ushering the two detectives into plastic seats set beside the absent administrator's desk.

"Do you want to be in here?" said Beattie.

Reeves looked torn, finally shaking his head, stepping back outside and closing the door.

"Not stupid our Solomon, he's after deniability. Can't blame him really but I digress," Beattie faffed his hands in the air. "Apologies for the lack of hospitality but any port in a storm as they say."

"Most people think you're at death's door," said Macpherson, shuffling his seat away from Beattie to put what small distance was available between their knees.

"Think or hope, Doc?"

Macpherson raised an eyebrow indicating his personal opinion but Beattie just gave another grin.

"It does no harm to have people assume the worst. That way they put stock in nature finishing you off for them so they'll not go to the trouble of getting their hands dirty or risk sending some halfwit to do the job. Speaking of which, how's your soldier friend, Veronica?"

Taylor chose not to react, taking time to check her surroundings. She couldn't be certain the office wasn't rigged for audio or video but she wouldn't put it past Beattie to be making a record for posterity.

"Tom Shepard is missing presumed dead," she said eventually, and although she was sure her tone and her body language matched the content of her words the gleam in Beattie's eye told her he supposed different. He leaned forward, an elbow on his lap, voice lowered.

"You know this is going to go a lot smoother if we are honest with one another."

"What the hell do you know about honesty, Monster?" snapped Taylor.

"I know that it's a mistake to confuse it with the truth," he said sitting back in his chair, his expression hardening a little. He let out a breath and the lines softened.

"Look, let's not get off on the wrong foot." He raised a palm in surrender. "I know Shepard's alive, and I know he pulled Harry out of that caravan and he's only still breathing because of that."

The two opponents held eye contact for a few silent seconds. Regardless of how he looked and where he was, it seemed Beattie remained as sharp and as connected as ever.

"I wanted to say thank you," said Beattie.

Taylor bowed her head and Macpherson huffed an inaudible grumble.

"Whatever you think of me, Veronica, I'm only here because, like it or not, you saved my life. And I owe you."

"You don't owe me a damn thing."

"Relax," chided Beattie. "I'm not about to offer you a bloody holiday home and a suitcase of cash."

Taylor blinked. No, that would be too simple for someone like Beattie. He would start with something innocuous, enough to pique her interest and get her to bite before leading her on his line until the point came when he would reel her in. She wasn't about to fall for it.

"I've had a lot of time to think—'

"If your conscience is getting the better of you, call in Slippy Reeves and we can arrange a confession to be drawn up. Beyond that, I'm not interested."

Taylor stood, nodding at Macpherson in an indication he should do the same. In the weeks after his shooting the knowledge he had survived sustained her through the trials and tribulations which had followed, a reassurance that she hadn't been robbed of finally bringing him down and seeing him face justice and a life behind bars. Now, manipulated into a meeting to display the continued extent of his reach, her skin crawled.

Beattie slapped the armrests of his chair in frustration, not used to having his command ignored.

"For fuck's sake sit down the pair of you," he shouted.

Taylor remained where she stood, nonplussed at the outburst. The door swung open and Reeves' concerned face glowered in.

"It's okay, Solomon," said Beattie, then to Taylor. "I'm sorry, please. Sit down a minute."

"I'll stand, and you have one minute," she said, deliberately checking her wrist.

"I don't blame you, you know?" said Beattie after a pause in which he composed himself. "In not trusting me, but I mean it when I say I owe you. Wallace would have done you and then me. No question. What you did took balls."

"I did my job," said Taylor. "You've forty seconds."

"Harry is going to pull through if you're interested. He'll be out of it for a week or thereabouts apparently, so you'll have a bit of time to come up with any questions you want him to answer."

Taylor shrugged one shoulder. "Harry's luck is going to run out the longer he dances to your tune."

"Veronica, I can appreciate the bravado but you're going to want to hear what I have to say."

"Am I? Or is this just another way to hedge your bets?"

"In a way, yes. It is," said Beattie honestly. "I might be stuck in here but I've plenty of eyes and ears that aren't and I'm reliably informed my business is going to shit."

"Your business is drugs and prostitution. People trafficking and guns too, last I checked, so forgive me if I don't shed any tears."

Macpherson interjected. "Somebody was going to fill the

vacuum whether you ended up in the grave or behind bars, so why are we interested if you're losing your grip? Are you hoping we can spare you from taking a bullet behind the ear by cutting a deal?"

Beattie gave the DS a cool look. Taylor scoffed.

"You want to play the same hand you dealt Ken Wallace, don't you? You inform on your competitors and hope we want to ride the prosecutions and your coattails to the big corner office?" Taylor shook her head. "I'm sorry to disappoint you but I don't have the shoulders for epaulettes and he's too close to getting his pension."

Beattie chuckled at Macpherson's tart expression.

"Aye, fair enough," he said. "I can see why you'd think that but you have my word when I say that I didn't know about those kids and the guns."

Taylor spat a laugh. "Why don't I quite believe that? And even if I did, if you think I'm going to run the competition out of town to save your business, you've another think coming."

"Believe what you want, but here's the thing. I arranged for you to be here because the people who were behind it haven't stopped and things are only going to get worse unless something is done."

"Jesus. Gordon Beattie to the rescue. Poacher turned gamekeeper. Do us a favour. What are they giving you in here?" scoffed Macpherson.

"He has a point," said Taylor before Beattie could respond. "What's with this sudden display of conscience? You have more people on your payroll than the bloody civil service and they're still out there ruining lives, because of you."

"I told you before there was worse than me, and you've seen it for yourself."

"So cut the hyperbole and tell us why you think bringing us here can do anything about that?"

Beattie looked tired. Taylor could see under the glare of the overhead light, despite his apparent recovery and continued influence, the stress and the toll of his injuries had aged him.

"There's going to come a day when you wake up and the city as you know it has gone, Veronica. And I don't mean there's a new kid on the block peddling a new high. I'm talking about a slide back to the bad old days, people so worn down by poverty, depression and hopelessness they are going to place the blame on the old enemy again. The day is coming when they realise that the hope they were clinging to was lies spun by men and women they were supposed to trust but who were really only interested in lining their own pockets. When that happens, it'll be you and yours put out the door to protect the deception."

"Did your trip into the light let you glimpse the future, Monster, or is this the morphine talking?" grunted Macpherson.

"I've had a lot of time without distractions, Doc. Time enough to cut through the crap that politicians are spinning us all as gospel truths."

"I don't have time for conspiracy theories, Monster," said Taylor.

"Good. Wallace told you in that undercroft how we got to where we are. Police, judiciary, government appointees, press, all of them culled in the months before our wee country's feted peace deal was signed. Why? Because they were putting pieces together and they were close to blowing open a scandal like you'd never believe."

"Like what? Collusion? Corruption? We've had those headlines for years—"

"And who has ever been convicted for any of it?" snapped Beattie. "Nobody, and why? Because to bring it into the light exposes the whole fucking sordid affair and brings down their house of cards."

Taylor shook her head in frustration. Maybe Macpherson

was right. Maybe it was the morphine or the after-effects of a brush with death but she couldn't drop the notion Beattie was closer to speaking honestly than she could ever have imagined he would. Thoughts of the dead-end investigation following the Hoey operation, Wallace's involvement redacted, and now Oliver Maddox and the investigation into his suicide being placed in the hands of, who exactly, swirled around her head.

"Why have you changed your tune now?" said Taylor, searching Beattie's eyes for another grain of honesty. "Why are you suddenly intent on biting the hand that's fed you all these years?"

"Truthfully, because I don't like being used and I never wanted to be a pawn in their game."

"So, you're after revenge?" scoffed Taylor.

"It's funny how that seems to be the thread that binds us together. You. Me. Shepard. Oliver Maddox."

"Maddox?"

"I'm sure you heard his speech, hard on the perpetrators of organised crime, hard on their enablers."

"I know what he was proposing."

"He was a marked man," said Beattie, something in his tone suggesting the observation was more than an off-the-cuff comment.

"And what would you know about that?" said Taylor, equally cryptically, wondering how much Beattie knew of Oliver Maddox and the brand that scarred him.

Macpherson's eyes narrowed and he scooted forward in his seat.

"I know, you know, Veronica." Beattie's eyes bored into hers. So, he did know. Maddox had been selected, groomed for office if her hunch was correct. Beattie continued. "Maddox's mistake was to think that what he knew would let him get away with murder."

"Are we talking literal or metaphorical here, Monster?" Taylor held the stare.

"Oh, both. Maddox died because he decided he wasn't going to be used anymore either."

"And what makes you think the two of us won't end up the same way if I act on whatever it is you are planning to tell me?"

"Because I'm going to tell you where you need to start digging. What you'll find will be incendiary enough to blow a hole below the waterline and hopefully get the two of us back to where we both want to be."

Taylor frowned. "And where exactly is that?"

Beattie eased back in his wheelchair and grinned.

"A good honest cop chasing an ordinary decent criminal."

"Do you think that was worth the risk?"

Solomon Reeves watched from the doorway of the admin office as the two detectives exited through the double door back into the corridor.

"Taylor is a like a bitch with a bone when she gets going. It was worth it," said Beattie. "

Reeves' face said he wasn't convinced.

"Sol, if the rumours are true they are coming for me and the only way that ends is with me dead. I didn't spend half my life grafting from the ground up to have a bunch of two-faced fuckers think they can hand it over on a plate without a fight."

"Sometimes, it's better to cut your losses and start again."

Beattie wheeled on his legal adviser. Reeves put his hands up.

"I'm just saying, there is enough put aside to set you up far away from here and when things settle and you are one hundred per cent recovered, you can reassess your position."

Beattie sneered. Reeves was great at the job he was

employed to do, but at times he lacked the vision and the guts to take the big gambles. Perhaps it was because he was too used to winning, no matter the cost, even to himself.

"I'm only going to say this once, Sol. I'm staying put and they can come all they want. They're only going to find out that now I've nothing to lose I'm twice as fucking dangerous as I used to be."

Beattie held the lawyer in his steely gaze.

"I'm taking back what is mine, and if doing it sees the twisted bastards who thought they could use me to boost their balance sheets pay the price, then this city will be all the better for it."

41

"Mr Finnegan? Paul Finnegan?"

Reilly leapt out of the car as the man who matched the photograph on her phone struggled to pull a set of keys from a shoulder bag.

"Ah, yes," he stammered caught unawares. "Who are you?" A wary expression was plastered on his face.

Reilly flashed her warrant card and indicated Walker as he approached.

"DC Reilly. This is DC Walker. We hoped you could spare us five minutes?"

Finnegan looked to each, not committing to a decision but rather making a show of searching through the bunch of keys in his hand.

At about six foot six he stood much taller than both detectives but looked like he would pose no threat until he'd had his first soy latte of the day. He had a shabby chic which suggested he should be chained to a railing or glued to the road rather than the principal mouthpiece behind a flourishing community protest group. Reilly gave a patient smile when he glanced up from her identification, remembering that appearances could be deceiving.

Turning away, Finnegan slotted a key home and unlocked a deadbolt, pushing a shoulder into the door to force it free of the swollen wood frame. "Can I get a hint of what this might be about?"

"Routine enquires. We're looking into some complaints regarding Corry Developments," said Reilly.

"You'd better come in then, and it might take more than five minutes."

SCAR, or Stop Construction and Redevelopment as the bold signage over the front window proclaimed, took up the ground floor of a converted Victorian townhouse located just off a main arterial road in the south of the city. The building was shared with a lettings agent and an independent mobile phone repair man. The other businesses were both accessed via the communal hall and a set of uncarpeted stairs.

Finnegan fussed with another internal door and then led the two detectives into what would at one time have been parlour and scullery but had been knocked into an open-plan office that smelled of rising damp and instant coffee.

"So, I take it this is about Corry impeding our right to protest and assaulting our members?"

"Sort of," said Reilly. She looked around the office space containing a few desks that may have been repurposed from a classroom. On top of each was a monitor and keyboard, a vine of wires twisting to large PC towers underneath. The desktops were strewn or stacked with paperwork depending on which you chose and the walls were covered in posters explaining the virtues of trade unions and health and safety. A number of placards decrying the poisoning of local river systems and the destruction of community for profit were propped in a corner.

"We hoped you could explain your interest in Corry Developments?"

"My personal interest or SCARs?" said Finnegan. He had taken a seat behind one of the more cluttered desks, Walker noting he had failed to offer a seat let alone refreshments.

"My personal opinion of Geordie Corry is probably on record somewhere. He's an arrogant bully, has no concern for the communities he bulldozes yet somehow..." Finnegan wagged a finger to make a point. "Somehow planning rules and regulations don't seem to apply to him."

"Surely as a developer, he has to abide by local planning restrictions and the like—"

"You would think so," said Finnegan cutting Reilly off. "However, Geordie Corry seems to have a blade to the jugular of those in council planning and their masters who are supposed to be representing constituents because more often than not, any opposition doesn't see the light of day. It's a joke that a judge can grant consent for forced evictions and condemn a swathe of housing when they haven't been able to make landlords uphold their obligation to ensure it was safe in the first place."

Reilly glanced at her colleague. Walker was straining to read an upside-down copy of an email transcript. She returned her attention to Finnegan who had busied himself booting up.

"So it's fair to say you believe SCAR's only recourse is to protest and attempt to actively delay or block construction?"

"It's a citizen's right."

"There's a line that isn't clear cut between protest and obstruction."

"What is clear cut is common assault on peaceful protestors," snapped Finnegan, leaning forward with elbows on his desk clutter. "I'm sorry, constable, are you here to follow up on my complaints about Geordie Corry and his goons or have his cronies got you to deliver a threat of their own now?"

"We're just making enquires and trying to gather information on the contentions around the development at MacArthur Court," said Reilly

"Apart from the fact it's a monstrosity?" Finnegan swatted away Reilly's reply before it had left her mouth. "Don't tell me you haven't thought it looks like an oversized caravan."

Walker just about caught himself giving a short nod, inwardly pleased though that his own earlier views had been vindicated.

"Are you telling me these protests are over an architect's inability to ensure the design is in keeping with the area? With MacArthur Court?" said Reilly.

Finnegan rolled his eyes and stood, taking a few steps to where several plans she hadn't noticed were pinned to the office wall.

MacArthur Court sat slap-bang in the centre of a community interface. It was situated approximately one mile from the city centre and consisted of red brick terraces that had at one time predominantly housed the families of those who worked in the shipyard, rope works and linen factories that exported their goods around the globe. Now the jobs were gone, the factories derelict or demolished and the contemporary residents were segregated from one another. The boundary between orange and green communities was maintained by a thirty-foot concrete and iron fenced wall, the tale and perspective of the Troubles and beyond daubed along its length, a large section of which ran through the new development.

The activist stabbed a finger into the area in question.

"I've had four families who say they have been intimidated out of their homes to make way for the car parking. This area is crying out for regeneration. Most of these properties haven't been updated since the housing executive sold them off to private landlords. The residents are living with a plague of black mould, streets that are rat infested, and drains that flood because farther upstream more work has narrowed the channel."

"How come things have been left to deteriorate for so long?" asked Reilly, genuinely interested as Finnegan lifted a flapping plan drawing to show the two detectives snapshots of the narrow and squalid entries around the residential area.

"Money. Well, greed more accurately," said Finnegan. "Those who invested got the dwellings at knock-down rates with no provision in the agreement of sale to refurbish or update the stock, that's a scandal in itself by the way. MacArthur and the surrounds may be areas of social deprivation but accommodation is at a premium so the power has been in the hands of the landlords and they've allowed the area to rot until now." Finnegan held his hands aloft. "Praise Jesus, Geordie Corry and the need to build a bauble to satisfy the followers of some bloody cult rather than attend to the real problems these people are facing." He dropped the blueprint's showing Corry's design for a new religious outreach centre and walked to the window, hands on hips, looking out at traffic stalled on the way into the city even though it wasn't quite rush hour yet. He shook his head, frustration in his voice as he continued. "And if that's not good enough they want to knock down a site of listed buildings to erect a so-called Mega-Church not five miles away too."

Reilly looked at the site plans he indicated. She had heard of New Light, a quasi-religious group that was a branch of Christian fundamentalism. It had been the subject of a documentary programme she'd seen on television, the film attempting to expose some of the more dubious practices they were alleged to carry out alongside investigating their strict beliefs on healthcare, pregnancy, marriage and same-sex relationships.

There was a similar New Light church to that planned at MacArthur not far from her own apartment. She had never really given much thought to the flyers that sometimes dropped through her door, and so far she was lucky to have avoided the occasional doorstep sermon some of her neighbours complained about as visits from the happy clappers.

"Your complaints relate to the contractors being heavy-handed in moving you on?"

Finnegan nodded. "Contractors. Local thugs paid to protect the site." He gave a light shake of the head, the gesture signalling he considered those were one and the same thing.

"What about the end client? Has there been any communication with them directly to resolve your dispute?"

"Apparently, what God wants, God gets. We've had a few moments of verbal sparring across the barricades with opposing protests set up by their congregation but really the only dialogue is via their solicitors."

Reilly considered what Finnegan had told them. So far, on the surface at least, it was as expected, an ideological dispute between two parties whose priorities were miles apart. Walker cleared his throat.

"Mr Finnegan, would it be fair to say your protests are organised rather than ad hoc rallies if that makes sense?"

"We do our best to notify the appropriate bodies when necessary if that's what you mean?"

"More so the personnel involved. I'm assuming you need stewards, that sort of thing?"

"We do, and we would mobilise a number of activists both directly and from interest groups like ourselves, alongside those affected directly. At times the numbers may swell, people see a spectacle unfolding and want to know what's going on. We do our best to control any rogue elements but…" Finnegan gave a shrug. "You know what it's like."

Walker nodded, a well-placed expression of understanding on his face. Reilly stayed quiet, letting him continue. It sounded to her ear like an excuse to allow troublemakers to push the boundaries of the official protest.

"Would you recognise either of these men? Perhaps from the protests at MacArthur or elsewhere? Maybe they've expressed an interest in your group?" said Walker, drawing out a printed page with photos of Steven Scott and Finn Abbott.

Reilly watched as Finnegan scrutinised the images, noting a minor twitch that may have been a tell.

"Are these the people behind the vandalism?"

"We're just conducting enquires and ruling out suspects at this stage, sir," said Walker.

Finnegan returned his eyes to the paper. "I've never seen this man." His finger tapped on Abbott. "This other one has been in the news lately."

Walker gave a nod but didn't elaborate. "You don't recognise him as being part of any protest you've undertaken against planned works by Corry, or at these New Light sites?"

Finnegan shook his head. "I don't but you have to understand, we see so many people. Either of the two may have taken part at one time or another but they're not SCAR members nor do they have any direct affiliation to us."

Again Reilly felt a niggle of excuse and wondered if Finnegan was being evasive but then he spoke again.

"This one? Those allegations against Oliver Maddox."

"Nothing we can comment on, sir," said Reilly.

"Yes, of course. It's just that Maddox is, was, quite actively involved in the New Light movement. Perhaps, if this man," Finnegan tapped on Scott's image. "If he knew or had involvement with Maddox or indeed New Light, someone there may know if he was at any of those counter-demonstrations?"

Finnegan returned to his desk and began to shovel through the untidy stacks of paperwork, finally drawing out a Sunday tabloid marked at an exposé on New Light and a separate magazine article. Reilly wasn't surprised that he was compiling a dossier on Corry's client, information that he probably hoped might offer some ammunition in his fight against their developments.

Walker scanned the pages and glanced urgently up at Reilly, who was reading the article over his shoulder.

"Would we be able to take a copy of this?" she said.

42

The entrance foyer of the Royal Victoria Hospital was busy as day staff arrived and those not necessary for the change of shift handover hurried homeward. The small concession store had just rolled up its shutter and customers began to wander inside in search of breakfast tea and coffee.

Avoiding the outflow of bleary-eyed souls, a contractor weaved through the atrium heading towards the stairs and the bank of passenger lifts at the rear of the wide concourse. As he walked, he shrugged on an unmarked hi-vis vest and consulted a clipboard, pausing to glance up at the overhead signage to orientate himself and put on a plain white hard hat.

The Royal was in a state of flux. New building works continuing to expand the huge site. Temporary cranes and contractor compounds wrapped around the southeast corner, and the plethora of trades needed to add additional ward and specialist services blocks swarmed into the concrete and cladded shells of the half-finished buildings like columns of fluorescent-backed ants.

Adding to the upheaval of new construction, remedial maintenance to ensure the old Victorian sections the hospital continued to be up to standard was never ending; the replacement of legacy materials and equipment was running behind schedule, service calls to repair reported faults were stacking up and then there was the never-ending painting and making good.

As the contractor approached the lifts he casually changed direction as two uniformed PSNI officers made their way down the adjacent stairs. He stopped at a vending machine and browsed the choices available.

The lift doors nearby dinged, and in the reflection of the glass, he noted a man and woman exit. Neither looked happy.

The man offered a grunt of acknowledgement to the officers who responded in deferential greeting and with that the two pairs went their separate ways. Uniforms towards the shop, the mismatched pair towards the front doors.

Kevin Cullen tipped the peak of the hard hat a little lower to shade his features and walked to the lift, entering the empty cabin and taking up a position where the internal camera would have a limited view. He selected the floor below his intended destination with a knuckle and waited for the doors to close. It was force of habit even though the cut-proof PPE gloves he wore ensured no prints would be left and blended in with the rest of his attire.

The fourth-floor corridor was quiet when he exited, a few nursing staff far ahead and a domestic cleaner buffing the floor at the other end, the orange cable of her machine spiralling behind her. Cullen stopped at the halfway point and entered the stairwell, heading up to the fifth.

What he was about to undertake may have seismic repercussions but in the short term, he agreed with his master. Colm Casey was right, better to put a wounded dog down than wait for it to come out snarling.

"Morning," he said breezily as he held a door open for a nurse on her way out. She gave a weary smile of thanks. "Is the ward sister about? I'm just surveying for some new cable runs if that's okay?"

"They're having their handover, she'll be free in about fifteen minutes if you want to just crack on. You won't be drilling or anything will you?" she added as an afterthought.

Cullen held up his clipboard. "Just a visual inspection and making notes at the minute. Safe home." The nurse gave another brief smile and nod of thanks and left him to it.

Voices drifted from the ward office and it was easy to avoid an interaction with the lone nursing student sitting at the ward nurse base. Cullen nodded and she waved back, more interested in her phone than a lone building contractor. He continued past the multi-occupancy bays and towards the north-south corridor of single-person rooms.

It was easy to blend in, people saw what they wanted to see and rarely queried anything that didn't stand out too far from the norm. Rounding the corner he made a show of checking the ceiling tiles, scratched a few notes and then surveyed the corridor half expecting his information to be wrong and there be a police guard. But there wasn't.

The corridor was deathly quiet and empty save for a porter's wheelchair parked outside one of the rooms.

Gordon Beattie's room.

Cullen took a breath, putting aside thoughts of any potential repercussions to deal with the job at hand. He strode purposefully along the corridor, peripheral vision and senses heightened to recognise anyone showing more than a passing degree of interest. It was still early so there was little to worry about; the domestic staff had yet to reach the ward and the breakfast trolley would still be getting loaded in the kitchens.

Cullen placed a hand on the door and eased it open a crack.

The curtains were drawn and what light filtered through the material did little to lift the deep gloom. A few LED lights blinked on a trolley of observation equipment but otherwise, there was little noise or sign of life beyond the gurgle of heating and the outline of Beattie's form under the thin hospital sheets, partially obscured by one of the bedside privacy screens.

Cullen took a final glance left and right and stepped inside. As he allowed his eyes to adjust to the darkness, he reached inside his jacket and removed a large hypodermic needle, the contents of which he was assured would send Beattie swiftly to the afterlife. It was a generosity Cullen believed the Loyalist gangster didn't deserve but it suited the task. He didn't need to make this kill uglier or more violent than it had to be.

Popping the protective cap from the needle, he approached the bed. Beattie hadn't moved, still either deep in sleep or, as the persistent rumours claimed, lost to a coma.

Standing over the bed, Cullen couldn't make out more than a shape, no arm had fallen loose of the blankets and neither was a convenient ankle or leg exposed. Gently, he reached down and eased back the sheet.

His breath caught, his mind racing to connect his expectations and what his eyes were seeing. His heart sank after realisation struck, a high-pitched whine filled his ears, and he was kicked into the black void of unconsciousness.

Cullen sniffed away the acrid smell that dragged him back from the blackness.

He commanded his eyes to open but for some unfathomable reason, they wouldn't respond. The mother of all migraines split his head, every breath was constricted as though somebody was sitting on his chest, and the pain between his shoulder blades felt as though he had been stamped on.

Slowly his senses and knowledge of where he was began to return and he was gripped by a sudden panic.

"Relax, you've had quite a shock."

The disembodied voice had a mocking quality. Cullen

made to rise but found he had been lashed to Beattie's bed by makeshift bonds made from bandages. The observation trolley had been moved closer and a mobile defibrillator lay on top. His fractured thoughts began to piece together what must have happened.

"Beattie?" Cullen barely recognised his own croaking voice. As his vision began to clear further he saw a man standing at the end of the bed wearing the light green tunic of a hospital porter.

"Lucky for you, no." Tom Shepard regarded the man he had followed from Casey's fuel yard.

"You aren't a porter?"

Shepard nodded. "Two can play at that game." He indicated the hard hat and clipboard which he had set at the foot of the bed.

"It seems like you've found yourself in a bit of a predicament—"

"What do you want?" interrupted Cullen, straining against his bonds.

"I did want to know where you had taken Steven Scott but now we're here I think there's a more interesting story."

"Fuck you."

Shepard gave a half-hearted chuckle at the bravado, Cullen flinching as he reached forward to collect an object from the bed. When his hand came back up it held the hypodermic syringe.

"I bet this nips a bit," said Shepard, inspecting the hollow point needle. "What is it?"

Cullen clamped his mouth shut, eyes glancing towards the door. Shepard's gaze followed, pausing briefly on the wall-mounted clock as he turned back to Beattie's prospective assassin. The minutes were ticking past leaving him little time for finesse.

"Look, I'll tell you what I know. You fill in a few blanks

and I'll leave you here to shake off the shock and the nurses will find you shortly. You won't get a better deal today."

Cullen refused to look up.

"Colm Casey sent you here." Shepard made a point of holding up the syringe. "To murder Gordon Beattie. Now that's a brave move considering the people the Monster runs about with, so, I've been doing a bit of reading and here's what I think. Casey has a good thing going, a mask of legitimacy sure, but it's hard to shake a family name in this town and there's plenty of rumours about where his real money came from and where his allegiances lie."

Shepard waited to see if there was any response, which there was not.

"So like any good businessman, he spots an opportunity. A new market has suddenly opened up and the void needs to be filled. Now, I'm making the assumption he knows who to speak with to get a deal done and step into our missing friend's place." Cullen looked up with ill-disguised hate in his eyes. "I don't know where he is by the way," said Shepard, adding with a shrug. "And it's no skin off my nose if you kill him. I'd be happy to stick whatever this is in his neck myself."

Shepard let the silence hang between them for a few moments. Somewhere farther along the ward, he heard beds being moved about and a few welcome greetings being hailed.

"There's no point Casey taking something like that on if there's somebody able to connect him to a few murders, or maybe to tell a tale about what he is really about, so he sends a few halfwits like you to snatch the witness, just in case his trial isn't really over. Am I close?"

"You haven't got a clue what's going on."

Shepard pursed his lips, considering the response and the time constraints versus the reward that engaging in more dialogue might earn him. He decided on one last crack.

"Look. I'm sure on any given day you're a guy that gets things done. Casey wouldn't have sent you here to murder somebody like the Monster if you didn't have the reputation to back it up." He hadn't expected flattery would get him anywhere and he was correct. "But, I've seen and done things you'll never be able to imagine, and you don't strike me as the type who'll lie back, bite your tongue and die for your boss, your God or even your girl."

A sneer cracked Cullen's face. "Was there a question in there?"

Shepard sniffed out a breath in mild mirth. He clamped a hand down to stifle a scream and stabbed the hypodermic needle deep into the muscle of the would-be killer's thigh.

Cullen writhed around the bed in shock, eyes bulging from their sockets. The pain radiated out from where he had been stuck.

Shepard took his hand away and whispered.

"Where did your lads take Steven Scott and what do they want with him?"

"Christ. What have you done?" Sweat streamed down Cullen's face. "Take it out, please, get it out."

"Where is Scott and who gave Casey the green light to put down Beattie?"

"Please…"

"I'm guessing if I inject this, it won't end well."

"No, please don't…"

Shepard pressed down on the man's knee and placed his thumb on the plunger.

"You tell me now what you know or you take your poison."

"For fuck's sake… I don't know."

Shepard sank the plunger home.

Cullen went limp, the colour draining from his face in

terror.

"You probably don't have long," said Shepard. "I can walk out of here and get a team of medics in…" Shepard shrugged. "They might have a reversal drug and they might be able to save you, but that only happens if you talk, and you talk right now."

43

"We've been up all night, are you sure you want to do this right now?" said Macpherson, an uncharacteristic note of concern in his voice.

For a moment, he wasn't sure if Taylor had heard. Her reflection stared silently back at him, her concentration focused on the glass door of the building across the road.

They were parked in the heart of the St Anne's quarter, in a space outside a derelict shopping mall. The area, having been designated for redevelopment years earlier, remained languishing in the limbo of planning problems and public objections. The hoardings and boarded-up shops were scarred by vandalism and graffiti and the only people prospering were the architects and solicitors reviewing arguments and renewing design drafts.

A bit farther along, a cleaner tipped a mop bucket of dirty water into the roadside drain, her brushing and bleaching waking the few homeless souls who had spent the night in nearby doorways. The nineteenth-century public house for which she was working was closed at the early hour but come lunchtime, the place would be packed with regulars and tourists sampling the stout and traditional Belfast fayre and just as the thought occurred Taylor's stomach grumbled.

She let out a long yawn and peered with bleary eyes at her sergeant. Events at Ballyhallion seemed like they'd taken place days ago, while the last few hours had left her feeling like she had been abruptly woken from a dream and into, she reflected, a nightmare.

"I think we both need a few hour's kip but if we don't do this now the shutters will be down before we get another chance," said Taylor, rooting around in the centre console for any of Macpherson's sweetie chews or mints to rid her mouth of the taste of stale coffee.

"Maybe that's a good thing, Ronnie." Macpherson cracked the driver's window and let the cool air bathe his face. "We're playing with fire now, girl."

An understatement if ever there was one, she thought, turning back to the ground-floor offices.

Beattie's revelations, although not altogether new, did offer the possibility of not only shining a withering light on a series of historic atrocities but also, finally, holding individuals accountable. Something which over the years multiple failed investigations and numerous dead-end public enquires had not.

"Here we go," said Taylor, opening the car door as the first of two figures emerged from a nondescript office serving the Prison Service Federation of Northern Ireland.

Macpherson followed her out of the car but by the time he blipped the locks his inspector had nipped across the road and was in conversation with the men.

"Mr Nendrum?"

Michael Nendrum spun around. Caught unawares, the dour downturn of his mouth dipped further, his eyes dropping quickly to look at Taylor's hands, and then at Macpherson walk-jogging across the road. Something in his manner suggested he had perhaps expected the thrust of a microphone or the glare of a television camera.

"You have me at a disadvantage," said Nendrum, drawing himself up to tower a broad and intimidating frame over the two police officers. His brow furrowed and then relaxed in recognition. "Taylor, isn't it? I recognise you from the newspapers."

Taylor gave a short nod, uncomfortable with her infamy thanks to various tabloid tales of her run-ins with Beattie and embarrassed anytime she was recognised because of it.

Michael Nendrum wore a suit in charcoal pinstripe and a crisp white shirt with a plain navy tie. His companion, although in a similar formal suit, wore his shirt open at the collar and had taken a step away to offer a degree of privacy. He reached into his jacket, removed a mobile phone and made about distracting himself.

"Yes, sir. This is my colleague, DS Macpherson." The trio exchanged nods, Nendrum keeping his hands casually interlaced behind his back. "I'm sorry for catching you like this," said Taylor, as she inclined her head towards the offices. "I expect it's been a difficult time for you?"

"It has. Is this about Oliver?"

Taylor gave an almost imperceptible nod. "Can we buy you a coffee?" She indicated a coffee shop that provided a bookend to the old city centre street but Nendrum declined politely. Taylor had spent the drive and her time waiting in the car considering the questions she could ask the head of the Prison Service without seeming to impose on any investigation into Oliver Maddox's death or causing the senior official to clam up and close ranks with his colleagues. What she hadn't considered was having to ask them kerbside

"You knew him well?" said Taylor.

Nendrum bowed his head, his expression sombre and for the first time allowed his hands to fall free at his sides.

"I'd known Oliver since he was a junior officer and I'd the privilege to watch him flourish. When he left us, I was proud to see him continue to serve the community at large."

The platitudes sounded rehearsed to Taylor's ear but Nendrum's body language suggested a genuine sorrow.

"I expect the manner of his death came as quite a shock all things considered," she said.

"Oliver was steadfast in his desire for prison mental health reform and committed to his charity work with those affected by suicide. For him to…" Nendrum didn't finish his sentence, 'die like that.' He gave an exasperated shrug and sad inclination of his head.

"I'm sorry," said Taylor, offering a sympathetic smile but studiously examining the NIPS principal officer. To her eyes, he looked uncomfortable, which may be expected given the topic. He may not be on the reading list in the reporting of Maddox's death but she was sure he would be close enough to someone who was.

"Can I ask your opinion on recent allegations levelled at Mr Maddox?"

"Utter tripe," stated Nendrum empathically. "Not one iota of that drivel is reminiscent of the man I knew."

"And you aren't aware of anyone bearing a grudge from his time in your service? Maybe who wished to discredit him?"

Nendrum scoffed, the sound coming out as a bitter chuckle. "You know the sort of men and the associations they represent incarcerated in our prisons, inspector. To believe their influence remains behind the walls is rather misguided wouldn't you agree?"

Taylor silently did. Throughout the years of Northern Ireland's struggles, regardless of whether the paramilitary commanders were interned or serving time laid down through trial, they remained in absolute control of their factions, at times no doubt aided by coercion through the threat and intimidation of prison staff and their families or by bribery and corruption of officials. Nendrum continued unprompted. "Aside from Oliver's time in uniform, his role as justice minister likely brought with it a few enemies, and not solely from the criminal fraternity. Some of his views were not always best received by his political counterparts."

"Really? From what little coverage I've seen, his colleagues all seem to be of one voice in their praise?"

"Politicians!" Nendrum gave a small shake of the head, leaning in and lowering his voice to a conspiratorial whisper. "Imagine if either of us were so cynical as to question the falsehoods, contradictions or the duplicity of our lords and masters."

Nendrum returned to his almost-at-attention posture. "Oliver believed in rehabilitation and reform over punishment, probably spurred on by his religious beliefs. Quite in contrast to the fire and brimstone rhetoric you might associate with his peers. You'll never hear anyone from the party call him out on it in public though." Nendrum glanced back at the man with whom he had exited the building to see he remained on his phone. "Privately, I can tell you there were quite a few senior party figures uncomfortable with where he chose to worship."

"I see," said Taylor, the mood of the justice minister's final address quietly echoing in the back of her mind. Had the announcement of institutional reform and an acknowledgement of societal problems stemming from a lack of political resolve been a gong of warning to some of his own? Or had it been the throwing down of the gauntlet and the challenge to the rule of the kingpins of organised crime and their slavish sycophants which had him daubed in shame? If Beattie was to be believed, the truth lay somewhere between the two.

"I'm sorry, inspector. Unless there is something specific you need of me, I really have to go."

"Did he ever mention privately the root of the discord between himself and Colm Casey?"

Michael Nendrum's brow knitted into a tight V.

"Casey is a villain, inspector. You of anyone should know the frustration of pursuing and administering justice to that type of man."

The detective inspector kept her own counsel. Her world had tilted on its axis now Beattie had gifted her a dirty ribbon which if followed may lead to an uncomfortable truth.

"If Oliver knew him in younger days, they forged very different paths, and if you want my opinion," continued Nendrum, "Oliver wasn't a man to pursue a vendetta. If there had been an acquaintance, or a boyhood friendship that turned sour, any cause he had to pursue Casey would have been purely professional. Allegations to the contrary, I expect you'll find are baseless."

Nendrum offered a nod to each detective. "I'm sorry. I really have to go. Regardless of if the allegations are found to be spurious or not, in light of what has happened, the DPP and I have been asked to attend the deputy first minister's office to assess any impact on recent and potential convictions."

"Of course. Again my apologies for doorstepping you like this and our condolences for the loss of your friend."

Nendrum gave a solemn nod of gratitude, but before he could fully retreat, Taylor spoke. "Sorry, sir. One more thing I meant to ask. You lost two other officers recently, POs Townsend and Plymouth?"

Nendrum gave the mildest of tuts and then said, "Yes. A tragic loss to their families and the service. It looks like that sacrifice will go unpunished now."

"This may seem insensitive given their passing but would you be aware if either had any blemishes on their record? Disciplinary notes or the like?"

"It is insensitive, and off the top of my head, I wouldn't know nor be inclined to say if there was. What I will tell you is they were upstanding Christian men and a credit to their uniform."

Taylor raised a palm in apology for the line of questioning. "Could the two have been known to Mr Maddox? Served with him at one point perhaps?"

"I expect it's possible, in the past. Both men had in recent years moved to take up positions within the juvenile detention system though." Nedrum blew out a breath, his expression shifted now from irritated to reflective. "Which makes their murders all the more senseless. Years inside guarding the hard men of the Troubles and then on the wind-down to retirement they're cut down..." Nendrum inclined his head. "Sorry, I really must..."

"Thanks, sir."

"Sir," said Macpherson mirroring his inspector's nod of gratitude.

They crossed the road, pausing at the Volvo to watch Nendrum and his companion turn the corner into Royal Avenue, perhaps headed on towards city hall or one of the other government buildings, maybe even to pick up a car for the short drive to Stormont.

"What do you reckon to that?" said Macpherson. "He was laying it on thick there. If the two POs didn't know Maddox through work maybe they swapped chat over the collection plate."

"I think I need to speak to Diane Pearson and Professor Thompson about Maddox on the QT," said Taylor. "And we need to find out who did the casework on the Plymouth and Townsend murders and pay them a visit, even if it's just to confirm nothing on them was overlooked in the haste to rope in Casey."

She opened her door but didn't get in right away, her eyes straying to Church Street, the narrow thoroughfare which led to Writers Square and St Anne's Cathedral also home to the Police Ombudsman Office.

Macpherson interrupted her thoughts with a gruff order

"Well, I'm taking you home first. We've been out all night and I don't know about you but I need an hour's kip and shower before we go in and face the super."

Taylor climbed into the passenger seat, too tired and too wrung out to argue.

44

"…details remain sketchy with authorities not confirming the cause of the overnight explosion however eyewitnesses report a shoot-out, possibly between rival gangs who are known to be active in the area. With several men confirmed as injured, police are also asking the public to…"

John Barrett bit back an oath and set his tea down with a little more force than expected, his attention focused on the local morning news bulletin playing out on the wall-mounted television set. The contents of the mug sloshed over the rim to cause a wet ring on his desk. Thankfully the proposal agreements he had worked on for most of the previous evening were far enough away to avoid damage.

"…and in other news, the Health and Safety Executive are in attendance at the Royal Victoria Hospital this morning. A representative of the Belfast Health and Social Care Trust confirms a contractor was found unresponsive on the site and although valiant efforts were made by staff to resuscitate, the man unfortunately died at the scene. His identity has yet to be confirmed. We'll bring you more on both stories as they develop."

Barrett paused in his mopping up as the scene cut back from stock footage to the reporter on location at a familiar blustery site.

"…In other news, the go-ahead for the contentious New Light Mega-Church has been confirmed this morning by Geordie Corry of Corry Developments. The director of the

group issued a press release late last night stating pre-works to the site will now start as soon as this weekend. Environmental activists and green campaigners have responded saying they are disappointed in the overturning of a recent objection and vow to continue their fight to prevent…"

It seemed there was no letting the grass grow under either of the men who he hoped would provide a cross-community bulwark and ensure the laundering of revenue continued to fill the coffers of the consortium in the short term and perhaps, should they meet expectations, for the years ahead.

Casey, he hoped, would learn to become less impetuous. The potential aggravation at the quiet seaside caravan park could be lessened as long as no bodies turned up and Corry had no option but to assist in the smoothing of Casey's transition across the river if he wished to continue the growth of his property portfolio. Any objections he may have had were successfully nullified by offering him a share of the illicit profits that could be made in rebranding Gordon Beattie's empire

Barrett muted the television and sat, skim-reading the final draft of the agreement orders that would set in motion the transfer and distribution of funds that would make his masters and himself significantly wealthier. Satisfied with his perusal he added his electronic signature and sent the documents to a secure cloud server. From there the documents would be processed, and procedures followed so that the exceptional sum of money involved could be transmitted in the form of zeros and ones across the ether to various bank accounts controlled by the consortium.

In all, it was a good result and would return him to the favour of those who had voiced concern about his continued ability to control affairs after the debacle at Hoey Cargo. An episode, he reflected, that could have gone much worse had his VIP guests not been spirited away in good time and outrageously compensated for the inconvenience caused.

The only blemish in the entire affair had been the unexpected problems brought about by the egos and entitlement of men who had forgotten who anointed them with their power in the first instance. Their avarice and deviancy which had begun to threaten more than the exposure of their sins could now be quieted and the equilibrium restored.

With the reputation of the justice minister now buried alongside the rest of the bodies and the Glenrafferty project proceeding, Barrett had again shown he could, for a price, grant whatever those loyal to him and his masters coveted.

That price, be it monetary, in the admission of unscrupulous secrets or in blood, had to be paid and now those terms had been made abundantly clear and that no one was exempt, he hoped he would have no need to risk further displays of discipline.

Shepard pulled the motorcycle to a stop, pausing kerbside at the top of a long sweeping descent. Below, a large sandstone structure stood out prominently above the treetops while adjacent outbuildings and paths were half hidden by the overgrowth of out-of-control foliage.

The wash of a low loader buffeted him as it passed. The cargo bed bore a large excavator and steamroller and the brake lights bloomed and air lines hissed as it slowed to take the side road towards the abandoned private estate, following as it was in the wake of two minivans of building contractors, a dark SUV and a police car.

Shepard double-checked the location address he had thumbed into the map feature on his phone and, sure enough, the red marker sat in the centre of the parkland below.

He sat far enough away to be of no concern to the men

now beginning to disembark from their vehicles and mill about, a few taking the opportunity to spark up cigarettes and chat. The driver and passenger of the SUV, more urgent in their step, crossed the square of gravel parking to have an animated discussion with the police officer who stood at the centre of the site's antiquated wrought iron gates.

The appearance of the PSNI was unfortunate but the presence of at least one of the men from Ballyhallion confirmed there was some truth in the garbled confession of Beattie's would-be killer.

Shepard scanned his phone, reading through the search results that had flashed up, clicking through to read several articles on the history of the estate and then a few more contemporary news stories on its decline and proposed future use.

One headline caught his eye. An article detailing intransigence and bitter division over what should be done with the site and others of similar infamy. The debate was bitterly contested with one side arguing the memory of what the bricks and mortar represented required them to be scraped from the earth like cancerous cells, however, there was something telling in the desire of the other party, nothing tangible but a sense that these buildings and their grim histories should not be hidden, or bulldozed and buried under tons of concrete, but rather exorcised of their ghosts and exalted towards a loftier goal.

He couldn't put his finger on it exactly but seeing the leering faces and clasped hands of Colm Casey, the project developer Geordie Corry, and an elderly gentleman representing the new owners of the former Glenrafferty Home for Troubled Boys sent a chill up his spine.

45

In the end, Taylor had neither sleep nor sustenance. The cornflakes were soft, the loaf of bread mouldy and the milk, which might have been good a day or so ago, glooped out like yoghurt.

So, a cold shower and a change of clothes followed by a couple of cups of black coffee to wash down two paracetamol had been the extent of her breakfast. A further two ibuprofen were swallowed dry as she crossed the pedestrian footbridge over the River Lagan heading towards the Waterfront Hall, all but blind and deaf to the city moving around her as she ruminated on the last twenty-four hours.

She had decided she needed the walk to process events and to form her opinion on the veracity of what Beattie had divulged, his true purpose for doing so, and also more practically, to align the details she would need in the debrief of events at Ballyhallion Caravan Park.

It was a short walk from her apartment in a tree-lined South Belfast suburb to the bus stop, where she had a short wait and a short journey before stepping off to walk the Lagan towpath into the city centre.

What had started as a routine investigation into vandalism was fast becoming mired in something much darker and entirely more unwieldy and unmanageable in the hands of a lowly detective inspector. Did her desire to unravel Finn Abbott's ramblings of conspiracy, Oliver Maddox's death and

Steven Scott's disappearance even matter if she was unable to galvanise support from her superiors let alone the higher institutions of the justice system in tackling what may link all three?

The larger issues which gnawed at the pit of her stomach were the same as those which had over recent times begun to slowly devour her trust in the offices and institutions to which she had pledged her loyalty and to honour and serve, each falsehood and cover-up undermining her oath to discharge her duties with fairness, integrity, diligence and impartiality. An oath that she held as close as the memory of her father, the man who had inspired her to follow in his footsteps, and who had died fulfilling his duty.

The chains of deception entangled her, and it felt like they were dragging her deeper into the swamp of corruption and collusion, the filthy waters closing over her head and threatening to drown her. Those feelings, manifested in a choking despair, contributing to the fear she was allowing herself to become a pawn in Gordon Beattie's desire for revenge and rebirth, which in her mind made her no better than any of those others she couldn't name but despised.

A long sharp note of a car horn pulled her from her waking slumber. She leapt back up to the kerb as traffic flowed quickly along Oxford Street in the direction of the law courts and St George's market. Across the road, the facade of the nineteenth-century Christian Brothers School was sandwiched between modern civil service and retail buildings.

Seeing a break in traffic, Taylor strode across the four lanes. The sandstone frontage of the old school still bore its name and insignia although it had been repurposed as a tattoo artists' studio for many years. The vision of Oliver Maddox's branding flashed through her mind and she resisted the temptation to peer through the arched windows to the salon beyond. To her right, Thanksgiving Square was bathed in sunlight, the iconic statue officially named the Beacon of Hope welcomed those crossing the Queen's Bridge from East Belfast but as Taylor approached, a cloud passed over as though even the elements had sensed the weight of hopelessness she was carrying.

A few minutes later she had entered the pedestrian gate of Musgrave Street Station and was badging through reception.

"Excuse me, inspector?"

"Sergeant?"

Taylor paused with one hand on the door which would take her through to the stairwell and the lifts, turning to face the duty sergeant. Harris was a burly man with a shock of red beard that was trying to compensate for the lack of hair up top. Ruddy cheeks and a broad belly drew the imagination to infer that replacing the uniform cap with a horned helm, would see the man at home in the bow of a longboat or pillaging hamlets.

"DS Macpherson wanted me to give you the heads-up the chief superintendent is looking for you."

Taylor nodded her gratitude for the warning, feeling the first spits of rain from the imagined cloud that hung over her head.

Harris gave a tight nod to the visitors' book. "We've a guest from the Ombudsman's office in already,' he said.

"I appreciate the warning, sergeant."

"Good luck," said Harris, a frown drawing a line between his brows that could have been cut by a battle axe.

Taylor signalled her gratitude with a grimace and then her eyes settled on a poster taped on the reception information board.

"Sarge, can I ask a favour?"

"If you're going to ask me to tell them I've not seen you—"

"No," said Taylor." Nothing like that." She pointed to the

poster. "Can you put out a request for information like that for me? Dashcam or doorbell footage from the evening of the thirteenth through to teatime the next day. The corner of Castle Heights and Loughview Avenue."

Harris was nodding as he scribbled the addresses, knowing a long shot when he saw it. Still, it wouldn't be the first time a call to the public provided valuable information or context missed by body cam or CCTV footage. His frown deepened as he dropped a pin in a mental map. "That isn't anywhere near your hit and run?"

"Just let me know if anything comes back," said Taylor, in her own mind plotting the area around Maddox's home as she walked away to meet her fate.

"Veronica, thanks for coming in. If you'd like to grab a seat."

Chief Superintendent William Law rose from his desk with a nod and tight smile, indicating the more social double sofa and armchair set-up that overlooked the Coroner's Court, the High Court, and across the vaulted roof of St Georges to the cramped low-rise housing of the Markets.

An offer of water knocked Taylor off kilter as the expected tirade for any number of potential grievances failed to materialise.

There were already two other guests in the room. Macpherson was huddled at the end of one sofa, his eyes were red and he sipped from a heavy glass tumbler, avoiding Taylor's eye.

Opposite him sat a woman. She was mid-thirties, wearing a well-cut business suit in emerald green. The colour matched her eyes. Rising to her feet she extended a hand which Taylor shook.

"Detective Inspector Taylor. I'm Rosie Bush and I'm here representing the Police Ombudsman's Office."

"Good to meet you," said Taylor, declining a second offer

of water.

"We understand you've had a busy evening and likely haven't had time to enter a full report," said Bush, glancing at the chief super.

Taylor kept her face impassive as Law spoke.

"DS Macpherson has apprised us of events as they happened at the Ballyhallion Caravan Park and the preliminary investigation from the follow-up team confirms the vehicle discovered at the scene is the same as that involved in the fatal hit and run of Finn Abbott."

Taylor let out a slow breath and nodded.

"We understand that although the suspect suffered gunshot wounds your quick intervention is likely to have saved his life," said Bush.

"Which means he'll face the consequences of his actions. Well done, Veronica. Well done both of you," said Law with a curt nod to each officer.

"Thank you, sir," said Taylor.

Macpherson mumbled something similar as he placed his tumbler on the glass-topped coffee table.

"There'll obviously be a degree of follow-up based on your official reports and the formal questioning of Mr…"

"Harry Carruthers," said Taylor.

"Yes," said Bush with a note of thanks, adding, "I'm pleased to say that following an investigation into your version of the events of the day, the preliminary forensic reports showing Mr Abbott's intoxication and now the acquisition of physical evidence, no further action is likely to be taken. While Mr Abbott's death was unfortunate and avoidable, I believe we can safely concur that there were no contributory or negligent factors due to PSNI conduct."

"Which is what we knew all along, but are very grateful to hear," said Law. "Thanks for coming in, Miss Bush. Your time is appreciated."

The ombudsman's representative gave a wide smile and stood, taking the chief super's outstretched hand. She turned to the two junior officers and gave a nod.

"Once the final analysis is complete and any outcome evaluated and recommendations given, I'll make sure you hear right away. I know these things can weigh heavily and impact on your day-to-day."

"Thank you, we'll make sure to get our reports completed as soon as possible," said Taylor. Outwardly she exuded a mixture of relief and reassurance but inwardly she was piqued which added to the sourness in her gut.

"It's a pleasure," said Bush, beaming.

"I was wondering," Taylor began. An audible intake of breath from Law and a dull groan from Macpherson fell in the gap between her opening and her question but she ploughed on regardless. "During your preliminaries, did you uncover any investigations into historic allegations made by Finn Abbott? Against the police, other public bodies, private citizens even?"

Bush's radiant smile remained stuck to her face but the light behind it died.

"I am aware of several complaints but thorough examination determined Mr Abbott was not a credible witness so no formal investigation was launched. As Chief Superintendent Law will no doubt agree, we must be seen to ensure our budgets are best spent in areas where prosecution is assured and witnesses are able to withstand the robust nature of a trial."

"Absolutely. Absolutely," spluttered Law. "Please, Miss Bush, let me see you out."

A moment of small talk passed as Law showed her to the door.

"Thank God for that," said Macpherson blowing out a sigh of relief.

"Can you not just be glad that you've seen a stay of execution, inspector?" said Law, his tone and expression beginning to take its familiar dour turn.

Macpherson, making to defuse the storm, rubbed his eyes and chuckled. "Rosie Bush. By Christ, her ma and da would have been better off giving her a number. Can you imagine the grief the wee girl got growing up?"

"Your restraint in not highlighting your amusement is noted, sergeant." Law sat in the armchair. "What the hell was that about, DI Taylor?"

"Sir, do you not think that investigation resolved itself a bit quickly?" said Taylor.

The mirth on Macpherson's face evaporated with her observation and the chief super swung one leg over the other. "I wouldn't look a gift horse in the mouth, inspector."

"I'm not, and while it was a clear-cut hit and run, we've all seen less complicated ombudsman investigations stretch to months. Especially when the deceased had placed numerous complaints against us in the past. For God's sake, they could have taken it the Article Two route if they'd really wanted."

Law's face flushed with anger. "And if they had you two would be sitting at home and I'd be two more officers down when we're under pressure as it is." He blew out a frustrated breath. "Veronica, take the bloody win and stop looking for a conspiracy where there is none. Abbott was delusional, he spent too many years under the influence of God-knows-what and stepped into traffic. There was nothing to find then, and nothing you could have done now."

Taylor chose not to press the issue as Macpherson gave her an arch sideways look. Law cleared his throat, smoothing his tie as he scrutinised them individually.

"Now, can either of you begin to explain how you came to be in the midst of another gangland gun battle that, but for the grace of God, didn't claim any lives?"

"Just good luck I guess—" said Macpherson sardonically.

"Sir," Taylor cut in before Law was able to vent the irritation that should have been aimed at her. "A routine patrol reported a disturbance at a fast food outlet not far from the hit and run. Our follow-up enquiries highlighted Harry Carruthers as a person of interest. DC Cooke was able to provide us with a number of addresses and we just happened to be following one up."

"Really? You just happened to be pursuing a tenuous link in which Abbott's death was perpetrated by one of Gordon Beattie's chief lieutenants?"

"Chief muppet, more like," scoffed Macpherson.

"What was that, sergeant?"

"DCI Reed's orders, chief inspector," said Taylor. "She gave us a clear brief to close the hit and run on Finn Abbott and prioritise the ongoing vandalism against Corry Developments. I only asked Miss Bush about earlier complaints in case Corry was featured too."

Law made a sound somewhere between a grunt and a groan. "So, a merry coincidence Gordon Beattie's man was involved at all?"

"Yes."

"Well, that is welcome news," said Law, sounding like he was trying to believe it.

"We're primarily looking at possible links to environmental and anti-expansion protestors who have extreme elements in their memberships," said Taylor.

"And you've not received information on any further sightings of Mr Scott?"

"We've no information on his exact whereabouts at this time, sir." Taylor kept her tone and her gaze even, not quite lying.

The chief super broke the look first, glancing to his left to find Macpherson studying the back of one hand. "Keep the

DCI and myself up to date with your progress." Law tilted his head in rueful cognisance of the pressure his officers were under and gave the smallest huff of a sigh. "I know you are both long enough in the tooth to understand there are aspects to recent events which place us in a difficult position with the justice department, the press and our political masters. I am equally frustrated by the establishment of an independent investigation, not just because of the implications which may arise in being sidelined but by the damage that may have on us reputationally."

Taylor and Macpherson both offered nods of agreement.

"DCI Reed has already expressed to me your thoughts surrounding Abbott's unverified claims in regard to Corry Developments amongst other things, and your feeling Steven Scott has the potential to shed light on that investigation. Given what we have collectively been through in the last months, I wanted to highlight that I appreciate your understanding of the sensitivity surrounding matters and the constraints by which we must operate in the short to medium term."

Macpherson looked at his shoes waiting for Taylor to say something, but she held her voice. Law continued into the silence.

"I want to reassure you that any details coming to light during the course of the investigation that can be shared and might assist, will be disseminated to your team at the earliest opportunity."

"Thanks, sir," said Taylor after a moment. "Will that be all?"

"For the time being anyway," said Law, rising from his seat and heading back to his desk. "Keep me informed. Geordie Corry has the ear of enough people up the hill to make my life more bloody miserable than it already is if he remains the target of these fringe lunatics."

Taylor felt a pang of regret as Law gave her a self-deprecating smile but accepted that at that moment, withholding what she knew, was the right thing to do.

46

Neither detective spoke until they were ensconced in the lift and heading to the fourth floor.

"I thought you were going to come clean," said Macpherson.

"So did I, right up until Rosie Bush whitewashed the whole Finn Abbott affair in a heartbeat. Have you ever heard of an ombudsman's investigation wrapping up so quickly, especially when the suspect is too ill to be questioned and considering everything else that it would have dredged up? Jesus, how quickly was Abbott branded as not a credible witness?" Taylor flinched as she recalled the expression Abbott had used himself.

"I'm inclined to agree with you," said Macpherson.

"But?" Taylor noted the tone in his voice.

"But it would have been worse if it dragged on, especially after our 'meeting' last night," said Macpherson, dropping a set of air quotes around the loose term.

The lift car pinged and shuddered to a stop, doors opening on their floor. A uniformed constable stepped aside to allow their exit and Taylor paused in the corridor.

"Okay, I'll give you that, but it still doesn't sit well with me. It's as though everything even tangentially connected to the allegations against Oliver Maddox is being buried."

"You know what the politicians are like, Ronnie. This isn't new."

"No, but it's not right and it only gives credence to the Monster's story," said Taylor.

Macpherson could see the conflict his DI was feeling physically manifesting. She was pale, drawn and agitated. "So? What are we going to do?" he said.

"What we always do. Start digging and see how many bones we manage to unearth. Let's just hope we manage to piece enough of them together to stop the next skeleton that lands at our feet being Steven Scott's."

Butler's Breakfast Café was an institution squeezed between a bookmaker's and a barber's shop on one of the city's oldest cobbled streets.

Less than five minutes' walk from Musgrave Street the café was hidden just off the bustling thoroughfare of High Street, which itself was bookended by two of the city's infamous landmarks; on the Lagan side, the Albert Clock leaned precariously towards the contemporary apartment development of Queen's Square. Both feats of architecture loomed over the seventeenth-century square and one of Belfast's oldest surviving public houses, McHugh's. Opposite and city side, the old bank buildings remained cloaked in construction hoardings following a devastating fire which had gutted the once-thriving business within.

The footpaths joining the two ends of High Street had, at one time, been severed by the polluted waters of the River Farset, but were now reunited by a tarmac road built over the river which had lent Belfast its name, and although lost to sight, the waters of the River Lagan's largest tributary still flowed far beneath the modern landscape of retail shops and office blocks which had taken up residence in the old seventeenth and eighteenth-century buildings.

Inside the café, stationed at their usual table set in the alcove farthest away from the door, Macpherson had foregone the belly buster fry and instead tucked into a Belfast bap stuffed with sausage, bacon and fried egg. The rest of the team had settled on toast topped with one or the other, while Taylor had ordered two slices of potato bread which she had set about carving into small squares before dipping each into a dollop of HP brown sauce en route to her mouth. She was also the only one drinking coffee, an Americano; the rest had tin mugs of tea beside their plates.

The decision to relocate had been two pronged. The first was of simple necessity, Taylor's hunger needed satiating if she was to engage her mind to navigate the labyrinth that was slowly revealing itself, and the second was the need for discretion. Even though there was no immediate sense they were under scrutiny, Taylor didn't want to discuss the last twenty-four hours inside the walls of Musgrave Street, and she wanted to give anyone on the team who wished to raise an objection the chance to be able to do so without drawing attention to dissent in the ranks. In that regard, as it turned out, she hadn't needed to worry.

"It must have been a shock all the same, coming face to face like that?" said Walker as Carrie Cook stacked the empty plates at the edge of the table to better assist the waitress in their removal.

"What was more surprising was his story and his desire to share it," said Taylor after a greedy slug of her coffee, and giving a self-deprecating smile. "Look, I appreciate the support from each of you, but I'll say it again, I'm asking that we fly a bit close to the sun on this one and I'll understand if anyone wants to skip it."

Macpherson didn't offer acknowledgement; he had already laid out his hand. Where she went so he would follow. Reilly, Walker and Cook also palmed off concerns. As the waitress arrived to take the empty plates and take the order for refills, Taylor paused, waiting until she was gone to continue.

"We'll share what we've got and the details in a second but to recap, the investigation into the allegations against Maddox and his death is to be handled independently. You also know Finn Abbott identified Stephen Scott as someone with knowledge of the crimes dogging Corry Developments and possible historical abuse carried out at the Glenrafferty Home for Troubled Boys, a location at which we know Maddox, Abbott and Scott were likely known to each other."

There was a frisson of anticipation and enthusiasm around the table, a sense that even though they had been instructed to get on about their individual assignments and concentrate on other cases, each of them was finding those apparently disparate investigations seemed to be drawing together with common links.

"You also know Beattie is a sore point for me." Taylor took a breath, conflict welling up again. "He's got away time and again, quite literally, with murder, and the reason he has managed that is through maintaining shrewd connections inside a number of institutional establishments, including the police service."

"Fat lot of good it did when push came to shove," muttered Walker. More loudly, he said, "It just shows that it doesn't matter how much dirty money you've got or who you're paying off, it doesn't stop a bullet."

Taylor gave a small nod. Each of her subordinates had stood firmly behind her and worked hard to convict men like Gordon Beattie for their crimes, to interrupt their illicit business models and to offer the victims of their reign a sense of justice. The realisation the deck was stacked smarted. More than that, it poisoned the soul. That the hours, days and weeks spent building a prosecution could be shattered because those in the upper echelons of the system had fragile moral principles or could succumb to avarice wasn't anything new, but to those charged with wielding the spear and shield in defence of the public, it left an emptiness and sense of despair that was hard to communicate much less live with.

"Why would he reach out at all?" asked Cook. "If his information leads us somewhere then he must know that someone will figure out who talked, and he above all should know how the groups he associates with deal with informers?"

"Be in no doubt pursuing this will benefit him." Taylor tapped a finger against the tabletop. "How exactly I'm not sure, but right now, the enemy of my enemy is my friend, and you've no idea how sick that makes me feel."

"We're working on the hypothesis he isn't going to have to worry about reprisal, Carrie," said Macpherson. "If we follow this through to an outcome, anyone with an axe to grind will have booked themselves on a flight to a non-extradition country or be more concerned that they've dropped the soap in the communal shower. If you want my opinion on Beattie worrying he'll be branded a tout"—the DS pulled a face—"he won't. The bugger will have sent an unequivocal message that no one does him dirty and those who do will pay for it. If not with their life, then their reputation."

"But I don't get why now?" said Cook. A look from Walker suggested he was thinking similar while Reilly remained impassive.

"Oliver Maddox made a speech recently," said Taylor.

"Although some might have taken it as a declaration of war," added Macpherson.

"His stance was not just on organised crime but on their enablers," said Taylor. "If we take Beattie's information at face value then looking into the court case against Colm Casey is the most likely to bear fruit."

"And that's conveniently been thrown out?" said Walker, a knot of frustration forming between his eyebrows.

"Because of the smear against Maddox," said Taylor. "Who

instigated it in the aftermath of three killings which until now looked unconnected and completely random."

She was interrupted by the waitress returning with their drinks, and once she had gone Taylor looked around the table, her expression pensive. Each of the faces looking back was determined. It was Reilly who broke the silence.

"Guv, we might have got a lead from our visit to SCAR," she said, passing out the copied pages from Paul Finnegan's dossier. Taylor gave them a speed read, passing them on to Macpherson who gave a harrumph of approval.

"Call it good luck or bad fortune," said Taylor. "But what started as looking for little more than a junkie window-breaker has landed us slap bang in the middle of something that's going to reshape the landscape of this city for years to come." Each of her team shifted in their seats, the electricity of imminent action sending a jolt of motivation through them all.

"So, here's what we know for sure," she continued. "And here's where we're going to start…"

47

"John. An unexpected pleasure. I don't suppose you're here to give me some good news on the rates I'm paying for imports?"

Barrett gave Colm Casey a cool look, waiting until his PA had closed the door. Casey chuckled and offered a chair.

"What about a bloody big pair of scissors to cut the red tape holding up my shipments from Europe? Whoever agreed to run a bloody border down the Irish Sea needs stringing up."

"Pressing issues no doubt, Colm, however, I'm sure you know why I'm here," said Barrett, easing himself into the proffered armchair.

"Drink?"

"Before lunch is a bit too early for me," said Barrett.

"It's never too early for a drop of Jameson. My oul man had it in his porridge every morning and didn't do him a damn bit of harm." Casey slugged a measure of the peaty spirit into a tumbler and took a sip.

"Maybe if he'd postponed the pleasure until the end of the day he might not have been so concerned with driving straight that he missed the UFF kill squad following him." Barrett's tone held no animosity, just simple logic.

Casey's eyes narrowed at the statement which skated precariously between insult and poor taste. Then he laughed.

"It was his downfall, alright. He loved his whiskey more

than he loved us."

"Then perhaps you should learn from the lesson and avoid making decisions when emboldened by a belly full of liquor."

"Ah," said Casey, taking another sip, a nod accompanying the pointing of a finger in the air. "You're here to offer your condolences."

"I am here to remind you of the terms of our agreement."

"I don't remember signing any contract," said Casey, slipping behind his desk.

"Colm, I told you I didn't want a turf war, and that discretion was paramount." Barratt's voice raised an uncharacteristic octave. "The reports coming to my ear are that you not only missed your target but you left behind a corpse who will be identified as one of your close acquaintances. Now where do you think we go from there?"

"No one will be identifying Kevin."

"Oh really?"

"Yes, really. You're going to make sure of that because if anyone comes asking me questions about what he was doing in Beattie's hospital room, then I'm going to have to mention our gentleman's agreement."

Barrett gave a reptilian smile. "You think because of that I am beholden to protect you now?"

Casey took a few moments to ponder the question, coming to the decision he was owed much more than protection. Yes, Barrett had engaged him to make The Crossed Keys problems go away and he had been well paid, then when that went awry Barrett again had seen him slip the charges. If anyone knew the risks and consequences of doing squalid deals with duplicitous people it was John Barrett, so, Casey reflected, he should have known it was a slippery slope from the outset.

"I'm sure you understand the need for me to have insurance; look what happened with Maddox," said Casey, then in a gesture of peace he offered open palms and a shrug.

"Look what happened to The Monster when his term was up, maybe if he had put in some safeguards you wouldn't be letting me piss on his patch."

The two men stared at each other in silence, Casey breaking off with a reflective pout.

"Full disclosure, I'm as surprised as anybody Kevin had the tables turned on him. He was a loyal friend and I'll miss him. But there are bigger issues in play now."

"Colm, the people we work for..." Barrett stood and moved to look out of the window at Casey's yard and the hustle and bustle of the morning's ongoing efforts to unload a docked freighter. "They don't like independent thinkers, much less those who might raise questions of trust before any partnership has had a chance to adequately mature." He turned and studied Casey who, unperturbed, continued to sip his morning livener. "In the spirit of cooperation and to cement our future partnership, I'll have Mr Cullen's corpse taken care of. In return I want any more planned deviations shelved. There is a place for you, as long as you toe the line. Understood?"

"John," said Casey, with a tone of levity. "I am a ready and willing partner." He stood and offered a hand. "And in return for your assistance, I'd like to invite you to a celebration I'm planning, a wee soiree I hope will resolve many a bad feeling."

"And what's the occasion or can I guess from this morning's headlines?"

Casey's chuckle broke the darkened mood; the early bulletins and first editions had all run articles on the cross-community collaboration which would chase away the shadows of the past under the new light of sanctity.

"Think of it as a rising of the phoenix," he said. "And after the cleansing fire, we'll scatter the ashes of the past and usher in a bright new dawn together."

48

"Morning."

Shepard offered the greeting and a tilt of the head as he exited the convenience store, sidestepping to allow two contractors room to enter for their ten o'clock bacon rolls and takeaway teas. The men returned the gesture by way of thanks.

The shop backed onto a nearby housing estate and was fronted by a small car park, presently chock-a-block with vans and private cars from the construction site on the far side of the council pitches and an untamed green area which bordered the forested grounds of the former boys' home.

The location was far enough away to be discreet but close enough to observe the comings and goings which had quickly ramped up in the last twenty-four hours, not just in terms of site traffic and personnel but, at first individuals, and then in the last couple of hours small groups of onlookers who had amalgamated into one solid mass. The throng had been vocal as they were pushed back to where the green space met the roadway by the installation of interlocking crowd control barriers, a temporary solution it seemed as contractors set about driving posts to accommodate a semi-permanent and altogether more robust safety hoarding around the work site.

The man Shepard had struck up a conversation with amidst the crowd, and who had joined him in the walk from the field and up to the shop, waited at the edge of the car park. Shepard glanced to his left as a builder in a JCB digger rumbled across the pitted tarmac to undertake some groundwork. The area around the vehicle was cordoned off, discouraging access to the convenience store's neighbouring unit which was in the middle of renovations.

"It's a bloody sin," he said, anger, despair and a lifetime of weariness etched on his features. "They should be tearing the place down, not turning it into a place of worship."

"Beggars belief, alright," said Shepard.

"There's not a night goes past that what went on beyond those gates doesn't haunt me, and even in daylight, it's still there, mocking me. Where is our new beginning, eh?"

Shepard knew the question was rhetorical and just placed a hand on the man's shoulder in what he hoped was a gesture of comfort and compassion. The stranger had introduced himself as Colin, striking up a conversation as Shepard mingled with the crowd in an effort to get a closer look at what Corry Developments were doing during the initial phase of works which had begun, as promised, at a lightning pace.

Colin had explained that he, and several of the crowd, had been one-time residents of the home. They were now classed as survivors, at least in the physical sense. Shepard had seen enough comrades return from war spiritually and mentally damaged to know what it looked like to be dead on the inside. He had listened in silence as Colin relayed his tale in a whisper, and when the tears fell he had guided the man away from the barriers and across the grass for a coffee and some reprieve from the weight of his memory and the shadow of the old boys' home.

From what he had seen, the works were focused on sprucing up the main sandstone building. The gravel drive was being cleared of overgrowth and weeds, and several dumper trucks had deposited new stones which were presently being laid and raked to cover the old potholed lane to the main house. Beyond that, several outbuildings were hidden in the tree line, one or two illuminated from within suggesting either a similar clean-out was taking place, or an assessment was underway to establish how bad the dereliction had got.

Aside from those scarred by their experiences behind the gothic gates, a section of the crowd was also made up of protestors and placard bearers decrying the damage that the construction was wreaking on bio-diversity, nesting birds and the greater negative environmental impacts that would unfold when traffic increased tenfold once the new 'Super Church' was finally completed and began to welcome its faithful.

While he held opinions on both, neither particularly were of interest to Shepard at that point. What was, was trying to establish if Casey's man was to be believed and Stephen Scott's captors had transported him here for what he had loosely termed, 'a final gathering'. If so, where would Scott be corralled? In one of the immediate outbuildings or somewhere else, a discreet location set in the depths of the heavily forested grounds perhaps. That idea was more likely now since the carnival of contractors, protestors and police had arrived.

Those were the thoughts that occupied his attention as Colin continued to pour out his frustration that those who had endured so much had been left without recourse, remuneration or even an apology. The words washed over Shepard as he scanned the site, his years of military experience sifting scenarios as he planned his next steps, and then he paused, considering that his actions to save the life of one man may yield the opportunity to ease the torment by which so many others remained afflicted.

49

Taylor glanced at the clock and not for the first time recently found herself reflecting on how twenty-four hours could blend into a seamless blur.

The final round of discourse at their offsite summit the day previous had necessitated another round of tea and coffee and, in an attempt at meeting his five a day, a large peach melba for Macpherson. Reilly and Walker's update from their visit with Paul Finnegan looked promising so, adding that to the other leads which they hoped might establish a foothold in the uphill climb that faced them, Taylor had divided up the immediate tasks they needed to undertake. However, the frustration of inaction had blighted what had been a good start as during the day, they ran into roadblocks and delays in their attempts to schedule appointments or track down the contacts they had listed over the table at Butlers.

Taylor's phone pinged with a text message, drawing her back to the present. A quick check confirmed both the sender and that she could finally get underway in addressing the first item on her list. Her destination was a short walk via the canteen corridor and up a floor, the route taking her around to the shaded side of Musgrave Street Station overlooking the city's commercial centre and where, she hoped, a meeting with a colleague might add some meat to the bones of her theory.

"Jesus, are you serving your time with that one, Jim?" said

Taylor, coming to a stop alongside one of the blue baize cubicles that housed the team of Section Eight. The harried detective inspector sitting at the desk was poring over files and clicking and cancelling links on a joint operations portal.

"Can you please remind me how a good deed led to me dealing with your mess?" said Jim Collins, indicating an A4 list of names and headshots attached to a thick file full of material relative to identifying the women and children rescued from Hoey Cargo and Signal Foods. Carefully aligned alongside and fastidiously marked up were their statements on the criminal gangs who had trafficked them. "I mean this is bad enough, but when you factor in the work in following up on the drug-related that are dropping every bloody day and the grief over this Casey balls-up, Christ, I'm beginning to wish Happy would just fire me and get it over with."

Taylor gave a sympathetic wince. Leonard 'Happy' Gilmore was Section Eight's inspector, his nickname granted in ironic acknowledgement of his predisposition for being in a foul mood ninety per cent of the time and his hangdog expression. She shrugged and patted Collins on the shoulder.

"Bryce Baxter was your lift and it all led back there," said Taylor. "I guess me getting distracted with Rab Millar being gunned down was just your good luck."

Collins blew a raspberry of irritation knowing she was likely correct but no less thrilled about it. When Taylor had been called away in the aftermath of the murder of Gordon Beattie's right-hand man, he had been the arresting officer of an intoxicated and violent Baxter who had been threatening to set fire to his family. When Taylor's subsequent investigations into the murdered gangster Rab Millar had linked local solicitor Baxter, his father, and a number of other prominent individuals and charities to the trafficking gangs, Collins had been handed the unenviable task of collating information that would further aid the PPS in bringing the case to trial.

He spun his chair away from the workload and ran a hand through his floppy fringe, then smiled in spite of it all, a row of straight white teeth at odds with a nose that had seen one too many breaks and a set of cauliflower ears.

"Your messages made it sound like you needed something urgent?"

"I do, and I'd appreciate it if you kept this conversation between us for the minute."

"Go on then, you've got me on the hook now," said Collins. He reached across to the empty cubicle opposite and dragged over a seat. Taylor sat and asked her first question.

"How well did you know Oliver Maddox?"

Collins flinched at the name drop, peering around the edge of the cubicle to make sure they had the modicum of privacy he hoped they had.

"Ronnie, I'm pretty sure you got the same memo as me…"

"I'm just asking your opinion. You knew him in sporting circles, right? How did he come across to you?"

"Did I in a million years think he'd be outed as a child molester? No." Collins took a breath and considered his opinion. "He was a stand-up guy; charming company, good tighthead prop. I heard his speech the other week on tackling OCGs and thought things were looking up for once."

Taylor nodded in agreement.

"Did he have much to do with the investigation into Casey once it was up and running? Have the team sending reports, updates that sort of thing?"

"Are you thinking he was checking for the holes the Echo article blew up? That he had put Casey in the frame?" Collins shrugged. "We weren't sending anything more than normal. What's going on, Ronnie?"

"I'm just trying to get a handle on the man. I've something

on the go and the Echo article and some other information put him on the periphery. How did you end up on Casey? Was it an indirect targeting instruction from above as the paper alleges?"

Collins shook his head. "Christ, no. We took a tip from HMRC. The firm was already under scrutiny. The perp in an embezzlement conviction was trying to broker a deal over sentencing and they offered a route to pursue Casey on illegal fuel manufacture and tax evasion. It was during the course of that operation that phone and financial records linked Casey and a couple of prison officers. The follow-up identified the officers were deceased, initial reports suggested suicide but the HMRC informant provided information they were killed on the instruction of Casey. "

"What was the motive?"

"The thinking was they were hired muscle and they tried to negotiate themselves a better payday for their silence."

"So, the scope changed and HMRC handed it on?"

"There was a load of back and forth first between HMRC, our higher-ups and justice. They had to get the families to agree to an exhumation and it turned out one widow was keen enough. She was adamant her partner wasn't the type to sign off that way and he had been seeking help."

"Help?"

"For sex addiction. Not with her"—Collins raised an eyebrow and gave a small shrug—"And a gambling problem. Townsend had recently lost the house and their life savings."

The image of Maddox hanging by the neck flashed into Taylor's head.

"How did they present? The suicides I mean?" she asked.

"Townsend hanged himself. Plymouth gassed himself in the car."

"And Plymouth's story?"

"A drinking problem saw several disciplinary issues

culminating in an immediate suspension pending a conduct investigation. That exacerbated the boozing and he got lifted for being drunk and disorderly in a public space."

"What was the final straw that prompted his suspension?"

"He assaulted an inmate. The victim claimed it was a shakedown over money he was owed from Plymouth who was a mule bringing phones and drugs in from the outside."

"If Townsend had lost everything why was the partner so keen to believe he hadn't hit rock bottom and took the easy way out? Same for Plymouth? A PO heading for the inside would have his cards marked."

Collins nodded his agreement, the gesture suggesting this was a hypothesis that had been followed. He shifted his seat and opened another database on the computer screen, clicking through to the relevant pages of information.

"The two were enrolled in a rehabilitation scheme run by a local Christian group. Both men had been doing well, the scheme managers and the sponsors reporting both had made significant progress in their recovery."

Taylor scanned the appraisals, and although sanitised to protect the privacy of Townsend and Plymouth, the reports gave a good overview and prognosis of their continuing battle.

"Kicker came when we got toxicology back. Samples taken from both men post-mortem had identified an unusually high level of a synthetic opiate. It rang alarm bells because part of the rehabilitation was regular screening and both had supplied negative samples throughout the course and on the day before their deaths."

"Could the samples have been faked?"

"Yes, or they both could have legitimately fallen off the wagon but the consensus was both were taking their recovery seriously. Ronnie, here's a thing if you're going down this route…" Collins paused and skimmed through several more links in the database. "Both men had Oliver Maddox named as a sponsor."

Taylor didn't react, instead choosing to read through the enrolment documents and pledges Collins had brought up on the screen as he continued.

"Not a massive coincidence considering they were all in the same service at one point and Maddox has been pushing himself as an advocate of prison and mental health reforms over the last few years, is it?"

"What was the organisation running this scheme?" said Taylor her eyes squinting as she speed-read the remainder of the available information.

Collins gave a cough of derision. "One of these evangelical, Christian fundamentalist-inspired places. They call themselves, New Light."

"You sure?" said Taylor feeling a surge of adrenaline.

"Yes, New Light. One hundred per cent, did you never see the Spotlight Special on them?" Taylor shook her head and Collins continued. "I can give you details on the treatment facility if you promise not to say it came from me."

"Thanks. I owe you one, Jim."

Collins flashed a grin. "In that case, you can take some of these case files away with you. What'll it be? Unidentified drug overdoses or missing persons?"

"No inspector with you today, sergeant?"

"I'm afraid not, Professor. She's let me out on my own so she has." Macpherson offered a hand and the two men shook warmly.

"You drew the short straw you mean?" said Thompson with a chuckle and Macpherson gave a pained nod.

The detective sergeant wasn't a fan of the abattoir as he only half-jokingly referenced it, but he had long ago resigned himself to the fact that visiting was an occupational hazard.

The sterile and clinical smell of the cutting room had met him the second Thompson had opened the frosted entrance door, the persistent odour of ruptured bowel and open body cavity refusing to be overpowered by the scent of lemon disinfectant. Once white tiles now looked a little tired after years of soaking up spilt blood and gore but thankfully today, the centrepiece of the room, the four ominous steel tables, stood absent cadavers.

"Come on through, I've laid out some of the notes you requested on your call."

Macpherson followed the pathologist into the glass box overlooking the mortuary where a third assistant would record any specifics Thompson would note during the post-mortem: organ size and weight or the detail of particular injuries which might allude to the cause of death. The professor had taken up position beside a small, wheeled table which normally offered a space to bag and archive any physical evidence removed from the body so it could be analysed further. Now though, spread out on the surface, were a selection of photographs, charts and marked-up anatomy templates.

"I appreciate this, Professor, especially considering the time constraints you've been put under to generate a full report on the minister's death," said Macpherson.

"Thank you, sergeant. I have to say your colleagues on the new inquiry team were not so gracious in their request."

"Pressure from above." The DS gave a knowing nod. "I find people lose the run of themselves when the bosses start spraying the brown stuff down the hill."

Thompson chuckled, fully aware of how Macpherson at times endured an abrasive relationship with his superior officers.

"Is there anywhere, in particular, you want me to start?" said Thompson.

"The inspector was interested in the historic injuries to Mr Abbott and the minister? If there are similarities or specific injuries that could show an association?"

"The answer to that is yes, and no." Thompson followed up on the cryptic answer by selecting two of the anatomy mark-ups and a selection of photographs showing sections of both bodies.

"From the visible physical injuries, the scarring and suchlike, I can be confident in deducing both these men endured a prolonged period of abuse. The X-ray images we took corroborate that. They show up a wealth of internal damage, healed bones, prominent areas of scar tissue, et cetera. Interestingly, both men suffered a left-side fracture of the tibia. Experience tells me the injuries were the result of blunt force trauma on a downward arc of trajectory by a hard, thin object. Therein lie the similarities."

Thompson eased two headshots side by side.

"By measuring skeletal anomalies and various other factors we can determine these injuries were likely sustained between the ages of eight and sixteen, which although a bit broad gives you a window of time to look at. Unfortunately, due to the age differences it also rules out these men being abused at the same time so your window opens significantly."

Macpherson nodded. Maddox was older than Abbott, so both being tortured at the same time had never been a line they were following. Had they been abused by the same group however was a very different question. Maddox's abuse had also culminated in one very different aspect.

"Can you tell us anything about the branding?"

Thompson picked up another photograph, placing it on top of the others. It showed a close-up of Maddox's pubic bone and the branded symbol.

"As you can see, the brand has been burnt into the skin using a heated object. The symbol itself is not one that I recognise, but it appears to be intricately designed. As macabre as it sounds, it's possible that it could be a mark of ownership, indicating that the person who branded Minister Maddox saw him as their property."

Macpherson nodded slowly, the brutality of the marking on what would have been an adolescent or child even, sickened him. "Is there anything else you can tell us?" he asked.

Thompson hesitated for a moment before answering. "There were a few other things that we found during the autopsy." He shuffled through his documents until he found what looked to Macpherson like a complex maths puzzle; horizontal bar charts of varied colours were overlaid by a line graph and his stomach sank at the thought of the imminent lengthy explanation. Thompson continued.

"There was evidence to suggest the minister was a recreational drug user. Hair and blood samples provided a positive result and the liver, pancreas and wider endocrine system showed damage we would associate with low level, albeit long term use." Macpherson tried to follow as Professor Thompson's finger cross-referenced what he was saying to the detail on the charts, distracted by the thought that given the level of violence and the mental anguish that likely followed Maddox's abuse was it any wonder the man needed something to get him through his days. He tuned back in as Thompson's tone shifted.

"…more significantly however we discovered traces of a particular synthetic opiate. The primary drug is more normally associated with the medical industry and being a narcotic analgesic as it's primarily used for severe pain relief or anaesthesia. Considering the concentration, on balance, with not knowing what other medicines it had been mixed with, or the victim's tolerance levels, it is possible that the administration of this drug could have led to disorientation and physical incapacity which would then have been a contributing factor in Minister Maddox's asphyxiation."

Macpherson felt a chill run down his spine as he considered the implications of what Thompson had just said.

"So this isn't a substance you'd generally associate with a functioning addict?"

"No, this is the hard stuff."

"Is there evidence that might suggest someone other than himself administered this dose of…"

"Furanylfentanyl," said Thompson, offering a non-committal shrug. "It's possible but it would be difficult to prove."

The idea that Maddox had given himself a lethal dose of the drug in the wake of the allegations levelled against him was possible, yet something gnawed at Macpherson. Gordon Beattie's conspiracy theories and the whisper of mystery deaths picked at the scab of suspicion that was beginning to form around the investigation. If this was not a suicide, then it was likely the justice minister had been murdered. And if that was the case, was it possible it was linked to his announcement on tackling organised crime or because of what he knew from his time at Glenrafferty or even further back, in a darker past?

"Thank you, Professor," Macpherson said, feeling a sense of urgency to straighten out his thoughts and build a hypothesis that he could take back to Taylor and the team. "I appreciate your help."

Thompson nodded, and Macpherson turned to leave the room.

"You're welcome, sergeant. Send my regards to the inspector."

Macpherson gave a wave of goodbye, the cogs slowly whirring as he walked away. Thompson followed him out into the cutting room.

"I can make sure you get a copy of this. Just in case the inquiry team misplace it or forget to add you to the mailing list?"

The DS paused, his hand on the door which led back to the warmth of the reception corridor.

"The DI would be very grateful for that, Prof. Thanks."

Thompson gave a salute and shuffled back into the glass box.

Leaving the chill of the mortuary behind, Macpherson walked in a daze back towards reception, his thoughts jumbled, seeking a way forward through the sprawling labyrinth of complexities that were stretching out to link a series of cases now beginning to blur at the edges.

Exiting the building, he took the pedestrian stairs up to a higher level and as soon as he had a signal he placed a call to his inspector.

50

"Yes, I can talk. I've just finished speaking with HMRC and then I'm travelling back across town to see Eleanor Hammond," said Taylor into the hands free.

"The housekeeper?" Macpherson sounded surprised and interested in equal measure. The decision to approach the woman given the sensitivity surrounding the Maddox case and the review by the independent inquiry team was a ballsy one. Taylor picked up on his tone.

"I need to speak to somebody close to Maddox. Someone who knew his state of mind in recent weeks," said Taylor.

"Why?"

"Because something isn't sitting right about all this. Maddox was a campaigner for mental health, and you were with me when Michael Nendrum said he wasn't the sort to take matters into his own hands, so to speak." She exhaled heavily. "Eleanor Hammond saw him every day, she's bound to have clocked if something was off."

"Do you not think whaling in there uninvited is asking for trouble?" warned Macpherson.

"I'm not exactly cold calling," Taylor objected. "When we spoke to arrange it she told me she's been having some difficulties with the press intruding onto the property. Given the accusation levelled against her boss, I've a concern over her safety. Well, that's my excuse and I'm sticking to it."

"You don't need me to tell you the sort of toes you're

stepping on."

Taylor gave a snort of grim laughter given her partner's abrasive manner when it came to handling authority.

"I'm serious, Ronnie—"

"So am I," said Taylor more sharply than she intended. "Finn Abbott told us his crimes against Geordie Corry stem from something else. Now we have him, Scott and Maddox all linked to this boys' home, allegations of historical crimes and the bloody justice minister abusing his position to get a case up and running against a well-known Republican family. It can't be a coincidence that not a week after making a public announcement on a crackdown Maddox is dead and Casey's lads are free to snatch the person who supplied the information against him."

"Are you sure you're not putting more trust in what The Monster told us than you should be?"

"I don't trust a word that bastard says," said Taylor through gritted teeth. "But, I can't rule out that in his desire for self-preservation what he told us is true."

"That there is some ulterior motive lurking behind the Casey trial falling on its arse?" said Macpherson

"It's all horribly tangled but, yes, as surprised as I am to say it, I believe him. Look, I'm nearly here so I'll fill you in on a few details later that have got me thinking."

The silence that drew out was long enough for Taylor to think the line had dropped. "Doc?"

"I'm still here," he replied, choosing to trust her judgement. "Well, tread lightly, won't you? She'll already have had the third degree from the jackboot boys and the last thing we need is another complaint from a pissed-off victim."

"I will. Just a few routine questions about his state of mind and any recent changes to his routine. Where are you anyway?" said Taylor, keen to get off the subject of overstepping boundaries.

"I've just wrapped up with the prof."

"And?"

There was another prolonged silence from Macpherson and Taylor sensed he was trying to frame his answer based on what had just been said.

"Okay, don't shoot the messenger but you might want to ask Ms Hammond if she was aware of the minister's wee habit and if she's worried the hacks are snooping through the bins for evidence."

"Drugs?" said Taylor, struggling to keep the shock from her voice.

"The prof reckons he was a functioning addict." He paused and Taylor was again left with the hum of traffic. The news, while coming as a surprise, triggered a memory.

"There was a syringe on the floor when SOCO took us to view the body," said Taylor. "Was the tox report ready when you were over there?"

"Aye, and it shows our man was saturated with a narcotic analgesic. Some synthetic mix of premium opiate and God knows what other shite," confirmed Macpherson.

"Christ!"

Taylor slammed on her brakes. The traffic light ahead had turned red and the line of traffic had stopped. Macpherson's update had diverted her attention from the road.

"Ronnie?"

"I'm okay," she said, heart racing but moving off again with a wave of apology to the car behind her. "Those details I was talking about? I spoke with Jim Collins this morning and according to him, off the rugby field and in the bar Maddox was exactly the man his public persona presented."

"Hair and blood traces are painting a different picture," said Macpherson.

"Aye, well here's something to wrap your head around," said Taylor, indicating across lanes to take the slip road that would lead onto the A2 and the high road to the Maddox home. "Maddox was a sponsor for a drug rehabilitation programme."

Macpherson harrumphed an acknowledgement of the irony.

"And, the two prison officers named in the Casey conspiracy trial were being supported in that programme by Maddox. Both men initially presented as suicides with tox reporting an overdose of a narcotic analgesic during the secondary examination when the deaths were re-classified as suspicious. From the records, it's a substance often associated with sedation or anaesthesia."

"Thompson confirmed the same for your man," said Macpherson, sucking in a breath. "Ronnie, we need to start thinking about taking some of this to the DCI."

"I agree, but what have we really got to give her? Nothing that's going to have us re-investigate anything as a result of new information. There's the stink of something rotten, but at the minute that's it."

"Ronnie—"

"Have you had any luck getting an appointment arranged with our friend from the Echo?"

"No, he hasn't—"

"Keep trying, we need to talk to him about his sources and those previous articles they ran. The organisation Maddox was engaged with as a sponsor was New Light."

"New Light?" Macpherson's tone shifted. "Do you want me to let the kids know?"

Taylor considered the suggestion but decided that not clouding her two detective constables' thinking was the better course.

"No, let Erin and Chris come to an unbiased conclusion first. Once I've done speaking with Eleanor Hammond I promise we'll all sit down and work out how to present this to Reed."

Macpherson was quiet and Taylor could picture the deepening frown and the drumming of fingers as he thought. "Have you heard from your other friend?" he said finally.

Shepard's face flashed up in her mind. "No, so until he has a lead on Steven Scott's whereabouts we keep digging."

"You know the way this is going, we're probably digging our own graves?" said Macpherson.

"It wouldn't be the first time," said Taylor.

The DS grunted. "Aye, well let's hope it's not the last."

The rest of Taylor's journey passed without consequence and she had time to let her thoughts percolate on what they were beginning to uncover. Finn Abbott's paranoid ranting on the motive for the attacks on Corry Developments had, through the Echo's exposé, uncovered historic links between Abbott, Scott and Oliver Maddox with those connections going back to their time at Glenrafferty.

For Taylor, the former boys' home was fast becoming the lynchpin locking each disparate element together, first with the relationship link between the property and the three men, secondly through what Reilly and Walker's enquiries at SCAR had uncovered about the redevelopment plans, and now, armed with the information she had gained from Jim Collins, she had a new name entering the mix from a second direction, the contentious religious group, New Light, and the ties continued to bind. The organisation had appointed Geordie Corry as their principal contractor for the works at the infamous site and were, if the headlines were to be believed, ushering in a new dawn of cross-community cooperation in a philanthropic deal struck with Colm Casey. The same white-collar criminal had been implicated in the deaths of the two prison officers enrolled in the New Light rehab programme and one of the group's spiritual leaders,

James Phelan. These three, like Abbott and Scott, all linked back to Oliver Maddox.

She held the image of a snake feeding on its tail as she considered the overlaps. The unease was not helped by the information passed on by Gordon Beattie of a greater scandal just waiting to be uncovered at the heart of the establishment, with those at the centre fully engaged to ensure any chance of the truth meeting the light of day was extinguished. As each aspect swiftly gained a life of its own and opposing theories spun like opposite sides of the same coin, Taylor found herself agreeing with her sergeant that despite the potential for conflict, they needed to make DCI Gillian Reed aware of their findings.

As uncomfortable as she was with Beattie's theory she couldn't help but sense the timing of Maddox's public humiliation and his death coming so swiftly on the heels of his declaration against organised criminality and his pursuit of Colm Casey was fortuitous for those he had placed in his sights. What the catalyst had been for Maddox's sudden challenge to the criminal status quo remained a mystery, and now the man was dead and she could only hope Eleanor Hammond might offer some clue to the minister's mindset in his final weeks.

Her hour with HMRC had revealed little she hadn't already got from Jim Collins but had provided some context and a broader background to Colm Casey and the familiar inter-agency miscommunications that often ended an investigation before it could get out of the starting blocks. The customs inquiry into the Republican family's counterfeit fuel and laundering business had been kickstarted with a tip-off, the investigation quickly grinding to a halt on the morning a series of raids on border premises had been planned.

As the teams gathered for their briefing, word came down that a judge had reviewed the warrant and declined the request. With protests logged, it transpired the informant, a convicted fraudster, was also a source for the paramilitary crime task force and the information he was supplying them on the Casey family's involvement with dissident terrorism trumped grabbing Casey on tax evasion charges. Disappointed but not despondent HMRC had quietly continued to gather intelligence, identifying several shell companies already implicated as fronts for organised criminal gangs smuggling contraband and people into Northern Ireland and Casey's dodgy fuel outlets. Cross-referencing the company accounts with details they had garnered from their informant had flagged transactions linked to an Eastern European bank, to Casey Bulk Fuels and to several nominals now noted as persons of interest. A forensic dig through the paper mountain identified a number of these as regular payroll payments to several of the nominals. When a deeper dive into the affairs of those in receipt of the monies discovered two of the individuals were recently deceased, the case officer, already smarting from losing the chance to slap the cuffs on Casey, gathered what she could and passed it up the chain of command. Shortly thereafter, word came back that the justice department had made recommendations to open a new case. Soon after, Casey had been lifted and with hindsight, it didn't take a genius to work out who had instigated the operation.

As Taylor pulled into Maddox's street it was quiet.

A single police car was parked kerbside at the bottom of the driveway and a few other vehicles were parked farther along. Slowing, she flashed her lights and eased to a stop beside the patrol vehicle, lowering her window.

"Everything okay here, constable?" she said through the open window.

The man looking back wiped crumbs from an embarrassed face, the cupcake in his hand missing a large bite.

"Quiet enough now the rowdies have gone," he managed through the mouthful.

Taylor nodded. "I have an appointment to see the housekeeper. Can you log me in as a visitor? Detective Inspector Veronica Taylor. Musgrave Street."

The constable set the confection on the carefully arranged napkin protecting the dashboard, wiping his fingers on the front of his body armour before retrieving his notebook.

"Where's your observer?" said Taylor.

"She's up at the house," he said. "We're taking it in turns to keep an eye on the property after a few of the hacks tried to get photos through the living room window."

Taylor gave a knowing nod. "Is that where you're getting the free buns?" A timid smile said it was and Taylor knocked the Vauxhall into gear, offering a wave of goodbye as she drove off.

Pulling up outside the house, the second officer peeled away from the porch to meet her as she exited the car. Taylor showed her ID.

"DI Taylor. I've an appointment to see Ms Hammond."

The constable peered at the badge and gave a nod. "Youse must have heard about the buns?" she said with a grin. "There's been detectives coming and going all morning."

Taylor chuckled. "Any more hassle with trespassers?"

"No," said the officer, inclining her head towards the road. "There's a couple of photographers lurking in their car but they've not tried anything since we gave them an earful."

"Good on you," said Taylor. "I'll hopefully not be long."

The constable smirked. "You say that but be warned, you'll not get out of there without a cup of tea and a slice of something."

The constable's words proved to be true.

Taylor set a china cup of Darjeeling back onto its matching

saucer as Eleanor Hammond offered another slice of Battenberg cake.

"Oh, not for me. Thank you though," she said, the scent of marzipan competing with the gingerbread and citrus candle overwhelming her sense of smell.

So far nothing of consequence had been exchanged beyond pleasantries, Eleanor Hammond preferring to talk about the weather and the wider headlines rather than discuss how she found her employer hanging by his neck, naked and very dead.

"Miss Hammond," said Taylor, deciding the time to press the point had arrived. "I wanted to talk about the minister. Are you comfortable filling in some details for me?"

Hammond's knuckles were bone white as she cut herself a ragged slice of the cake, the knife clattering off the stand as she placed it down.

"I'm afraid I don't know if I've anything much to add," she said with a slight waver to her voice. "I told your colleagues earlier everything I thought they should know about that morning."

Taylor took a beat, hiding her thoughts behind a sip of the hot tea and finding Hammond's answer evasive. "I'm sure I'll receive their report in due course," she said, not totally sure that she would. "I was more interested in how the minister was in himself during the weeks leading up to that morning."

Hammond fussed the cake around her plate with a fork but made no attempt to eat any of it. "Uh-huh."

"Did he come across as overly stressed? Pre-occupied? Might he ever mention to you if he was or if it was due to any of the things he was working on?"

"Would none of his colleagues be better placed to tell you that?" said Hammond.

"Possibly," said Taylor. "But I think you're in a much better position to judge."

"Oh?"

"People are more likely to talk freely in the confines of their own home to people they trust, Ms Hammond. And in my experience, those people will pick up on slight changes of mood or manner that work colleagues would never spot."

"In your experience?" Hammond eyed Taylor across the table, still nervous but Taylor could sense an edge developing. Macpherson's words of warning echoed and she was reminded the woman had already endured the questions of the inquiry team and was bound to be prickly. Hammond continued. "Have you hidden your own pains from colleagues and superiors, Inspector?"

"Me?"

Hammond flicked her eyes towards the living room window. "The press haven't given you an easy time over the last wee while. Dragging up all that business between you and that horrible Beattie man."

Taylor felt the heat rise to her cheeks as she always did when she was recognised or acknowledged due to the reams of ignominious press cuttings written about her.

"I'd imagine in those instances you'd rely on the people you worked with? You're not alone in facing the fallout, I mean. You have colleagues who went through it with you," said Hammond.

"The service offers me the support I need," said Taylor, unsure if it was a deliberate observation to throw her off her line of questioning or a roundabout way of asking how one deals with sudden press intrusion. "What about you? Is there anyone you can confide in about the experience you've been through? It can't have been easy discovering the minister like that."

Hammond blinked hard, as though smashing her eyelids together might erase the horror of the memory. When she picked up her teacup her hand was trembling.

"It's not the first suicide I've seen," she said. "My sister killed herself when I was a teenager. I found her."

"I'm so sorry to hear that," said Taylor easing forward in her chair.

"It was a long time ago as you can imagine," said Hammond with a self-deprecating smile. "But I'd be lying if I said what happened to Oliver hasn't brought all that back."

"Of course." Taylor reached out across the small table and laid a hand over Hammond's. "It's completely understandable."

"The thing is she was a troubled soul, Rebecca. Nowadays there would be a medical diagnosis for it but then it was just bad behaviour. She had my parents at their wits' end."

Taylor said nothing, letting Hammond talk and hoping the confession may continue to reveal parallels with the present. "In the end, it was my grandfather who stepped in. He was a clergyman and used his influence to get Rebecca treatment." When Hammond looked up, her eyes were glossy with tears.

"Ms Hammond?"

"Rebecca confessed things to me. Dreadful things. Abominations carried out by the people who she had been sent to for help."

Taylor's blood ran cold, the hair on the back of her neck prickling, Finn Abbott's rage and frustration for those with no voice echoing from beyond the grave. "Did you tell your parents about what she said?"

"This was a different time, Inspector. A time when those with influence were held in higher esteem and anything to upset the status quo was swept under the carpet. Especially if it was coming from a difficult child. I told my mother and she said she would deal with it. I was never to speak of it again."

The weeks of investigation and the days of recent revelation blurred as Eleanor Hammond chased her tea around the cup with a teaspoon. For Taylor, the sound and the action triggered deep memories; those of her father's wake surfaced, his colleagues and family doing the same while talking in whispers, the same sound coming from the kitchen in later days as her mother stirred her tea in a trance until it was cold. Macpherson's confession about her father raising questions over the boys' home she now believed held significance in Abbott's allegations, Scott's kidnap and possibly the murder of Maddox, his prison service colleagues and a religious pastor all left her feeling adrift.

"Ms Hammond, this might be important," she said, easing closer to the housekeeper. "Did you ever tell this to the minister?"

She had expected hesitation but there was none. Hammond nodded. "Yes. I told Oliver about my sister."

"Okay. I know this is difficult but do you remember if you told him or he asked you?"

"What difference would that make?"

"Humour me," said Taylor.

Hammond thought about it, her eyes closed as she pondered.

"I told him my sister had died," she said eventually with a shrug. "A general conversation, quite early on in my tenure working here. It was a discussion about family, did I have siblings, were my parents still alive et cetera."

"Okay," said Taylor, nodding.

"It was more recently he asked about specifics and I think it has a bearing on your original question."

"His demeanour?" said Taylor.

"Yes, and why he asked about Rebecca." Hammond cast a look into the middle distance. "He had been championing mental health provision in prisons and other judicial settings and trying to address this ghastly rise in drug overdoses. I presumed he felt some first-hand context might assist him."

Taylor bit down on her lip, trying to unpick the loose

thread from a myriad of competing thoughts as Hammond continued. "When I met him, Oliver was a man full of verve with the desire to move society onto a better path but he was becoming frustrated. I could see the effort was wearing him down when support from the party or his cross-community partners was not forthcoming. Some of these frustrations you'll be well aware of."

"Me?"

"Yes. He followed your struggles against organised crime quite closely."

Taylor must have looked surprised, Hammond asking, "You never met him?"

"No," said Taylor with a shake of her head.

"Well he knew of you and I believe he was as frustrated as you are that these people seem to continually find ways to evade justice."

Thrown slightly by the revelation she had been under quiet scrutiny but buoyed by Hammond's growing candour Taylor decided to move onto a more sensitive topic. "Ms Hammond, Eleanor, what I'm about to ask you will be taken in the strictest confidence. It won't be entered into any reports I write up."

Hammond offered the slightest of nods.

"Were you aware the minister was using narcotics?"

"As I said, his work was wearing him down." Hammond offered a reflective shrug. "I empty the bins and yes, I think perhaps he had become more reliant on prescription painkillers and Cabernet Sauvignon of late."

"But you're not aware of anything else? No sign of other paraphernalia, foils, needles, syringes?"

Hammond's expression soured. "Only that one morning…"

"You're sure?"

"I'm sure given all I know about Oliver Maddox that the

man was not a hard drug user," said Hammond, nodding. "His goal in life was to put a stop to the cancer of it poisoning the community and lining the pockets of thugs."

Taylor gave a short nod and allowed the woman a second of composure. "Eleanor, I'm considering a theory and depending on your answer it might help me in identifying if there was a catalyst for the minister's death."

"Oh, there was a catalyst alright."

Taylor blinked, sat back in her chair and regarded the woman. Hammond sat with her hands in her lap, her eyes downcast as though embarrassed at the outburst. "You think you know a reason why Oliver Maddox killed himself?" said Taylor.

"Or was backed so far into a corner he felt he had no other choice, Inspector," she said quietly, before adding. "There will be those, like your colleagues earlier, who believe it was the burden of those cruel stories in the paper. It's all too easy for some to believe there is no smoke without fire and you know what happens next, what do they call it these days, cancelling somebody?"

Taylor waited as Hammond rubbed her hands over her knees. "Others will blame his decline on the collapse of recent trials, and the failure to find any traction in addressing the epidemic of drug overdoses and the rise of service suicides. They'll say that pushed him over the edge, but I believe the catalyst was your recent success."

"I don't understand," said Taylor.

"I've told you he was down, stressed. Depressed maybe, but he was re-energised when you disrupted that trafficking ring and rescued those women and children."

Taylor shifted in her seat. The revelation was not one she had been expecting to hear.

"He seemed to find a clarity the aftermath which he hadn't had in recent months. I don't mean to embarrass you."

"No, it's just…" Taylor paused unsure what to say, self-consciously aware of her own frustrations in the aftermath of Hoey Cargo and in finding herself on the sidelines of the major inquiry into finding those ultimately responsible. Yes, they had achieved some success and rounded up bit players but the organisers remained free. If Maddox had felt the same, was it because he had realised his own powers of office were equally impotent in digging out the rotten roots of corruption or was it more acute, a pervasive guilt over past transgressions that had suddenly and very publicly come back to haunt him. Could it be the desire for absolution which led to his pursuit of Colm Casey and to those others he had mentioned in his speech, those he referred to as the organisers of crime and their enablers? Taylor felt the ethereal touch of past and present descend like a fog to draw an impenetrable veil over each thread she was trying to unpick and stitch onto the next.

Hammond seemed to sense the uneasiness and brushed down the hem of her skirt. Rising to her feet she beckoned Taylor to join her.

"What you must know, Inspector, is faith was important to Oliver. Faith in the systems he represented and faith in God." Hammond led the way from the formal living room out into the reception hall and then along a short wood-panelled hallway.

"His ex-boss, Michael Nendrum mentioned to me the minister's faith may have been a barrier in garnering support from party colleagues in pushing through his reforms."

"Only because Oliver had chosen a church which sought to promote the tenets of forgiveness and mercy. One that chose to redeem those cast out rather than coddle those who could place the most into the collection plate."

Sentiments that were not quite what Taylor had gleaned from Collins and her DC's inquiries about New Light but she kept the opinion to herself. "I understand several of those who worshipped with him have passed quite recently too," she said instead. "Might those bereavements alongside his other frustrations have been a setback and led him into taking uncharacteristic risks?"

"What does your gut say about Oliver?" Eleanor asked.

Taylor looked at her. The housekeeper's gaze was steady as she delivered the question. Was it a test? Would the answer dictate whether the door was opened or it was time that she was shown out? Hammond had paused at the last door on the right, her palm settled over the brass handle.

"I don't think the minister killed himself," said Taylor. Hammond gave a tired smile, as though finally she could pass over her burden and take some rest. Taylor continued into her silence.

"I think the minster was beholden to others who were directing him to do their bidding. Whether he was under duress or not, it's my belief the revelations in the Echo bear some degree of weight and that either through action or omission the minister was equally culpable in the crimes that took place at the boys' home. I think something finally broke the hold over him and he planned to expose those who were manipulating him and likely other figures of high standing."

It was as Hammond had asked, her gut feeling. Everything seemed to hinge on Maddox and Glenrafferty.

"I have something you need to see," said Hammond, opening the door to offer access to the room beyond.

Taylor's brows lifted in surprise as the visit in which she had hoped to learn more about Maddox the man continued to prove altogether more illuminating. The inspector took a quick glance before committing, then stepped into what could be described as a snug.

"What is it I'm seeing?"

The room had no windows. A bookcase dominated one

wall and opposite, Hammond indicated a nest of tables beside a sagging twin sofa. On the uppermost surface was a collection of pocketbooks not dissimilar to her own, a dozen or so piled neatly beside a plastic document folder.

"After the conversations I had with your colleagues earlier today, I think you are the only one who will be willing to make use of them."

"Them being?"

"Oliver kept meticulous notes," said Hammond and made to close the door, offering Taylor some privacy to read Maddox's diaries, if that's what they were and as she did a wave of emotion caught in the housekeeper's throat.

"Rebecca carried that mark, Inspector," she said in a hoarse whisper. "The same mark I saw branded on Oliver."

With that, the door closed and with a hand trembling in anticipation Taylor picked up the document wallet. The page inside had the trappings of a legal document, signed by Oliver Maddox and witnessed by two others, the first being Steven Scott and the other, Pastor James Phelan.

'I, Oliver Charles Maddox, in sound mind and in the presence of the undersigned, hereby submit a true and accurate record of events. This is my confession…'

51

Buoy Park sat in the heart of the city centre, a stone's throw from St Anne's Cathedral, Belfast Central Library and the site which since 1886 had been home to The Belfast Telegraph.

Now though, The Sixth, as the newspaper HQ had been renamed, offered a state-of-the-art workspace for global brands seeking a prestige property in a prime location.

"Sad to see the old girl sold up. Those walls have soaked up more stories than ever hit the front page."

Taylor thought Reg McGarrity might shed a tear as he looked across the road from where they sat on a bench in the park. The three large buoys which stood in honour of Belfast's maritime past and lent the park its name cast shadows towards the old media building. The industries both represented had suffered a long decline over the years, unable to keep step with the march of progress.

Shipbuilding had been thrown a lifeline in the growth of renewable energy, the Harland and Wolff shipyard once renowned for producing the iconic Titanic was now constructing wind turbines, while the tactile touch of newsprint was rapidly being replaced by the cool glow of digital media for which the city was becoming a mecca.

"At least they didn't bulldoze her and build more of those monstrosities," said Macpherson indicating the recent soaring glass and steel towers which had sprung up to shadow a cityscape once dominated by church spires, linen mills and

Venetian gothic architecture. He seemed to have been gripped by a level of nostalgia, gazing out at the buildings which had once formed the backbone of Belfast.

Taylor let her own gaze drift and in doing so was left with no doubt that the precious past was losing the war to the onslaught of modernity, and she suddenly felt fearful that if the questions she had for the Echo reporter couldn't offer her some clarity, it wouldn't just be bricks and mortar lost to history but the truth and an opportunity to put right the wrongs which had been allowed to penetrate the foundations on which modern Belfast had been built.

It had taken much more time to track McGarrity down than it had to entice him into a meeting. When Macpherson called to say the reporter was interested in talking she was working her way through Maddox's notebooks, and eagerly suggested they needed to meet immediately. At first, McGarrity was suspicious but then the incentive she had offered was so well sugared it would have taken the most puritan of hacks to turn their nose up. With all arranged, Taylor had taken a brief detour on her way, depositing the items Eleanor Hammond had gifted her with the one person in the city with whom she believed they would remain safe.

Now they were sitting opposite the great door to St Anne's and just across from The Belfast Echo's small offices which ironically shared the same block as the police ombudsman's office. The breakfast at Butler's following her confrontation with Rosie Bush felt like it had taken place a long time ago now, the varied threads running through each loosely connected case seemed to be drawing together all at once.

Beattie's tale that Maddox's untimely accident was likely suspicious seemed, at least in part, to hold weight, especially when considered alongside his contentious speech on reforms and the deaths of Pastor Phelan and the two prison officers to whom he could now be linked. All of which had thrown up a number of unpalatable coincidences and an equal number of unanswered questions.

As a foil to the suggestion of foul play and to ensure they were steering around any potential bias, Carrie had presented Professor Thompson's findings and the SOCO report from Seapark. While both Finn Abbott and Oliver Maddox presented with old wounds that, it could be argued, stemmed from similar adolescent abuse and trauma, the cause of Abbott's death was clear cut: a result of impact injuries. Maddox's verdict was open. As explained to Macpherson, although there was evidence of drug use, the manner of the death could not be proven as drug related and, physiologically speaking anyway, by means of strangulation with the evidence leaning heavily towards an episode of auto-erotic asphyxiation gone tragically wrong.

Neither of these facts helped Taylor resolve her immediate problem of answering why Geordie Corry was the recipient of Abbott's ire or in proving foul play in respect of Maddox. The historic bent could potentially serve to launch a re-investigation surrounding events at Glenrafferty but only if she could convince her superiors it warranted the spend and it was in the public interest. In the end, it had been Reilly and Walker's discovery in Paul Finnegan's office which had provided some momentum and it was that which had led Taylor and Macpherson to be brandishing photocopies of old Echo headlines to the man named in the byline.

"You know I can't reveal sources? Not off the record, not even in court," said McGarrity.

Taylor nodded. He appeared slovenly. He had a receding chin that was unshaven and there was the redness of eczema under the five o'clock shadow. His hair needed a good wash and dandruff dusted the shiny collar of a suit that was held together more by fortuity than fineness of thread. It was a look that reminded her of a certain shambling television detective, that, along with a shrewdness that lay behind his beady eyes.

"At the minute we're interested in the background and build-up to your hatchet job on Oliver Maddox and his connections to the New Light Church."

"New Light?" McGarrity's eyes narrowed and his nose twitched, the scent of a story in the air.

"You've written a few pieces on the rise from culchie cult to big-time enterprise." She offered up the photocopy of McGarrity's story on the organisation's funding crisis, the piece detailing several donations from questionable sources. Front and centre of the accompanying piece was a photograph of the justice minister and one of the founding members, Pastor James Phelan.

"Not much for me to add," said McGarrity with a petulant pout.

"But it was you that broke the story," said Taylor. "Even though the big boys managed to muscle you off the scoop."

McGarrity tried not to look bitter but couldn't hide it, Taylor's assessment being crudely accurate. The reporter's nose often led him away from the safe harbours of abrasive political stalemate or regurgitating the same headlines as the rest of the press pack. In seeking the story behind the headlines, McGarrity regularly placed himself in danger, often reputationally as he confronted those at the heart of Stormont over spending anomalies and political donations, but also physically when it came to shining a spotlight on crimes as diverse as counterfeit fuel laundering, puppy farming and paramilitary-led Ponzi schemes.

"They did that alright. Arseholes," grunted McGarrity.

"That's why they say never trust the press," said Macpherson with a wry smile.

"Funny how you can change that to police and it works just as well."

Macpherson chuckled, offering acknowledgement to the barbed touché. McGarrity held the copied article at length and scanned his words.

"They thought they had scored a thirty-yard free kick getting you lot to investigate Mickey Mallon but he was a stooge. Yes, he was named as the treasury secretary but he'd no more free rein than the man on the moon. He was a scapegoat and shifting the story to focus on him meant the real story died," said McGarrity. He placed a dirty fingernail on the image of Phelan. "There weren't too many on the inside who shed a tear when they heard what happened to this one either."

"What led you to be looking at them in the first place?" said Taylor.

"Just what you said. I started to hear more and more about this tight-knit, happy-clappy clan expounding their version of the gospel from the peat bogs to the big city. At first, I was interested in how quickly they were adding recruits. This was back when I started to notice people handing out Bible tracts to the homeless, in addiction shelters, and outside schools." McGarrity paused in his reminiscence. "When I spoke to a few of them they were charming enough, full of the fervour of the believer doing God's work. I suppose I wanted to know how they could suddenly afford to be buying up swathes of Belfast with little or no legitimate source of income."

"Which brought you Mallon?"

McGarrity nodded. "It's like any commercial entity, really. They have to report finances, funding, and expenses, and appoint people to the usual positions. When I saw Mallon was involved it got me digging. He had been done for tax evasion and fraud which is what got him drummed out of politics. It didn't stop him from being able to open and close a dozen businesses owing significant debts and holding on to his clients' money though."

"Were you thinking he was siphoning revenue and pushing it through New Light?"

"There was a small group of founding members who had big designs on what New Light could become. Phelan being one." McGarrity paused to consider the right word. "This board of elders laid a foundation where members donated a significant portion of income to the church. That was to guarantee growth and to ensure ascension to the Big Fella's garden in the sky when their time came." McGarrity tutted and aimed a finger skywards. "These men were orators, good bloody salesmen too and it didn't take long before they'd convinced a few faces to sign up; their attendance drew more personalities until it became the place to be seen of a Sunday and where backroom deals could be struck in confidence."

"A brand new old-boys network," said Macpherson.

"One like I've never seen before. Judges and politicians rubbing shoulders with reformed criminals." McGarrity grunted, waving a hand as though conducting an orchestra. "Media hounds and the cream of the business community holding hands and singing hosanna with ex-paramilitary gunmen. It's quite the menagerie."

"I came not to call the righteous, but sinners to repentance," said Taylor "The Gospel of Luke," she added, as the two men turned their eyes to her. Eleanor Hammond's description of New Light and McGarrity's assessment fit tidily within the context of the verse.

McGarrity scoffed. "There's been plenty of that." He rummaged in his pockets, lost in thought for a few moments, and not finding what he wanted, he continued. "After the Good Friday Agreement, if you didn't choose charity, you chose the Lord. Now, I'm not saying everybody should be tarred with one brush, but you'll know yourselves, every gangster no matter their flag exploited it for all it was worth."

McGarrity rubbed thumb and forefinger together in the universal sign of money.

Taylor held her counsel, her thoughts drifting to one specific example of the manipulation he alluded to: Gordon Beattie, chair of the Inner East Community Funding Initiative before events spiralled out of his control and put him in a wheelchair. Accusations around the misappropriation of funding and the occasional headline aiming the spotlight on dubious financial affairs appeared regularly but failed to gather enough traction to secure a conviction. McGarrity's attempt at drawing open the drapes surrounding New Light had ended with Micky Mallon being cast out and the curtains being pulled back tight.

"Mallon carried the can because he had form but there were those who never really wanted him on the inside in the first place. He was a human sacrifice and the full story was buried under injunction. I wasn't allowed to go to print. Your lot wouldn't touch it with a barge pole and the PPS didn't have enough evidence to make a case in the public interest."

"Sounds like this was all to save embarrassment," said Taylor, not trying to keep the scorn from her voice.

"There were too many people of influence involved in the organisation by then to have any suggestion of malfeasance see the light of day," said McGarrity. "Everyone was happy to tear chunks out of Mallon. He was never the sort to make and keep friends so there were only too many willing to come out and pour fuel on the flames."

"You said something about Phelan?" said Taylor.

"What happened with Mallon was a catalyst. The fallout saw James Phelan attempt a coup to seize control of the board. Rumour was he had never been a fan of using influence to buy favour. He believed the aims of the church had been distorted, with the faithful becoming more interested in using the status membership bestowed to promote their own agendas."

"And Maddox was an ally?" said Taylor. The image in the picture suggested as much, arms round shoulders and warm smiles.

"That he was." McGarrity nodded. "Not that it mattered. Maddox had to withdraw support when the story about Phelan leaked." McGarrity flipped to another copied headline.

"He might have survived an extramarital affair even with it being with one of the faithful," said McGarrity. "But there was no chance once news leaked it was with one of the junior leaders."

PAEDO PREACHER PAWS PARISHIONER.

The headline didn't pull any punches, but then the accompanying image could do little to dull any blow. Although grainy and zoomed in, there was no mistaking James Phelan with his hand on a girl's backside and his lips on her neck.

"He wasn't that concerned about how his church might be perceived when this was taken," said Macpherson.

"Seduced by temptations of the flesh," said McGarrity.

"Could he have been set up?" said Taylor.

"Maybe, maybe not. The more digging I've done, the more rumours come up out of the muck. Let's say New Light policies and guidelines on professional and pastoral boundaries are loose, to say the least. "

"Is there any chance you were able to substantiate any of this? Formally, I mean."

McGarrity shrugged at Taylor's question. "It's there in black and white. That image isn't a fake. It is Phelan. Unfortunately, he wouldn't give a direct quote, and soon after, well, you know what happened."

She did. Phelan was killed in a road traffic accident. A hit-and-run by what transpired to be a stolen vehicle. The driver was never traced and the case remained open until Oliver Maddox had rounded on Colm Casey as a principal actor in his friend's demise. She now knew from his diaries how that had come about.

"Did you get the New Light take on Phelan's behaviour?"

"They offered a hollow apology for the harm caused and the promise they would strive to ensure that the broken trust in what should have been a safe place to experience God's love was restored."

"And the girl?"

McGarrity pulled a sour face.

"What?" said Taylor. "Is this where you going to tell me she was welcomed back into the fold in return for her silence?"

"She died. Drug overdose."

"Died?"

"Found a few days after Phelan by workers at a construction site."

"Jesus," muttered Macpherson. "You never thought that was suspicious?"

"Even if I did, a wee girl dying of an OD?" McGarrity had another rummage through his pockets as he thought. "There's a drug death every other day at the minute. It's an epidemic. This girl was turning her life around after a troubled start and then found herself in the spotlight. She was bound to fall back into old ways."

"She only found herself under scrutiny because of your exposé," said Taylor sharply. "Come on, Reg, surely you can't be totally heartless."

"On the contrary, Inspector. She ended up on the front page because James Phelan pursued a relationship with her and more than one of his so-called friends used that against him to further their own ends."

The three sat in silence for a moment, Taylor trying to sort through the mist of thoughts surrounding New Light, Phelan's downfall and Maddox's outing and subsequent death. On top of all that she was burdened by how far outside her own boundaries she now found herself. The core belief she'd carried for so long that the truth would out and justice prevail had soured with the realisation that not everyone who should wish for that to be the case, did.

"Do you think the same people held a grudge against Maddox? Made sure the allegations against him found their way to you too?" said Taylor.

McGarrity considered it. "Maybe. The thing with New Light is that there are factions within factions. Are they all bad?" The reporter shrugged. "I don't think so."

Taylor watched the reporter for any indication he wasn't offering an honest assessment, but she didn't see any. McGarrity continued.

"That being said, there is an element of sexual, political or financial exploitation being used to further ambitions and hiding in plain sight behind this religious facade. They'll tell you theirs is the new way to commune with God and not be burdened by the dogma and division of the old church while at the same time improving the wellbeing of those on the fringes of society."

"It's a nice thought," said Taylor. McGarrity grunted.

"You haven't come to me because you believe it. I've followed your battle with Gordon Beattie, Inspector. I'm willing to put my neck on the line and say your gut and mine are telling us the same thing, that inside that organisation is a controlling cabal willing to do whatever it takes to ensure their associations and the secrets they have accumulated in building their brand and their benefaction stay buried."

"What if I could give you those secrets for the front page?" said Taylor. McGarrity looked confused. "You're not offering that for nothing."

Taylor inclined her head in agreement. "I need the name of your source on the inside,"

McGarrity puffed out a nasal breath, his lips drawing into a tight line. "I already told you—"

"It's not just the happy-clappy who need to sacrifice a few scruples for the greater good," said Macpherson.

"Help us out and I'll give you an exclusive," said Taylor.

"Your bosses won't let you near a microphone—"

"Not me," interrupted Taylor. "But give me what I'm asking and I can put you in a room with Steven Scott."

McGarrity's eyes narrowed and he licked his lips.

"This is time sensitive, Reg, and it comes with the added bonus of me giving you a copy of Oliver Maddox's diaries." She nodded towards Macpherson who gave the reporter a tight smile.

"And I'm told they make quare reading so they do," he said. "You play this right, my friend, and my money says not only is Mr Scott going to be naming names, but you'll get to throw two fingers up at everyone who muscled you out of the limelight the first time round."

"We just need to know who is feeding you information from inside New Light," reiterated Taylor.

"Who says I've a source inside?"

Taylor gave him a look that dared him to refute her. "You didn't write those pieces without help," she said.

"And that photograph didn't take itself," added Macpherson nudging the grainy image in the reporter's hands.

McGarrity stared up at the huge buoys that decorated the small city centre green space, jaw twitching as he considered the potential payoff.

"Okay," he said eventually. "I'll give you a name but I don't know how useful it's going to be for you."

52

The administrative offices of New Light were situated in rented office space within a turn-of-the-century listed building overlooking a prestigious Belfast grammar school and adjacent to a popular city centre hotel.

"Sorry to keep you waiting."

The woman who ambled across the parquet had a pleasant smile and a warm demeanour. Her hair was pinned up and her fashion sense owed a lot to the fifties: a canary yellow blouse secured at her throat by an oversized ribbon was twinned with a plaid green below-the-knee skirt.

"We appreciate you finding the time to see us," said Erin Reilly, rising from the chair in which she had waited, and offering a hand. "DC Erin Reilly, this is my colleague, DC Walker."

"Pleasure. Sheila Mercer. I'll take you through and we can have a look at what you have brought."

Mercer beckoned them to follow and guided them out of the reception area through an oversized doorframe and along corridors which were resplendent with original features complemented by contemporary furnishings and design.

"This is lovely," commented Reilly.

"Yes." Mercer seemed to bloom at the compliment, pausing to take in the high cornices and some of the oil paintings mounted along the walls. "It's a beautiful building and it will be a shame to leave but how exciting to have a new start."

She beamed and ushered them into a room. It was large enough not to be dominated by a huge walnut conference table around which Mercer bade them sit. Arched windows allowed in bright sunlight, offering views through the trees bordering the playing pitches of the adjacent school where a groundsman meticulously mowed the grass of a cricket pitch. A side table held a jug of water and upturned glasses alongside some silver-framed pictures of the New Light board meeting with local and foreign dignitaries from across the political and social spectrum and faces from the media.

"I'm sorry, it's just me and not anyone from our board," said Mercer. "With the announcement and the planned unveiling of our new home, it has been all hands to the pump so to speak."

"It's grand," said Reilly in reassurance. Truth be told she would have liked to have got into a room with a few of the men who smiled out from the photographs, if only to get a true sense of how they came across without the glitz of what could only be described as religious celebrity, and to launch a loaded question in an effort to establish the firmness of the facade.

"Let's hope this is a fresh start and your good news doesn't suffer the same unfortunate business as the lot at MacArthur Court."

Mercer's mask slipped and for a moment her eyes burned, then she slipped back on her smile.

"I hope not. When you are fortunate enough to be gifted so many generous donations the last thing you want to see is those funds and the contractors' hard work go to waste. Such senseless vandalism, and although it's heartbreaking to us, to the congregation and to our sponsors, ultimately it is those who stand to benefit the most within the community that are really losing out."

Well rehearsed, thought Reilly, a nod masking the internal

voice wanting to ask about those sections of the community whom New Light deemed unfit to enter their temple. Walker preoccupied himself with looking along the row of picture frames.

"Have you ever met him?" he said suddenly, pointing out a photo of an Irish actor; the snap wasn't posed and captured a moment in conversation. The participants also included an Irish TD, a minister of the Stormont Assembly and two New Light board members. Each had smiles and glasses of bubbly in hand as they listened to a sixth man; Reilly didn't recognise him. He had an air of importance and wore tortoiseshell glasses and a five-grand Cartier wristwatch. A sponsor to be courted she presumed. Walker continued. "I was watching a drama with him in it last night."

Mercer giggled, her tone light. "I know the programme you mean, but rest assured he's nothing like the character. A delight actually, and incredibly generous in giving his time to help with our community outreach programmes."

"What sort of projects do they undertake?" said Reilly, more as a means of pulling the conversation back as opposed to being wholly interested.

"All sorts," said Mercer with a puff of breath. "We try as a church to make a difference in people's lives, by focusing our mission on homes, schools and charitable organisations where our ministry can make a positive difference." She turned the warmth of her smile on each of them and continued. "As you'd imagine, we offer scripture study and classes to those who seek to explore faith outside the confines of their traditional ministries. Our congregation boasts members of all faiths and none. Outside the spiritual, our help runs the gamut from the most essential by offering help to those in need of food and heating assistance to the more frivolous but no less needed, cookery clubs, book reading groups and date night assistance."

"Date night assistance?" Reilly couldn't keep the surprise from her voice and Mercer chuckled in a light tone.

"Maybe not quite what it sounds. It offers couples an opportunity to explore their relationship with God through their love of each other without having to worry about the cost or the effort of finding childcare."

"So it's a babysitting service?" said Walker.

Mercer nodded. "Of a fashion I suppose."

There was silence for a few moments as they all exchanged polite smiles. Mercer had yet to offer tea, water or any other form of refreshment and it was a tactic Reilly had seen employed by those wishing to bring the point of her questions to a head or to get things over with.

"We've been involved in the investigations into the vandalism against Corry Developments' recent works, and more specifically against your planned building at MacArthur Court," she said.

Mercer nodded. "I'm aware of the setback and the contractor assures us we can be back on track with minor delay."

"We've identified a number of people during the course of our inquiries and hoped you may be able to tell us if they were, or at some time had been, members of New Light?"

"I can try, constable, but you do appreciate people come and go? Some are not yet ready to take the love of the church into their heart."

"We'd just be grateful if you would take a look?"

"Of course."

Reilly placed the printout of Abbott and Scott on the table and Mercer, to her credit, made an effort in studying both.

"I'm sorry, constable," she said with a slow shake of the head. "Neither face leaps out."

"Neither of the two?" said Reilly, battling to keep the scepticism out of her tone.

"Perhaps if you were able to leave this I could pass it around. Maybe one of the more senior members or someone on the outreach teams will recognise one or the other?"

Reilly had the gut feeling the picture was going straight into the bin but she nodded.

"Thanks. I'd appreciate that." She folded the printout and passed it across, reaching into her pocket to retrieve a card. "I can be reached at those numbers or by email."

Mercer accepted both. "Can I assist with anything else?"

"You wouldn't be aware of anyone with specific grudges against New Light?" asked Reilly, unsure if Mercer would name specific names or throw out a suspicion but she thought it was worth a punt.

"Those who seek to spread the gospel find doubters and non-believers at almost every turn, especially now. In these difficult and secular times we seek to remain a beacon in the storm," said Mercer. "There have been minor incidents. Our street preachers were coming under verbal attack at one point, and some spurious claims have been made regarding our interpretation of God's word and his practices which some have deemed regressive or even repressive by others." She paused and shrugged. "Such is how people choose to think and we can only argue our case and shine by our example." Finally, Mercer stood. "I'm sure we will have enemies as long as darkness seeks to spread."

Reilly followed her lead and rose from the table, Walker likewise guided himself from his chair. They followed their host to the door and back out along the corridor. Approaching the front hallway, Reilly noticed an exhibition display she had missed on the way in. A tall banner, unfurled, with a collage of images under the New Light logo. A myriad of faces grinned out, captured engaging in various physical activities or taking receipt of certificates.

"My condolences on your loss," said Reilly, pausing and

indicating the smiling face of Oliver Maddox in life. He was surrounded by a group of teenagers who looked to have completed a charitable challenge.

"A tragedy indeed," agreed Mercer, pressing on to open the door to the reception and exit beyond. "Sorry I couldn't be of more help but rest assured if anything comes of this," She wafted the folded image of Abbott and Scott. "I'll be in touch."

Reilly nodded but her eyes remained on the banner, scanning the display and the individual snapshots.

"Thank you, and if anything comes to mind please get in touch. It could prove helpful in putting a stop to the vandalism," said Walker, filling the silence left by his colleague that was beginning to border on the uncomfortable.

Reilly shook herself from her scrutiny of the exhibition piece. "Anything at all, no matter how insignificant," she said. "We'll see ourselves out from here."

Carrie sat at the keyboard with Walker looking over her shoulder. Reilly marched impatiently back and forth behind.

"Erin, will you take a seat, you're stressing me out," said Walker.

"Anything yet?" said Reilly, pausing her pacing.

"I've got social media accounts, press releases, the New Light website and a dozen Christian bloggers. I'll find it."

"I know. I'm sorry," said Reilly.

"While I'm sifting through this, do a general media search. It might throw up a commentary or a statement from someone within the church, and it would beat wearing out the soles of your shoes," said Cook.

Reilly gave a snort of frustrated agreement and thumped down on a chair, logging in to her laptop.

While the visit to New Light hadn't yielded anything on Scott, Abbott and their suspected grievances against the movement or its members it had revealed something unexpected and potentially revealing. Reilly's interest, having been piqued by the image of Oliver Maddox on the display banner, had quickly been drawn to another face she knew from the team's discussions, Pastor James Phelan. The two were surrounded by a youth group and each young face was holding a certificate of accomplishment. One of the faces was instantly recognisable. A second, after some quick research she had also identified.

The first was Dylan Masters, a young man whose life had been tragically cut short and whose death continued to reverberate in the media and around political circles. His family, supported by a number of local MPs and sections of the press continued to call for an independent inquiry. Their conviction was that the verdict of misadventure was a whitewash due to an incompetent investigation or, more dramatically, a cover-up, the allegations playing out with regularity in the pages of the tabloids and on local radio talk shows.

The second was another victim, this time a girl called Joanne Gould. She hadn't had the privilege of the life or the support in death that Masters had. A victim from a young age, she had been removed from her family and grew up in the care system. Adolescence brought several stints in juvenile detention and a journey through addiction, which she survived although it didn't stop her life coming to an early end. Gould's body was found on a building site. She was nineteen years old, had been beaten, and died with a needle in her arm. Just one of the many recent cases that remained unsolved.

53

Taylor studied the dull swirling pattern on the worn carpet and began to think perhaps McGarrity had been correct in his parting assessment. The reporter had in the end not only offered a name but had generously scribbled out an address too.

Standing in the lobby of the named establishment her stomach was tight with disappointment and she tried to mouth-breathe rather than take in the heady scents of dirty mop water, boiled vegetables and bedpans.

"Detective Inspector?"

Taylor looked up. The woman who approached was in the process of removing a disposable plastic apron and wadding it into a ball.

"Denise Chambers," she said by way of introduction, dropping the used apron into a large pedal bin. "I'm the care supervisor this afternoon. Apologies for the wait, but we've finished lunch now and the colonel is being brought out to the garden for you."

"The colonel?" said Macpherson.

Chambers shrugged. "It's a nickname that seems to have stuck."

Macpherson pursed his lips and returned the gesture. "I did hear after the Good Friday Agreement he ended up in Iraq but I only ever knew him to be a copper."

"I wouldn't bother yourself over it. If it's not tales about the Troubles it's war stories from the desert. It'll be somebody's idea of fun but he seems to like it." Chambers beckoned the two detectives to follow her.

The route passed a nurses station then through a common area off which four corridors of single bedrooms ran at right angles and Macpherson found the layout strangely reminiscent of the old H-blocks at the Maze prison. A set of double doors led from the centre of the shared social space to a paved area and small garden.

"The folks will be straightening him up after his dinner. They'll be out in a second," said Chambers, offering the two detectives a seat on a worn wooden bench overlooking a bed of hydrangeas.

"How is he?" said Taylor, a waver in her voice. She caught Chambers' expression and expanded. "Is he lucid, I mean?"

"Good days and bad," said the supervisor. "He's had his belly filled so you can be sure he'll be in good form as long you keep him entertained enough to avoid his nap."

"Do you not remember him?" said Macpherson as Chambers retreated inside.

"Vaguely but only from the news or you and my daddy talking about him. He was long gone before my time," said Taylor.

"Aye, I suppose he was." Macpherson squinted into the sun which had crept above the perimeter wall and was bathing the garden in warm light, his thoughts searching for the last time he would have seen his old chief.

Vincent Edwards had risen from constable to detective inspector of Special Branch before heeding the call of senior management and undertaking the role of first district operational commander and then acting assistant chief constable. After eighteen months in the role, his superior suffered a bout of unexpected ill health which saw him promoted to the vacant position of chief constable.

Macpherson remembered him as a bear of a man, his broad shoulders topped with a boulder of a head. A hairline ravaged by male pattern baldness had left him with a glaring dome but it did little to thwart the thick black hair that wrapped around the back and sides nor affected the huge walrus moustache in which he had so much pride.

The DS caught a breath as he recognised his former colleague in the guise of a frail old man being wheeled out by a young member of the nursing staff. The years had not been kind. Macpherson could see the physical toll left by Edwards' diagnosis of lung cancer, an illness the policeman had battled in his own inimitable bloody-minded style, losing half of one organ on the way. Any joy in survival though had been lost as he was struck down by the onset of dementia in his recovery.

The nurse eased the wheelchair to a stop and engaged the brake, pausing to wipe the corner of Edwards' mouth.

"Here you go, colonel," she said in a bright Welsh lilt. "A couple of your old colleagues are here to see you."

"I didn't think there were any of them left," he grunted, voice box ravaged by too many years on sixty Bensons a day.

Edwards leaned precariously forward but was safely restrained by a lap belt. He favoured one eye, the other squeezed shut as he squinted at his visitors. Somewhere in the space behind the rheumy eye, a light went on.

"Robbie?"

"Good to see you, sir," said Macpherson clearing his throat.

"Robbie Macpherson," exclaimed Edwards with a chuckle. "Have they never managed to get rid of you yet?"

"Not for want of trying," said Macpherson, reaching out to place a hand on the other man's. The skin felt cool and paper thin.

"Who's the youngster?" said Edwards turning his unnerving squint to Taylor. "She looks familiar."

Macpherson and Taylor exchanged a look. Edwards' grunt turned into a staccato cough. He pulled his hand back and waved away Macpherson's sudden concerned expression.

"I'm fine," he said. "And I've not lost all my bloody marbles yet, no matter what they've told you in there." He jerked a thumb at the nursing home. "What's your name, love?"

"Veronica Taylor."

Edwards silently rolled the name around his mouth, both eyes narrowed to slits. A few moments later the good eye popped open.

"You're never Derek's wee girl?"

Taylor nodded, caught off guard even though she knew her father had been in Edwards' orbit.

"Thank God, she took her mother's looks, eh?" said Macpherson.

"Your mummy and daddy were special people, Veronica," said Edwards. "How long has it been now?"

"Nearly twenty years."

"Twenty years," echoed Edwards, his eyes closing and his head nodding forward. He stayed like that for a time and Macpherson thought he had drifted off.

"Sir?" he promoted.

Edwards looked up. "It's not a social call, is it?"

"Afraid not, we hoped to ask you a few questions."

"I'm not as sharp as you remember me, Robbie. My old memory, it plays tricks on me," said Edwards, tapping his temple and his voice breaking slightly in the explanation.

Taylor swallowed hard. The policeman was a tenuous link to her past and as she observed his frailty, the sadness of losing her father in his prime met the imagined grief of nursing him through a long and debilitating illness and the loss of everything he was.

"We wanted to ask about your involvement in the New

Light movement?" she said.

Edwards seemed taken aback, then shrugged. "When you get a diagnosis like mine you tend to suddenly appreciate the need for spiritual guidance. In our line of work, it's easy to forget there's a bigger picture."

"I understand," said Taylor honestly. Each of them had seen the worst humanity had to offer. Engaged in the investigation of beatings and rapes, infanticides and homicides, it was hard to square the idea of a benevolent deity when faced with the bestiality of humanity day in and day out.

"We spoke to Reg McGarrity," said Macpherson.

Edwards gave the DS a wry glare. "Not beating about the bush, are you?" He grunted. "So much for protecting your sources."

"It's as well he wasn't a peeler," said Macpherson, eliciting a chuckle from the former chief constable. The wheeze developed into a cough.

"What do you want to know?" said Edwards once he regained control of his breathing.

"Why you decided to feed stories to The Echo rather than raise any concerns you had with us?" said Macpherson, turning a hand to encompass both himself, Taylor and the PSNI at large.

Edwards dabbed at the corner of his mouth with a handkerchief and considered his answer. "Who knows you are talking to me?" he said, adding, "Apart from McGarrity?"

"Nobody," said Taylor, receiving a nod from her DS.

"Good," said Edwards popping the hanky back up his sleeve. "Good for me, better for you."

"That's a bit cryptic, isn't it?" said Taylor.

"I'm going to ask you two something," said Edwards, a gust of wind caught the tufts of hair that still stuck to his scalp. "Do you really want to know why I chose McGarrity over my former employers?"

"Yes," said Taylor empathically.

"Really?"

"Yes," reiterated Macpherson.

"Even if it means opening old wounds?"

Taylor and Macpherson peered at each other in confusion. "I don't…"

Edwards put up a hand and quieted Taylor. "Wheel me over to the pond, I like to hear the fountain and see the fish."

When neither of the two detectives made to move, Edwards rapped his knuckles on the arm of the wheelchair and poked out a bony finger.

"Just you two youngsters remember who holds the rank here. C'mon, the pond. And that's an order."

"Are you sure you're alright?" said Taylor, concern creeping into her tone as she shot a look back towards the doors to the nursing home's communal area half expecting to see one of the staff stalking towards them but, there wasn't. The garden around the pond was more exposed than their previous seat and clouds had rolled across the sun, plunging the spot into shade and dipping the temperature enough to notice.

"Most people think that taking the cancer was the worst thing that could happen to me," said Edwards leaning forward to watch the carp weave through the water under the protective netting stretched over the pond. "It's not even losing my mind. Things just haven't been right since I lost Blythe."

Taylor had never known Edwards' wife, but evidently, Macpherson had. His face pinched in a sorrowful frown.

"I'm sorry, boss…" he began but Edwards waved the condolences on.

"A time's coming when I'll not remember her. Or you, Robbie. But if you're adamant you want to burden yourselves and while I've what remains of my marbles then I owe it to her to tell you what I know."

Neither of the two detectives spoke for fear of nudging Edwards off his train of thought, both of them concerned at how much time they had while the older man was still lucid.

"A couple of the old boys convinced me to go to New Light when they heard I'd taken ill. The doctors hadn't much hope so I thought why not cleanse my soul of some demons and maybe beg the big fella upstairs for a few more months." Edwards gave a chortle and looked at the two police officers. "Never in my life have I seen a more dysfunctional group of individuals come together in a more incongruous setting. You remember the Hilltop pub bombing?"

The question was addressed to Macpherson who nodded. A small country pub had been packed with Christmas revellers when a Loyalist hit squad tossed pipe bombs inside in retaliation for a spate of Republican shootings. A wave of tit-for-tat violence bookending another year of Ulster's violent troubles.

"Imagine my face when I was introduced to the boyo behind that by one of your old superintendents and then the two of them taking turns on their knees to pray for me."

"There's enough have found a new start after the Troubles by turning to the church, sir," observed Taylor.

"Don't you kid yourself, lassie."

Edwards focused his good eye on her and cocked his head to the side as he regarded her expression.

"Oh, you're your da's wee girl alright. You no more believe in second chances than he did."

Taylor didn't reply and it was Macpherson who broke the silence.

"Reg McGarrity. Why did you go to him with rumours of Micky Mallon?"

"Because they weren't rumours and no one was going to

come investigating New Light for fraud and money laundering. Not with their who's who of members tossing pensions and God knows what else into the coffers. Imagine the lengths they'd go to to make sure that stink was covered up."

"So you thought if you leaked a few stories and McGarrity made enough noise it couldn't be ignored?"

"I didn't give a toss about Mallon and the money," said Edwards and at that moment Macpherson saw the spirit of his old chief constable overwhelm the fragile form he now inhabited.

"So what were you interested in?" said Taylor. "Actually before you answer that let me ask you something else. Do you remember anything about allegations of impropriety at The Glenrafferty Home for Troubled Boys?"

Edwards twisted in his seat to give a stern look with his one good eye.

"I had a look at the historical review notes," said Taylor.

"Aye, well. That's not one even the dementia is likely to let me forget," he said and Taylor nodded.

"Your name is prominent as one of the senior investigating officers."

"For my sins."

"Not much of an enquiry back then as I read it? Wasn't until years and maybe hundreds of victims later the truth came out."

Edwards' mouth opened to respond but before the words formed he collapsed into another fit of wheezy coughing.

"Colonel?" One of the care workers had popped their head around the doors of the common area. Macpherson was rubbing his old superior's back and Edwards raised a placating hand.

"He's okay," said Taylor with a wave. The carer didn't look convinced but further gesticulation and an unintelligible grunt from Edwards confirmed he was.

"Why do you think I'm seeking solace in the arms of New Light, Inspector?"

"Some might think you are trying to assuage your guilt for the part you played in a cover-up?"

Edwards dabbed the corner of his mouth again, a tired smile creeping over a face ravaged by the years and illness. "She's a sharp whip, this one, Robbie," said Edwards, then back to Taylor. "Go on then, girl. What is it you think I'm hiding?"

"I think the initial Glenrafferty investigation was shelved to protect sources or informants working for Special Branch or the security services."

"It was a dirty war alright," observed Edwards, the response not quite landing as confirmation.

"We've been looking into a series of attacks on New Light property and against a developer, Geordie Corry."

"Is that so?"

"Do you know him?"

"I do."

"Much to tell us about him?"

Edwards spat on the ground and Taylor took the gesture as answer enough.

"You see, I think you started to see familiar faces in New Light. Maybe you started to hear rumours of things you hoped you had left in the past."

"You're are like your da. He did a lot of thinking too."

"DS Macpherson says my old man had his suspicions about Glenrafferty and he was told to cease and desist."

"He was. I was the one that told him."

"Why?"

"Orders from on high, Veronica. For what it's worth you aren't a million miles away. I did see people who I knew were rotten to the core and I'm not far enough gone yet not to recognise when history is repeating itself."

"When Mallon got offered up as a convenient scapegoat you tried again, this time exposing Phelan and Maddox to McGarrity because you knew they were in some part involved in the Glenraffery scandal and you hoped somebody might recognise them and come forward to get the ball rolling again. We're in different times now, aren't we? You can't hide institutional abuse in the age of the internet and cancel culture."

"Maddox was as green as grass," scoffed Edwards. "If he had wanted to he could have turned, made a formal statement about what he'd seen happen at the home but he didn't. In hindsight, he was already broken by then. He was an adept, an acolyte. He was there because they had put him there and his career ever since had been directed by the same people."

"Who?"

"They call themselves The Crossed Keys."

Taylor felt a flush of nausea as Maddox's brand and the words of his confession flashed through her head.

"You understand that exposing him likely signed his death warrant?"

"I could see he hadn't forgiven himself for his part in what had happened all those years ago. Once he saw me, I knew it was only a matter of time before his conscience kicked in and he'd see the light, if you'll pardon the pun."

"The shame and regret followed him to his grave. He left a confession."

"Fat lot of good it will do you now he's dead."

"Maybe, but we have an individual I believe will substantiate the claims. He's an eyewitness. Another victim."

Edwards seemed to perk a little in his chair. "All's well that ends well then, that is if you can convince your lords and masters to re-open an investigation into the original complaint."

"This is what you wanted, isn't it? You sacrificed Oliver Maddox in the hope it might expose New Light as a safe harbour for paedophiles and rapists?"

"This isn't about New Light. It's about the men at the heart of it."

"Men like Geordie Corry?"

"Men like the ones who butchered Barry Toms and countless others to get their sick kicks," snarled Edwards, spittle spraying from his lips and dripping down his chin. "Men who got away with murder because they were willing to inform on their own side or do anything that was asked of them to keep their position of influence even if it meant sacrificing their own flesh and blood."

"Barry Toms?" said Macpherson, unsettled at the memories which surrounded the boy's name.

"Aye, that wee boy and a hundred others like him died to protect The Crossed Keys and their dirty little secrets," said Edwards. His eyes fell to the pond and then came back up to meet Taylor's.

"And so did your daddy."

54

"That's very kind. Thanks," said Carrie Cook, accepting the mug of tea. "You shouldn't have gone to all the trouble."

Her host gave a dismissive shake of the head as she placed a plate of delicately cut sponge cake on a small nest of tables.

"It's no trouble." The woman sat down. She masked a moment of concern with a sip of hot tea. "Have you news about my sister?"

Roberta Gould was a few years older than the murder victim Cook had come to enquire about and from the pleasant middle-class surroundings she had stayed a very different course to that of her sibling.

"I'm sorry for your loss, Ms Gould," said Cook, placing the daisy-pattern mug down beside the cake. "Your sister came to our attention during an ongoing investigation and I wanted to follow up with a few questions."

"Drugs, is it?" said Roberta, the conclusion dripping with disdain.

For the moment, Cook refrained from specifics.

Since Reilly had identified Dylan Masters and Joanne Gould from their pictures at the New Light HQ, she and her detective constable colleagues had trawled social media and newspaper and online archives for stories and links detailing the church organisation and their outreach programmes. As she sat this afternoon, Joanne Gould's sister was the third relative Cook had visited and she wondered was the story, or

357

the denial, going to be much different to what she had heard so far. A tale of tragic loss. A life wasted. A troubled teen trying desperately to turn their circumstances around. Cook took out her notebook

"The information we have from social services says Joanne was living with you prior to what happened. Can you tell me how she was? If she was having any particular difficulties around the time? You mentioned drugs?"

Roberta warmed her hand hands on the mug.

"Technically she was living here. By that I mean this was her registered address since leaving the unit."

Cook scanned her notes. 'The unit' referred to Joanne's most recent stint in the regional mental healthcare facility on the outskirts of the city. "She was well enough in the beginning but then after a few months began to withdraw," continued Roberta. She looked at Cook with an expression of sad resignation. "You have to remember neither of us had the best start in life. I was lucky to get away without suffering as much as Joanne did."

Cook nodded. She'd reviewed the family history and had memorised the lowlights of Joanne's time in the fold.

"There began to be periods when she would go days without coming home and we found out she had been associating with some of her old…" Roberta trailed off and Cook could see she was struggling to find a description of the people with whom Joanne had been associating. Friends certainly not being the correct one.

"She'd fallen back in with old acquaintances?"

Roberta nodded. "Joanne had been ground down by life. She was easily influenced and although I like to think she was dragged back, I know she was just accepting the easy route to oblivion."

The woman blinked away a frustrated tear. "We, my husband Paul and I, did our best to talk some sense into her but it was Joanne's decision in the end to come and ask for help."

"Do you know what prompted it?" said Cook.

"There was a spate of deaths in the city. Overdoses. I think she probably knew a few of the kids who died."

Cook nodded in understanding; the shock of her friends dying and the sudden realisation she may follow a similar path holding a mirror up to the troubled young woman. She was about to speak when Roberta continued.

"She spoke about being approached by a street preacher. Whatever he said seemed to wake her up to herself. She brought home a Bible tract and some information. When Paul and I looked into it they were running a family support group and a residential service for addicts who wanted change. It turned Joanne around. She was a different girl a few months later."

"This group? Did they have a name?" said Cook, already knowing the answer.

"New Light."

"And she'd seen the outreach scheme through?"

Roberta Gould nodded. "She did, and she was happier. That's why I can't accept what happened to her. How she died."

"Have you any idea if something had changed? If she was slipping back?"

A shake of the head and a look offered Cook an emphatic no.

"I want to think she was going back to help. To find some people she'd left behind and offer them help to face their demons."

"Is that something she was doing for New Light? Helping identify others like her?"

"I don't know… maybe," said Roberta, the words mumbled behind a tissue.

Cook made a mental note to follow up on New Light's recruitment measures.

"I can't cope, knowing she had made it through the worst but her old life still killed her in the end, and all for trying to do the right thing."

"Do you know any of her old acquaintances? People in that community we might be able to ask about her coming back and offering help?"

Roberta Gould shook her head again. "She never named names. I guess they had a code of silence to cover up the things they got up to to score their drugs." She blew her nose gently and cleared her throat. "I'm sorry…"

"No," said Cook, reaching out a hand and placing it on the woman's forearm. "I'm sorry we haven't got you answers yet."

Roberta Gould patted Cook's hand and wiped away more tears.

"When she went walkabout we used to find her under the Lagan flyover. Near City gate and the railway station. Always the same spot. A strip of waste ground below the bridge, out the back of some retail units."

"I know where you mean," said Cook.

"That might be the place to go if you want to find anybody who knew her."

Five minutes later, Cook was in her car, heading northwest, indicating onto the ring road and driving back towards the city centre.

55

The site traffic and the number of spectators had increased as works to prepare the old Glenrafferty mansion house in advance of an imminent press announcement continued. The breaking news coming through the New Light and Corry Development websites and social media pages was that representatives of the church, the developer and those who had assisted in greenlighting the project would be in attendance to officially break the sod of the redevelopment and announce the timeline to repurposing the former children's home followed by an evening of promotional engagements.

Shepard's eye divided the growing gathering into four distinct segments. The greatest remained the various contractors who now included electricians raising spotlights that would illuminate the driveway and the front of the main building where the photo opportunities would take place. As darkness descended, the glow would highlight the best of the old building's features while throwing the more dilapidated areas into deep shadow.

The sandstone facade to serve as the backdrop was currently getting a spray down by a team towing a bowser and power hose through newly-laid decorative aggregate. The crushed gravel, a mix of pink granite and quartz, was being offloaded in barrows by a bull of a builder in a shortened hi-viz tabard and then raked over and hosed clean by a colleague.

Next, roughly equal in numbers but divided by the roadway and their sentiments towards the project the two opposing sides to the development faced off. Taking the pitches and hemmed in by the main road, which hadn't yet been cordoned off, those opposed linked arms and chanted slogans calling for transparency and truth. The environmental protestors who had been forefront earlier had conceded ground, their messages replaced by homemade placards which bore slogans declaring 'EXPOSE THE COVER UP', 'NO ESCAPE FOR RAPE' and 'SILENCE=COMPLIANCE'.

Unseen to Shepard from where he stood near the back of the crowd, but vocal over a loud hailer, someone near the front called for an enquiry into the Glenrafferty scandal and the immediate cessation of works to protect any evidence of systemic abuse from destruction.

Across the tarmac strip of no man's land, the verge tapered up to a patch of weed-covered hardcore which served as unofficial parking for the forest trails which wound around the periphery of the home. Atop a soapbox and aided by an amplifier, another voice called out Bible verses and prayers for those in need of salvation. More placards waved in defence of the development, the signs bearing scripture and calls for repentance and to turn back to God. The voice of both mobs rose and fell in a concert of conflict.

Caught in the middle of the two and at a significant numerical disadvantage, just holding calm between the sides, stood a thin line of uniformed police officers.

"…and rest assured brothers and sisters Jesus hears your pain. He suffers as you suffer… as you have been failed so he shall lift you out of the misery of your doubt and shame."

Shepard slowly pressed his way through the group of protestors, feeling the tension and bitterness rise as New Light's speaker continued his sermon to a crowd misaligned with his message.

"…*Shame? It's those perverts who should be hanging their heads in shame*…"

"…*Monsters. They were just kids*…"

"…*Took their mummies away and then took their childhood*…"

"…*I'll never forget them finding that wee boy*…"

"…*Sure they never even found enough of him for a decent burial*…"

As he moved through the throng, the sense of injustice and hopelessness seemed to distil into a pressure wave of anger.

"Here, mate."

Shepard felt a hand tug at his jacket.

He turned to see Colin, his face flushed and a gleam of tears and fervour in his eyes. The man twitched, indicating the shop across the road where a couple of unmarked vans had pulled up in the car park.

As Shepard watched, the doors opened and several men got out. Several more bled from the alley at the side of the shops. None of them looked friendly.

"Colin? What's the craic over there?"

"Fuck that lot, mate," he spat, indicating the opposition. "Bible bashers covering up for their paedo mates. You coming?"

"Coming where?" said Shepard.

"The frigging peelers are doing nothing…"

"And what are you doing?" said Shepard, eyes on the vehicles and the men in the car park, quickly deducing what was about to happen.

Colin spat on the grass and when he looked back up his sneer slowly morphed into a snarl.

"If the bastards want fire and brimstone we're going to give them it."

56

"…as tensions escalate at the Glenrafferty site. The former boys' home which has been sold to New Light sees the evangelical church group's rapid expansion across the province continue… in laying out plans a spokesman said the development of the so-called 'Super-Church' will not only bring jobs to the local area throughout the redevelopment phase but will also see the organisation cater to those in spiritual need regardless of their current background be it religious or secular. Sources believe an eleventh-hour deal was struck between the church board and the site's current owner, Colm Casey, with developer Geordie Corry negotiating as intermediary…"

The news report continued to drone from the wall-mounted television screen as Taylor took her seat at the conference room table. Her body language and mood matched the sombre timbre of the reporter's voice. Macpherson squeezed her shoulder as he took a seat to her right. The rest of the team was equally subdued as they watched the pictures streaming preparations from the site.

"…Casey, who has seen recent charges of conspiracy against him dropped has called a press announcement at the site for later this evening. The controversial businessman had been identified as having links to underworld figures by the former Justice Minister Oliver Maddox who recently took his own life amid accusations of alleged historic abuse…"

"Will I turn this off?" said Walker, pointing towards the

remote control which sat beside the conference phone.

"Please," said Taylor, then changing her mind added, "Actually, just mute it."

The knot which had formed since the meeting with Vincent Edwards lay heavy in her stomach, a dead weight of unanswered questions and accusations following Edwards' revelations concerning the manner of her father's death.

Her frustrations aimed at the old chief constable were quickly deflected by Macpherson's reminder of where they were and that she was berating a man without the capacity to completely answer for a service and decisions long distant. The detective sergeant's half-hearted attempts to alleviate Taylor's deepening brooding on the journey back had not fared much better, not while he also struggled to come to terms with Edwards' bleak suspicion surrounding the historic events.

"Did none of you youngsters think of bringing any buns? My stomach thinks my throat's been cut," said Macpherson, reverting to type to break the silence and the tension.

Cook, resourceful as ever, slid a packet of shortbread biscuits across the tabletop. The DS forced a grin onto his face and offered his thanks. "So, did the holy rollers manage to sign up a couple of new recruits?" he said, managing to shower the tabletop with sugar as he fought with the wrapper to free a biscuit.

"I'm not sure Chris is the calibre of person they're looking for," said Reilly with a sardonic chuckle.

Walker placed the remote back on the table and pulled a face, huffing in agreement. "There's no way I'd survive if I was making their monthly tithe on my wages. They're not short a bob or two you know."

"Or friends in high places," added Reilly.

Macpherson wiped crumbs from his beard and regarded Taylor, whose eyes remained fixed on the screen showing the end of the report from Glenrafferty.

"Aye, and don't forget the ones that scrape around the bottom of the barrel," said Macpherson through a mouthful of biscuit. "They're not short of those friends either."

Taylor shifted her gaze. "Did they give you anything on Abbott or Scott?"

"A big fat zero," said Reilly.

"The woman we met played it cool. Didn't know them by name, didn't recall seeing them at any events or services. She did say she would pass out the descriptions and mugshots to their outreach teams," said Walker. "Not that we're expecting it to achieve much."

"But it wasn't a totally fruitless visit," Reilly offered to the bleak expressions around the table.

The DC sorted the paperwork she and her colleagues had worked on in the intervening hours since they had last all been together. Walker stood, assisting in laying the documentation out across the table which included the finds which Cook had helped in detailing.

"New Light runs several community outreach programmes funded by congregational donations and also from local sponsors," explained Reilly. "These range from food and heat assistance for those in need, and school runs and nursery services to non-denominational faith-based programmes helping those trying to turn their lives around."

"The druggies, drinkers and delinquents?" groaned Macpherson.

"Not the most politically correct way of putting it, but yes," said Reilly with a nod.

"One of the programmes focuses specifically on troubled teens. Those under the influence of gang culture or who have fallen into substance abuse or homelessness," said Walker, sliding a copy of the New Light mission statement and two photographs from the spread of documents.

"Joanne Gould," said Cook, taking up the briefing.

"She didn't die of an overdose," said Taylor, eyes narrowing as she recalled the severity of the young woman's injuries and the attempt to mask them with the insertion of a dirty needle. Before Cook could elaborate, the inspector recognised a second photograph from the selection Walker was fanning out. Another that had been handed over by a grieving parent.

"She did not," confirmed Cook. Reilly had taken a step back to stand beside a city map tacked to the wall. Several sticky dots and Post-its highlighted areas of interest.

"Over the last eight months we're all aware of the increase in drug-related deaths in the city centre," continued Cook.

Reilly indicated a dense pattern of yellow dots stretching south from the underpass of the M3 bridge into the streets of the city centre.

"These images are of eight confirmed drug overdoses of teens and young adults investigated since the turn of the year. We've been able to confirm that each of the victims had a connection in some form to New Light."

Reilly made a point of indicating eight separate red markers spread out from the rest.

"What sort of connections?" said Taylor, sliding the second picture towards her and lining it up with that of Gould

"The majority of this group were or had been enrolled in one of New Light's outreach rehabilitation courses," said Cook. "I met a few of the victims' families and spoke to a few people in the homeless community. New Light is actively recruiting from that base, and from conversations, they've been in all these areas."

"This young fella was a saint from the articles I read," said Macpherson. "I'd bet you a bottle of Bush his mother and half of the peacocks on Stormont Hill will spit feathers if they hear we're putting him into this group." His eyes shifted from the picture of Dylan Masters under Taylor's fingertips to Reilly's map.

"He volunteered with the outreach group. Dylan Masters was a peer counsellor and that brought him into direct contact with the rest," said Cook.

Reilly moved from the wall to the table and the display of information the three DCs had pulled together.

"He's here in most of the press and social media posts alongside nearly every one of the other victims," she said. "And with Oliver Maddox."

Taylor and Macpherson took in the snapshots and cut and paste of online archive articles.

"Should've figured he'd be in there too," whispered Macpherson. Taylor followed his eye and caught what he was looking at.

"James Phelan." The A4 printout showed a promotional image from an outdoor pursuits day. It also included a casually attired Oliver Maddox, Dylan Masters and three of the other young people in Walker's line-up.

"From what we can glean from all this he was the driving force behind New Light's youth programmes," said Walker.

Taylor felt a familiar tug in her gut as a previously unseen pattern slotted into place. She hadn't as yet retrieved Maddox's diaries and wouldn't until she had support and confirmation from DCI Gillian Reed that they wouldn't disappear into the evidence locker of the independent inquiry team.

Maddox's confession had started to lay the truth bare, and from her discourse with Edwards and his leaks to McGarrity, she knew Phelan had an eye for younger women. Did that predilection also fall on younger men? Although the girl he had been pictured with was certainly over the age of consent, whatever the relationship had been it was now complicated by her death and the passing of so many other young people who it seemed were closely connected to the pastor and his church. Maddox had protected Phelan and covered his transgressions, but that paled in contrast to the cover-up of the crimes which had ultimately led to their deaths.

Taylor removed the *Echo* picture of the pastor and his ladyfriend. "Add her to the list," she said. "Mr McGarrity tells us she found her way to a similar end as the rest of these poor kids."

"An OD?" said Reilly.

"Sometime shortly after Phelan died," confirmed Taylor, adding. "and pass this list on to Jim Collins. He's working to identify a number of missing teens and overdoses and I'd like to know if there's any more with connections to New Light that we haven't identified yet."

"Toxicology found a high dose of fentanyl in each of the young victims," said Reilly.

The image of the syringe lying at the feet of Maddox's swinging corpse again flashed vividly into Taylor's mind and then she imagined similar being forced into the arms of prison officers Townsend and Plymouth.

"If you cross-reference with Professor Thompson's preliminary tox findings on Oliver Maddox I'm willing to bet breakfast for a month that it's the same batch, or close enough," she said.

The shocked silence didn't last long.

"Something doesn't add up," said Walker. "We've got a group, all of whom would have been well known to others within a limited organisation and—"

Taylor finished for him. "And no one has thought to start joining the dots."

"Or somebody has been deliberately muddying the waters to ensure that doesn't happen," suggested Cook, Reilly nodding along to show her agreement.

Taylor stared at the wall-mounted map and then again at

the documentation spread out on the table.

The headway gained was cutting through her earlier mood for different reasons. On one hand, it looked like the steer Beattie had given her was kosher, on the other it was producing evidence and opening up investigations that were going to cause problems for a lot of people who would rather the spotlight fell elsewhere. And perhaps that was the point.

"This is good work considering the obstacles you've been up against," she said.

Cook's ingenuity coupled with Walker's inquisitive mind and Reilly's tenacity made a formidable mix.

"Thanks, ma'am," said Cook, speaking for each of the subordinate officers.

"If we stay the course and continue to treat Phelan's death as deliberate and Maddox's as suspicious then what's the connection to…" Reilly waved a palm across the spread of photographs, the question as much to herself as the team around her.

Walker broke the silent reflection after what felt like a long half-minute. "Are we looking at some kind of drug ring inside the church? Somebody utilising the outreach to recruit vulnerable young people to have them push product?" he said.

Taylor exchanged a look with Macpherson. The muscles of his jaw flexed and with a sigh, he slumped back in his seat. "Go ahead and get it off your chest for the good it'll do any of us," he said.

Taylor took a seat at the head of the conference table and bade Reilly to sit.

"When Beattie told us to look at the Colm Casey prosecution I thought I was going to discover Maddox was just another bent politician lining his pockets by shafting the competition for a friend. Closing down Casey and declaring war on organised crime left the field wide open for Beattie to make a return, especially if we cottoned on Maddox's death wasn't a tragic accident and found out who was behind the allegations."

"But who would—" began Walker only for Macpherson to interrupt.

"You hang on to your horses, son. There's a big but coming."

"Thanks to the articles you dug up, Reg Mcgarrity gave us some unvarnished truth about the goings on within New Light," Taylor began, following up with a summary of what the reporter had told them of the schism which had opened as Phelan attempted his coup to take over the board and reset the direction of the church.

"McGarrity also gave up his source on the inside and since talking to them, I believe Phelan and Maddox didn't die because of what they did, but because of what they knew."

57

The increasing bitter war of words that was waging outside the former Glenrafferty Home for Troubled Boys was interrupted momentarily by the blare of sirens and honks of airhorns as a police Land Rover and liveried patrol car ran the gauntlet of the narrow no man's land between the opposing sides.

Several of the faces around Shepard watched the two vehicles pass on the road below with nonchalant expressions, while standing at the back of the recently arrived van, one man was loudly derided by an accomplice for failing to shut the doors to the payload quickly enough. His actions to the layman perhaps lent an air of paranoia due to the increased police presence, but to Shepard's eye, he recognised the practised movements of maintaining operational security, even if it was just lip service.

Having walked the short distance alongside an increasingly agitated Colin, Shepard found himself on the periphery of a furtive group unloading plastic milk crates full of mixed glass bottles from the van. The cargo was quickly ferried away into the alleyways behind the shop which threaded into the bowels of the housing estate.

Growing up in Belfast and serving in most of the globe's low spots including Libya during the Arab Spring and Kabul during the worst of the Taliban's counter-offensives, the former special forces operator knew what the signs of imminent civil disturbance looked like.

"Alright there, Col?" said a man recognising Shepard's newfound acquaintance. He had a pinched face, eyes full of suspicion and a rat's tail of hair creeping over the collar of his bomber jacket. An unlit cigarette was tucked behind one ear.

"Sammy," acknowledged Colin.

"Who's your mate?" Beady eyes turned on Shepard and he felt the tension among the group crank up a notch.

Colin shrugged. "A mate. He's alright so he is."

"He looks like a peeler to me," said Sammy. His beady rodent eyes turned on Shepard and he unconsciously reached for the comfort of the nicotine stick. He pointed it, growling an accusatory question before jamming it between his teeth. "Are you here to tout on us, peeler?"

There were no flies on Sammy and it seemed his aggression wasn't going to end on the rough edge of his tongue. Although the van door remained closed, Shepard caught the whiff of fuel in the air and he knew then, and with certainty, it wasn't just attitudes that were becoming incendiary. Eyeing up the confrontation and overhearing Sammy's words, the group of men and youths standing around the car park became visibly more aggressive in their manner, their shoulders hunching and fists balling for a fight.

Shepard chose to indulge the accusation in the way he had found to be most effective. "Go fuck yourself," he said with a derisive shake of his head. "And take that fag out of your gob unless you plan to send us all to the burns unit."

The cigarette drooped from Sammy's lip and the murmuring of the bystanders stalled in a sudden silence, the tension palpable as the mob waited on their leader's permission to hand out a beating to the stranger.

Colin put a palm on Shepard's forearm, guiding him back a step. Sammy's high-pitched howl of laughter broke the spell.

"I like him, Col," he said through wheezes. "You're alright, so you are. What's your name?"

"Steve," said Shepard, unsure which pocket he had plucked the ad hoc alias from. "Planning a warm welcome are you?"

Sammy chuckled.

"Come here with me," he said, a gesture passing to one of the other men as he guided Shepard and Colin away from the van and over towards the edge of the car park where they could look out over the scene beyond.

"Do you know what the problem is here?"

Shepard didn't reply, quite sure that the question was rhetorical and Sammy would soon enough explain the exact nature of his grievance against his new neighbours and how he was going to solve it with three score of petrol bombs and the help of some manipulated and militant youths.

"It's the fact they've never apologised for what happened in there," said Sammy. "Did Col tell you what they did to him?"

Shepard nodded and Colin looked at his feet.

"Bastards. All the kids round here were scared shitless growing up. Your ma and da told you all sorts and then when you thought you were old enough to know better, you saw for yourself the cars coming in on a weekend and if you thought you were brave enough to head into the woods for a juke you soon changed your mind when you heard the screams."

Sammy's face twisted into a bitter mask of disgust. "Everyone knew about it and nobody did a thing about it."

"Whatever you say. Say nothing," Shepard muttered the mantra, a code of silence that hid all ills. He looked at Sammy.

"So, are you planning on paying back the sins of the past by burning out the new owners?"

"You think this new breed is any different to the old breed?

There's fuck all different about them. First, they'll ingratiate themselves into the community and next, they'll be grooming your kids."

"Bit of a stretch isn't it?" said Shepard.

"Is it?" said Colin sharply. "I can remember every face and every filthy second."

Shepard paused. Playing dumb would stave off any suspicion that his being there and his striking up of their initial conversation was anything other than social, when in fact, it had been completely intentional, a means to source information and to blend in. Lone men stuck out in a crowd. As the cogs began to whir in his head, he decided the meeting of Colin, and his aggressive friends, might open the gate of opportunity. He just couldn't be too obvious about it.

"So the plan is to start lobbing Molotov cocktails into the crowd and hope the outrage of burning families on the six o'clock news wins you support and this gets abandoned?" he said.

Colin resumed the examination of his toecaps and Sammy gave a gruff chuckle.

"That'd be something to see. Might readjust a few perspectives, getting to taste a bit of hell on earth, I mean."

"Seriously though," said Shepard. "Is that it? That's your big plan?"

"Minimum effort. Maximum impact," said Sammy with a savage leer.

Shepard ran a hand through his hair and puffed out his cheeks. "Colin, I'm sorry…"

"All mouth, no balls."

Shepard shifted a hard stare at Sammy who rolled his cigarette along his lower lip.

"Look, I sympathise," Shepard continued to the top of Colin's head. "I do." He held up a hand to stave off Sammy's next barb and relieve Colin's sudden pained expression.

"I had a brother. We went through the system after our parents died. He wasn't as lucky as me."

Shepard looked back at the crowds gathered outside the old boys' home, patiently waiting as the lie sank in. It didn't take long.

"He was a survivor?"

Shepard nodded. "He wasn't right for years after. Took to the gear, he overdosed in the end."

"I'm sorry," said Colin, his jaw flexing after a moment's reflection. "But do you know why he did it?" Tortured eyes stared at Shepard. "I do. I've thought about doing away with myself but it's the hate that stops me. Seeing people like those hypocrites down there standing by and allowing the abuse to happen. It gets inside your head and twists it so you are to blame for what they did to you. They put their claws into me when I was a kid. I didn't do anything to deserve it."

"Ninety-nine per cent of those people down there come to these places because they believe in whatever the marketing department has hooked them on," said Shepard. "Maybe they get a sense of community, or a way to turn a blind eye to reality, and think that by being part of it they are helping the world one sinner at a time."

"Doing nothing about it makes you as guilty as the bloody rapist hiding behind his scripture." Colin was becoming agitated again. "They killed your brother."

"My brother killed himself," said Shepard taking a gamble

"No, people like that fucked your brother up so badly he would rather die than wake up to another day of the memories," snarled Colin.

"Aye, the lad's right." Sammy encouraged his acquaintance with a slap on the back. "I say burn the bastards."

"And I say you're wasting your time."

Colin's fists balled in frustration and Shepard was aware of the glowing glint in Sammy's eyes as he anticipated the prospect of the disagreement escalating into a physical confrontation. Breaking first, Sammy glanced back over his shoulder towards the rest of his cronies, the movement telegraphing what Shepard already knew, the man's front and bravado were only as strong as the group around him. He was a bully, preying on the weak and no better than those he purported to despise.

A convoy of three cars sweeping down the road interrupted the immediate tension and reoriented their attention to the scene below them.

The vehicles slowed to a stop, momentarily mired at the mouth of the access lane by the bottleneck of people until a group of police officers pressed back the crowd and the cars limped the short distance to the police line which opened to allow them entry to the site beyond.

"If you want to make a difference, that's who you need to bring the hammer down on," said Shepard, jutting his chin forward as the three cars lined up on the newly laid turning circle. As the doors opened, the sound of engines rounding the sweeping corner to their right announced the arrival of another two blacked-out saloons followed by a police escort.

"There's no point in culling the lambs when it's the lions you need to be hunting," said Shepard.

"That's a great notion but in my experience, it's easier to start hacking away at the bottom of the tree," grunted Sammy.

Shepard quietly took in the scene below and shifted the permutations of the evolving situation through in his mind. He was positive Casey's man in the hospital had been telling the truth and that Steven Scott was somewhere within the confines of the Glenrafferty Estate. The burning question which he kept returning to was why?

If Scott could put the finger on Colm Casey then why had

he allowed the witness to be brought here in the midst of growing scrutiny? Did Casey relish the risk involved or was there another motive? Was he making a point and if so to whom? And did his attempt on Beattie's life factor into any of it? The questions kept coming and then fading away to be replaced by more.

As a third cavalcade of cars rounded the corner and eased down the gears on their approach to the site, Shepard started, something from the conversation alongside the wreckage of Carruthers' caravan coming back to him. The exact words were hazy but the implication of them began to coalesce into something tangible.

The mobile phone in his pocket and his obligation to keep Veronica Taylor in the loop both weighed heavily. The inspector was as invested in an outcome as he was, perhaps more so considering the wider implications of what arrests and trials may bring out into the open. The discoveries at Hoey Cargo had only been a catalyst, the explosive event illuminating how far back and how wide-ranging organised crime and corruption had been burrowing into the foundations of their small, green corner of the British Isles.

If Scott was given the opportunity to publicly declare what he knew about Glenrafferty, or if whoever was truly behind the attempted murder of Gordon Beattie and the character assassination of the justice minister could be identified and put on the stand, might that offer the key to a permanent change? A re-balancing of order.

A gust of wind lifted the heavy odour of fuel from the back of Sammy's van, the smell shrouding Shepard in dark memories and the raw pain of an imagined and agonising death.

The saloon cars, like those preceding them, had to pause at the end of the lane. Shepard's eyes bored into the heavily tinted windows. Images of bubbling paintwork and the rapid spread of flames blurred out the unseen faces within.

"If you want to do this," said Shepard suddenly, "then we're doing it my way."

"Who do you think you are granting permission and dictating what way we're—" Sammy's superior chuckle caught in his throat as Shepard roughly grabbed his bicep.

"If you do exactly what I tell you," hissed Shepard. "Then that eyesore down there will be bulldozed before the week's out and the people you really have a problem with, the bastards in the backseats of those cars, they will either be on the run, in jail, or dead."

58

For a fleeting second, as he regained consciousness, Steven Scott thought it just might have been another of the nightmares that had plagued him throughout his life, but, as the drowsiness cleared and he adjusted to the subtle cues in the environment around him he knew the truth of it. He had come full circle.

His hands and feet were numb and he had an itch on his nose that he couldn't scratch. The coarse fabric hood over his head was the cause of the irritation and coupled with the predicament of having wrists and ankles bound to a chair meant any relief was impossible.

Scott was shoeless, his shirt torn through rough manhandling, and his trousers were damp. His bladder, weak in the face of the violence and fear of what lay ahead, had released the crippling anxiety he was feeling during the bumpy car journey. His captors hadn't been happy when they popped the boot lid, but at least he hadn't shit himself.

It was as he was dragged unceremoniously from the car, bare feet sinking into cold stony gravel, that the crippling sense of familiarity skewered the pit of his stomach. At first, Scott put the loss of equilibrium down to the sudden shift from lying in a cramped foetal position to being half marched, half dragged and blind across unforgiving terrain.

Why he had been taken and by whom was somewhat clearer amid a whirl of desperate thoughts. The press arriving on his doorstep, his involvement with Olly Maddox and Harry breaking the news that Maddox had died suggested all roads led back to Colm Casey, and that his destination was likely an unmarked grave in a lonely forest or peat bog.

As those thoughts preoccupied him and just before he stubbed a toe on smooth concrete steps, a haunting ballad of wind whistling through the branches of tall poplar trees brought his mind to a crashing stop. His worst fears were confirmed as a set of doors were hauled open, the hinges squealing and the acrid smell of harsh floor polish penetrating the hood.

Scott lashed out wildly in an attempt to stop himself from being propelled any deeper into a hell he had thought he had escaped. The effort proved futile as a stiff and unseen punch landed through the hood, sending his senses reeling and leaving his legs limp.

The time between then and now was indeterminable. It could have been minutes, hours or days but he knew exactly where he was. He could hear the groan of the pipes and feel the heat radiating from the incinerator. Under the hood, tears welled and fell down his face and his shoulders shook in silent sobs. A tut broke his train of catastrophising thought.

"You dirty wee beast."

The blood froze in Scott's veins and he jerked upright. The chair was bolted to the floor and didn't sway an inch. The voice from his nightmares chuckled into his ear.

"The prodigal son returns."

Scott then sensed more than one presence and flinched as hands dropped onto his chest and began to unbutton his torn shirt. His mouth was sandpaper dry and his respiratory rate rocketed.

"The evening has come, and it is the Day of Preparation," quoted the voice, moving away but remaining close enough to observe the rough cutting of the rest of Scott's clothes. The cold touch of scissor blades on his skin sent goose pimples along his arms and legs. With the garments removed and discarded to the floor, the hood was then snatched from his head.

"Welcome home, Steven." The brogue was as coarse as it had ever been, even if the cruel mouth speaking the words had lined with age and excess.

Each of the three rapists standing in front of his chair looked vastly different, time and lifestyle taking its toll upon each, but at that moment, for Steven Scott, not a second had passed since the last time he had been passed between them.

"I'm pleased you're here to be our guest of honour this evening, Steven." The oldest of the three stepped forward, leaning heavily on a brass-tipped cane. His tongue poked out between yellowed teeth, moistening his lips. A jackal about to feed.

"There are a lot of people looking forward to seeing you again."

Scott was hyperventilating, palpitations drumming a tattoo inside his chest as a liver-spotted hand reached out to tilt up his chin. With fear gripping every sinew he tried to arch away from the nicotine-stained fingertips, his memory assaulted by the vivid recollections of perversion upon an unholy altar and the fog of incense that drifted between the cloaked order and their naked acolytes in a ceremony of ritual abuse and child sacrifice.

Mercifully, as the hand touched his skin, the room swayed and Scott felt himself dragged into a sweet, dark oblivion.

59

The room was silent save for the hum of the muted television monitor and Walker's too-heavy breathing.

Macpherson pushed back his chair and walked to the door. Opening it a crack, he peered out into the corridor, then with a satisfied snort he closed the door quietly and took up position with his back against it, giving Taylor a nod the coast was clear for the meantime.

"Well this is ominous," said Cook.

"We have talked to the source feeding The Echo their information on personalities within New Light and their motivation is the belief there is something rotten at the heart of the organisation," said Taylor. "Something far more insidious than we may have thought initially."

"Is this witness making an official statement?" said Cook.

Taylor shook her head. "It wouldn't stand up. He's suffering from dementia and has terminal cancer."

"Why do I get the feeling we're all about to regret hearing what you're about to tell us?" Reilly leaned forward in her seat, propped up on her elbows with intrigue pinching her elfin features.

"You don't know how close you might be with that crack, Erin," said Macpherson in a coarse undertone.

"The witness's allegations are corroborated by several diaries written by Oliver Maddox which detail his connection to what can only be described as a child abuse ring whose crimes go back years, and include the coercion of perpetrators and victims in covering it up and Maddox's own omissions which saw him and a number of other prominent individuals benefit from opportunities the ringleaders bestowed on them."

"Jesus Christ!" breathed Walker. The other DCs' faces held expressions of equal measures of disgust and incredulity.

"I've been trying to work back to a starting point over the last couple of hours so this might sound incoherent at first but bear with me," said Taylor. She spread her palms out on the table and took a calming breath. It didn't help. Her mind whirled and she felt agitated and on edge, unable to stop herself from thinking of her father and if this was how he felt when his suspicions around Glenrafferty continually met a brick wall.

"This all started with a spate of vandalism, aimed we thought, solely against Geordie Corry," she said.

"Now, Corry by his actions has pissed off half of his own community and most of the opposition with his desire to slash and burn in the name of gentrification or 'Orange' expansion." Taylor dropped the quotes over the term, referring to Corry's overstepping onto traditional nationalist ground in his pursuit of real estate. "When you add in his ability to ride roughshod over planning regs and get away with it, there could be a queue forming of people who wanted to give him a taste of his own medicine."

Heads bobbed around the table. Like it or loath it Belfast was changing, and in some ways that was expected and largely for the good. But, like the debacle in recent times over in the Holylands which had seen the snatch and grab of generational family homes to become sub-divided student accommodation or the 'Inner East Regeneration' and its widespread evictions and the tearing down of social housing to throw up rent-a-chain commercial properties without putting anything back into the local community, Corry's masterplan stuck in the craw of those displaced, disenfranchised or swindled out of their dividends. Especially when it was netting millions for the developer and his faceless financial backers.

"Now, I would normally assume he does this with brown envelopes or greasing the palms of intermediaries he meets through his extracurricular activities." Taylor dipped her chin at Walker, acknowledging the information he had gleaned from close observation and a simple handshake with the abrasive developer.

"One nil to the fat cats, boss," said Walker. Taylor answered with a grudging nod.

"Up until now, we've been looking at reasons why Geordie Corry is the target but what about his clients," said Taylor, getting back on track. "One of which is New Light, a little-known evangelical group that blows up out of nowhere and begins to snap up big chunks of the city. A few teething problems and scandals swept under the carpet but regardless they are managing to grow in status. Press cuttings and your visit confirm the membership is bursting at the seams with a who's who of industry, finance, local government, and media personalities. Not so well publicised but not that well hidden in the roll call is a subset of Belfast lowlife and ex-paramilitaries turned 'entrepreneurs' and it looks like they are burning through the cash reserves like it's Christmas."

"Money laundering leading to blackmail?" said Cook. Taylor steepled her hands, setting her chin on the index finger spire.

"On the face of it most of this investment is being wheelbarrowed over to Geordie Corry to build their houses of worship and community outreach centres, and given who he is, the thought did cross my mind," admitted Taylor, adding, "It wouldn't be the first time an organised crime group washed their dirty money through the collection plate so why not a group like this one Maddox was part of."

"Really?" said Walker, his tone indicating he was taken aback by the claim.

Taylor shot Macpherson a look, thinking back to a time when she, still in uniform, had supported CID in a raid on a church manse.

"You'd be surprised at what you find down the back of a church pew never mind shoved under the cushion in a confessional, son," said Macpherson.

"Corry could be one of those conduits," said Cook. "Given the story we got from Paul Finnegan at the SCAR group it makes sense. Bullyboy tactics, buying up land and getting it through planning objections. He has gangs of migrant site workers and access to any number of contracting and supply firms that he could be filtering cash through."

"In all likelihood, yes, but this isn't just about money laundering," said Taylor. "Segue back to what we know. We have Abbott as the principal perpetrator in smashing up New Light property, and he names Steven Scott as instigating the targeting of Corry, which he says is revenge for historic crimes against them. Abbott's PM shows signs of significant abuse. Scott is a former resident of Glenrafferty. We know from speaking to Eddie Faulks that after the home, Scott ended up in the grip of Billy McBride, aka The Mad Monk, who aside from leading a UFF hit squad was well known to fraternise with underage boys and had a history of extreme violence. The Monk also managed to conveniently escape prosecution throughout the Troubles. There's nothing concrete in his file but I think it's a fair assumption he may have had ties to Special Branch."

"An informer?"

"I think it's likely, but maybe not for the stories he could tell about his paramilitary mates."

"So what are we saying here?" said Reilly, a heartbeat later expanding on her question. "We all know the stories about collusion between Loyalist paramilitaries and the RUC to target suspected IRA members, but covering up child abuse? To what end? Intelligence gathering? Blackmail?"

Macpherson grunted. "It was a dirty war, Erin, and there's always bad apples. Part of our job is to make sure they don't ruin the whole barrel."

"Everything, all this," said Taylor, indicating the paperwork now spread over the table. "Leads back to the Glenrafferty Home for Troubled Boys."

Taylor selected various articles and photographs and lined them up as she continued.

"Geordie Corry has negotiated the purchase on behalf of New Light from Colm Casey, and a common denominator between those two, James Phelan and Oliver Maddox, is Steven Scott."

The eyes around the table didn't waver from her as they sat quietly waiting for elaboration.

"Steven Scott and his alleged historical abuse at the home, the accusations against Maddox from his time as an officer there and the press archives you dug up show they were all known to each other. To supplement that, Maddox's diaries indicate Corry as a personal friend of several key officers within the boys' home and he also documents Joe Casey. Colm's father, was a regular visitor to the estate in the time before his murder." Taylor then touched the pictures of Dylan Masters and Joanne Gould. "These two, and the rest, all link tangentially although more recently and, at this point, only through their association with New Light."

Taylor sat back.

"I think the facts we have at the minute offer a reasonably explanatory narrative to take to the DCI with a view to re-opening an investigation into crimes carried out at

Glenrafferty and in securing more evidence and the questioning of those individuals, named in Maddox's diaries and by our source, who are now potentially implicated in the abuse and murder of some more recent victims."

Her audience remained grim faced but each member of the team offered a nod, resolving to contribute with whatever was needed.

"Prepare everything you've found to be presented in the next hour to DCI Reed and Chief Superintendent Law. DS Macpherson and I will work to write up the pathology and toxicology links alongside the witness testimony."

No one spoke, each officer knowing what was needed at the moment. Taylor glanced up at the muted monitor; on screen, the tension ratcheting up outside the site of the former boys' home was building to match the pressure she felt constricting her chest.

She retrieved her mobile phone from her jacket pocket and checked the screen. It was blank and her thoughts settled on the most likely outcome regardless of the information which had come to light. Without Steven Scott as a living witness, the written testimony of Maddox or that from Vincent Edwards would offer little to secure her the result she needed to commemorate her father's determination to expose the horrors which had occurred at The Glenrafferty Home for Troubled Boys.

60

"…and I think we should look to expand the request for information to include other UK forces and our colleagues in the Garda."

"Do you now?" spluttered Chief Superintendent William Law, his expression showing Taylor just how warmly her request had been received.

"Sir, I'd urge you to at least consider it. We know groups like this rarely remain confined to one geographical boundary and the nature of the crimes we're looking at suggests association with other criminal networks. People traffickers. Drugs. Similar groups with the same sick interests."

To their credit, Taylor's junior officers had pulled together the multiple threads they had uncovered into a succinct and well-presented set of case files in record time.

The DCI and chief super had acquiesced to a hastily arranged briefing on what she had told them offered a resolution to the vandalism and the targeting of Geordie Corry, his wider business interests and clients. The last hour had involved Taylor's briefing her supervisors, the presentation of the evidence they had gathered so far on Corry and his relationships, Maddox's interest in Colm Casey and the details linking the minister to his former colleagues who had died of drug overdoses, and Pastor James Phelan. Both Law and DCI Reed had then spent time examining the files and asking questions.

"I don't know, Veronica," said Law, a touch of sympathy in his tone. "I still think it's a bit flimsy."

"Which is why we need to expand the request and re-open the old files." Taylor drew out the pathology report on Oliver Maddox, thrusting the mortuary examination images front and centre of the discussion.

"Maddox was branded. I've one other witness who corroborates a case of institutional abuse where similar branding occurred. You can't argue that's not a specific MO. We need to find other examples of victims branded in this way, I don't care if they're living or dead, but we need to know about them."

"Oh, yes, Ms Hammond and her sister. The independent inquiry team is quite interested in talking to her again considering their first dialogue seems to have been absent some of the more compelling information you managed to extract from her."

"Given what we around this table know about ACC Wallace and the potential for elements of the group to have penetrated policing or justice is it any wonder she kept her mouth shut?" said Taylor.

Law said nothing in response. The muscles of his jaw flexed as he bit his lips. The scandal of the former ACC's long-standing links to organised crime was still contained to a small number of well-briefed and trustworthy individuals.

"You suggest we'd be going back years here," said Law instead.

"Yes," agreed Taylor, her voice steady amid the raging tide of emotion that threaten to swamp her. "We're talking a prolonged case of systemic physical and sexual abuse. Rape. Conspiracy to pervert the course of justice, misconduct in public office and the murder of at least one police officer."

Law puffed out his cheeks. Up to that point, the other senior officer in the room had kept her own counsel. DCI

Gillian Reed removed her glasses and set them on the desk.

"Do you think your judgement is clouded on this?"

"No!" snapped Taylor.

Reed raised her eyebrows. "You do understand that pursuing cases like this is mired in contention." The DCI's tone was even. "That's not to mention the difficulty there would be in securing convictions. Currently you only have these diaries which could be argued at best as the work of a fantasist and at worst as a means to distract from the allegations directed at Oliver Maddox himself."

"We've the word of former Chief Constable Vincent Edwards and that of Steven Scott," said Taylor.

"We don't even know where Steven Scott is," said Law, exasperation beginning to cut through his uncharacteristic patience.

Taylor felt her blouse clinging to her back, hoping the musk of stress she caught was confined to her own nostrils. She leaned into the unnatural calm she was feeling to double down in her desire to make her superiors see there was mileage in pursing Geordie Corry and those hiding at the heart of New Light, if not for what was happening in the present, then for the litany of pain they had left behind them.

"My father raised concerns about this group and they were pushed aside to maintain the cover of Special Branch informers. He may have died because he kept asking questions and we might now have the answers. Not acting is a dereliction of duty."

"Veronica, your dad was a victim of the Provisional IRA," said Law.

"That was an easy assumption to make at the time," said Taylor, "And a convenient peg to hang his murder on, just the same as suicide in the wake of a scandal was for Oliver Maddox."

Law blew out a breath as he considered arguing against the

conspiracy theory.

"Derek Taylor pursued Barry Toms' killer and the allegations around that home like a dog with a bone," said Macpherson, breaking into the brief lull. "I know because I traipsed down dead end after dead end with him and I can stand by what Vincent Edwards said, the brass at the time received the call from on high to put any enquiry on the back burner."

Reed and Law shared a look. Some of the groundwork that had been presented was compelling, some of it raised valid questions and some presented them with a step back into the past neither were inclined to take.

"You don't need me to tell you who some of the people named in this are, Veronica." Law prodded a section of the case file as though it might at any second burst into flames.

Macpherson cleared his throat. "With respect, why should that protect them from answering a few questions?"

"Doc," said Reed, trying to maintain the equilibrium and bring clarity to the reality of the situation. "You know why. This isn't something that can be kicked out the door without proper consideration of the potential fallout."

"Reg McGarrity isn't going to worry about any fallout," said Taylor. "The Echo has its teeth into this story and it's coming out. Do you not think we'd be better leading the charge rather than mopping up a mess like Hoey Cargo?"

"Frankly, Veronica, yes, I do think that. However…" began Reed. Taylor couldn't help but roll her eyes and Macpherson took the opportunity to stand and stretch out the kinks in his back. The DCI continued to speak as Law massaged his temples in a bid to loosen the migraine that was beginning to grip.

"We are looking at an entirely new investigation here, one seeking multiple charges against multiple suspects. Notwithstanding, we have the historical allegations which will require an acknowledgement that mistakes were made in the past, mistakes we all have to live with as the consequence of decisions made during a difficult time."

"Don't dare try and divert what was going on then as a Troubles-era necessity," snapped Taylor, her previous calmness evaporating and her challenge to authority boiling over. Reed didn't flinch and kept her collected tone.

"The original investigation lacks the capacity to include most if not all of the theories you are presenting not to mention, as we've already touched on, we have no witnesses and those we may persuade to come forward are likely to be unreliable if it ever comes to putting them up in front of a jury."

Taylor balled her fists and batted them on her thighs, leaning forward to look directly into the faces of her superiors.

"We are talking here about a prolonged and active case of physical and sexual abuse on a scale and of a duration that is frankly mind-blowing." Taylor's voice had resumed the eerie calm of earlier. "We have the chance to bring down a high-level abuse ring that has been the cause of immeasurable damage for decades."

Reed's lips were pulled into a tight bloodless line. William Law was as pale as his shirt, eyes blinking rapidly as they flitted between Taylor's hard stare and the provisional evidence laid out across his desk.

"There has to be something we can do for fuck's sake?"

❖❖❖

"Uniform. Uniform. Sierra-Seven to control. Over."

"Go ahead, Seven."

Police Constable Leigh-Anne Arnold inched her mouth closer to her TETRA radio and thumbed the send key. "Sarge, it's getting hot and heavy down here. Any chance of getting some backup? Over."

PHILLIP JORDAN

As though to add emphasis to her request another bottle soared over the barricade to thump viciously on the roof of her patrol car.

"We've had a couple of RTAs and other priority incidents come in over the last hour, Sierra-Seven. All call signs are presently tasked but as they come free we'll reassess and advise available support."

"Fucking great," mumbled Arnold, eyes tracking another youth threading through the crowd, hood up and hands low. She lowered her head to the radio to aid being heard over the opposing battle for vocal superiority raging between the protestors. "Roger, control." As control's response warbled in her earpiece the young man exploded into action and launched a half-brick over the heads of those pushing up against the fence line in front of him. Bombs away, he melted almost instantaneously into the crowd. Somewhere behind her, the angry roar of a near-miss rippled through the crowd.

"We have an escalation of protest in progress. If there's an evidence gathering wagon free we could use it, over."

Control's response on despatching a CCTV-enabled armoured Land Rover to the scene was non-committal.

"Jonty, did you see where that wee shite went?" called Arnold. Her nearest colleague, wide eyes meeting hers, shrugged.

"Fuck's sake," she said.

There wasn't much she or any of her colleagues could do other than hold the line between the two groups, and stern looks and angry challenges were slowly losing the battle to the bitter diatribe and indiscriminate violence. More regular attempts at shoving down the steel barriers were becoming the norm as was the bombardment of the vehicles carrying those to the inaugural event inside the old home. What had started as a deluge of catcalls and spittle was now turning into a hail of stones, bricks and broken bottles.

With the guests and dignitaries all now safely sheltered behind the thick sandstone walls of the main building and the last of the contractors spirited away, attention had turned to the small contingent of police officers and vehicles barring access.

Arnold flinched as another missile bounced off her patrol car windshield, the impact spider-webbing damage across the reinforced glass.

A unifying roar of glee erupted across both sides of the conflict.

"Oi!" Arnold waded towards the barrier and pushed a hand into the chest of a cheering protestor. "Get back from the barrier!"

A flurry of flashes momentarily blinded her as somewhere amid the chaos the press was making sure the carnage was being captured for the morning's front pages and the late news while scores of mobile phone lights weaved through the crowd like fireflies and added to the illuminations, participants in the protest recording the police actions to be replayed across social media or, if one of their own were to be hauled across the barrier and arrested, the footage would help with claims of heavy-handedness.

Away to her right, a section of protestors clamoured, their shouts muted suddenly by the dull crump of an explosion which preceded a plume of black smoke rising into the evening air. Arnold backed away from the barrier and strained to see what had happened, her position preventing her from placing the seat of the blast but experience and her gut telling her someone's car had just been set on fire.

She glanced up to the higher ground and the shops where a group of hooded youths and other men had been gathering to look down on the protests. The younger contingent whooped and cheered. The older men were now conspicuous by their absence.

"Leigh-Anne!"

Arnold twisted at the warning shout from her colleague, expecting to find a cohort of protestors had breached the fence line, mentally preparing herself for the ensuing hand-to-hand melee.

But the ground behind her was empty, the barrier secure. PC 'Jonty' Johnstone's finger was however stabbing the air urgently.

Arnold's eyes widened as she took in the unfolding scene and she scrambled for her radio.

"Uniform-Uniform Sierra-Seven to control. Immediate assistance required!"

"Veronica." Reed's voice carried a warning that a loss of self-control, even under the circumstances, wouldn't be tolerated.

"Let her speak freely, Gillian," said Law. His eyes settled on Taylor and he took a moment to regain his composure. "I can understand why what you heard from Vincent Edwards may have presented a challenge to your view of authority, however, and as abhorrent as it sounds, a certain discretion is going to be required in discussing how this proceeds."

"Discretion?" Taylor spat the word. "Why, so reputations can be spared or spouses kept in the dark about the gory details? Sir, it doesn't matter who these people are, or what position they held or currently hold. What matters is doing the right thing and putting every effort into making sure they face justice for whatever part they've played."

"You know as well as I do, Veronica, people like this rarely face the kind of punitive justice you are thinking about," said William Law. The chief superintendent looked defeated. Damned if he did and damned if he didn't. He considered the options and when he spoke it was directly to Taylor.

"Firstly, moving any of this forward has to begin with a conversation with the chief constable, but…" He raised his fingertips from the desk to temper the swift nods of agreement from Taylor, knowing his next words would curb her hope he was about to go all in on what was an unsuited low pair. "Given your primary evidence is in the form of these diary entries and the testimony of a terminally ill man, I can't in good conscience officially re-open the original Glenrafferty case."

Taylor opened her mouth to protest but a glance from Gillian Reed stalled her; the DCI had a look in her eyes that communicated a concession was taking place. Law continued.

"That said, we can probably start an internal inquiry to establish if any opportunities were overlooked or deliberately mismanaged. If that bears fruit then your new evidence can be taken into consideration."

"Don't be putting yourself out," grunted Macpherson, returning to take a seat beside his inspector who although deflated hadn't yet yielded the battle.

"It's a welcome start," added Taylor, earning a magnanimous nod from both her superiors. Her emotions were ragged but she was hiding them well, wearing the detective's disguise; that series of almost schizophrenic masks she could slip on to distract the mind from the onslaught of the daily occupational horrors. The ordeals and atrocities could chip away at an inner humanity forced to repeatedly deal with the inhumane.

She could feel a simmering anger radiate off Macpherson and remained surprised she didn't feel the same. Derek Taylor had been his best friend and colleague but, he had been her father. The idea his gut feeling about Glenrafferty had been right and that his pursuit of those with knowledge of the home's secret had led to his death should have lit a burning fire of rage. A rage like Tom Shepard's? The question rose briefly and then she acknowledged the emotion would cloud her judgement in finishing what her father had started.

"Where do you see a review into Oliver Maddox's death considering the links to the others and the association to New Light and Geordie Corry?" she said finally.

"I assume no one from the organisation came forward after any of the appeals that we ran?" The question came from Law, fingertips scanning the case notes.

Taylor nodded. Correct. Nothing. "Nobody from New Light has admitted Joanne Gould, Dylan Masters or any of the others were involved in their outreach schemes or offered information on their movements in and around the times of death."

Law pursed his lips and gave a slow dip of the head.

"Then, I think, based on the information you have unearthed there is room to question those in supervisory positions over those particular outreach schemes."

"Thanks, sir," said Taylor.

"That doesn't mean you go running off half-cocked," said Law with a stony look at both his subordinates to make sure the point had landed.

"Well, they're all gathered down at their new church. Can we not strike while the iron's hot?" said Macpherson with a glint of devilment.

"It might be harder for them to lie to us while they are standing in a house of God," said Taylor.

Law paused, ignoring them both, instead shuffling the particular sections of the notes reserved for Geordie Corry. "Corry is a different matter. We need to tread carefully but I think a forensic look into his tender and procurement processes is acceptable. We'll also seek assistance from forensic accounting. Let's see if he's anything further to hide."

"And Finn Abbott's allegations?" Taylor was not about to let that one go.

Law gave a slight shake of his head. "Bring me Steven

Scott and once we've heard what he has to say, we'll look at expanding that avenue."

Before Taylor could reply, there was a knock on the door. The rap was urgent. A rat-a-tat-tat that didn't wait for an answer.

"Do come in, constable," said Law, a more natural scowl coming to his face.

"Sir. Ma'am. Guv." Erin Reilly was breathing heavily from the short sprint. She had left the door ajar and held an iPad at arm's length.

"Guv." She addressed Taylor, setting the tablet on top of the briefing materials. "You need to see this."

"What is it, Erin?" said Reed rising from her chair to move beside the young officer.

"It's a social media feed from Glenrafferty."

"Live?"

"Well, this is now a couple of minutes delayed but it's ongoing. Sergeant Harris has prioritised all call signs to attend and is calling for support from TSG."

Macpherson caught the urgency in Reilly's voice, swapping a look with Taylor and his superiors. If the call had gone out to the Tactical Support Group then the situation had deteriorated rapidly since they had last observed the news reports.

"Play it," said Taylor.

Reilly prodded the icon and they were assaulted by the tinny sounds of protest and unrest. The camera panned to see a uniformed constable duck an incoming missile which shattered part of the patrol car windscreen behind her. The uproar rose in pitch and then the camera panned around. The crowd which had overspilled from the containment area into the narrow lane leading up to Glenrafferty was scattering.

The whine and roar of a diesel engine intensified as a JCB digger marauded along the lane, the front scoop lowered like a battering ram.

"Fuck!" Macpherson's oath went unchallenged as the image distorted, the camera shaking wildly as the operator was caught in the skirmish of those trying to flee and those rushing in behind the vehicle as it breached the barrier and smashed into the first patrol car, momentum and the lowered scoop throwing it aside to narrowly miss the retreating officers.

Law's landline began to ring. Reed's mobile too but they ignored the calls, their attention rapt as the marauding construction vehicle continued to crash through the blockade of police vehicles until it came to a jarring stop, the tines of the scoop stuck in the door of an unmarked van.

The cockpit door flew open and a man leapt out, taking little time to right himself as his feet hit the gravel drive before he sprinted for the old home in the background of the unsteady shot. A split second later he was lost in the throng of other protestors now racing towards Glenrafferty. Just out of focus a petrol bomb exploded.

Taylor snapped out a finger and the footage scrolled back ten seconds. She let it play and did it again, this time pausing on the figure mid-flight from the cockpit to the ground.

"In the name of Christ, I thought he was dead. What the hell is he doing there?" said William Law, the colour draining from his face only for his complexion to be rapidly suffused by scarlet.

No, thought Taylor. Very much alive and doing what he did best. From the screen, the face of Tom Shepard glared back. His expression was resolute and set on violence.

61

"Is this absolutely necessary?"

John Barrett held the hooded garment at arm's length, a look of bemusement on his face.

"Not a fan of fancy dress?" said Colm Casey.

Barrett glanced at the man who was in the midst of disrobing. Casey was barefoot and stripped to the waist, his own garment hung over the back of a sturdy chair.

The room was illuminated by a single lightbulb hanging from an antiquated ceiling rose and operated by an equally ancient brass switch.

The low wattage did its best to disguise the dilapidation of the surroundings. Wallpaper curled from the high skirting boards and drooped in the corners of the ceiling where it peeled back from ornate cornices. The smell of damp was pervasive.

"I'm an observer, not a participant," said Barrett, the latter emphasised with sour distaste.

"If you're feeling a bit queasy, John, you can always go back to the party," said Casey with a chuckle.

Barrett draped the ankle-length gown around his shoulders and fastened the collar. The fabric felt heavy, and worn over his suit, he immediately felt uncomfortable. With the cowled hood up, it would be stifling.

"I need to bear witness, Colm." Which was true and as uncomfortable as Barrett felt with what lay ahead he wasn't about to share his misgivings. "I'm fine," he added.

"Aye, well, tell your face."

Barrett narrowed his eyes and bit back a retort as Casey continued, stripping off his trousers and laying them over his jacket and shirt. "You know what happens in this country when you start trying to fuck about with traditions."

Barrett winced. Unlike much of what he viewed as the professional peril of operating with the criminal classes, the ceremony that was about to take place in the unholy sanctum buried in the bowels of the Glenrafferty Estate wasn't one he would normally volunteer to oversee, but a message needed to be sent to those who had lost sight of the risks. The message? The consortium is watching.

A breathy sermon interrupted Barrett's train of thought. The speech, heavy with Bible quotes praising the power of forgiveness, emitted from a small speaker in the corner of the room, the device relaying the inaugural launch event ongoing in the main sandstone building a few hundred metres from the area where Barrett was watching Casey prepare himself.

New Light, as an organisation was, in the round, legitimate enough. The desire to make change and offer hope to an aggrieved underclass and an alternative to more traditional teachings had garnered a surprising level of cross-community support, and although in general the membership and many of those installed in boardroom positions were true believers in the good they were doing, the real power behind New Light were the few at its poisoned heart; those lions who preyed on the lambs of the flock and who for decades had slaked their lust for power and debauchery under the guise of philanthropy, the membership enabled and indebted to those in the consortium who had bought their loyalty by ensuring their anonymity and freedom from prosecution.

Those members of The Crossed Keys summoned to attend the evening's event had played their part well, mingling with those massed in the large function room to enjoy a champagne reception and to regale the crowd, the black truth at their heart unknown to those with whom they pressed the flesh and swapped anecdotes and professional gossip. The few handpicked members of the press corps who had been in attendance had been courted with equal relish and the obligatory photographs would make their way into the morning editions and onto the websites to assist the New Light PR machine as it continued to seek out prospective members and future donors. New blood.

As the reception wound down and the speeches began, many, already drunk on the fervour of the evening, failed to notice those who had left. The small groups were ushered away by orderly or acolyte in twos and threes to travel the short distance from the main home along the now graffiti-strewn tunnels to the repurposed rooms where, like Casey and Barrett, they would be prepared for the real ceremony: a ritual where oaths would be sworn to pagan effigies and innocent blood would spill.

62

The flash of another overhanded Molotov cocktail exploding illuminated the tree line as Shepard raced across the gravel driveway, his feet seeking the firmer swathe of grass border and the gloom of the overhanging branches.

The plan had been crude but effective. The theft of the JCB had been more of a hijack, the crew offering up no resistance when Sammy had demanded the keys with menaces. Setting fire to several other cars had created enough misdirection to ensure the element of surprise in breaching the first barricade, giving Shepard the head start he needed and now, as he worked his way rapidly toward his destination, Sammy and his contingent of supporters followed by the more militant protestors provided further distraction. The crowd had overwhelmed the skeleton-staffed police line and were taking up rock, branch and bitter voice in their march towards the main Glenrafferty school building which stood near defenceless behind a turning circle crammed with chauffeured cars, minivans and a panicking cohort of drivers and minders who were suddenly out of their depth.

Shepard took deep and controlled breaths, his sprint easing to a steady jog, snapping out a hand to ward off low-hanging branches now he had weaved off the main drive and into the trees. The ground underfoot was littered with leaves and deadfall, and a carpet of mossy vegetation made for going that while not perilous still required care to be safely passable. His route angled him away from the protest and the prominent building which had been the focus of the clean-up for the New Light event taking place. From the conversations with Colin and his recollections of his time at the home, there was a collection of smaller villas and outhouses set in the grounds on an axis to the main house. Colin had described how the low structures were set in small clearings, each linked to the main house by large underground tunnels that had served as shelters during the Second World War or beside meandering forest trails. The buildings were used for different spiritual classes or as retreats for visiting staff and guests during the summer months. At other times though, their use fell to more debauched practices. Bonfires and boozy parties where older men plied the young charges of the home with alcohol and drugs, encouraging them into woodland walks that would routinely lead to rough sex and vicious beatings. Sometimes it was one on one but at other times multiple participants shared the victims.

Shepard pushed the images away and pressed on, pausing briefly as the trees thinned and he had to cross a narrow rutted track. His gut feeling continued to guide him towards the probability that Steven Scott had been brought here and that he would be sequestered away from the festivities at the main house to be secured somewhere deeper in the grounds Somewhere for Casey to question him over what he had revealed about the horrors of Glenrafferty and then deal with him quietly, or pass him along to his friends.

As Shepard continued in his search of the outhouses, heading in the general direction provided by Colin, he heard the sound of distant sirens drift through the trees.

❖❖❖

"What the hell was that?"

"Christ knows," said Frankie peering out from the lodge window to the forested grounds beyond. The jeers and roars of protestors down at the gate were muted by distance and the dense vegetation.

"It sounded like an explosion."

"Ack, wind your neck in, Malkie," said Sean. The smaller man was hunched over a table rolling a cigarette. His nerves had settled quicker than his cohort's after the shooting and explosion at Ballyhallion Caravan Park. He put the cigarette to his lips and licked the papers. "Are our eardrums alright?" Chuckling, he flipped the roll-up between his lips. "It's a bunch of paranoid tree huggers versus the holy moly brigade. It'll be handbags at dawn, that's all."

Frankie turned his attention away from the direction of the noise to look to where the bullet-marked BMW was hidden under the boughs at the end of the rutted lane, hoping Sean was right. Something about Colm Casey's orders wasn't sitting well with him, and neither was the conspicuous absence of Kevin Cullen.

He pushed the thought away; more likely than not it was a case of self-preservation. It didn't help that the kid they had grabbed from the caravan had seen their faces before they'd hooded him and handed him over to the grim-faced men in the old school building. He'd recognised the dour face of the old yellow-toothed man lurking in the shadows as they passed the wriggling prisoner across. His presence was disturbing.

Equally, the fact that the news hadn't reported fat Harry Caruthers dead was eating at him. There had been witnesses at the caravan park. Too many eyes had seen the BMW flee the scene and with Chalkie White in hospital and the cops holding a description of the car, he could only hope his confidence that the kid wouldn't be talking to anybody and that things would blow over soon was well founded.

Malkie had pulled open the lodge door and took a step outside, a rattle at the window and excited garble of words coming a few seconds later.

"There's smoke."

"Fuck's sake, Malkie." Sean rose to join his counterparts. Frankie was already outside. Above the trees, a thin column of black smoke drifted into the sky.

"Bit early for the bonfires," muttered Sean, tilting his head back and huffing a cloud of tobacco smoke into the air.

"Should we call Colm?" said Malkie, a nervous quaver to his voice. He'd already told them he didn't like the woods.

Frankie kept his eyes on the rising smoke. It was close enough to be on the edges of the estate that bordered the Glenrafferty grounds.

"No, we stick to the timeline. It won't be long before we need to make our move," he said, giving Malkie an encouraging pat on the shoulder.

The words and the gesture did little however to reassure himself as the distant moan of protests combined with the forbidding groan of the branches and the eerie gloom of the woods exacerbated the fear which had begun to wallow in his stomach.

63

The siren's blue lights flashed mutely as the Volvo raced along the A24 towards Glenrafferty.

In the passenger wing mirror, Taylor could see the reflection of the eight armoured Land Rovers strung out in their wake. Ahead, other road users peeled from their lanes to edge up against the pavement or central reservation to let the convoy pass.

"All call signs en route to the former Glenrafferty School. Be advised Silver Command advise Section Four are re-establishing a perimeter but reports significant public disorder. Tactical Support Groups are inbound from Strandtown with additional units standing by. EGT have taken a position on the north end of the housing estate overlooking the playing field and entry road…"

The in-car speaker crackled as the distorted voices of other call signs acknowledged the report and the positions of their colleagues in the Evidence Gathering Team. Taylor picked up the microphone as Macpherson glanced quickly left and right before ploughing through the red stop lights of the busy intersection.

"Charlie Six-Four, acknowledged. Two minutes out," she reported.

Off to the east, beyond a suburban shopping centre and cinema complex, several plumes of rising smoke marked the Glenrafferty Estate.

"So much for keeping us in the loop," grumbled Macpherson. "Although I suppose you have to admire his enthusiasm." He flashed the Volvo's headlights, signalling to allow a duo of green and yellow liveried ambulances held up by traffic to edge out onto the carriageway and then flicked on his wipers, the steady mizzle since leaving Musgrave Street threatening to become a full-on downpour. With a response not forthcoming, he sighed. "Hopefully this rain will send them all scattering to the pub."

"I should have known better," said Taylor.

Macpherson glanced across, a shake of his head taking back the previous comments and indicating his belief that what was unfolding wasn't her doing. "At least somebody is willing to put the cat amongst the pigeons."

Taylor's jaw clenched. So far, their knowledge of Tom Shepard's involvement remained between the two of them. The former special forces operator's explosive second coming had however thrown Chief Superintendent William Law into near apoplexy, Macpherson at one point taking his superior's elbow to steer him back to his chair. The sergeant had been convinced the man was about to have a stroke and as the Volvo rounded the final corner to finally offer a view of Glenrafferty, Taylor thought if Law could see the scene unfolding now, he probably would.

A stream of New Light supporters and legitimate protestors negotiated the pitched battles being fought as they tried to move towards the minor safety of the main road which was fast becoming clogged with police and support vehicles. The more selfless of the able-bodied aided the walking wounded while those more self-serving charged headlong and panicked in their attempts to get away from the surging scrum of an angry mob who were clashing with their opposite numbers. On occasion, amid the chaos, a uniformed officer could be spotted. Overwhelmed and outnumbered they were buffeted around in the tide of bodies like a float cut loose to the waves.

Most of the time public order disturbances were a calendar fixture, with the days leading up to the dates filled with an increased tension on the streets and a rise in operational and tactical preparation for what usually proved to be the inevitable escalation. Policing a riot was a right of passage for any PSNI officer, so much so that it was incorporated into basic training at the Garnerville police training centre with further advanced practice taking place at the former British Army site of Ballykinler on the County Down coast.

Whether it was marching season and interfaith conflicts when the sectarian divide and bitter enmity over flag and culture saw neighbour battle neighbour and the ability to submit leave was impossible, the overtime budget was thrown out of the window, or more recently the agitating effect created by the Northern Ireland Protocol which had disaffected Unionism and placed a border in the Irish Sea, civil disturbance was part of policing the province. The protests over the latter and what was seen as the segregation of Northern Ireland from the rest of the United Kingdom had formed a catalyst for civil protest, and for those who wished to exploit a still divided community, it provided enough tinder to start a fire.

Not that any of that really mattered though; in Northern Ireland there was always time for a spontaneous recreational riot.

Macpherson swept the Volvo off the road and onto a set of hard core pitches, directed towards parking spaces by a yellow-jacketed police constable. The Land Rovers behind carried on, the officers inside kitted out from head-to-toe in protective gear moving closer to the pandemonium where they would disembark and, under guidance from the bronze commanders on scene, work to support the cordon before other teams moved in to establish order in the crowd.

Taylor stepped out of the car, the smell of burning fuel and plastics and the noise assaulting her senses. She adjusted the Velcro straps of her body armour and carried out a radio check.

"Charlie Six-Four, on scene."

"Roger Six-Four, Inspector Sheehan is briefing arrest teams on identified individuals at the southwest edge of the sports field and Glenrafferty Road. He's your point of contact."

Taylor confirmed as Macpherson inhaled a deep nasal breath and slipped his hands under the straps of his vest to observe the carnage. "Don't you love the smell of four-star in the morning?"

"It'll be unleaded," said Taylor wryly, checking her weapon was securely fastened in its holster and her extendible baton was in the pouch.

"Right enough, you'd have thought the bloody price of it would have put the wee bastards off."

On cue, another double flare arced into the air to impact the side of a police Land Rover rushing to the forward cordon. The vehicle slowed briefly as fire engulfed the armoured flanks and windshield, then roared on spewing gouts of black exhaust fumes to add to the toxic mix of smoke and burning fuel.

It took them a minute to reach the huddle on the far side of the pitch. Several uniformed officers were joined by colleagues in riot armour and on the periphery of the huddle stood a select group of private individuals, themselves marked by plain clothes with some wearing hi-viz tabards or mid-length reflective coats. A mix of marshals and community representatives who were on board but out of their depth in trying to restore calm.

As they arrived, the inspector was finishing up his brief to the quartet of officers next for assignment. "Davis, you're the arresting officer. The rest of you are in support with proportionate response to resistance. You're sweeping this area for these three men," The inspector's finger marked out a box section on the map spread out on the bonnet of a patrol car. "The evidence-gathering team confirm they are orchestrating a section of younger youths."

Taylor marked Sheehan out by pips on his epaulettes before she read the identity tag pinned to the centre of his vest. She knew of the man but had only limited professional dealings given they operated out of different stations.

"Alright," said Sheehan, with a dip of the head to both newcomers followed by a raising of eyes to the sky. "Bloody great night for it, isn't it?"

"Has the order come in to go dynamic?" said Taylor, accepting a handshake and cocking her head at the retreating officers.

"Had to," said Sheehan with a nod. "It's out of control. The intelligence we're getting back from the crowd is there's a group of protestors aiming to storm the property and there's a concern over serious injury and threat to life."

"Came too late for some," mumbled Macpherson, looking out as a small group carried one of their number out of the melee. A once-white handkerchief waved the signal for mercy as they manhandled the patient between them, a blood-soaked scarf wrapped around a head wound.

"Be that as it may, we're trying to round up the main rabble-rousers." Sheehan cut to the chase. "Gold Command says you're looking for a specific nominal you identified as a ringleader in the riot?"

Taylor gave a half nod. "We're fairly certain the man responsible for the initial breach is a suspect in a number of high-profile murders," she said, pulling out her phone. "We also have a suspicion a witness in another case may be being held somewhere on the estate."

Sheehan gave a gruff nod and eyed the screengrab Taylor had brought up of Shepard and a second photo of Steven Scott taken from his apartment. "Are the two connected?"

Taylor offered a noncommittal shrug.

"Constable?"

"Sir." The voice came from behind the row of civilians where an officer was trying to establish who they were and then the best use of the resource they were offering.

"Jesus, would you look at the state of you?" said Macpherson, a flash of concern giving way as the constable's beaming, albeit bloodied smile, met the two detectives.

"Better late than never, Sarge," said Leigh-Anne Arnold, accepting Taylor's brief hug of concern. "I'm fine, Inspector."

"Child, you've a bump on your napper that looks like you're trying to grow a new head. Have you been seen by…" Macpherson took a step towards the woman and peered down at the swelling.

"Triaged and cleared for duty." Arnold fussed Macpherson away.

"Constable Arnold has refused to stand down, so we've moved her back to help with the coordination effort," said Sheehan interrupting the reunion. "These folk are members of New Light and marshals who were in place to oversee several of the protest groups. They've offered to help with the transition of the injured from the locus and to try and mediate a dialogue with those up at the main house intent on doing their worst. Constable Arnold was on the main drive when the attack came."

"It was all over in a heartbeat really, ma'am," said Arnold, playing down the initial mayhem and hand-to-hand that followed the digger skewering the gate. "We were lucky."

"Did you see what happened after the vehicle broke through?" said Taylor. Arnold nodded.

"Fella jumped out and ran like the hammers towards the

big house before disappearing into the trees."

"The trees?"

"He ran into the woods, yes."

"Mr Gough," called Sheehan. "A second of your time please."

The civilian who stepped forward wore a black raincoat over a pinstripe suit. One knee was muddy and the jacket had seen better days. He was in his mid-fifties, hair askew and looked like he'd been in the same wars as Arnold.

"This is Ned Gough. He was to join the New Light festivities but given the depth of feeling among the protestors was attempting to alleviate their concerns and open a productive dialogue."

"Love thy neighbour has never really taken off in these parts, sir, " said Macpherson, taking the man's hand.

Gough cleared his throat. "This is desperate. Not the sort of thing we wanted at all."

"Mr Gough's other duties ran to liaising with local authorities and he was fire and emergency warden for the inaugural event. The fact the main building and several of the outlying properties essentially remain building sites at the moment brought a level of concern."

"Mr Gough?" said Taylor, seeking explanation.

"We were asked to offer contingencies in the event of fire or other emergencies, one of which was the evacuation and assembly of guests." Gough hesitated. "Obviously, we have several VIPs present this evening."

I bet you do thought Taylor. "Go on," she said.

"I… I explained to your colleagues. If these people are intent on entering the building and causing mayhem they don't need to batter down the front doors to do it."

Taylor shifted her stance and took a beat to look back at the ongoing pitched battle between the New Light supporters and protestors. A line of tactical support officers had strung out like a row of black beetles, riot shields raised as they began a slow march to encircle and remove offenders.

More flames erupted nearer the big house and the dull crump of an explosion made Gough flinch. The prestige cars outside on the turning circle had, by the sound of it, met with the anger of the mob.

"There are several wartime tunnels that feed out to a number of glades and outdoor cabins which were used during the summer months so, by their nature, also offer a way in. Of course, our security compliance was robust but if there was a leak, anyone with ill intent could get into the building the way we planned to get out."

"Or set a mob loose to bait a trap," said Sheehan. "How dangerous is your man, inspector? Has Gold Command requested ARU and aerial support?"

"Chief Superintendent Law has briefed command on what we know," said Taylor. "Mr Gough, how secure are these egress points? Are they locked or guarded?"

"May I?"

Sheehan conceded his map to the New Light man and he took a second to orientate himself. "These three are blocked up," he said, indicating the positions and further explaining. "Apparently after the council services left there were issues with vagrants and local teens trespassing onto the property." Taylor gave a nod of understanding as a manicured fingertip moved along a highlighted walking trail. "This one is open but blocked by a collapse which leaves these two which extend towards the edge of the estate. Neither are locked and we have people manning them this evening."

"It brings you out quite a ways," observed Taylor, peering at the map. She could see the positives in why the tunnel escape had been chosen. It ran to a secluded area bordered by a bend on the Lagan and a car park for the nearby Meadows Nature Reserve and although accommodating for the numbers, more expeditious means of escape existed. When she looked up she was surprised to see Gough nodding.

"It's quite far for those engaged in the public confirmation of faith in the main reception buildings perhaps, but this exit is for the private consecration ceremony. In the subterranean altar."

Gough pointed a finger equidistant between the main building and the edge of the estate. Gradient lines placed the location under a grassy knoll surrounded by the woods.

Taylor felt a sudden need for expediency.

"What private ceremony?" she said.

64

John Barrett started. The padded drumbeat which played a soporific rhythm stopped. The tempo in combination with the dim atmosphere and stifling warmth had been nudging him towards the jaws of an unintended doze but now that alertness had returned, Barrett found he was just as uncomfortable as he had feared he would be. An increasing sense of dread was creeping over him but it was nothing to do with the claustrophobic nature of being underground.

The amphitheatre, although buried several metres below ground level, was augmented by the addition of a soaring beamed ceiling making the space seem larger than it actually was. What it lacked was any natural light and was instead illuminated by a central brazier and rows of ensconced torches along the walls. A second, smaller, copper firepit was aglow on the raised dais at the head of the chamber and hundreds of candles flickered.

He tried to convince himself it was the heat from the burning lamps and the suffocating confines of cloak and hood that was smothering him or the closeness of the other members of the select congregation who sat either side and close behind. What little draught offered ventilation came from the three archways leading into the chamber. The surrounding masonry was ornate and formed into bleak black mouths, chiselled with the iconography of a twisted religion. As the drum beat took up again and the procession loomed out of the yawning darkness he was forced to confront the true nature of his discomfort.

They ranged from very young to adolescent and walked barefoot in pairs from the left-hand tunnel entrance to form up around the edge of the raised platform and altar. Each wore a thin grey cloak with the hood down around their shoulders, the garment unable to hide their nakedness underneath. The youngest was perhaps eight or nine and they all wore subdued expressions that only came from the administration of opioids. The oldest, late teens or very early twenties, was a girl with long red hair tied back in braids.

Following the initiates came the acolytes, their garb a deep crimson, and as they paraded to their positions behind their young charges, the higher orders of The Crossed Keys began to file in from the central tunnel mouth to take up position by the grand altar, the three most senior of which took their place at the head of the oblong altar stone beside which the firepit glowed.

The two men and one woman stood over the select gathering, their robes a deep black with vermillion and gold trim The high priest, marked out by intricately detailed vestments, had both hands clasped and leaned on a blackthorn cane while his two counterparts held a copper-tipped wooden staff and a large halberd, the medieval weapon draped with a linen sigil depicting a set of crossed keys.

Barrett could feel the frisson of excitement run through the assembled gathering. They knew how the ceremony would progress and the anticipation of the rituals to come and the joy of flesh to be enjoyed afterwards was palpable. He could feel the intoxicated tremor from the leg pressed against his own.

"Faithful brothers and sisters, dear friends and distinguished guests," The high priest shuffled a step forward and smiled from under the hooded cowl, the flickering candlelight lending his age-worn features a demonic cast. "We come together in this place today in celebration, an occasion that marks the end of our sojourn and a return home."

There was no ripple of applause. Honoured guests, sworn members and those chosen as vessels for the evening's sacrifice maintained an obedient silence.

"I welcome you to honour the divine power that flows through us, a power that through dedication and unwavering devotion has enabled us to reveal and find our purpose in this mortal realm. Tonight we free these initiates from the ties that bind them, casting aside the malignancies of the material world to send them on a path of enlightenment. Through the offering of their flesh and the bequest of spirit shall the truest salvation be attained."

The slow drum beat once again thumped out the funeral tempo and from the right-hand tunnel, two scarlet-garbed acolytes emerged, guiding a naked man between them. The high priest continued as they took the offering and laid him on the altar. His head hung over the edge to face the congregation, eyes rolling in their sockets.

"Today as we gather in this most sacred space, let us pledge ourselves to renew our cause within and without, mindful of recent challenges and facing those ahead together."

A final figure emerged from the central tunnel, a cool smile the only feature evident under the black robes. He strode purposefully to the altar taking the several steps quickly to kneel and offer his hand to the high priest. The older man accepted the hand and when he spoke, his words carried the tremor of near ecstasy.

"Through the searing of flesh let our bodies be joined, by the sharing of blood let us be one."

In turning away from the crowd, he exposed an unabashed nakedness, a thin hand and arm slipping from the cloak to remove a glowing poker from the burning coals of the firepit. He held the implement aloft.

"Let our sacred fires alight. May their flames consume our enemies and fuel our desires."

Barrett watched in horrified fascination as the twisted old judge beckoned the kneeling disciple to stand. Colm Casey did as requested, accepting the red hot poker used to stoke the firepit.

As rehearsed, he took a step back, and as he did so his cloak fell open. Revealing his own scar.

"To those who walked before us, to those who walk after. We humbly offer the first of these tributes to honour your faithful devotion."

The high priest raised a hand in the air and the congregation stood, their low chants filling the chamber as he withdrew a second instrument from the flames. The long thin rod radiated heat, the tip gleaming deep red in the dull light was fashioned into the shape of two crossed keys.

The hand dropped and for a brief moment, silence was restored.

65

Events may have transpired very differently for Shepard if it hadn't been for the squawk of radio transmission. Halting abruptly at the sound of it had also likely saved his life.

The peal of sirens had lowered in intensity as he got deeper into the trees, sticking mainly to the wood but occasionally crossing a beaten-down trail or wider overgrown service road. The first of the estate villas appeared out of the gloom unexpectedly, the branches thinning and the canopy opening to a large almost circular clearing.

Shepard had taken an orbit, remaining inside the cover offered by the overgrown ferns and moss-covered tree trunks to circle the property which looked, from a distance, derelict and unguarded. As he wound around the western edge he spotted one of the tunnel entrances Colin had described, an angled concrete wedge protruding up from the earth about ten metres into the undergrowth. The entrance was bricked up.

Satisfied he was alone bar the caw of rooks in the overhead branches, a closer search of the building revealed nothing but rotten timber, discarded beer cans bleached white by age and every other sign of abandonment he could think of. Unperturbed he continued, pressing east but having to pause and drop to cover when the sound of an engine filtered through the trees closer than he anticipated anyone would be.

The next clearing offered a cabin that was much less

ramshackle and looked to have recently been given some degree of repair. The rotten wood was in the process of being replaced and the service road leading from the opposite side of his approach showed signs of use, the grass flattened down all around the front of the property by the passage of vehicles. Focused as he was for signs of life, Shepard almost missed the wedge of a tunnel entrance, fallen trees and wild overgrowth hiding it until the last second but unlike the previous entrance, this one was accessible. A quick peep inside revealed a dank space falling down several steps to a dark corridor beyond and slimy walls covered in garish graffiti.

Choosing to investigate the shack for any sign it may have been used to accommodate Steven Scott, Shepard backed out of the tunnel and crossed the glade using as much of the already tamped-down grass as possible to mask his tracks.

A few large builders' safes littered the frontage and some hand tools had been temporarily abandoned on the veranda. Claw hammers, crowbars, a twenty-four-volt circular saw and a nail gun were balanced on a tarp covering a collection of new decking boards, and a set of ladders were propped against the gable. Rolls of roof repair felt and pots of tar were piled nearby.

The door to the property was ajar, and as he edged along the wall, attempting to peer through the window, he heard the squawk of transmission and froze.

"Two-Eighty. Status?"

Shepard hunkered down under the cover of the tarp-covered decking stack. A window pane of the outhouse offered him a mirror image of the new arrival.

The man who marched out of the tunnel entrance was oblivious to his surroundings, crunching heavily through the deadfall to stop a brief second and survey the clearing.

"Two-Eighty. All clear," he reported, then dropped the mic

to his belt and rummaged through a pocket to find a cereal bar. As he fought to free the contents from its wrapper the low rumble of an engine and the sound of tyres over a rutted road interrupted him.

The approaching vehicle stopped just out of the convenient sightline offered by the window's reflection so Shepard chose to stay where he was for fear of being unintentionally spotted.

A rough skid and the clack of doors opening preceded the killing of the engine. Shepard tuned in his senses and eased to a new position, lying prone and trying to get one eye on what was unfolding. Two doors thudded closed. Multiple occupants.

The tunnel guard spoke out as he left his overwatch.

"There are restrictions in place today," he said, voice dropping an octave in warning.

Shepard used two fingers to lift a corner of tarpaulin. A dark SUV blocked his view.

"The protestors have broken through and have encircled the main house," said a new voice.

"Just stop where you are." The guard's voice again. Emphatic. Shepard could visualise him reaching for his mic. "I'm aware of what's happening. This is a restricted area for the duration of the…"

"We've been sent up to assist…" A third voice interrupted.

"Two-Eighty, control—"

The tunnel guard never got to finish. The echo from the initial crack of gunfire hadn't time to fade before a secondary barrage followed.

Shepard flinched, the sudden movement knocking a crowbar from its perch to hit the deck at the same time the dead tunnel guard hit the grass. He held his breath, the call of rooks fleeing the branches the only sound in the clearing.

Shepard watched as a leg strode into view. The toecap of a

boot prodding the shoulder of the fallen guard. He held his breath.

"Will I move the car?" The tone was questioning but unconcerned.

"No, leave it where it is. We're running late." An impatient response. "C'mon, the tunnel should be over there somewhere."

The retreating footfalls were muted by the vegetation and Shepard lay where he was for a full five minutes until there was only the sound of the wind in the trees and the returning birdlife. Shuffling from his space he picked up and hefted the crowbar, handy if things got up close and personal. Rising to his feet Shepard looked out at the dead guard and the bullet-marked SUV from the caravan site at Ballyhallion. The tunnel entrance was just visible through the trees.

A knot of confusion knitted between his eyebrows. While he was grateful to see his hunch playing out, why Casey's men had killed the guard was a mystery. So too, their need for haste. Was it to do with their prisoner? Where was Steven Scott and were there other factors in play he didn't know? He looked again at the crowbar and then the direction he needed to go, the words of an old movie coming back to him. Never bring a knife to a gunfight.

The men were armed and save for a crowbar, he was not. As he considered his next move he spotted the woodworking tools laid out on the decking boards. He picked up a battery-operated nail gun and thumbed the power switch. Three of five bars of charge illuminated on the grip.

Shepard aimed the device at the BMW and squeezed the trigger. An electronic whine and then a hiss of compression sounded before a hard thwack sent a four-inch nail rocketing towards the car with a whump as the zinc-coated shaft embedded up to its head in the side wall of the tyre.

Shepard gave an impressed half nod. Desperate times

called for desperate measures and nor could beggars be choosers. Stepping from the porch he fired a second projectile into the rear passenger side, the SUV beginning to loll as the two tyres rapidly deflated. Just as an amused grin was beginning to crease his face, it evaporated.

The birds fled the treetops again, frightened from their roost by an inhuman howl of pain erupting from the mouth of the tunnel.

❖❖❖

"Shit!"

"A fox?" offered Gough.

Macpherson looked at his shoe, an expression of disgust etched on his face. Gough, peering at the squashed scat, amended his first guess, nose wrinkled in distaste.

"Maybe a badger?"

While the trek through the woods had mostly been on rutted track and wider rough service roads the last few minutes had, for the sake of expediency, been cross country resulting in Macpherson falling victim to a feral booby trap.

"Maybe a bloody grizzly bear by the size of it, for God's sake," snarled Macpherson, scuffing the excess off the edge of his shoe on an exposed tree root.

"Some people say it's good luck," offered Taylor with a suppressed grin, pushing through the last of the undergrowth. "Mr Gough?"

Ahead of them was a clearing, at the centre of which stood a cabin and a BMW X5. As Taylor led the way out from under the dense canopy and her field of vision widened she spotted the body on the ground.

"Shit."

Macpherson trampled through the undergrowth with all the grace of a rampaging gorilla.

"Ha." He gave a wry chuckle. "Serves you bloody right for taking the piss out of… Oh shit."

Taylor raised a hand, warning Gough to stay where he was then drew her sidearm. Macpherson did likewise and focused his attention and aim on the abandoned vehicle.

"Matches the description from Ballyhallion," he said.

Taylor nodded. The scene was quiet but they would need to clear it. First things first though, preservation of life. She crossed the open space quickly, using the vehicle for cover, coming to a crouch at the rear quarter panel. She popped up to peer inside. Empty. Trying the door, it was unlocked.

"Clear inside," she said, Macpherson acknowledged and moved to join her from the tree line, weapon covering the cabin.

Taylor took a knee beside the victim. The body was still warm, the surrounding grass soaked in blood from the series of gunshot wounds to chest and abdomen. She checked for breathing and circulation.

"Charlie Six-Four," she said into her TETRA. "Body discovered in clearing approximately one kilometre northwest of the main Glenrafferty building. Multiple GSW. Life extinct. SOCO and support crews to this location."

She waited while the call was acknowledged and responded to the possible delay due to the ongoing operation to quell the protest at the main house turning into a riot. Opening the map software on her phone she sent GPS data for the location and then snapshots of the immediate locus, the body and the SUV.

"Six-Four, received. Suspect vehicle from Ballyhallion Caravan Park incident is also in situ. No sign of occupants. Six-Four securing scene."

With an acknowledgement from control buzzing in her earpiece, she gestured to Macpherson and they approached the cabin. A cautious three-sixty route around the perimeter and then a rapid entry confirmed the place was deserted.

"Mr Gough, you can come over here now," called Taylor,

holstering her weapon and gesturing to the preferred route. "Stay on the edge of the trees and then approach through this area."

"Are you sure he's dead?" Gough was pale faced as he approached.

"As a dodo," said Macpherson.

"Mr Gough, we're going to have to remain here and secure the scene until relief arrives. I need you to have a look at this photo and tell me do you recognise the man. Can you do that for me?"

The New Light liaison gave a reluctant nod and Taylor showed him her phone.

"Yes, I know him. One of the security team. Not sure of a name."

"Have you any idea who would know this was your VIP emergency assembly point?" said Taylor, putting the phone away.

"Our organisational list was relatively small but the risk assessment had to be distributed to local authority and emergency services so…" said Gough, trailing off with a shrug.

"Are you aware if anyone who might be present at the ceremony had received any recent threats?"

Gough gave a bewildered shake of the head.

"Not that I was made aware of. Obviously, as we've seen, there are those in some quarters who oppose our beliefs and what we are trying to do by repurposing this estate, but murder?" He tried not to look at the dead security man.

Taylor wasn't sure she agreed. All the roads which had brought her here were tainted by death: Finn Abbott's accusations of hidden crimes tragically silenced; Oliver Maddox's character assassination and dire ending too. Would similar be found following the disappearance of Steven Scott? The case building against Geordie Corry and New Light would be littered with it.

The trail of victims now ended in a wooded glade with another body. Had this one been Shepard? She tried to dismiss the thought as soon as it crossed her mind, but it nagged. Had the soldier, in his pursuit of Scott, found others to focus his raging grief on? She hoped that she was wrong. That Shepard remained engaged to fulfil his side of their loose bargain and save Scott from his fate so that he could help them both. Regardless of which, for good or ill, there was a gunman somewhere in the dark tunnel, his aim centred on the heart of New Light.

Gough's words broke into her thoughts, echoing her own misgivings.

"Inspector, is there nothing you can do to warn them?"

It was a question she had been asking herself as she focused on the mouth of the dark tunnel looming in the trees. Every fibre begged her to take some form of action, the impulse to do something pulling against the priorities of preserving the scene and securing what evidence may have been left by the killer or killers.

A short squelch of static preceded the radio call that tipped the scales and saw her unholster her sidearm again. A decision taken out of her hands.

"All call signs, be advised… Protestors have breached Glenrafferty House. Reports on the net of multiple fires inside the property. Fire and Rescue are currently impeded by blockages on the route in…"

"Doc," said Taylor, running through a mental checklist of her personal equipment. Vest, torch and body camera.

"Aye, I heard it too." Macpherson moved away from his inspection of the cabin, catching sight then of her determined expression. "No way, Ronnie. We stay put until the cavalry arrives."

"Standing orders, sergeant. Preserve life."

"Ronnie," warned Macpherson.

Taylor gestured at the wooden framed structure on which they were standing. "Hold the fort."

"Ronnie!" Macpherson snapped but without waiting to hear further protest she stepped off the deck and strode purposefully towards the tunnel.

Somewhere inside was a gathering of The Crossed Keys and someone was trying to smoke out the rats.

❖❖❖

Silence hung in the air for what seemed like an eternity and then a horrified scream tore through the amphitheatre.

The high priest's eyes bulged in horror as he looked across the dais. His hand holding the branding iron over Steven Scott's abdomen wavered wildly as he bore witness to the sudden and unexpected violence desecrating his unholy ceremony.

The last time The Honourable Mr Justice Pollock and Colm Casey had been as physically close could be measured in the distance between dock and bench.

Casey pulled the red hot poker from the throat of the female priestess, the gasps and the sudden rush of the congregation rising from their seats masking the thud of her body and ceremonial staff hitting the flagstones.

It was incredible, he thought, how suddenly the veil of ceremony and theatricality could vanish. How the grotesque and evil could so very quickly be replaced by the mundane and ordinary. The congregation of brooding cultists and lifelong sadists had vanished, replaced by the ashen faces of middle managers, civil servants, political aides and other professionals who had used membership of their secret club to satisfy twisted urges and ascend the greasy pole of power. Each now wondering how the planned evening of incestuous drug-fuelled debauchery and the pleasures of inflicting pain and humiliation on their handpicked harem of innocents had gone so terribly wrong. In many an eye the fear and horror of what had just unfolded was eclipsed by something else, an acute realisation that their sins and their monstrous deeds might no longer be hidden.

The woman who lay at Casey's feet was wide-eyed and white with shock, writhing in a vain attempt to breathe but hampered by the catastrophic injury. Ironically, not only was she was a figure of note in human rights circles, a well-heeled and respected professional but also the one who that not long ago been at the tip of the spear defending Casey's conspiracy to murder charge. Just as he had been the subject of Pollock's perversions Casey had witnessed Margaret Jury KC abuse her playthings with a ruthless zeal. She was vicious. Revelling in the brutality, and the more extreme the torture the more it aroused her although, unlike the majority of her peers, her lusts were not finally satisfied by sexual gratification, that peak was ascended by seeing the light leave the eyes of her victims. Not that death spared their bodies from violation. There were enough deviants in her harem for her to indulge watching that particular abomination as a denouement.

The smell of singed hair and burning flesh rose to his nostrils, followed by a more subtle tang of wood smoke, the scent taking him back to his youth, to the woods. To his rape at the hands of the other two men on the platform. To the overseeing eye of his treacherous father. He couldn't remember exactly how it had begun but he remembered the first time Joe had brought him to the Glenrafferty Estate, how he had flattered him with loving compliments, how he was different to his brothers. A special boy. Casey hadn't wanted to be special after that and his vain attempts to emulate his brothers, to be like them, untouched, free from the clutches of his father and his friends had not been ended by his inability to be useful to their cause or through poor luck. His own father had informed on him. Sacrificed him to a system from which there was no escape and into the hands of those who would ultimately break him.

"You?" The hatred radiated from Pollock's eyes. The crossed keys brand with which he had marked the young Colm Casey's skin moved to point at the Judas.

"You treacherous wee bastard!"

Casey sneered, stepping over the woman's writhing body, placing himself between Pollock and an enraged Geordie Corry. Her chokes and grunts were more urgent now but proving futile.

The crimson-robed acolytes were hurrying their young charges out of the ceremonial hall and back towards the tunnels, the desire to protect their flock overwhelming. The congregation meanwhile was in tatters, chairs were overturned and those who weren't cowering at the spectacle were hurrying away. Not that they would get far. Casey met John Barrett's eye. Surprised to see the man seemed to be intrigued more than fearful, the consortium's man broke the gaze first, moving against the crowd towards the tunnel from which the grand order had arrived.

"You're surprised?" Casey spat, attention focused on his abusers. "You had me cleaning up your mess for years and the first opportunity you got you tried to hang me."

"A noble sacrifice and the fact you failed to embrace your destiny highlights you're unworthy of your mark," hissed Pollock.

"Unworthy," spat Casey. "I didn't have a choice!" He held his cloak open, the day they seared the mark as stark in his memory as it still was against his nakedness.

"You always had a choice," said Pollock.

"The same choice you gave Oliver Maddox?"

"Maddox made his choice." Corry hefted the halberd and took a step closer to Pollock and the offering still recumbent on the altar. "He knew the consequences his actions would bring."

Casey supposed he did, but the difference between his old childhood acquaintance and himself was that Maddox was weak. He had allowed himself to be carried along until the day when his resolve returned, and he thought justice would come in traditional fashion, by exposing the group using the likes of Steven Scott and James Phelan. That through the publication of their testimony and evidence it would lead to trial and conviction. He had been weak and naive, thought Casey. The Crossed Keys was too powerful with their members too deeply embedded in the fabric of the country to ever be allowed to be exposed.

A scream distracted Corry, his attention drawn to the exit tunnel back towards Glenrafferty House where those fleeing in that direction had stalled, murmurs growing to shouts. The smell of burning was now heavy in the air.

"It's over," said Casey.

A gunshot rang out. The crowd surged backwards, bodies tripping over themselves in their hurry to flee as the gunman was framed in the tunnel entrance; a moment later he had heaved the heavy portal closed sealing the exit.

Corry looked at Pollock, the old judge's features were twisted in hate. The congregation was now a frantic mob, desperate for an escape Casey had ensured would never happen. They were trapped like rats in a barrel.

"Fuck you both." Corry cast down the ceremonial halberd in disgust, self-preservation winning over his desire for vengeance. Casey watched him go, manhandling others out of his way as he made for the central exit.

Pollock's fury erupted, lips curled back in a silent scream as he lunged, brand raised high and arcing down at Casey in an axe blow.

It was an easy parry.

The crash of poker and ceremonial tool echoed across the

amphitheatre and the shock of the impact tore the brand from Pollock's grasp.

Casey didn't blink. He grabbed his tormentor by the clasp of his cloak and pushed him backwards.

Pollock tripped over the now-dead King's Council, his arms flailing as he fell to land on the glowing coals of the brazier.

The scream which tore from his lungs was as shrill and piercing as those of his many victims. His cloak started to smoulder as he struggled to sit up, each attempt to right himself thwarted as he burned on the red-hot rim.

Casey stood for a second and watched, the old man's eyes begging for a mercy he had never shown then, taking a firm grip on the poker he stepped between Pollock's legs, thrusting the poker hilt deep into the man, hoping that in his final moments, the violation saw the twisted bastard experience infinitely greater pain than that which he had inflicted on countless others.

66

There was something otherworldly about the vision swaying before his eyes and it took several long seconds for Steven Scott's drug-addled brain to separate the shapes and piece them into a coherent order.

A bang had roused him, then the piercing screams. Smoke and the acrid stink of cooked meat brought tears to his eyes and he forced himself to move from the spread-eagled position he had been placed into, something almost foetal. The movement made his stomach swim but he held the threat of vomit back.

A few feet away a figure loomed over the firepit, thrusting something black and heavy between a set of disembodied legs which writhed and sizzled on the rim of the brazier, each backswing spattering blood and bodily fluids onto the smooth concrete dais.

A wave of nausea gripped Scott again as he forced himself off the altar, landing heavily on his side. The stone was cold against his naked skin. He peered about, trying to orientate himself. The memory of the last few hours was hazy but as lucidity slowly returned and shock blunted the effects of the drugs his senses coalesced, leaving him horrified to find himself back at the heart of the black church. The familiar octagonal steps fell away to the lower floor. Over the course of many ceremonies he had been forced to stand as witness to the horrors of what happened on the altar but now as he looked down, abandoned on the polished stone, lay the cruel iron brand of The Crossed Keys, an item responsible for so much of the torment that had blighted his life and many others.

Scott slumped, wrapping his arms around his knees, fear rooting him where he sat, the overwhelming desire to escape igniting nerve endings but his brain unable to fire the required motor functions.

All around chaos unfolded as the congregation of cultists and visitors tried to escape the hall, pushing and shoving in an attempt to reach one of the tunnel exits leading to the initiate dormitories or the number of other cells and spaces set aside for the preparation of sacrifice or the velvet-bedecked playrooms ensconced along the eastern passages. The main double entrance doors which led back to Glenrafferty House were closed and Scott could make out the slow creep of smoke puffing from under them. Those who remained didn't seem to know or care which of the other exits they chose, hastened in their flight as the drift of acrid toxins started to noticeably fill the chamber.

Scott coughed too. The fire was getting worse. He imagined it must be in the main house, the tunnels acting as makeshift extraction vents both fuelling the flames and acting like narrow chimneys to remove the smoke.

He knew he had to move, and he knew the route he must take if he were to feel fresh air and sunlight on his face. On the other side of the altar, a clang rang out, a fearful glimpse around the edge offering a hint of the high priest's remains slowly cooking on the brazier. The coals had charred his skin black, burning away what hair he had left on his head and twisting his limbs into caricatures of what they once had been.

The figure backlit by the glow had discarded whatever he had brutalised the other man with, his shoulders and back were slick with the sweat of his exertions, and his right fist and forearm were soaked in blood.

In that second Scott was emboldened and he forced himself to hands and knees, pushing himself up to take stumbling steps away from the demonic figure who was laughing at his gruesome handiwork.

Shepard paused and took a breath. Not because he was fatigued or due to the hundred or so zig-zagging concrete stairs which had deposited him at the end of a deeper and much wider tunnel than the one leading from the clearing. He did it to take account of his surroundings and make sure he wasn't about to surprise, or be surprised by, Casey's men who had entered the subterranean complex before him.

In their haste, they had not locked the galvanised steel gate which separated the graffiti-strewn upper access tunnel from the stairs so his pursuit through the gloom had been silent and uneventful. The nail gun felt reassuring in his hand but he was well aware that he was blind to the situation he was walking into and that he was both outnumbered and outgunned. And not for the first time. He thought back to his most recent escapade, a brutal fight with Freaky Jackson in the landing bay of Hoey Cargo and then before that to another life, ingrained memories resurfacing of the freezing mountain burrows of Tora Bora and his months of tracking down and liberating captured Yazidi in the northern deserts of Syria. Remembering too the anxiety and fear that accompanied the claustrophobic and painstaking clearances of those booby-trapped hideouts and rocky caverns. He had taken for granted then the tools of his trade; assault rifle, night-vision equipment, and the weight and scope of Western military might. Right now, as he listened to the drip of ground water penetrating the ceiling cracks, he silently cursed himself that he hadn't had the foresight to look in one of the builders' toolboxes for a proper torch. The light of his mobile phone screen was doing little to penetrate the darkness.

From the base of the stairs, the tunnel extended about thirty metres before doglegging right. A central channel carried waste water and detritus which had blown down from above to a barred grate set into a pitted wall behind him. The stink of mildew and decay rising from the drain was overlaid by the faint tang of smoke. All was quiet save the scratch and occasional squeak of rodents.

Shepard edged along the wall until he arrived at the bend, surprised to see the gloom begin to dissipate slightly. Taking a peek around the corner revealed little more than a longer tunnel this time doglegging left. Now though, a series of cobweb-encrusted bulkheads offered pools of dull light at regular intervals.

As he moved around the corner a draught brought a stronger smell of burning and an indistinct low murmur of voices. He was halfway along, doing his best to stay in the shadows, when the unmistakable report of automatic gunfire echoed along the walls.

John Barrett reacted instinctively as the bullet struck the wooden upright and sprayed splinters into his cheek and forehead. Throwing up a protective hand to shield his eyes, he stumbled on the feet of the person in front and crashed heavily to his knees. The ground was wet and slimy with moss and he skinned a palm arresting his fall. The channel which ran up the middle of the tunnel was full of waste water with a slick of ooze floating on the surface.

"Everybody inside!"

The lower section of the gunman's face was obscured by a scarf bearing a grinning skull motif. The folding stock of the machine pistol was secured in the crook of his shoulder, the barrel indicating the chamber opposite the ante-tunnel he had appeared from.

Thinking better than to follow the strict instruction one man pushed on, heaving several cloaked acolytes and initiates out of the way, determined to press on in the direction of assumed freedom.

The blast of gunfire was deafening in the enclosed space, bullets riddling the man from hip to neck, his body dancing like a broken marionette. Finally, he slumped down the wall leaving a smear darker than the damp stains already marring it.

"Inside!" No remorse. No compassion. Simply an order.

No one else broke free. The stream of people loosely veered into the chamber, muffled sobs and self-pitying moans rippling among them. Barrett hauled himself up, his hands and knees smarting. Keeping his head low he blended into the surge.

Had Casey lost his fucking mind, he thought, replaying the ferocity and the surprise of the sudden strike. Barrett had watched wide-eyed from his seat as the red-hot poker skewered Margaret Jury. Had he missed something in Casey's demeanour? Were there signs the man was unhinged? Maybe, he decided. After all, he was the product of the loins of a twisted father, and brother to a pair of demented siblings. Perhaps there was a familial deficiency. An illness of the mind. He reflected on the gains achieved through the barbarity of old Joe Casey and his membership of The Crossed Keys and how they had been the source of his usefulness to the consortium over time.

The salacious information gained on policemen, politicians, judiciary and even royalty of stage, screen and noble birth from within the hallowed vaults of places like Glenrafferty; or other less salubrious middens, had helped guide the direction of a policy which had held together a fragile truce between legitimate government, those seeking anarchy and the organised criminal fraternity. Fear, favour and the ever-present threat of blackmail the consortium's currency to propagate their wider agenda.

Was it knowledge of all this that had brewed the recklessness Colm Casey had shown in his youth? A disregard for consequence that followed him as he assumed the mantle as head of the family, an ill discipline most recently highlighted in his attempt to murder Gordon Beattie in his hospital bed. Was this his final attempt to break free of a damaged past and shed the chains of confederation he believed to be holding him down? Barrett's mind settled on that point as the amorphous group of cultists, victims, visitors and honoured guests were herded at gunpoint over the threshold and into what he could now see was a much smaller space than the ceremonial hall. It was roughly half as wide as deep, the roof battened flat rather than an elaborate concave and it was ringed by decorative vestibules which overlooked the floor space.

A chill rose up his spine as he remembered Casey's earlier words, the feeling of dread increased by the smell of smoke which was now pervasive throughout the underground complex. *"Think of it as a rising of the phoenix,"* he had said. *"And after the cleansing fire, I'll scatter the ashes of the past and usher in a bright new dawn."*

As several other gunmen appeared above, Barrett quietly considered, with the benefit of hindsight, how perhaps he had chosen the wrong path in abandoning Beattie to his fate. After all, better the devil you know.

67

The plume of smoke rising from Glenrafferty House breathed embers high into the evening sky. A strengthening breeze fanned the flames and sent flurries of the burning ash to descend over the continued melee between protestors rallying on the playing pitches for a counterattack against the phalanx of PSNI officers battling to restore order.

The roar of the flames increased as the fire feasted furiously on the old building's timbers, its long tongues snarling, threatening to leap across and ignite the branches of the woodland trees. From her vantage point, Leigh-Anne Arnold could see those who had planned for an evening of ceremony and celebration trapped in windows and desperately calling for help.

The Northern Ireland Fire Service had arrived but their tenders remained blocked on the road by abandoned vehicles and hooligans launching salvoes of whatever ammunition could be plucked from trash can or grass verge. The only thing limiting the inferno from running rampant was the PSNI water cannon, the riot dispersal vehicle damping down the roof of the property rather than the fight in the protestors.

"Arnold?"

"Sir?" she said, turning away from the spectacle to the approaching Inspector Sheehan.

"Your guv and sergeant have called in an incident in the

woods."

"Are they okay?"

Sheehan shook his head. "It's not them. Victim's been provisionally identified as site security for tonight's event. Take Pearce and Fairfax to help secure the area until SOCO and an undertaker can get up there and retrieve the body. I've asked command to release an armed response and dog team to support."

"Do well," said Arnold, collecting her riot helmet from the ground and retrieving a bottle of water. The liquid cleansed her palate but didn't take away the smell of burning.

"Be careful," said Sheehan.

"Aye, good luck up here too," replied Arnold, formality abandoned amidst the ongoing battle.

A second later a roar mixed with jubilation and horror rose from protestors and the gathered onlookers as part of the Glenrafferty roof collapsed. The twisting plume of black smoke intensified.

She nodded at her colleagues and turned to face the darkening woods.

They were all going to need it.

Taylor coughed into her elbow as the smoke caught in her throat and quickly considered if it remained sensible to press deeper into a space that was becoming more confined and with a rapidly deteriorating air quality.

Any link with the outside world had gone. The last message had been a garbled report of fire spreading at the main house and a repurposing of resources to tackle the blaze and assist in the rescue of those trapped. Now her TETRA was just hissing a dull static as the concrete and tons of earth pressing down on her head masked any chance of a signal getting in. Or out.

The dark descent had revealed little other than an exodus

of rats which scurried in ever-increasing numbers along the raised walkways on either side of the grim central channel. When and where they could the rodents slipped down drain holes or into the grates that fed the overflow out to the wetlands surrounding the estate. There was no sign of Shepard, or anyone else and for a moment she wondered if the tunnel and her search might come to a dead end.

Then the rat-a-tat of gunfire, screams, and the rise of panicked voices was amplified along the rough walls. Any detail was muted by the slime and moss clinging to the walls but the emotion was distinct. Fear.

She gripped her sidearm tighter and ignited a mini-maglite torch, shining a narrow beam of pale light along the walkway, eventually illuminating an exit from the tunnel about forty feet away on the opposite side of the walkway.

As she continued on a careful approach, a sudden rush of rats spewed from a series of pipe heads running laterally along the waste channel, their skitters and squeaks loud in the darkness, their flight quickly followed by the sluicing of water and debris from the open tubes.

Taylor stopped dead in her tracks.

The mildewed and putrid smell of stagnant water was mixed with something else.

Fuel.

68

Steven Scott snatched up a discarded robe and shrugged into it.

The action was an effort as he was carried along in the scrum of bodies squeezing through the carved archway into an already packed space, although the benefit was that the bullet-riddled corpse was largely hidden from view.

Fighting the after-effects of his sedation it took him a moment to find his bearings, eventually placing where he was in relation to the altar room and the rest of the subterranean vaults by the decorative vestibules which overlooked the crowd.

No, the prisoners, he decided instead. The half dozen masked gunmen aiming assault rifles down at the circling crowd confirmed where the balance of power lay. Scott slowly eased as discreetly as possible towards the periphery, trying to get as far away from the man covering the doorway and close enough to the walls to make it difficult for those directly above to shoot down with any degree of accuracy. What had happened replayed as a fevered dream, the man he knew as Colm Casey instigating the bloodshed with the murder of the priestess he had seen partake of the macabre delights enjoyed in the room they were now trapped inside.

Each of the alcoves was accessed by a set of stairs that cut from the main tunnel up to what was in essence, a VIP box. Those dignitaries of The Crossed Keys who wished to, in privacy and with whatever predilection they savoured to hand, would watch proceedings unfolding on the floor and like the masters of Rome they could, and often would, decide on the fate of the individuals involved.

The iron beds and implements of torture had long ago been moved out, perhaps destroyed as rumour had started the search for truth, or more likely they had been closeted away in a private collection. Secure inside another house of horror where they had continued to fulfil their vile purpose.

Scott bumbled through the spiralling mass seeking the edges of the room, his gentle shoves earning grunts of indignation or bitter snaps of anger. He didn't care and pushed on, eyes searching the floor so as not to trip on the bolted iron rings which had once secured the initiates or those children collected from other institutions for the pursuit of entertaining The Crossed Keys membership.

The men in the upper alcoves were busy, shuttling back and forth between the balconies, but there were enough to keep a watchful eye on their captured prisoners. As Scott squeezed aside a poe-faced woman he found himself at the edge of the room. Her chagrin at being forced out of the way turned to ire as she was swept up in the mass and bustled away.

A moment later the thud of the outer door being heaved shut, followed by the sound of a heavy locking bar being set into place, threatened to cause total pandemonium.

The crowd surged forward. People screamed as they fell, their calls for help muffled as they were trampled.

Scott used the sudden space to crab around the edge, quickly coming upon the compact waste grate he had been seeking. It had been a chore for his small group to clean the chamber after the weekend orgies, sluicing blood and bodily fluids from the equipment and floors, hosing it down the various drainage holes, at one time forced to venture into the broad pipes in pursuit of a misplaced wedding band, and facing brutal retribution when it couldn't be found.

The drain offered access to a filthy sub-network of feeder pipes that eventually fed out to the wetlands and the sewage treatment facility on the outskirts of the Glenrafferty Estate. Like others around the complex, it provided those brave enough with one of the many hidden holes and surreptitious pathways to navigate their prison. That was until they found out Barry Toms was using it to escape on nightly sojourns to terrorise the wildlife and children from the local estate. After that, locks were renewed, screws replaced and security much tighter.

Scott inspected the grate which remained padlocked; the hasp was rusted and years of dereliction and neglect had left the grille looking weak. The vertical bars were warped and the area around the fixings crumbled. Taking a firm grip Scott pulled hard.

It didn't yield a millimetre.

Scott stole a glance at the alcoves overhead but he was hidden by the bodies surrounding him. Setting his feet on either side of the bars he reset his grip and heaved, jerking as violently as he could but the result was the same.

"Fuck!" He looked around the floor for anything which might be used to attack the fixings but there was nothing. Focused on the removal of the grate he was distracted until something wet sloshed down his back.

"What the hell?" His fingertips came away sticky, he didn't need to place his hand anywhere near his nose to catch the reek of fuel. Panic surged through his chest and he scrambled back to the grate.

Above the maddened crowd Casey's men had settled thick rubber hoses on the sills, which now spewed a viscous off-pink slime. Those with their faces upturned screamed as the fuel mix seared their eyes, those more fortunate still choked and spewed as the fumes began to overpower the desperation to escape.

Scott sprawled onto his back, his fists slipping from the rusted bars. Driven by fear he sprang back to the grate, narrowly escaping a drenching and being trampled to death. He heaved again, imagining he felt some give.

"I'll help you."

Scott started, he hadn't seen the man approach. He didn't know him. Didn't care.

"Go that side, use your feet," said Scott, the bare soles of his own leaving bloody marks on the pitted wall.

John Barrett did as instructed, feeling the strain through every sinew in his forearms, shoulders and legs as he wrenched at the grate.

He felt a slip and then both he and Scott sprawled backwards in a tangle of limbs.

"Again," screamed Scott.

They repositioned. Barrett focused on securing his grip, fixated on the screws. Had the bars bent a little? Were those cracks there before?

"One, two, three…" Scott counted down and they heaved again.

'After the cleansing fire…'
'Rise from the ashes…'
'A new dawn…'

Casey's words beat out a mantra as Barrett gritted his teeth, muscles screaming as he pulled, the rough iron biting into his palms, blood making it harder to maintain a grip. The fucking madman meant to burn them all. Was it poetic justice? A preliminary experience as a starter for an eternity in hell for their crimes on the mortal plane? They all probably deserved it, himself included he thought.

"But not like this," he said, the words to himself, Scott deaf to them under the tumult of noise.

"Again," screamed Scott.

The spray from above had stopped, the screams of fear and pain around them had not and then there was a moment of weightlessness as the grate hauled free.

There was no time to rejoice, no congratulatory words or a second to breathe in relief. Barrett shoved Scott head first into the exposed tube and followed immediately behind, plummeting down a shallow forty-five-degree drop into a putrid morass of God-knows-what.

The extract pipe was cramped, but large enough to rise onto haunches. It was pitch black and he could hear Scott scrambling forwards, splashing through the effluent. The younger man's voice echoed, his words urgent.

"Quickly."

Then Barrett felt his breath catch, Scott's filthy back was illuminated briefly as a wash of heat radiated through the pipe carrying with it the howls of a hundred agonies.

69

Shepard had the minor advantage because he knew from bitter experience it was only a matter of time before he made contact with the enemy.

His opponent, however, secure in his belief that command of the old subterranean complex hidden below the grounds of the Glenrafferty Estate was complete, would find the split-second delay in reaction would cost him his life.

After the crackle of gunfire, the harsh commands, and sounds of fearful protest that followed, Shepard had quickened his pace. The entrance tunnel brought him to an open steel hatch, a portal he found reminiscent of a bulkhead door on a naval warship. A sign beside the hatch was headed with the insignia and contact details of the local water company and he recalled from his earlier research on the site they had bought up a section of the estate after its closure, utilising some of the old air raid shelters and service infrastructure to house equipment and to re-lay pipework that siphoned off the overflow from the wetlands bordering the estate.

The hatch led from the tunnel to an open-plan storage area, another sign pinned on a galvanised guardrail warned of deep water and closing to inspect he found a metal grille set into the floor. Fast-flowing water passed two feet beneath, the overflow of groundwater being carried out through the drainage tunnels or storm drains to the treatment works.

The walls of the room were racked with antiquated metal shelving housing numerous sections of pipe, bends and other components from pumps to filtration devices. Scattered atop a grimy workbench were a number of electronic time clocks alongside an equal number of discarded plastic packing wallets. The rest of the floor space was overwhelmed by old iron water tanks and their more modern composite replacements, the latter still wrapped in protective plastic.

As he continued through to the next room there were signs of more recent labours. Shepard, casually taking inventory, deduced the cable reels, tools and other equipment shoved in haphazard piles had been brought down and hastily stored after the rapid push to get the main house ready for the New Light dedication. The bicep-thick armoured electrical cable laid on the floor and the overhead contractors' lights slung in loose arcs pointed to a job half done, but complete enough to facilitate the evening's event.

Stepping into the third space brought him face-to-face with his enemy.

The man was as broad as Shepard but a head smaller, giving him a stocky appearance and after a split-second of indecision, he dropped one of the jerry cans he was carrying and launched the other at Shepard who took a side step, adding a flourish of the hips which a matador would have been proud of.

The empty can sailed through the air to clang loudly as it struck the floor.

His opponent who had dipped a bovine brow and charged to tackle the intruder, now checked his momentum, throwing a wild swing in an attempt to gain something from his misjudged error.

Shepard raised the nail gun and fired into the back of the man's exposed head as he whipped past.

He dropped like a stone.

Putting a boot into his shoulder, Shepard rolled the body over. He was dead, the point of the projectile protruding from just below his left eye, an expression of shock frozen on his face. Turning back from the corpse Shepard caught an overwhelming scent that eclipsed the stink of smoke which had been steadily accumulating. It was a sweet oily bouquet that was pervasive and as he paid more attention to the storage room he realised why.

Several fire hoses snaked from a huge storage tank and there was no mistaking the heady scent of marine gas oil. An electric pump hummed nearby, and placing a boot on the nearest hose he could feel the transfer of fuel was underway. Stacked next to the uncapped storage tank were four large wooden packing crates. A crowbar used to pry them open lay beside and each was empty save for an armful of pink styrofoam packing pellets that remained in the bottom, the rest being liberally scattered around the floor.

Shepard took stock.

The man he had just killed was unarmed, but it was unlikely he would be as lucky again. He looked back around the room and finding nothing further of note followed the hoses out into another corridor. He had gone no more than ten feet when he was forced to throw himself into the cover provided by more stowed construction material and stacked hoarding, none of it any use unless he wanted to try and use a section of steel conduit as a makeshift javelin.

Preoccupied with keeping their prisoners in check, the two gunmen missed him as they rounded the corner, herding a group of adults and children towards another vault accessed by a reinforced steel door. The group was fashioned as though they'd been in attendance at some bizarre masquerade ball. Men in dinner suits, women in expensive couture, and many others naked beneath outlandish hooded capes but all had a look of terror etched on their faces.

"In there," said the lead, the barrel of his weapon indicating the way.

"Please, you don't need to do this. We have the means to pay you, just name the price—"

The pleading petition was silenced by a vicious pistol whip and a snarl of indifference. "Get the fuck inside."

From somewhere close by Shepard could hear wailing, a sound of horrible agony given voice.

What the hell was going on here? He searched the group for any sign Steven Scott might be among them but from his position he couldn't be certain.

As the man was picked up by his fellow prisoners and helped inside the room, Shepard continued to scan the pinched and fearful faces who were harried and harassed by their captors. His eyes briefly settled on one of the hoses which coiled away from the rest to sweep up in an elongated S shape, a coupler connection and heavy tap breaking its length just before it disappeared into an open vent two-thirds of the way up the wall beside the doors.

"Are youse serving your bloody time? Get the evil bastards in there!"

The booming voice poured vitriol at both custodians and their captives. "Come on, it's time these ungodly fuckers were sent to hell along with the rest of their number."

It took a second for Shepard to recognise the man. Like others in the group Colm Casey wore an outlandish hooded cloak, and he seemed uncaring of the nakedness beneath. His fists and forearms were blackened in blood and his face was spattered with gore.

"Can you hear that?" he called at the group. A sudden urgency sprang into the steps of those who recognised the figure stalking forward. Casey's words dripped with something approaching glee. "A cleansing fire to sear away your sins, that's just what you need." He was flanked by two other gunmen, submachine guns slung across their chests.

Shepard considered his options. Outnumbered, unarmed and lacking any support, a positive outcome from confrontation was unlikely.

As Casey reached out a hand to one of his men, Shepard recognised the item being passed across, hand to hand like the passing of a relay baton. Casey accepted the flare.

The pieces tumbled into place in Shepard's head.

The fuel, the styrofoam packaging pellets, the hoses. The mad bastard was pumping hundreds of litres of homemade napalm under the foundations of Glenrafferty, and throwing those he had caught into his homemade furnaces.

The recipe was simple. Casey's heavy fuel oil mixed with the pellets which would dissolve to then create a gel-like incendiary, the volatile and sticky mix burning longer than the fuel itself and at temperatures up to and exceeding twelve hundred degrees. If sprayed along the supporting structures or on any flammable surface and ignited, the chemical reaction would be intense enough to burn through steel, and as for exposed flesh? Shepard shuddered at the prospect. Anything left buried underground in the collapse would continue to burn for days.

Screams and cries for mercy rang out from inside what would soon be an incinerator. Casey's men took a few steps back as he approached.

"I'll see you all in hell," he said, slamming the door closed and spinning the lock. Then, a nod to the guard who manned the tap.

A dull tattoo beat on the locked metal portal. As the hose twitched savagely and began to disgorge the flammable jelly onto those trapped inside terror-stricken squeals echoed from the vent grilles.

Shepard thought of Colin, of the tales of torture and abuse he had shared, of the pain and shame he would never shed.

Then, of Steven Scott, and Taylor's desire to have him speak his truth and bring those who had perpetuated decades of evil crimes into the light to face justice. Those prosecutions perhaps opening the door to others, a legacy of Oliver Maddox's last wish. A way to hang Gordon Beattie.

Casey bid his man to stop and ably assisted by one of his accomplices the two began to extract the hose. Casey approached the vent.

Shepard thought of his wife Cara and young son Thomas, burning to death trapped inside their car.

It was no way to die.

70

"Go to hell!" Taylor wasn't sure if they were the exact words but the sentiment fitted the tone as she slid along the wall, sidearm in hand and approaching the corner.

The smell of fuel persisted as she moved in the opposite direction to the fleeing rats, the walkway ending at a small metalled stairway which on descending brought her out into a space that was more corridor than subterranean tunnel.

Orange sodium lamps illuminated the way, the bulkheads spaced evenly and granting enough light to spot intersections and doors as she moved. Along the route were loose collections of paint tins, stained coverings, step ladders and a detritus of construction materials, all the signs of hastily wrapped-up work placed to one side until it was required again. Kicked into the corner, where floor met wall, a number of thick fire hoses twisted over each other.

The rooms she passed were empty, rudimentary in function with peeling paint and the smell of mildew. Mostly they could be classed as storage spaces; in one instance shelves and boxes of leather-bound Bibles and hymn books rotted, their spines and pages mottled with mould.

The distorted screams which had followed the short burst of gunfire had quieted, but as she approached a T-junction another noise attracted her attention, the scuffle of feet and the occasional harsh bark of instruction. She followed the sound, noticing as she did another hose had been laid out along the floor of this section of corridor. Taylor paused at the shout and peeped one eye around the corner.

About twenty feet away two men manhandled another of the hoses, dragging it along the corridor to form a long U shape. Two other armed men stood slightly closer, near a sealed doorway. Inside, pitiful screams for help escaped through an unsealed ventilation grille. She had to double-take the fifth man, her recognition muddled at first but as he turned to speak, the left side of his face was clearly illuminated under one of the bulkhead lamps. Colm Casey, attired in an elaborately decorated robe, split the two groups.

As he motioned to one of his men to lift a locking plate roughly the same size as the open vent, Taylor started at a sudden crack and flash of light, the intense glare blinding her for a brief second. When her vision returned the corridor was awash with light and Colm Casey was readying to deposit the flare into the locked room of crying people.

As he raised his arm a section of hoarding stacked along the opposite side of the corridor collapsed.

❖❖❖

Shepard knew he would only have a brief second of surprise and so he had better make the most of it.

Casey held the flare at arm's length as the phosphorous raced up to temperature, his henchman close by and readying the heavy plate which would seal the furnace and the fate of those inside.

At the last possible second, Shepard heaved the steel conduits, timber batons and hoardings to send them crashing to the ground.

Casey checked his throw. His men on the hose and the one holding the plate flinched as the heavy objects scattered and bounced across the floor. The remaining gunman, equally caught off guard, dropped his aim. He was the primary threat, but Casey was the target.

Shepard exploded out of his cover, the nail gun raised and blindly peppering the air around the gunman with projectiles as he raced across the hallway to plough full pelt into Casey's back.

The impact crashed the two men against the wall, the flare falling from Casey's hand to spiral across the floor.

For a heartbeat, they all stared at each other.

"Fuck!" It was Casey who had noticed the prospect of imminent disaster first and he scrambled for the flare.

Shepard, springing back to his feet, slapped a boot out, sending it bouncing off the wall to tumble end over end in a shower of sparks.

The two men on the hose were oblivious as they scrambled for their weapons. Casey's protest was drowned out as automatic gunfire erupted from his man a few metres away. "NO!"

Shepard rolled as the bullets zipped around him, splinters of concrete and puffs of impact filled the air, the noise of the fusillade deafening but the flash and the intense wash of heat which followed eclipsed what had come before, and knocked the breath from his lungs.

"What was that?"

"For Christ's sake, Malkie, you need to see a doctor about your nerves," sneered Sean.

Malkie took a few steps away from where his partners worked and cocked an ear. "I'm fucking telling you I think I just heard one of those pop." His complexion was pale as he considered the consequences.

"You heard the pipes creaking or something," added Frankie, passing another time clock to Sean who crouched and stripping the end of a small gauge wire with his teeth. Spitting the excess sheath onto the passageway floor, he then twisted the bare ends around a pair of brass lugs protruding from a fist-sized electronic timer. A gentle tug to ensure connection and then he reached out a hand to his anxious accomplice. "Batteries?"

"Aye, here." Malkie passed some over. "I'm telling you though—"

"The rest of the timers are set exactly like Colm asked," soothed Frankie.

"What if one was faulty?"

"They're not faulty," said Frankie, teeth gritted, patience wearing thin.

"That's us now," said Sean, another set-up almost complete. "What's the numbers for this one?"

Frankie unlocked his phone, scrolled up the screen and recited a set of digits. Sean prodded in the digits. "Done, is that them all?"

"One more," confirmed Frankie.

"Do you think you can keep it together until we get the last charge set?" said Sean, standing up to face Malkie.

The condescending expression on his face fell when they all heard the echoing blast of automatic gunfire

Taylor stepped out and took aim as the gunfire erupted. The shooter was oblivious, and judging by his aim only loosely focused on his target. Shell casings spat from his submachine gun in a lazy arc and the sparks of impact downrange danced off the walls and ceiling.

She watched Shepard kick the flare and heard Casey roar a protest. Adjusting her sights she saw why and threw herself back behind the corner for protection a second before the whump of ignition and the sudden vacuum as oxygen was sucked out of the air. The blowback showered her with dust and debris.

Spluttering, with her pistol in a two-handed grip she peeled off the wall into the corridor. It was ablaze.

The gunman had been thrown back and lay against the tunnel wall and although disorientated, he had enough clarity of mind to notice her as a threat and scrambled to aim his weapon.

Taylor squeezed her trigger first, rounds striking the man just below his sternum and shattering his collar bone. Satisfied he was no longer a threat she ran forward.

"Shepard?" screamed Taylor. "Shepard!"

She threw a hand up in front of her face. The heat radiating from the inferno was so intense it pushed her back. Flames were devouring the material scattered around the floor and leaping to savage any and all combustible material.

Moving sideways, desperately struggling to protect herself from the intensifying heat and trying to see through the flames, her brain pieced together the last things she had seen before the explosion.

Shepard's rush. Casey dropping the flare. A scramble. The damaged hose.

"Jesus," she breathed, recalling the moment.

The hose running away from Casey had been damaged by the wooden hoarding and materials pushed over in Shepard's attack. She had noted the puncture a second after Casey, a ragged split spraying pressurised contents up the walls and along the ceiling, the gunfire and sparks igniting the fuel, severing her side of the underground structure from Shepard's and each second that ticked past saw the inferno become more enraged, the thick hose feeding the flames and fuelling the destruction.

"Taylor, is that you?"

"Tom!"

"You alright?" A shadow moved on the other side of a wall of flame. His voice sounded slurred.

"I might need my eyebrows seen to," she said, suppressing a nervous laugh. "Casey?"

"He's alive," Shepard shouted over the roar. "These other fellas aren't though."

Taylor grimaced, visualising the three men cowering before they were showered in the spew of fuel mixture.

"Can you get out?"

"I'm going after him—."

"Tom, it's over."

"Steven Scott is here, the men that took him from Ballyhallion killed a guard in the clearing."

"We found the body. You're sure it was Casey's men?"

"One hundred per cent. Casey's been pumping some kind of accelerant through this complex. If this fire spreads or he manages to ignite the rest it's going to collapse the estate buildings and bury this place."

"So forget Casey and get out."

"Are you going to leave Scott?"

Taylor didn't respond. Shepard shifted as tongues of flame whipped about him, his mind was whirling; he was becoming hemmed in by the flames and conscious of Casey launching a sudden retaliation.

"There's a door on your side. Can you get to it still? Is it damaged?" He cupped both hands around his mouth, shouting to be heard.

Taylor confirmed she could see the sealed portal and it was not damaged.

"He's trapped people inside, you need to get them out. I didn't see Scott but he might be among them."

Taylor frantically pulled some of the burning hoardings aside, casting a look around for anything that might help fight the fire, something to bridge the gap between them. But there was nothing.

"Taylor? Did you hear me?

"I heard you."

They were feet apart but may well have been on different

planets.

"Tom…"

"Get them out. You might end up with more than one person willing to talk if you're lucky."

"What about you?"

In an ominous reply, a section of galvanised cable tray collapsed from the ceiling with a howling screech, the fixings melted by the intensity of the blazing napalm. The crash threw up a wave of heat forcing Taylor to retreat. Sweat streaked her face, her hair stuck to her scalp, and her shirt was drenched under her body armour, the material clinging to her.

"You worry about you," said Shepard, backing away from the twisted metal and several cables which drooped dangerously, their plastic sheaths dripping molten fragments. "Good luck, Taylor."

"Tom, wait!" Taylor called but she received no response.

71

"Tom!"

Taylor repeated her calls several more times until the smoke and the heat saw her gripped by a fit of coughing. She doubled over, hawking up sputum as she tried to clear her lungs, the spittle was black and Shepard was gone.

Hopefully, if he had any sense of self-preservation he was searching to find a way back to the surface, to clean air and the cooling breeze that swayed the huge birch trees. She hawked up more black phlegm, resigned to the fact that it was more likely the soldier would be searching the tunnels for Casey, trying to buy her and those he had said were trapped time to make their escape.

She moved to the door and grabbed the locking wheel.

"Shit!" Taylor snatched her hand back, the metal heated to the point of scorching. Pulling down her sleeves for protection she tried again, needing a few attempts to get the cams moving. Once the wheel hit its stops, she hauled the door open and looked inside.

At a rough guess, there were a couple of dozen individuals and they ranged from young to later middle age. They had all fled to the recesses of the small room and were huddled together. Some were clad in ceremonial robes while others huddled in suits and finer gowns. Several soaked by the influx of accelerant were being comforted by others. There were screams of pain from those blinded or in agony as the corrosive fuel burned their skin. A ripple of terrified cries ran through the assembly.

"I'm a police officer. You need to follow me now," said Taylor, mag-lite searching the faces. "Steven? Steven Scott?"

No one acknowledged her instruction or identified themselves. Taylor flinched as another section of containment crashed down in the corridor behind her, the explosion of sparks bringing a collective cry of alarm from the group.

The heat was building. They had to go before they were cut off completely.

Taylor holstered her weapon and beckoned forward the nearest woman who was kneeling and under the protective arm of an older male.

"Up you get. Let's go. We have to move right now!"

❖❖❖

Shepard retreated the way he had come, quickly ducking under sagging sinews of melting cables that threatened to entangle him. His thoughts were with the detective inspector and his failure to wholly deliver on his end of their bargain to rescue Steven Scott. On the upside, he was sure Scott was here. Somewhere anyway, and hopefully still alive so that she might yet have the luck to find him. On the downside though, even if she did, the odds that any of them might make it back above ground were narrowing.

The punctured hose had ripped along its length and the fuel mix was well alight, the flames, having caught all the loosely stored material along the route, making progress slow and treacherous. The air although tainted by the smell of burning plastics was surprisingly clear of smoke; the draw of air along the passageways while acting to spread the flames also seemed to double as extraction. As he weaved along the passageway the previously bright bulkhead lamps flickered, several had blown and sparks spewed from shorting electrical equipment as the fire cut through cables and connection boxes. It took a few more minutes before he was back in the room where he had first met resistance. The man's body lay where he had fallen and the pump still ran to push Casey's potent mix out through Glenrafferty's underground passageways.

Futile though it might be, Shepard moved to kill power to the pump and disconnect the remaining hoses before the flames could work back along their length and blow the huge storage tank.

He was almost at the electrical board when he sensed movement.

Without senses honed through years of fighting wars and primed to anticipate danger the blow might have been devastating, but his split-second reaction combined with the adrenaline coursing through his veins limited the impact of the initial blow, Shepard managing to twist away enough that the descending crowbar missed his head by an inch to instead crash mightily onto his right shoulder. The blow sent his arm numb to the wrist. With his heart pounding he rolled away from the surprise assault.

Colm Casey stalked forward, swapping the long iron crowbar he had recovered from beside the crates from hand to hand. The flickering lights added a malevolent quality to an already vicious expression.

Shepard scrambled to put some distance between them, seeking anything that he could snatch up and use in defence.

The flames from the corridor had worked rapidly along to lick at the open doorway, seeking sustenance to further fuel an unquenchable appetite.

The two men faced each other a few metres apart. The tension crackled, as tangible as the sparks spraying from the malfunctioning electrical distribution boards.

Neither spoke. They both knew only one of them could leave, and that was if the growing inferno didn't kill them both first.

The able-bodied led the injured, their hands supporting those who were lame from trampled limbs or helping guide those who had been blinded by the sticky mix of fuel oil and dissolved styrofoam.

Taylor led them all. A temporary saviour guiding them through a hell of claustrophobic semi-darkness and the heat of hell fire.

She had ditched her body armour in the corridor outside where the captives had been held and stripped to her vest, the heat sapping her as the organising of the group's exit took far longer than it may have done in normal circumstances; a necessity so that those drenched in fuel weren't suddenly turned into human torches. Thankfully, the carefully choreographed exit succeeded with no additional casualties bar the sacrifice of her police-issued equipment which would by now have been claimed by the fire. The only items she retained were her weapon and torch.

After a thorough inspection, Steven Scott hadn't been in the group and any enquiry had been met with the mute blank stares of immediate trauma. There was nothing she could do about that or for Scott now except pray his death had come quickly. If he remained somewhere in the complex, chances were he was facing a grisly end.

She had travelled for several minutes now, trying to retrace her original route but had been forced to divert as smoke and the rapid spread of the blaze had blocked passageways or plunged them into total darkness. More confusing than the maze of passageways was Casey's agenda. His family had bought Glenrafferty when it came up for sale, so was the deal with New Light an insurance scam, or was he really bitter enough to cross Geordie Corry and burn down the Loyalist developer's blue ribbon investment on day one? Wiping sweat from her brow she decided those questions would have to wait, the answers only to be revealed if she managed to get herself and her party of misfits to safety.

Arriving at a T-junction she swore to herself. Did it look familiar? Had she travelled a looping circuit to end up no further forward? Spotting a dull glow, the dim outline of another heavy metal hatch opening off the passage gave her some hope so she moved forward confidently beckoning those behind along, sure now this was new territory and potentially some way closer to an exit.

Taking a steadying breath and readying her sidearm, she shouldered around the doorway.

It was a toss-up as to who was more surprised.

"Don't shoot—"

"Police—"

"We're unarmed." The words were spoken by the older of the two men, both raising hands in a gesture of surrender.

"Steven Scott?" Taylor moved closer, her tone echoing her surprise at finding the man she had sought since Finn Abbott's death delivered to her fingertips seemingly none the worse for his traumatic experience.

The two men were filthy and glancing towards an open grate she suspected their route had been a desperate one. Scott gave her a wary glance, but she knew it was him.

"Steven, I know you were helping Oliver Maddox. I'm here to make sure you get out and have a chance to tell your side."

Scott gave the slightest nod but he was tense, his body language timid and uncertain as he gauged the group following her.

Taylor acknowledged the look. "There's a fire spreading through the complex, these people were trapped and we need to find a way out."

"Casey killed them," said Scott, voice a vibrato of emotion. "He—"

"I know what he did," said Taylor. "He's no threat to you right now. Are either of you familiar with this place, can you guide us out?"

Scott looked about and the man he was with, bespectacled and suited did likewise, avoiding her scrutiny. Taylor thought he looked familiar, but couldn't place him through the grime and under the pressure of the circumstances. Taking a beat she inspected the room herself for the first time.

Roughly eight metres square it had two archways opposite the hatch she had entered. Parked beside the arch was a mobile scaffold and from the amount of contractors' tools and equipment strewn about it seemed to be the central dumping ground for the incomplete works to the upper buildings. If they were now closer to the main house chances were they were also closer to an exit. Smoke drifted in through one of the archways and the lighting around the room flickered.

"I'm pretty sure if we go that way it leads to an old service entrance. There's a fire break through the woods that doubled as an access road the deliveries would come down," said Scott. The archway he pointed to was wreathed in dull grey smoke. He didn't look certain. Taylor gave a reassuring nod.

"Okay, we'll try it." She cast an eye about the space. "They had to bring all this kit in somehow."

As she rallied them to move, several things happened simultaneously and in the chaos of events, she didn't see John Barrett snatch up a chisel from the nearest workbench.

❖❖❖

Shepard hauled a thick electrical cable from the open fuse board and thrust it towards a charging Casey, showering him in sparks and throwing his aim.

The ferocious overhead chop of the heavy iron crowbar deflected off the electrical cabinet as he tried to avoid the smoking cable and the exposed components inside.

The live cable crackled, showering both men in sparks and

as Casey lined up for a lateral counter-swing, Shepard knew he needed more than the flimsy cable for defence.

He lashed the cable out, whipping the live connections at Casey's head and then he let it go, using the distraction to spring forwards, aiming to get under Casey's wild backhand and wrestle the crowbar from his grasp.

The men crashed together, Shepard pinning his opponent's arm, the two pivoting around each other as each tried to gain an advantage.

Their faces were inches apart and twisted into masks of bitter aggression, both evenly matched as they crashed into the sides of the electrical cabinets, dislodging the thin aluminium doors and loose stacks of equipment.

The encroaching flames made short work of snapping up the scattered tools and boxes, the heat building as the inferno followed the fuel back towards the storage tank.

Shepard's grip on Casey was slipping on a mixture of sweat and blood slicking the man's arms. Feeling the pressure ease, Casey launched a headbutt, scoring a crunching impact just above the bridge of his opponent's nose.

The impact flashed bright behind Shepard's eyes and he stumbled, trying to maintain purchase but Casey found leverage, pushing the crowbar forwards in both hands and driving him back towards one of the old iron water tanks.

Shepard, temporarily giving up on the struggle, let himself fall. The unexpected lack of resistance overbalanced Casey and he tumbled, landing heavily on top of his slightly smaller adversary.

With teeth gritted against the battering of the bar and sudden weight pressing on him, Shepard launched an uppercut, the open heel of his palm catching Casey under the chin and rocking his head backwards.

Unperturbed, Casey slid both fists down the shaft of the metal bar and raised it above his head.

Shepard writhed wildly, trying to shake off his opponent or at the very least upset the strike.

The blow came down with a wicked anger behind it, Shepard managing to buck enough to see the blow glance off his shoulder but not enough to unseat Casey who was resetting, winding up a second attempt to crack his skull like a nut.

All the while the creep of flames was closer, the ferocity scorching the skin, filling their lungs with super-charged air and the pollutants of burning embers.

Casey's hips pressed down, his back arched, arms extended overhead.

Shepard snaked out a hand and caught a rope of melting cables, the plastic burning his palm and wrist as he snatched it from the flames, hurling the length towards the face grinning down at him.

Casey screamed as the sticky plastic struck him; the exposed outer sheath had melted to goo and the more he tried to free it the more it clung to his skin and hair. He jumped to his feet wrestling the tentacles of burning material from around his head in a wild rage.

Shepard struggled back to his knees, seeking a weapon and trying to dampen down the sleeve of his shirt which had caught on fire.

Casey, half blind, half maddened lashed out. Blow after blow rained in on Shepard who covered up when he could and rolled with the impacts when he couldn't. Blood trickled from the cut above his nose. The vision in his left eye blurred, his cheekbone perhaps broken from a clean strike which had evaded his defences, the area swelling rapidly, one nostril blocked with gristle or blood, and his hands felt aflame.

Casey was unrelenting. Shepard tried to grab at the crowbar, snatching at the man's arms and hands but was unable to gain purchase.

As the fury continued, Shepard could hear Casey's huffing wheezes increase. At first, he put it down to the physicality of the fight exacerbated by the noxious fumes but then he realised, Casey was laughing.

Behind every blow, his lips were curled to reveal bloodied teeth, plastic smouldered on his skin and his right eye was welded shut. The pain of his injury was driving him on, his laughter mocking Shepard who knew he couldn't keep on absorbing the blows.

Desperately weaving to the right, Shepard almost walked right into the frayed and sparking electrical cable he had first used to distract Casey.

His opponent had seen it too, batting the dangling cable towards him and Shepard felt the shower of sparks on his face as the cable sailed perilously close, the exposed wires shorting in blue-white arcs as they crossed his eye line.

He scrambled backwards but was rapidly running out of room, Casey forcing him back towards the bank of electrical cabinets, closing off his retreat and forcing a mismatched last stand.

Shepard looked for a way out, a way past but the fire was raging now, igniting all in its path, continuing its progress along the old linen-wrapped pipework and heavy cable trays above.

Shepard glanced overhead as Casey stalked forward, determination to finish the job etched on his face.

The crisscross of metal containments feeding the electrical cabinets extended in all directions. Flames devoured a good seventy per cent.

It was a last resort and a long shot at that.

Shepard leapt up, grabbing at the edges of the nearest section, and let his weight and gravity do the rest, jerking his shoulders and legs wildly, furiously hauling at the fixing and joints.

The basket had never been designed to bear the weight of a person in the best of circumstances, but weakened by a fire intensified by Casey's concoction of fuel oil and packing pellets it could only offer minimal resolve.

Shepard felt the bolt heads sheer and he tumbled to the floor, a large section of the containment peeling away, the freed weight adding to the wave of momentum as it ripped from the ceiling. Casey managed a wide-eyed look of horror before he was buried under the twisting metalwork.

Gasping from the impact of landing flat on his back, Shepard struggled to sit up, pushing aside some of the mangled frame which had collapsed across his legs.

He didn't feel any pain but both shins and his upper right thigh bloomed blood.

Casey was pinned, one arm twisted unnaturally as the other weakly battled to shift some of the weight. Dust covered his face and when he coughed, flecks of scarlet marked his lips.

Shepard, having got to his feet, glowered down.

Casey's hand flopped. Sobs of painful laughter escaped in wheezing gasps. Shepard could see where a threaded rod which had held the trays in place had pierced his chest, probably puncturing a lung.

"Too little too late," gurgled Casey, his eyes rolling back as a violent spasm sprayed blood from his mouth. He grinned.

Shepard heard the roar of the flames intensify, the fire's rampage fanned by the collapse and rapidly seeking out the new feeding grounds it moved at pace towards the big storage tanks.

He didn't have time to catch his breath as, stumbling across the room, he forced his legs to cooperate.

When he reached the door to the water service storage area he collapsed over the threshold. It was an awkward leopard crawl to the floor grille and, biting down against the pain radiating from his burned hands, he hauled open the grate, tumbling into the dark void to then be snatched away by the torrent of raging water.

For several long seconds, he drifted through an icy bleakness, surrounded by a vast freezing silence and then the water around him and the tunnel above erupted in flickering orange light.

❖❖❖

"Get the fuck out of my way!"

The voice boomed behind Taylor and she spun to see a man shoving his way through her party of frightened evacuees.

Geordie Corry was bare chested under an open dress shirt and wore a pair of suit pants, black polished derby shoes, unlaced, and no socks. Dressed in a hurry.

"Mr Corry?"

"You have me at a disadvantage," said Corry as he approached, reeking an air of authority and self-importance. "Regardless, if you know who I am you know who I represent."

"I'm Detective Inspector Veronica Taylor, sir." Taylor raised a blocking palm as he made to stride past. Corry slapped it aside.

"I didn't ask for an introduction. Get out of my way if you know what's good for you, Inspector."

"Mr Corry—-"

"Is that you Barrett? Are your duplicitous masters behind all this?" Corry had turned his ire on the man who had moved away from Steven Scott. As Corry's rage became more focused the man looked like he wished he could melt into the wall.

Steven Scott scurried a few steps back as Corry approached.

Barrett? Taylor recited the name in her head and tried to

see past the filth and ruffled hair. Barrett? Where had she seen him?

A crack of gunfire echoed around the chamber.

Jesus! Taylor flinched, whipping her weapon up and scanning for the threat. A ripple of terrorised wails ran through her group, the air fizzed with tension and she could feel they were on the verge of stampede. She had heard a grunt as the bullet struck someone, sensed the body fall and others around it crouch to offer aid.

Scott had fallen to curl into a ball beside a tool locker and Corry and the source of his anger, Barrett, wheeled on the newcomers.

"How do we get out of here?" There were three of them, and although two were armed with pistols, the vocal and the most nervous looking seemed to present the most danger.

"Put the guns down," shouted Taylor, moving forward to cut an angle of interception between this new group and the rest.

"Fuck off." There was no acknowledgement a weapon was pointed at him. The man marched forwards, fear and panic in his eyes. "Which way—" But he never got to finish.

Taylor felt the tremor faintly at first, a vibration that built from under the soles of her feet to rise in a crescendo of ear-splitting magnitude.

The wave of pressure accompanying the explosion that ripped through the underground complex was exacerbated by the narrow passageways, their inadequacy to offer release rupturing like arteries blocked with the excesses of an Ulster Fry too many.

The three men were buried under the ceiling collapse as walls and passageways began to implode, the damage from the fire undermining the structural supports holding back the tons of earth above their heads.

The remaining lights in the room flickered, blinked out and

then came back on.

Taylor's ears buzzed and she made to move but found herself lying on her side. Her head was splitting and when she touched her hairline, her fingertips came away bloody.

Confused, she gazed around. The air was a haze of debris, dust and shifting earth. One archway was gone, the other holding fast, just about, with huge cracks in the surrounding concrete.

Scrambling over the rubble those who had followed her were now gripped in a pandemonium of panic, seeking the only way out now presenting itself.

Coughing, Taylor pushed herself to her knees, searching the ground for her weapon but seeing no sign.

Several further tremors rumbled through the ground then. The report of more dull explosions. Her teeth chattered, water poured in from the far wall where a huge scar ripped along its length and a deluge poured into the space. The flood waters washing equipment away and beginning to take hold, pooling in the lower section of the now off-kilter floor.

"Steven!" Her voice came out as a croak, and she expelled another lungful of dust and smoke in a hacking cough. "Steven?"

She spotted him as she stumbled towards where he had taken refuge.

Scott scrambled away when she reached out to him.

"It's Veronica." She had to shout over the pounding of the water, wiping the dust from her eyes to see better. "Come on, we have to go."

Scott let her pull him up.

She screamed. The impact was sudden. Savage. She toppled beside Scott. The kick to her kidneys radiated pain around her abdomen.

Geordie Corry looked down in contempt as he sent in another kick.

"Leave them!" The order came from the other man. From Barrett.

Taylor squeezed her eyes against the pain and made to rise.

Barrett, had she seen his photograph in her DC's report? Somewhere else? A vision of another soaring space then the chill of darkness. Of water.

Barrett. Alongside Gordon Beattie inside Hoey Cargo. A disembodied voice in the undercroft below before there had been bullets and bloodshed.

Corry relented, scrambling across the collapsed blockwork. Barrett followed.

Taylor bit against the pain, rising to her knees, lashing out a hand in a futile attempt to grab him.

Barrett stumbled on the uneven ground, Taylor capitalising to heave herself up and throw herself at him.

"Taylor!" The shout had a warning note, a familiarity.

Barrett punched her. She felt the impact and rode the sudden breathlessness, continuing to wrestle him.

His second punch felt different. The power went from her legs.

"Taylor!"

Barrett slipped from her grasp, scrambling frantically towards the archway like the devil was on his heels.

Arms gently cradled her head.

She looked down, her palms were bloody. Vest soaked with it.

"Taylor." The tone was comforting.

"Shepard…"

72

"Get this lot bloody moving and another ambulance up here!"

Macpherson stamped across the grass and wagged a furious fist at one of the uniformed constables who, in trying desperately to organise the chaos of paramedics, fire appliances and police vehicles, had managed to inadvertently cause a roadblock.

The walking wounded had begun to arrive shortly after the first explosion, the dull crump and subsequent tremors reverberating through the estate and causing half of the main Glenrafferty House to collapse into its foundations. The other half continued to burn and throughout the woods, trees had fallen into deep sinkholes and at the central motte, reports were filtering back that the large grass-covered mound had been completely swallowed by the earth.

"Walking wounded over there," said Macpherson to a pair of paramedics burdened by their large medical bags. "We've a gunshot wound and a few broken limbs over by the tunnel."

It was bedlam.

The DS looked around at the faces. Some weeping. Most shellshocked. Men, women and children in various degrees of dress and undress. The nature of why that was the case twisted in his guts

"None of these bastards gets to slink away without an officer cuffed to their wrist, do you hear me?" he shouted, indicating the group of adults.

Some trained crisis officers and hastily called local care teams had arrived to start assisting with the immediate treatment and safe recovery of the young boys, girls and adolescents.

Taylor was nowhere to be found amongst any of them.

"Sarge…"

He cursed himself for letting her go in without him. For letting her go in at all. Of all the half-cracked, half-baked schemes and scrapes he'd survived in nearly twenty years of policing, he should have seen disaster writ large.

"Sarge!"

Macpherson volleyed an empty first aid kit and turned to the call.

"Christ on a bike!"

Leigh-Anne Arnold was hobbling down the short, grassy bank from the half-collapsed tunnel entrance, supporting a young man. Behind her, Tom Shepard carried a body in his arms.

"She's been stabbed," he said, laying Taylor on the first available flat patch of grass.

Macpherson swore. She was deathly pale.

Blood soaked her vest top and slicked Shepard's arms and chest. He sank to his knees and began CPR.

"Medic!" screamed Macpherson. "Get me a fucking medic over here there's an officer wounded."

Arnold fell down beside them, ripping open a fresh first aid kit.

From the corner of his eye, Macpherson spotted a camera crew and photographer who had managed to evade the cordon. "Get them two out of here," he screamed.

As two uniformed officers sprinted across to intercept the

press duo Macpherson snatched up a ball of gauze and bandages and put pressure on the wound to Taylor's side. "Hang on, Ronnie. You bloody stay with me."

Shepard blew out a breath, positioned his hands and began counting compressions.

"Where the fuck are they?" Macpherson raged, looking back down the hill to where, beyond the tree line, the Glenrafferty Home for Troubled Boys burned.

Epilogue

"…Belfast wakes to news of tragedy this morning…scenes of chaos last night at the inaugural dedication ceremony at the site of the infamous Glenrafferty Boys Home…"

The dull hum and bleep of machinery which had offered a soothing lullaby now lured Veronica Taylor back to consciousness, the news reporter offering commentary and update on the intervening hours.

"…protestors opposed to the redevelopment of the home which would have seen the controversial religious organisation New Light establish its headquarters and so-called 'Super Church' at the site, managed to break through protective fences and overwhelm police lines…"

Taylor flinched as memory became pain, fleeting images of blue lights, water cannon and the choking veil of smoke. She moved a hand across the thin blankets covering her body, noticing her bare arms and the patterned sleeve of a hospital gown. A cannula was secured to the back of her hand by a cross of translucent tape. The movement made her ache and she felt disconnected, her memory muddy.

The television continued to drone as she took her bearings; beside her lay the remote to operate the hospital bed and looped on the safety rail was a self-administering morphine drip. More memory flooded back, seeming to prompt the reporter.

"…the outbreak of fire which claimed the main property and several outbuildings has now been brought under control…

unconfirmed reports suggest there are a number of fatalities...a
spokesman for New Light has condemned the attack, as have the
police and civic leaders..."

Fatalities, thought Taylor, feeling at once grateful that her name would not be included on the list but also overwhelmed, almost on the verge of tears at how close she had come to death. Mental images of those final moments projected onto the stark white wall of her hospital room. The flight through the flames. Finding Steven Scott. The sudden explosion. Dust. Darkness.

Barrett. John Barrett as she now knew him.

She had been lucky according to her surgeon. The thin chisel with which Barrett had stabbed her, had lacerated her spleen, resulting in a sudden and profuse bleed. If it hadn't been for immediate first aid and that paramedics were on scene to medically intervene it would have been touch and go. Miraculously the stabbing missed any other vital organs and structures so with care, her recovery wouldn't be prolonged.

Shepard lifting her from the rubble was her last memory before unconsciousness. Her next was Macpherson's red face discharging a sailor's repertoire of swear words as he encouraged expediency en route to the nearest hospital. She drifted off again after that, waking briefly in a recovery room and then again when her surgeon had come in to explain what had happened and to deliver her prognosis. She'd live to fight another day.

The television reporter continued to drone.

"An unnamed source reports developer Geordie Corry is helping
police with their enquiries. There has been no comment from Corry
Developments, however, this perhaps suggests there were a number
of shortcomings in the recent construction works to prepare for the
inaugural event. A spokesman for the Health and Safety Executive
has refused to comment while their investigation is ongoing."

She glanced at the clock, pointless as the hands were frozen at ten to two, unsure how long it had been since Macpherson had visited and briefly filled her in on what was happening in the immediate aftermath of the disaster at Glenrafferty.

The infamous sandstone structure was now a ruin, burned to the ground along with most of the outbuildings. A number of its new owners and Geordie Corry had been apprehended trying to leave the estate under cover of the ensuing chaos. They were all now in the process of answering difficult questions. Macpherson knew little other than that Corry remained petulant but considering the brewing media storm he expected it was only a matter of time before somebody's tongue shook loose.

Steven Scott was safe and providing a detailed witness statement on his working relationship with Oliver Maddox and what had happened to him in the horror chambers below the home, both in recent days and long years before. Carrie Cook, who had been sitting in, reporting back that it made for a sickening listen.

Taylor had dropped her head onto her pillow as Macpherson regaled her between chomping through the gift of grapes he had brought. She knew from Maddox's diaries it would be shocking. The fallout would be seismic. Over the next few days, she could imagine the sudden resignations, the early retirements and career breaks. It wouldn't be long before the call for a public inquiry came.

A migraine began to manifest behind Taylor's eyes as she considered the future for the victims. Could there ever be an unbiased and judge-led investigation into what had gone on? Glenrafferty wasn't the first place where institutional abuse had been uncovered, nor likely the last where the alleged perpetrators were those who should be leading the charge for justice. To date there had been no official apologies, and regret and promises to ensure more would be done to prevent future occurrences had only ever amounted to lip service.

In most other instances where predatory groups had been uncovered infiltrating safe spaces to abuse positions of trust, the result had been a whitewash. Prosecutions were resolved with misdemeanour charges off the back of plea deals or custodial sentences only for the lowliest of rank. The stink never travelled any higher than the first rung. Until now. The fallout from Glenrafferty, around New Light and those who had secreted themselves at its centre was surely too big a storm to weather.

And then there was John Barrett.

The grey man, a creature who it seemed spun the web and teased the threads of corruption.

Her urgent words in the ambulance were flecked with blood and pain, telling Macpherson of the name she had learned. Recalling Hoey Cargo. ACC Wallace. Beattie. Her wounds.

Macpherson's raid had come too late. The Titanic penthouse apartment was empty. Whoever John Barrett really was, he had cut the rope and walked away.

"You haven't lost your appetite then?"

Taylor, deep in contemplation, hadn't heard the visitor enter.

She looked at the few empty grape stems left in the punnet, and then into the penetrating cobalt eyes sizing her up.

"You look a lot better than last time I saw you," she said.

"I wish I could say the same." Gordon Beattie was up and walking unassisted. He offered a concerned nod towards the tubes, medical paraphernalia and bandages.

"Don't worry I'll live."

"Glad to hear it," he said with a look towards the television. "Your handiwork?"

"Not all my own," said Taylor.

"That's what I like about you, Veronica. You're not a glory

hunter." His smile faded to something more sombre as images of the obliterated care home played on the screen. "It's about time that abomination was razed to the ground and I'm not afraid to tell you I won't be shedding any tears for the bastards who ended up buried inside it."

"What do you want, Monster?" said Taylor.

"People tell me you were a regular visitor when I was upstairs. I'm returning the favour."

"I was making sure you hadn't died before I could lock you up and throw away the key."

The answer elicited a chuckle from her nemesis, the laughter sounded odd under the circumstances but she almost felt like joining in.

"Actually on that revelation, this is only a flying visit. I'm on my way to see Solomon about some compensation following your spurious claims and as a result of my terrible injuries." A mock flash of pain crossed his face, hand kneading his back

Taylor rolled her eyes, feeling weariness creep over her. Beattie continued, picking up a thin plastic folder she hadn't noticed him deposit on her tray table.

"Seeing as I'm in for a few quid, I brought you a present to say thanks."

"I don't need gratitude from you," she said, eyeing the paperwork archly.

Beattie shrugged. "Take it anyway. It might prove useful."

Taylor reached out and flicked open the cover. The first image she saw was a surveillance shot of John Barrett. Several more followed and the next few pages offered a summary of information. After that more faces. More details.

"Are you looking for me to do more of your dirty work?" said Taylor, one hand on the document wanting to hand it back but reluctant to do so.

Beattie noticed the hesitation. "We're different sides of the same coin, Veronica. People like us keep the peace here. We just have different ways of going about it."

"We're nothing alike," she snapped, the blip of the heart rate monitor increasing.

"You keep telling yourself that," he said.

"I won't be in here forever you know."

"I hope not." A grin split his face, slits of cobalt caught in the light as he turned to leave.

Taylor kept her hand firmly on the folder.

"I'll see you around, Monster."

"Not if I see you first."

❖❖❖

Dublin was bathed in sunshine and Tom Shepard paused to purchase a cool drink from a street vendor, then walked the short distance to rest at a standing table next to some railings overlooking the sparkling River Liffey.

The pedestrians and traffic crossing the Samuel Beckett Bridge on their commute were oblivious to his observations. On the water pleasure craft and water taxis cut along quietly while nearby, the staff of a renovated training vessel turned floating restaurant formed a human chain to load provisions from a delivery truck parked up on the cobbled dockside.

The sun was pleasant and under normal circumstances Shepard would have enjoyed an hour or so of people-watching, adding in a bite to eat and then maybe a beer and a stroll along the waterfront to work off the calories.

But these weren't normal circumstances.

Across the river, soaring steel and glass structures housed the headquarters of economy, infrastructure, telecommunications and international government liaison. Finding himself in the capital of Ireland, a hundred and something miles from the chaos unfolding in Belfast was as much a surprise as when Taylor's irascible detective sergeant had called for the ambulance to stop, opened the back doors, and told him to get out.

Shepard took the offer of liberty for what it was, gratitude for saving a life. A life precious to both of the men. He had offered a hand and Macpherson shook it fiercely, his eyes red rimmed in worry for the woman who only still clung to life because of Shepard's intervention.

He considered his and Taylor's shared history briefly and how it had stemmed from the desire to see Gordon Beattie answer for his crimes. How that goal had morphed into something much bigger than either could ever have foreseen and although the sheer scale of what they faced was vast, those involved largely faceless and their victims innumerable; what drew both him and Taylor closer was the suffering they had endured on the most personal level. The loss of kin. Of belief in a system they had invested their lives and their trust in.

The phone call had been unexpected, the offer intriguing. Although her voice was strained he could hear in it a resolute determination and he knew she would recover.

Draining the cola, he tossed the empty can in a waste receptacle before picking up the dossier he had placed on the table as he drank.

Walking to the water's edge he shook the pages free, watching them flutter to the waves below, drifting slowly on the current before sinking from sight. He had no need to read it again. He had already memorised it. In a final act of abandon, he committed the folder to the depths too.

Anyone watching him move off across the bridge would have noted his gait was stilted somewhat. He hadn't fully recovered from his injuries but he was eighty per cent and his mood was positive.

A few hundred metres away, inside one of the soaring towers on the opposite bank, was a man who could help him locate his quarry. He would protest of course, but Shepard would be persuasive.

Now armed with the information he needed and set on his path, Tom Shepard knew that after this visit, there could be no going back.

Historical Note

The book you have just read is a fictional work, and any resemblance to actual entities or persons either living or dead is purely coincidental in regards to the fictitious organisations mentioned or the roles and titles of the fictional characters within its pages.

Not far from my childhood home, a nondescript house once stood, inconspicuously blending in among the bustling streets of East Belfast. Adjacent to shops and residences, it shared a boundary with a primary school. Although unremarkable in appearance, the infamous Kincora House was the site of real horrors, the chilling accounts of which continue to horrify us even today.

In the 1980s, allegations began to surface publicly, detailing the horrifying abuse suffered by the boys at Kincora. An investigation conducted by the Royal Ulster Constabulary (RUC) confirmed the seriousness of the abuse and identified several influential individuals involved. Shockingly, despite the evidence, no prosecutions were pursued.

As public awareness grew and anger mounted, three staff members were eventually charged and sentenced to prison for their involvement in the abuse serving six, five, and four years. However, suspicions of a cover-up persisted, and allegations of a wider network of abuse emerged, including claims of high-profile individuals participating in gay orgies at Kincora and other locations, north and south of the border.

Attempts to uncover the truth have faced significant obstacles over the years. Various enquiries conducted in the early 2000s failed to bring justice, and as suppressed testimonies and evidence began to surface, some victims who spoke out were threatened with criminal libel charges. Former members of the security services also came forward, alleging that information about the abuse at the home was intentionally suppressed by their superiors and that paramilitary groups, government officials, and other influential individuals involved in the paedophile ring were being blackmailed by intelligence agencies during the turbulent times of the Troubles.

Despite ongoing efforts by victims and advocates, the truth about the crimes committed at Kincora has been difficult to fully expose. The scandal has been marred by controversy, bureaucratic obstacles, and alleged cover-ups. A comprehensive independent enquiry into historical child abuse, launched in the aftermath of the revelations surrounding Jimmy Savile's abuse, faced challenges including Kincora within its scope.

At the time of writing, a formal apology for the victims and a resolution of the long-standing scandal remained pending, further complicated by the political turmoil in Northern Ireland and the demolition of Kincora House. The fear persists that the authorities may now attempt to close this dark chapter without holding all responsible parties accountable for their heinous acts.

❖

Get Exclusive Material

GET EXCLUSIVE NEWS AND UPDATES FROM THE AUTHOR

Building a relationship with my readers is *the* best thing about writing.

Visit and join up for information on new books and deals and to find out more about my life growing up on the same streets as Veronica Taylor and Tom Shepard, you will receive the exclusive e-book 'IN/FAMOUS' containing an in-depth interview and a selection of True Crime stories about the flawed but fabulous city that inspired me to write.

You can get this **for free,** by signing up at my website.

Visit at www.pwjordanauthor.com

Afterword

THANK-YOU FOR READING 'THE CROSSED KEYS'

I sincerely hope you enjoyed the second novel in The Belfast Crime Series. If you did, please spare a moment to leave a review it will be very much appreciated and helps immensely in assisting others to find this, and my other books. The first book **CODE OF SILENCE** is available now.

Veronica Taylor and Tom Shepard will return

You can find out about these books and more by signing up at my website:

www.pwjordanauthor.com

Acknowledgments

I wish to extend my heartfelt thanks to the readers who have supported my writing throughout the past few years.

Thanks also to the members and administrators of UK CRIME BOOK CLUB who have welcomed me into their ranks and continue to offer unstinting support for which I'm incredibly grateful.

Writing a book is a challenge, getting it noticed by readers is so much more difficult so a massive thanks to the book groups who have allowed me to hijack their audience and promote the series week after week.

Thanks to Sean Campbell, Susan Hunter and all at Crime Fiction Addicts for their support, and to the blogging community who tirelessly assist in promoting the work of all authors, thank you Lynda Checkley, Deb Day, Nicki Murphy, Donna Morfett and Pete Fleming.

Special thanks to Maureen Webb- your eye for detail continues to amaze me- and to Kath Middleton, a fantastic author in her own right who very generously provided critical feedback to make this book the best it could be.

And last but not least, thanks to my very patient editor- Melanie Underwood.

* * *

The writing of this novel has been a long and difficult one as I juggled the increasing pressures of my day job and fitting in writing time. Continuing the story of Veronica Taylor and Tom Shepard with the writing of this second novel has been an ambition which I couldn't have fulfilled if the love of books had not been instilled in me as a child and for this, I will be forever grateful to my parents.

As with everything I do, I couldn't have managed any of this without the belief and encouragement of my family.

Thanks to Owen and Martina for your constant support and making it much easier to create adverts and cover designs.

And to Donna and Erin, thank you for helping inspire me to keep chasing the dream even on those days when writing was the last thing on my mind.

I love you all.

Phillip Jordan
July 2023

Also by Phillip Jordan

About Phillip Jordan

ABOUT PHILLIP JORDAN

Phillip Jordan was born in Belfast, Northern Ireland and grew up in the city that holds the dubious double honour of being home to Europe's Most Bombed Hotel and scene of its largest ever bank robbery.
He had a successful career in the Security Industry for twenty years before transitioning into the Telecommunications Sector.
Aside from writing Phillip has competed in Olympic and Ironman Distance Triathlon events both Nationally and Internationally including a European Age-Group Championship and the World Police and Fire Games.
Taking the opportunity afforded by recent world events to write full-time Phillip wrote his Debut Crime Thriller, CODE OF SILENCE, finding inspiration in the dark and tragic history of Northern Ireland but also in the black humour, relentless tenacity and indomitable spirit of those who call the fabulous but flawed City of his birth home.

Phillip now lives on the County Down coast and is currently writing two novel series.
For more information:
www.pwjordanauthor.com
www.facebook.com/phillipjordanauthor/

Copyright

FIVE FOUR PUBLISHING

Printed in Poland
by Amazon Fulfillment
Poland Sp. z o.o., Wrocław

23175545R10280